GIVE *a novel* ME
GRACE

GIVE ME SERIES, #3

GIVE ME GRACE

a novel

GIVE ME SERIES, #3

KATE MCCARTHY

Editing by Maxann Dobson, The Polished Pen http://polished-pen.com/
Cover Art courtesy of Okay Creations http://okaycreations.com
Cover photo courtesy of Scott Hoover Photography http://www.scotthooverphotography.com
In conjunction with Love N Books http://lovenbooks.com
Cover model is Colby Lefebvre https://www.facebook.com/colbylmodel
Interior Design by E.M. Tippetts Book Designs

Dedication

To Tammy.
This book wouldn't exist without you.
Thank you for standing beside me on Casey's journey.

Chapter One
CASEY

I woke to a hot, wet tongue stroking my cock with enthusiasm. It had been too long, weeks maybe, since I had the time for this kind of outlet. My groan was loud and deep. I felt the girl behind the busy mouth smile around my erection. She was good and she knew it.

I opened eyes bleary from a wild night and watched her work me over. My breathing got heavier and my hips thrust upward, plunging deep inside her willing mouth. She responded in kind, swirling her tongue and sucking harder. Hazel eyes glanced up at me, gauging my reaction.

Bingo, I thought when her name came to me. I gave her a lusty grin. "Morning, Morgan."

Her mouth popped off and her eyes brightened. "Morning, Casey." Her raspy voice indicated her booze consumption last night had been just as excessive as mine.

She sat up on her knees, her perky tits bouncing as she grabbed me with both hands. My cock flinched at her iron grip, but it cleared my head long enough to remember just who Morgan was.

Ah shit.

The Florence Bar. Vodka shots. Mitch Valentine introducing me to the newly appointed detective in the cybercrime division over at Sydney City Police. We had a policy at our firm: no fucking any female from any government agency we had a working relationship with. Morgan being in my bed had fucking disaster written all over it, pun intended.

Then I thought about that worn file in the locked drawer of my office. I had questions—ones that Mitch informed me on numerous occasions he wasn't able to answer. No one could, because all the information pertaining to the case had been wiped. All I had was an old case report that listed information I refused to believe was correct.

I needed answers. Real ones. So when Mitch introduced me to Morgan at the bar last night, I was just drunk enough to decide that maybe she could help. Morgan worked in cybercrime for fuck's sake. They were a division notorious for closing ranks to outsiders, so when her eyes had flared wide with obvious interest, I knew just the way to get those answers. So what if it made me an asshole for using her. After too many years of getting nowhere, I had no other option and nothing else left to go on.

No new information.

No leads.

Nothing.

Looking up into Morgan's face, I knew there was no other choice. She was a lead in retrieving the wiped information. It wasn't like fucking a sexy girl was a hardship. I stretched out an arm and grabbed for a condom off my bedside table.

There's always a choice, Casey.

Fuck off, I growled to the voice in my head. I held up the foil packet between my thumb and forefinger. For this, there is no choice.

Morgan stroked me a few more times with her iron grip. Waves of heat brought me to the edge, and I gritted my teeth as she let go and snatched it from my hand. Peeling it open, Morgan bit her bottom lip as she rolled it down my cock.

Breathing heavy, I watched her straddle me, positioning my head at her opening. Glancing at me, she paused. "Why me?"

"What?" She chose right this very moment, when I'm trying not to bust a fucking nut, to initiate a conversation? I fought against the urge to thrust upwards.

"Look at you, Casey." Her eyes roamed over my face and chest with admiration, assuring me that she was indeed, looking at me. "You're the guy that has it all. You could've had anyone in that bar, male or female. Why me?"

The guy that had it all? Jesus.

Was that all she cared about—that she was fucking someone she thought was hot and loaded? I hated superficiality, but she would likely hate the truth more. Why her? Because I was drunk, and when I left the bar, not only was she the nearest female willing to leave with me, she was also someone who could do something for me.

"Casey?" My eyes flicked from her well-endowed chest back to her face, and in that instant I felt hollow. I saw the love my best friend, Travis, had for his wife, Quinn. I watched how every touch between the two brought a light to their eyes. They put each other's happiness before their own. They mattered to each other.

I wanted that.

I gave myself a mental slap.

Remember the file, Casey.

"Why you?" I repeated. Grabbing her hips in a grip that would no doubt bruise, I thrust up and into her body, and I hated myself for it. She cried out, and I couldn't help the growl of pleasure when she clenched around me, squeezing me. "Because I like a girl who knows what she wants and goes for it."

At least that was the truth. She saw me at the bar, she wanted me, and she went for it.

Morgan's head lolled backwards and she moaned. Assuming I'd supplied a satisfactory answer to her ill-timed question, I rolled her over and ground my hips into her body.

"Harder," she ordered.

I'd barely got my cock inside her and already she wanted to go balls to the wall? Give a guy a chance to find his rhythm for fuck's sake.

"Bossy bitch," I muttered and pulling out to the tip, I thrust in again—hard.

"Oh yes," she breathed. Her hands slid over my shoulders and down my back. I felt the sharp sting of fingernails scratching over my ass cheeks as she grabbed at me.

"You draw blood and I'll spank you so fucking hard you'll see stars," I warned.

Her eyes lit up and her nails dug in harder. Jesus, this bitch liked it rough. I would've tied her up if I'd known, save getting my skin shredded.

My phone rang.

"You've got to be kidding me," I snarled, hearing the work ringtone on my first day off in three weeks.

The noisy, persistent shrill overtook the harsh sound of heavy breathing and the sound of skin slapping on skin as I rammed myself inside her, just how she said she wanted it.

"Don't answer it," she panted.

I thrust in once more. Damn it. I was so close. "It's work."

Reaching for the phone, I hit answer and put it to my ear. "Casey," I barked irritably.

Maybe I could get Morgan off before I wrapped up the call. I pumped my hips in short, sharp bursts and she cried out beneath me. I put a finger to my lips, silently shushing her as Travis replied in my ear, "Casey. You're up."

I bit back a groan as Morgan came, her walls contracting around my cock. "Yeah, I am. In more ways than one."

"Thanks for the visual. We've been called out on a job. Shake a leg." His voice might've been muffled, but the urgent tone came through loud and clear.

"I'll message the location."

Shit. Well at least one of us managed to get off.

"On my way," I replied and hung up.

I pulled out with a regretful growl and a cock still hard and aching for release. Ignoring it for now, I moved off the bed. Morgan rolled to her side, her lips forming a pout as she watched me peel the condom off. In a hurry, I tossed it on the floor with a grimace and grabbed a pair of jeans off the corner chair.

"Sorry, Morgan." I tugged them over my legs and yanked up the zipper. Half dressed, I leaned over the bed and slapped her on the rump. "Up you get."

"Nice," I heard her mutter. A bit louder, she said, "You want to try this again later?"

"Sure," I replied casually, my tone suggesting there was no way I wanted to try this with her again ever. Even if I wanted to, I had a barbecue to go to tomorrow at a friend's house and security detail for the well-known band Jamieson later that night.

The file, idiot!

I swiped a hand across my face. Feeling like a two-bit whore, I turned and tossed my phone at her while she was scooting off the bed. "Put your number in there. I'll call you when I wrap this shit up, okay?"

She grinned, her look victorious. I turned my back on it. Reaching for a shirt, I yanked it down my chest while she tapped in her contact details. Wallet, keys, and phone all went in my pockets while she was still at the stage of putting on her bra. I vaguely remember thinking her underwear sexy last night, but in the cold light of day, the tiny scraps of red lace did nothing.

Leaning in, I brushed a quick kiss to her cheek. "I have to go. Let yourself out?"

An hour later and I was crouched behind a large rock alongside Travis—both of us locked in position so our cover wouldn't be blown. My shirt was damp with sweat and I was itching to peel it off and feel a cool breeze on my skin.

"You dragged me away from sex, on my day off, for this shit?" I bitched. "Have I told you that I really don't like you right now?"

The day was overcast and the humidity was not only sapping away the last of my remaining energy, it was increasing the desire to strangle Travis until his eyeballs popped from his head—which I planned to do, just as soon as our target was acquired, taken down, and I'd stretched out the cramps in my legs.

"Have I told you that you're acting like a little bitch?" Travis countered.

I risked a glance sideways. Travis had his blond hair tied off his face. Arms up, gun cocked, he tilted his head to the side, bright green eyes flat as he tracked our target through his viewfinder. I knew without a doubt when he pulled the trigger he would find his mark. Travis was just that guy, the one who did whatever it took to have your back.

He'd had mine from the moment we met in our first year at Charles Sturt University. I took him down in an illegal high tackle in rugby league tryouts. Shoving me off, he growled a curse and threw a punch that would've rendered a lesser man unconscious. Not me though. I came from a background where crippling blows were the accepted form of communication. I could've taken it ten times over if I had to, but Travis wasn't looking to go another ten rounds. He'd simply held out a hand and hauled me to my feet. A slap on the back, a beer at the university's pub, and we were friends.

That was a defining moment in my life—meeting Travis Valentine—because just under a year later I almost died. God knows I should have. If Travis hadn't had my back, I would have. I'd wanted to.

Why? Because I'd made a promise I failed to deliver on. That didn't seem so bad, I know. Promises were made to be broken, right? Wrong. Not when breaking them meant you failed so fucking bad, you lost your entire world in the blink of an eye.

No words could ever encompass the magnitude of what that felt like. It was like you were somehow still breathing even though your heart wasn't beating anymore. It was like becoming a whole other person you didn't know. It was like losing yourself, and when you lost yourself, there was no coming back.

I was at the Coogee Bay Hotel on summer break from uni when it hit me that I didn't have to try and come back. I didn't have to pretend I was okay. I didn't have to live through losing everything. I didn't have to fight anymore.

The sudden realisation was a relief, and surrounded by friends at our table, I simply stood up and walked out. The bottle of booze in my hand slipped to the ground outside. Beer sprayed everywhere, glass shattering and skidding across the ground. Tripping over, I fell on the broken shards, but I was so fucked-up I didn't even notice.

"Come on, Casey. Up you get."

A hand gripped my bicep and I looked up. There was Travis, once again hauling me to my feet. I wanted to tell him to let go, just this once, because I didn't want to get up again, and I was okay with that.

"Travis," I slurred. Shrugging off his arm, I staggered to my feet and grabbed the beer out of his hand. I saluted him with it. "To the best friend a useless fuck like me could ever ask for."

Two girls walked by on their way inside. Bracing my arm against the wall, my eyes fell on girl number two. Long, wild red hair, miles of leg, and a full, curvy body showcased in a tight, black dress.

Looking me over, she smiled at me as they passed, but it slipped off her face when my hand gave out and I lurched sideways into the wall. They disappeared inside.

"Christ, Casey," Travis muttered, grabbing for his beer. "Haven't you had enough?"

I looked him in the eye. "You're right, Travis." *Just like you always are.* "I have had enough."

Panic flooded his eyes at my definitive tone. I hated letting him down. Travis had thought time out from classes, hanging by the beach and surfing, would be some kind of bullshit rejuvenation. It was nice getting away from everything. It was nice having a best friend as well, but not if it meant failing him too.

"No, Casey." Travis shook his head. "No."

"I tried. I fucking tried, but I can't do this, Trav. There's nothing there, and I'm tired of pretending there is."

"Fuck." Travis reached out and when I shoved him back, he stumbled. "You can't—"

Spying the beach across the road, waves crashing heavily in the dark night, I cut him off. "I'm sorry."

Travis made another grab for me, but even as fucked up as I was, I was too quick. I jogged across the road, my eyes focused on the water and nothing else. The ocean was rough and wild. If alcohol couldn't smother my demons, I'd drown them in the pounding waves.

"Casey!" Travis yelled from behind me but I didn't stop.

Gasping for air, I reached the shoreline and tripped in the wet sand. I went down hard and cold water gushed over my body, numbing me.

Fuck yeah. Now that's what I'm talking about.

I clawed my way in further.

Arms grabbed my waist and yanked me backwards. Travis staggered and we both went down. I tried struggling from his hold, but his grip was anchor tight.

"Why can't you leave me the fuck alone?" I shouted.

"Because if you go in there, you'll drown!" he yelled back.

"That's the point." I closed my eyes and swallowed. "Can't live like this anymore, Trav. I just can't."

"You can," he replied hoarsely.

"Give me one fucking reason why I can."

Please. I need something.

"Because there are kids out there right now who need you, you selfish prick! Do you want to see them go through what you went through, or do you want to make your life count for something? You can give them something you never had. You can give them hope. Doesn't that mean something to you?"

I exhaled heavily. "I'm just one person, Trav. What the fuck can I do?"

"You're not just one person because you have me. I'm your family now." His breath was harsh in my ear from the exertion, but I believed him. He was my family now. He was all I had. You would think that was too much pressure for one person, but Travis was rock solid. He always had been. "Just promise me you'll try, okay? I need you to promise."

The bastard. After what happened last time, he knew I'd never break another promise as long as I lived. Slumped against Travis in the sand, I stared up at the stars as water flowed around our legs, and I promised.

From that day on, I got out of bed every day, because I'd promised. I went to lectures and I ate when I was supposed to, and I dated girls, because I'd promised. I graduated with a dual degree in policing and psychology, and I moved back to Sydney with Travis, because I'd promised.

When he setup Jamieson and Valentine Consulting with his brother Jared and Jared's friend, Coby Jamieson, he wanted me in, but I couldn't do it. Travis had carried me for so long, I needed to stand on my own two feet. So I joined the police force and I trained, and I studied, and I worked so fucking hard I could barely stand from exhaustion. But after an entire year, I hadn't gotten anywhere. We hauled in criminals just to turn around and watch the system set them loose.

So I quit and became a partner in their business, and as usual, Travis was right. It was a perfect fit and where I should've been all along. Located in the Sydney suburb of Darlinghurst, the firm was extremely specialised: contracting to various government and private agencies for kidnapping, hostage negotiation, and security services. My primary role was to get kids out of abusive situations by whatever means necessary, and I took whatever means necessary to heart. God help any asshole who got in my way, because if there was one thing that should be feared, it was a man with nothing left to lose.

"Casey," Travis whispered furiously, startling me back to the present and our current operation.

"What?"

"Who'd you go home with last night?"

"Just some girl," I muttered.

Loosening the grip on my gun, I freed a hand and swiped it across my brow. His question reminded me that I needed to ring Morgan when I got home. My job might've given me a reason to keep going, but so did that file and its unanswered questions from the past. Whatever it took—fancy restaurants, jewellery, tying her to the fucking bed and taking a crop to her ass if that's how she liked to get off—I'd fucking do it.

Decision made, I resolved to swing by the sex shop on the way home just in case.

Travis glanced sideways, his brows drawn together in a fierce frown. "You're hiding something."

"No I'm not," I lied. Travis would pitch a shit fit about me going against firm policy by sleeping with Morgan. "I'm just getting too old for this shit." My legs were still cramped, and my cock reminded me with a dull ache that life was passing it by.

"Twenty-nine is old now?"

No, but after graduating, I'd done the one thing I swore I'd never do after Travis saved my sorry ass from drowning. I'd made another promise. There was no way in hell I would hit thirty without putting that file to rest.

"I'll be thirty before I know it," I replied.

"You know that worrying about your age makes you a girl?"

"You're a girl," I retorted, and right there my immaturity level reached a new low. I blamed it on my hangover.

"I don't have a clear shot," he told me. "Target is still armed and coming your way." Shifting slightly, Travis lowered his aim. "And go find your hookup after this and fuck her stupid if that's what you need to do. Unless your cock is getting too old for that shit too."

I resisted the urge to reach down and adjust it in my jeans. "Me getting too old for that shit? You're the one who's married," I whispered out the corner of my mouth. "You'll be needing that prescription for Viagra soon. Tell Quinn I'm available when she's ready to trade up."

Travis snorted. I tuned out his reply as I raised my gun with steady hands, the movement slow and silent. Taking aim, I waited, breathing softly until we heard the soft crunch of someone stalking through dried leaves northwest of our position. Five seconds later our target came back into view.

"Come to Papa," I murmured, my lips curving in satisfaction.

"Don't hesitate," Travis ordered, his voice lighter than the soft breeze that carried it.

I relaxed the gun in my hands and looked at Travis. "You're telling me how to do my job now, asshole?"

"Just take aim and shoot dammit," Travis growled.

"Now see there? I think you've got unresolved control issues."

Travis exhaled in a huff, his wide eyes busy telling me I was crazy. I probably was, but being called away from sex and morning coffee would do that to a man. "Fine. Shoot the fucker, don't shoot the fucker, but don't tell me…" he jabbed his finger for emphasis "…that I have fucking control issues."

I used my gun to shove Travis's jabbing finger out of my face. "For the record, I think you're lying to yourself, but whatever helps you sleep at night. Are you like this with Quinn?"

A vein started pulsing angrily in his temple. Biting the insides of my cheeks, I gave Travis my back as I lifted the gun, adjusted my aim to account for the wind factor, and refocused my sights.

"I'm not controlling, I'm confident and I like to take charge. Women dig that."

My brows flew up and I looked at him. "So now that you're married, you're suddenly an expert on women?"

"I like to think so. Maybe you should try getting married."

A knot formed in the pit of my stomach.

"Quinn can hook you up," he added. "She has plenty of hot friends."

I forced a grin. "Travis Valentine. Best friend, pussy whisperer, and part-time pimp. Thanks, but no thanks. I can arrange my own hookups."

"I'm not talking about hook—"

"Target acquired," I interrupted before Travis could take the conversation any further. He might've deserved every bit of his happiness, but I didn't deserve shit, and I wasn't prepared to have a deep and meaningful over it.

Exhaling softly, I followed my target, my finger steady on the trigger as I began the countdown. Three … two … o—

I jolted sideways, almost slamming into Travis as shots hit in rapid succession up the left side of my body. Short, sharp bursts of pain assaulted my ribs. I gritted my teeth, closing my eyes for a brief moment to gain control. Damned if I let anyone see how much that shit hurt.

"Take that, Hotdog!" came Evie's loud, high-pitched squeal to my left.

I rolled my eyes at the nickname. I surfed daily, and yeah, maybe I showed off a little because I was damn good at it. Evie found out it was called hotdogging when you surfed for flash rather than function, and now she refused to let the nickname go.

Evie was Coby's famous little sister, Jared's wife, and lead singer for Jamieson, but her biggest claim to fame lay in being a better shot than all of us combined. Today proved no exception.

Travis laughed loud and hard, gasping for air as the gun in his hand fell lax. Getting to my feet, I shoved my boot into his knee and watched him spill over, falling into the pile of leaves we'd scraped away earlier to create our hidey-hole. Turning, I lifted my goggles to rest on my forehead and gave Evie a murderous glare. It was entirely wasted because suddenly her body started jerking backwards. She stumbled, going down against the force of the rounds hitting her in the gut. Uh oh. Jared will be pissed.

Tim, my personal assistant at Jamieson and Valentine Consulting, staggered his short, slim frame towards Evie until he stood over her body, gun held up in the air like he was Wyatt Earp taking down the town. "Now who's the badass motherfucker, bitch?" he crowed.

Without hesitating, I fired off a quick round and took Tim out. His body exploded in a mess of blue and green paint. His gaze dropped, his mouth open in shock as he took in the chaos covering his outfit. Tim was precious about his clothes—even the old stuff he'd dragged out for today's occasion—so I knew shit would hit the fan at work next week. Sure enough, he was busy glaring at me, accusation in his narrowed eyes. "What the fuck, Casey? I'm on your team!"

I shrugged and grinned. "That's for being late to work yesterday."

"All of you be fucking quiet," Travis hissed. Our mouths snapped shut and we looked his way. "In case you don't seem to realise, you three are now dead, and guess who's left standing?"

"Um …" Tim's dark brown eyes flicked from mine to Evie's before returning to Travis. "You?"

"And?" he prompted. There was a brief silence after which Travis rolled his eyes. "Mac, buttheads. Mac!" Out of the four Valentine siblings, Mackenzie was the youngest, and the only girl. She was also a beautiful, golden pit bull and a really shitty shot, so the fact that she was one of the last two standing left us in shock. "Do you want her to win?"

Fuck no. We all shook our heads.

"So all of you shut your holes and get the hell off this paintball field so I can take the bitch out."

Evie promptly whipped off her goggles, turned around, and started puking in the shrubs behind us.

"Evie, honey, you okay?" Freeing one hand from my paintball gun, I rubbed her back in warm, soothing circles.

She shook her head, moaning a loud, "No."

Her legs were shaking so I handed my gun over to Tim and picked her up, noting her entire face under the war paint was green. She burrowed into my chest, and leaving Travis to deal with Mac, I carried her off the paintball field.

"I can't be sick or Mac will murder me."

"Why's that?"

"Because we have to play at that awards ceremony tomorrow night," she reminded me.

I brushed the hair out of her eyes with care. Evie and I were close, and she'd always held a little piece of my heart. "You leave Mac to me, sweetheart. I'll charm her into a good mood."

She managed a weak nod. "Hey, you're still coming to our barbecue tomorrow aren't you?"

Jared's face lost all colour when he saw me walking off the field with Evie in my arms.

"Sure," I murmured before he reached us. "I'll be there."

Chapter Two
CASEY

icking the front door of my loft shut with my foot, I tossed my wallet, phone, and keys on the kitchen counter. Next to that I set a bright yellow plastic bag with the well-known lettering, Naughty But Nice, printed gaily on the side in flowing, pink letters. Thank you very much, sex store, for your casual approach to discretion. There was nothing more liberating than shouting to the members of the public that you were a big, fat pervert.

My business partner and roommate, Coby, sauntered out of the second bedroom in nothing but a pair of boxer-briefs, hair mussed and scratching idly at his chest.

The loft we shared was a converted warehouse slash revolving bachelor pad. The ceilings were high with exposed red brick lining the wall of the open kitchen, living and dining area. Neither of us were cooks, so the stainless steel appliances, marble bench tops and saucepan racks were entirely wasted, but the huge outdoor deck with slight views of Sydney Harbour made it a valuable investment.

The space was owned originally by Jared and Travis, but I bought Jared's share when he and Evie bought a house in Bondi; Jared was the only one who didn't think the house should've been condemned by the local council. His intention had been for them to live in it while undertaking the renovations, but a year after completion something went wrong every other week. Last week, it was blocked pipes. Jared blamed it on Evie's long hair clogging the drains but after spending an entire day digging up the front yard, he found a collapsed section of pipe out near the road. That made it a council issue, and there was more likelihood of God stopping by their house for a beer than the council venturing out to fix it. The week before that it was five exploding outlets in two days, the last one almost setting Jared's laptop on fire. The only advice I could offer was to either cut their losses and move or take out better life insurance.

Then it was Travis's turn, only he was marginally smarter. Travis and Quinn lived in Coby's house while they did their renovations and Coby moved into the loft with me. Six months later, their Manly Vale house was beautifully restored and they moved in. Then Travis had the gardens and lawn dug up before finding out it was easier getting a ticket to the moon than getting someone out to do their retaining wall. Combine that with three weeks of torrential rain and their entire yard was now a mud pit, and not the good kind that featured naked women wrestling.

Considering the revolving bachelor pad status of our loft, Coby would be up soon. I smirked as he wandered into the kitchen.

"You're next."

He paused, eyebrows going up. "For what?"

"True love, Disney-style."

"Fuck that," he muttered, running a hand over the tufts of messy brown hair sticking up on his head. "I only just got Evie married off. She's Jared's problem now. Let me enjoy the moment for a good couple of years at least." He continued towards the fridge. "Besides, if the curse on this loft is anything to go by, you're the one that's up next."

I winced. "Yeah, that's not funny. Speaking of not funny… How did you get out of paintball today when I got called out, mid-sex, like it was a life or death operation?"

Coby shrugged, opening up the fridge door. "You brought someone home last night?" he said to the barren shelves.

"Just some girl," I said casually with the words that were somehow becoming my new mantra. Coby would also pitch a shit fit if he knew it was Morgan.

He dangled a beer over his shoulder that I didn't really want but took anyway. Getting his own beer, Coby shut the door and turned. With the simultaneous grace of ballet, we both twisted off the tops and flicked the caps towards the vicinity of the sink. Lips poised to take a sip, Coby's eyes fell on the pansy-ass yellow bag and froze. He looked from it, to me. "Just some girl, huh?"

Whipping out his phone from nowhere, Coby snapped a photo of the bag and started tapping like his fingers were on fire.

"What are you doing?"

Walking over to the couch, he flopped down and tossed his phone at the coffee table. "Informing the Twitterverse of your new predilection for dildos." He gave me a grin.

Snatching up my phone, I opened Twitter to read Coby's post. Casey's new acquisitions. I had no idea butt plugs came in extra large sat next to a photo of the damning yellow bag sitting on our kitchen counter.

There was no hiding when your sex life was exposed on social media, so instead I shrugged and retweeted his tweet. Any willing females up for being experimented on?

Done, I picked up my beer and wandered over to the couch where Coby was channel flicking. It was Saturday night, and with two missed calls from Morgan already today, I could only conclude she was trying to get something arranged for later. The thought of returning her call made me twitchy. Instead, I sat in the navy leather recliner with a heavy sigh. Tossing my phone on the coffee table, I flicked up the footrest and settled in.

"Anything on?"

"Nope," he replied, doing another round of the channels just to be sure. Then he sniffed. "Dude. You stink. You went into a sex shop like that?"

I looked down at my grimy, sweat-stained shirt and I knew that if I rubbed at my face, a layer of war paint would transfer to my fingers. I shrugged. "I didn't go there to pick up, asshole."

My phone vibrated, the sound loud against the thick timber of the table. Coby picked it up, reading the screen with widening eyes.

"What?"

He tossed it at me. Catching it in one hand, I checked the screen. Four notifications of replies to my retweet sat on the screen, all willing females seemingly happy to sacrifice their own ass for the greater good. Huh.

"I didn't even buy butt plugs," I told Coby.

He grabbed the phone out of my hand and started skimming. "Maybe you should have. Hell, get some for me when you go back."

"Buy your own butt plugs."

Handing me back the phone, he asked, "How do you even know that many people on Twitter?"

"I don't. I don't even know how to use it. Tim set it all up and now I'm stuck with it."

"Figures. There are hardly any guys following you on there, you know. Tim probably deletes them all so he can stay the number one man in your life."

"Tim's a good kid," I muttered, knowing Tim would be pissed if he heard me calling him a kid. He was only five years younger than I was, but sometimes it felt like fifty years when he let his personality fly. His ability to create drama out of thin air was legendary, and it often came back to bite me on the ass by default. Take his ongoing feud with the local barista near our office. This barista was the Rain Man of coffee. He made an espresso you'd give your left nut for, but when he slept with Tim's boyfriend's brother's cousin or what-the-fuck-ever and didn't call him back, Tim stopped leaving money in his tip jar. Now the usual miracle elixir Tim bought for me wouldn't revive a fucking flea, yet he still insisted on going there because the gospel according to Tim was that the man was hot. Now I was the one stuck with piss-weak coffee.

The loft intercom buzzed announcing a visitor. Coby flinched, the sharp sound waking him from a doze. "Who's that?" he asked, knowing we weren't expecting anyone.

"How should I know? My superpowers don't include seeing through walls."

I flicked the footrest back down and stood. Stretching my arms high, I felt joints pop with a satisfying crack. Coby stumbled off to his room, likely to find some pants, while I went to answer the door. Without flicking on the video monitor, I pressed the answer button with a, "Yeah?"

"It's me," Travis announced.

I shook my head. Travis had big balls stopping by after dragging me from bed for paintball this morning. Still feeling the need to hold a grudge, I replied, "I'm busy rubbing one out. Come back later."

A strangled cough came through the speaker, followed by his wife, Quinn, saying politely, "Sorry to interrupt, Casey. We'll um … leave you to it. Is half an hour okay?"

I didn't fight the grin. I'd missed Quinn at paintball today. She was one of my closest friends, not just because she kept Travis in line, but because she'd gone through the kind of hell that would've broken a lesser person and came out of it stronger. I admired her for that. Pressing the button again to speak, I replied, "Half an hour? Is that how long it takes your husband to get himself off?"

I heard Quinn say faintly, "Travis?"

"Are we really going to have this conversation," he growled, "or are you going to let us in?"

I laughed and hit the buzzer to let them up. Scratching idly at the stubble on my jaw, I thought about having a shower and a shave as I flicked open the locks and walked into the kitchen.

I was in the kitchen getting drinks by the time they came through the front door. Pale hair pinned up, Quinn was wearing some kind of navy thing that sparkled. She smiled.

"Casey!"

"Damn, I missed you," I told her, kissing her on the cheek as Travis followed her into the kitchen, "but you didn't have to dress up for me. I like you in anything, or nothing at all if you prefer."

Travis grabbed the glass of wine I'd just poured, slapped me up the back of the head, and handed the drink to his wife, who was busy laughing at my exaggerated wink.

If I wasn't so damn tired, I'd put him in a headlock and get his dressy clothes all dirty. I gave Quinn my best puppy dog eyes instead. "You're not going to let him beat me up, are you?"

"Of course she will," Travis interjected. "In the order of men in her life, I outrank you by a mile."

"Oh yeah?" My eyebrows went up as I looked from Travis to Quinn. "Where am I on this list?"

"Dude. You're so low on the list, you're not even on the list." He took the two beers I'd uncapped with him into the living room and handed one to Coby. "And really … butt plugs?" He sank into the perfectly worn groove of my recliner and smirked.

Ignoring him, I put the wine bottle back in the fridge and said to Quinn, "If you ever get tired of Mr Vanilla, you know where to— Oh hey!" My eyes caught the little cherub peeking out from behind Quinn. Mussed blond curls and brown eyes so wide it made you hurt just to look at him. Sam, the three year old foster kid I rescued almost two weeks ago, watched his mother overdose and die, and now he couldn't speak from the resulting trauma. What made the entire situation so fucked-up was that people like Travis and Quinn couldn't have kids. She was so badly beaten as a pregnant teen, she'd not only lost her baby, she'd lost the ability to have more. The bright side was that they were given the opportunity to be foster parents. To me, that alone made the world a better place. If they managed to adopt him, Sam would grow up with a future.

Crouching down to eye level, I gave him my best grin. "You came all the way over here just to see me, bud?" My eyes shifted to the big piece of paper clutched so tightly in his hands it was a wrinkled mess. "And what's this?"

"Well, that's the thing," Quinn began. I glanced up at her nervous tone. "We have dinner reservations at Mr Chow's, and really, we'd forgotten about them with … everything going on." She eyed Sam pointedly. "And obviously we weren't going to go because we don't want to leave Sam with just anyone, or leave him at all really, but then …" Quinn took hold of Sam's hand and gave it a squeeze. "Show him your drawing, Sam."

My heart swelled a little at the tentative trust in Sam's eyes when he looked at me. He offered up the crumpled bit of paper.

Taking it from him with care, I smoothed the edges out and held it up. My name was etched all over it in a chaotic scramble of colours. Nothing else. Just … Casey. My eyes burned and I swallowed the sudden lump in my throat. "Dude," I said affectionately. "You did this for me?"

Sam nodded wordlessly.

"There's more of those at home," Quinn whispered.

I met Quinn's eyes briefly and saw the sheen of tears. Clearing my throat, I said to Sam, "Well this is going on my fridge. Front and centre. You know why?"

He shook his head.

"Because when everyone sees my name all over the fridge, they'll know all the food in there belongs to me. That means no one else can eat it." Sam's eyes were solemn, as though what I'd told him was the most important thing in the world. "But," I added, "I'm pretty sure I saw some ice cream in there that had your name on it. Want some?"

Sam nodded again, and this time I was rewarded with the corners of his lips turning up slightly. Just that slightest reaction made me want to fist pump the air.

"But you have to do something for me first, bud, okay?" A frown started to overtake his face. "Give me a hug? I need one of those because it's been a long, tiring day," I told him with a meaningful glance at Travis. It was a wasted effort because football just came on the television. Kicked back in my recliner with a beer, Travis looked in no apparent rush to be going anywhere.

Sam walked straight into my open arms. I stood up, bringing him with me, and he burrowed into my chest. After helping put the picture on the fridge, we got the ice cream. Holding onto him with one arm, I used the other to get a spoon from the drawer.

"Bowls are for girls," I told him with mock seriousness. "We're men. That means we can eat it straight from the carton."

"Casey! You'll teach him bad habits."

I chuckled at Quinn as I handed the spoon to Sam. "Hey, I know how to take care of kids. Fill them with the sugar, show 'em how to jump on the bed, then send them home to puke all over their parents."

Quinn scowled and set her wine down on the bench. "Maybe this—"

"I'm assuming he has things, right?" She nodded. "So go get them and bring them up so you can go already." I shifted Sam in my arms so he could reach the ice cream carton, noticing Quinn's hesitation. "Hey. I got this, okay?"

She shuddered visibly. "Don't say 'I got this.' It makes me nervous. Last time someone said that, my life turned into an episode of The Sopranos."

"Blame Mac," Travis called without shifting his eyes from the screen. "Everyone has a catchphrase. That's hers."

"Oh yeah?" Quinn dug through her bag for the car keys. "What's mine then?"

Travis paused for a moment before saying, "Baby, you're so big." He smirked at her before licking his lips in a way that would give me nightmares for weeks.

Quinn rolled her eyes as she walked out the door. "Be right back."

"Take your time!" Travis shouted after her.

By the time she returned, the three of us were on the couch, Sam sitting on my lap as we watched the football.

"Look who I found downstairs just about to ring the bell," Quinn called out.

All eyes shifted to the doorway and tension rose swiftly in the air, thick enough to choke on.

Ah shit.

I lost my voice for a moment, and not in a good way. Morgan was standing beside Quinn, and I'd seen Band-Aids bigger than her outfit. The way she ran her eyes over me would make a porn star blush. I shifted Sam in my lap, feeling the urge to cover his eyes.

Stupid sonofabitch. I had no business being set loose in a bar, drunk. The evidence of that stood right there, waiting for me to say something. I was left with two options. One: I could pretend I didn't know her from a bar of soap—unlikely to work—or two: I could introduce her to the room and face the wrath of my business partners. Where was door number three when you needed it?

I re-introduced Morgan to the room. Then I handed over Sam, took Morgan by the hand, and with an, "excuse us for a minute," I led her down the back of the loft for privacy.

"You didn't return my calls," she began.

"Sorry. I got caught up with uh, work."

Morgan took in my filthy, dishevelled appearance with sympathy. "Tough case, huh?"

I thought back to our paintball expedition and the fact that Mac had somehow overcome all odds to come out the winner. "You could say that," I hedged.

"I know exactly what will make you feel better."

The gleam in her eyes left no doubt. "I bet, but I'm babysitting Travis and Quinn's little boy tonight. Maybe we could try this again another night?"

She shrugged and stepped a little closer, not seeming to mind the smell of sweat wafting off me in waves. "I can help. I'm good with kids. Want me to stay?"

Jesus. Morgan was persistent, I'd give her that. I glanced over to the living room to find all eyes on us. I shifted uncomfortably and smothered the heavy sigh. I really wouldn't mind getting laid. All that naked and willing flesh on display was making my cock sit up with interest. "Sam's not good with strangers."

Ten minutes later I managed to get her out the door. Then I turned to face Travis with his flat, knowing eyes and folded arms. "We need to talk."

I made a point of looking at the large clock on the wall in the kitchen. "Oh is that the time? You guys are gonna be late."

"Tomorrow," he warned me. "You and I are going to have a chat."

On that ominous note, they left, Quinn shooting me a look of sympathy before she disappeared out the door. I went back to the fridge for another beer and then changed it to a juice, getting one for Sam while I was there. I didn't like drinking around little kids when they were in my care. I'd experienced firsthand the damage alcohol could do to an angry parent around a child. I wasn't my father. When it came to kids, I knew the importance of responsibility.

Chapter Three
GRACE

"Tilt your chin up a little and look at me."

Like a good little soldier, I tilted my chin and faced John and his camera. With brows drawn, he crouched a little and changed his angle. "Narrow your eyes more, Grace. I'm supposed to be seeing your inner bitch, but right now you look about as pissed off as a bag of chips."

I gave a deep, heavy sigh before setting my jaw and narrowing my eyes. John shook his head from behind the camera. I don't think he was buying it. I couldn't blame him. I was a hardened professional in the modelling world, able to summon whatever look was required from me with ease, but today was not my day. Nothing was going right, and two days after flying in from a quick assignment in Italy, jetlag was still making me its bitch. Why was I so damn tired all the time? Exhaustion burned deep in my bones and I couldn't shake it.

A loud thump came somewhere from my left, followed by my assistant, Jemima, hissing, "Mitsy!"

I squinted, unable to see beyond the glare of the lights. Not that I needed to. Mitsy had been disrupting the entire photo shoot since he stepped paw inside John's Melbourne city studio. The damn dog hated the entire world and everybody in it. Now he was busy making sure we knew just how much. The fluffy, white dog slash furry beast belonged to my boyfriend Dalton, but Dalton was still in Italy, spending an extra week with mutual friends.

Dalton's mum had been taking care of Mitsy in his absence, but she stopped by unannounced this morning, claiming she had to go out of town for work. I suspected she was telling a big fat lie. Not just because she worked the counter at the local post office, but because she couldn't look me in the eye as she handed him over. That should have been my first clue that today would suck donkey's balls. The second had been when I put on my jeans and realised they were a smidge tight. Being thin was always the new black in the fashion world, and I hated having to watch everything I ate. The third clue had been the missed call on my phone and subsequent message. I hadn't listened to it yet, but I already knew what it would say and it scared the living shit out of me.

Just give me a few more days.

Please.

Feeling suddenly vulnerable, I'd taken pity on Mitsy and brought him along to the photo shoot with me. That was an obvious mistake we were all currently paying for.

"Grace!" John clicked his fingers to get my attention. "Give me some bitch, okay?"

Instantly I thought of Dalton's dog and the heat of my glare should've cracked the camera lens. Mitsy didn't travel well, as evidenced by the nasty message left behind in the cab on the way here. Too late, I'd remembered Dalton mentioning Mitsy's aversion to moving vehicles and that it helped if the dog had something to chew on. Arriving at John's, I'd had to hand over an extra wad of cash just to pay for the cleaning.

"Perfect," crooned my photographer and best friend.

John was early-thirties with short, dark silky curls and facial hair that wasn't quite a beard, but longer than stubble. What would you call that? Brubble? I tried not to snort. The brubble was new since I saw him last. It suited him, adding to the tattoos peeking out from his shirtsleeves. The man was rough and a little wild. All he needed was a Marlboro hanging from his lips and someone should've been photographing him instead of me.

"What?" he said.

Click. Click. Click.

"Nothing," I murmured, schooling the amusement that flashed in my eyes.

No one could read my expressions like John could, not even Dalton, who on more than one occasion accused me of being a cold, unemotional bitch with no personality. Not true, but something inside held me back from being my real self in a relationship, and it was something my boyfriend liked to bring up numerous times when drunk. Pushing the issue aside, I focused on John.

"I'm just wondering what you would call that growth on your face."

Click. Click. Click.

John changed the camera angle and squinted through the viewfinder. "Is that what's going through your head right now, Grace? My beard?"

I shrugged, ignoring the growls of hunger from my stomach and the ache of my tired body. "I was thinking brubble, but the word sounds a little abrasive, like I could use your face as an exfoliator."

He shifted position and my eyes followed his movement, making sure to keep my glare as directed. "I don't know if I should keep it or not. What do you think of it?"

"That depends."

"On?"

"On how far you plan to take it. I mean, beards are trending right now. I still watch Lord of the Rings just for Aragorn's facial hair, but if you take it too far..."

John paused, brows raised in question as he relaxed his hold on the camera. "Too far?"

I fought the grin. "No one wants to have sex with Chewbacca."

He laughed from behind the lens, his chuckle deep and sexy. Damn. Why wasn't I able to fall in love with John?

Bracing my hands on my knees, I glowered as directed.

Click, click, click.

John was my one true friend. I didn't want to ruin that. Neither did he. We'd talked about it and decided it was too weird. John's theory was that my one true love had been brutally murdered in a past life and I was waiting for him to come back to me. Admittedly, he came up with that when completely wankered from a bottle of wine. John was usually a hard liquor man, but that night it was all we had on hand after finishing a photo shoot in Broome at three a.m.

"Dalton doesn't fit the profile," he'd slurred, pointing his finger at me with a hand that held both his wine glass and a cigarette.

"What profile?" I slurred back.

"The profile of your gladiator." John hiccupped. "The warrior who's fought through the centuries to find his way back to you. You've just gotta lose the cold armour, Grace," he informed me, his closet romantic side escaping with every sip he took. "He won't be able to bust down your castle walls if you don't. Dalton's too weak. You need someone who's going to push your buttons, and not just the ones in your panties." He offered a meaningful look towards my lady parts as well as waving his hand in the same direction in case I didn't get the reference.

He was right about the cold armour. It never used to be there, but life had a way of changing you into someone you never imagined you'd be, and giving you a life that you'd never really wanted.

I came from a big family. Two loving parents, an older brother, Henry, and two younger twin sisters, Emma and Ava. Henry was lead guitarist in the band, Jamieson. I always knew he'd be famous one day. He'd been attached to that guitar from birth. Emma and Ava were fraternal, but similar, sort of like peas and corn. They'd decided at an early age to join the Air Force. Our house subsequently became fluent in Top Gun. For an entire year, they wouldn't answer to anything other than Iceman and Goose. And me? Every day was different. One day I wanted to be an Olympic trampolinist, the next a heavy haulage trucker. Only one thing remained constant: I was the sister that caused trouble. We were allowed ice cream if we ate all our vegetables, and I was always the one that fed them to the dog and said I ate them. When we went to the shops, I was the one screaming and causing a scene for the chocolate so craftily displayed at the supermarket checkout. I was the one that begged for a skateboard and broke my arm when I tackled the biggest hill in our housing estate. I was the one that wouldn't go to sleep at night without demanding at least five stories and a glass of water.

You probably get the point, but nothing fazed my mum, not even me. She was the person you could just look at and know she was someone who loved life. She radiated it from every golden pore, like some goddamn beacon that was too beautiful for words. My father worshipped at her angelic feet, but when she was diagnosed with breast cancer, everything changed, including me, and when she died four years later, everything inside my dad died too.

He'd spent years doing everything to prolong her life: surgery, radiation, chemotherapy, tonics and healthy eating. It was horrific, because at such a young age, even I could see there was nothing left of her. Watching someone so bright and vital fade into nothingness was unbearable; it was harder than saying goodbye.

Two months later at the age fourteen, I stumbled on a foreclosure notice from the bank. We were losing our house. Employing my best snooping skills—because I was the child that always found where the Christmas presents were hidden—I found out just how bad it was, and my heart broke for my father. We were left with medical bills so big they might as well have been Mount Everest. In that one horrifying moment, I saw Henry giving up his guitar, feeling obligated to work some boring, dead-end job to help support our family. I saw Emma and Ava's dream of the Air Force turn into working the check-in counter at Sydney's international airport. So when some random stranger at the local coffee shop took in my gangly, awkward frame and told me I could be earning big dollars on international catwalks and "hey, here's my card, call me," I didn't laugh in his face. I clutched that card like I was adrift in The Perfect Storm and it was my goddamn life raft.

I'd been working nonstop ever since, most of the time away from home with a tutor to help me finish high school. And while the money I made had paid the bills a thousand times over, the price I paid was horrendous. I didn't know my family anymore. We weren't close. I'd lost them at the same time I'd lost my mum. Henry, Emma, and Ava were out there living their dreams while I was stuck in a life I'd never wanted.

Now I was just the sister who was never there.

"Early lunch break!" John shouted, snapping me out of the past and making my stomach rumble painfully.

He murmured something to his assistant, who then disappeared from my field of vision. I hoped he wasn't getting fast food. If I had to stand there for another hour while breathing in the smell of fried fish and hot chips, I was going to smash John's camera against the wall.

"Hold that glare," he ordered swiftly.

I froze.

"Yap! Yap!"

A white streak of fluff blurred across the floor behind John. The rapid dash ripped a cord from the wall and all eyes went wide with horror as one of the lighting stands began to topple in slow motion.

"Mitsy! Godammit, Grace!" Jemima yelled and I winced. Her bright purple hair fell in her eyes as she made a grab for it, catching the expensive equipment before it smashed to the floor. John's second assistant rushed over to help and together they both righted the stand while Mitsy made his great escape.

Click. Click. Click.

John continued working, ignoring the chaos around him while I stood there praying for a swift end to a lousy day.

"Oh gross."

My eyes flicked left at the comment. Mitsy was now humping the shagpile cushion on John's studio couch. His doggy hips pumped like an aerobics instructor on crack. I cringed, seeing his little unneutered balls slapping madly as he made the cushion his bitch.

John paused, before muttering, "Oh for fuck's sake." He made a sound of disgust, calling to one of his team to burn the molested cushion. It was dragged from underneath Mitsy with a thumb and forefinger and taken away. Jemima rushed forward and clicked a leash on Mitsy's collar. He resisted, snapping and snarling as my beleaguered assistant dragged him away.

John sighed heavily and refocused his camera. "Why are you looking after the douchebag's dog, Grace?"

"You're too old to use the word douchebag anymore, John. It reflects poorly on your growth as a decent human being," I replied.

"My growth? Your birthday dinner last month. You paid for his food and drinks, and by drinks, I mean he cleaned out the bar," he reminded me in the stern, patient tone my father used to use.

I hated that tone. It reminded me of when I used to be a pain in the ass as a child. It made me wish I'd made my mother's life easier. I'd done my best to lose the attitude before she died, but it was a case of too little, too late. Now the thought of letting down someone I loved made me want to puke.

"He forgot his wallet."

"That's because he's a penniless douchebag," John retorted. "If he wasn't such a dick on set, people would hire him."

My eyes narrowed sharply. "Who told you that?"

John gave me his back, putting down one camera and picking up another that to me, looked exactly the same. If I hadn't been watching him carefully, I would've missed the casual shrug. "You hear things in this industry. You know that."

Why did it feel like I was missing something?

I opened my mouth, but the cockney twang of Lily Allen singing Fuck You interrupted me.

John put his camera down and turned around. "Answer your phone, Grace. It's a wrap here anyway."

With a shrug, I strode off set and towards Jemima who had Mitsy by the leash in one hand, and my phone in the other. "It's your brother."

My brows flew up in surprise as I took the phone. I put it to my ear as I entered the dressing room. "Henry?"

"Grace? I'm so glad I caught you."

My heart leaped to my throat at his panicked tone. "What's wrong?"

"Hang on." I heard the sound of a muffled argument. Sitting down in front of the mirror, I grabbed a makeup wipe, ready to strip off the layer of must have cosmetics on my face when he came back on the line. I paused to listen. "You probably don't know, but we're playing a song at the annual Australian TV Awards tonight." I knew, but he kept talking, so I didn't interrupt him. I had a date planned with my television and a less than exciting bowl of fruit tonight so I could watch them play. "The thing is, our bass guitarist, Frog, was in a car accident this morning. He's okay, but his left arm is broken. We need a replacement fast. Someone we can trust. You remember when we were young and you used to play bass to my lead guitar? You were so damn good at it. You—"

Panic fluttered in my chest at where the conversation was leading. I cut him off. "I haven't picked up a guitar since you moved to Sydney years ago, Henry. I don't know how to play your songs. I'll fuck it up. Don't ask me to fuck this up for you!"

"Gracie Bean," he said softly, using my childhood nickname. "I need you. Please?"

"Henry Bear," I whispered with a sigh. Henry never knew the real reason why I dropped out of school and slowly disappeared from my family's life. He simply made the assumption that a modelling career was something I wanted and I didn't correct him. Why would I? He would've pulled the big brother card, and who knew where he'd be today if he'd done that?

I mentally reviewed my schedule, knowing there was no free time in there for a side trip to Sydney, but something unfurled in my chest, and with Henry needing an answer, there was no time to pinpoint what it was. All I knew was that he needed me, and just like back then, I wasn't going to let him down. "Of course I'll do it."

"Thank God," he replied.

"Only God? What about me?"

Henry laughed and my lips curved at the sound.

"We'll pay you," he added.

"You know I don't need the money. Just … tell Frog he owes me dinner or something, okay?"

"Frog is not taking you to dinner. You need to treat him like he has leprosy, or the black plague. Wait! Are they the same thing? I suck at historic diseases. You—"

"Henry!" I heard his band manager, Mac, shout.

"Hang on," he muttered again. Another muffled conversation followed before he was back. "We don't play until nine tonight, but if we can you get on a flight this afternoon, that'll give us time for you to learn the song we're lined up to play."

"I can do that."

"Thanks, Gracie Bean. You know …" Henry hesitated.

"What?" I prompted.

"Well, Frog is going to be out of action for a while. We'd love to have you stay and play for us for a few weeks if there was some way you could manage it."

"A few weeks?"

"Yeah."

It wasn't a good idea. John would be pissed. But getting away was starting to sound really appealing. "Okay. Let me see what I can do."

After arranging the details, I hung up, startled when I caught John standing just inside the door, his arms folded. I met his brown eyes in the mirror, seeing anger burning in their dark depths. "Did you hear?"

He nodded wordlessly.

"John."

"It's a bad time with the shit you've got going on. I don't think you should go."

I closed my eyes against the censure in his voice. John's arms wrapped around me from behind and squeezed. I could feel the rapid thumping of his heart where his chest pressed up against my back.

"Grace—"

"I'm going, John. Henry needs me."

His arms fell away abruptly and my eyes flew open. "Goddammit!" he growled loudly. "You know what? You never listen to me anyway, so just go!"

I flinched when he turned around and punched the wall, leaving a dent in the plaster. Paint flaked off, fluttering harmlessly to the pale timber floor. After drawing a deep breath, he muttered something that sounded like, "stubborn bitch," before he turned and left the dressing room.

That right there, was the fourth clue that my day sucked donkey's balls. Surely it couldn't get worse, right?

With no time to change or take off the thick layer of makeup, I stood up, calling out, "Jemima!" as I left the dressing room.

She was at the small table by the window where everyone was now eating lunch, pulling all our things together between grabbing at food. Mitsy was by her side, chewing through the thick leather leash that tied him to the chair.

Shit. Mitsy.

"Jemima, I have to fly to Sydney. It's likely I could be gone for a few weeks."

Not pausing her packing, she replied, "I know. Your flight details just came through on email." She looked at me then. "And no."

"No? You don't even know what I was going to ask you."

"I'm not looking after Mitsy."

Dammit.

I looked at John. He sat at the table with a bottle of water, not eating. He reclined back in his chair and folded his arms. The tension was palpable as everyone eyeballed us, obviously having heard our brief argument just moments ago.

"John," I began. Feeling desperate, I started towards him.

He held up a hand and I paused. "You know I would," he said, and we both knew he was lying because no one would take Mitsy, not on a dare, or the knowledge of an impending tsunami, or even on the promise of cold, hard cash. "But I've got that job up north in three days, and then I'm going to be out of the country for the next couple of weeks."

"Are you sure?"

Still pissed, he nodded.

Half an hour later, I was on the curb of Chapel Street, waving goodbye to Jemima. She tried to look sympathetic for my sake, but the spring in her step exposed her inner jubilation at seeing the back of Mitsy and the prospect of a few weeks off.

John blew her a kiss before hailing me a cab. When it pulled up in front of us, he opened the door and shoved me in. The sudden jostling made Mitsy turn and bare his teeth in my face. I returned the sentiment until I saw the driver eyeing us through his rearview mirror. John hopped in beside me. Shutting the car door, he offered the man directions before I could say anything.

"What are you doing?" I asked as we zoomed into lunchtime traffic.

"I'm helping you pack, then I'll go with you to the airport. I still don't think you should leave, Grace. Are you going to tell Henry what's going on?"

"Are you kidding?" The very thought had my toes curling in horror. "No way."

John shook his head but let it go for now. "I wish I could come with you."

"Me too," I mumbled and my eyes burned. I averted my face to look out the car window. Thank God John could never stay pissed off for long, even when I was too stubborn to admit he was right. I had some bad shit going on. Leaving would only make it worse.

I reached blindly for his hand and he linked our fingers. That's how the drive to my apartment went—me staring out the window not seeing anything, John holding my hand in silent support, and Mitsy baring his teeth at the world.

Chapter Four
GRACE

Two hours later I waved goodbye to John and boarded the plane. The flight from Melbourne to Sydney only took an hour. For that I was relieved because Mitsy was travelling in style courtesy of Qantas Airlines cargo hold. Knowing his aversion to moving vehicles, I could only imagine his beef with an aeroplane. The only other option was to leave him on his own. As tempting as that was, animal abandonment wasn't an extra curricular activity of mine.

The elderly lady in the window seat next to mine eyed the colourful tattoos covering my arm and shoulder as I lifted my bag into the overhead compartment. I fought a sigh at her expression of distaste and tried for a smile but someone bumped me from behind. I stumbled forward and my bag fell, spewing its contents all over the floor.

"Seriously?" I griped.

"Sorry," a male voice mumbled. I glanced at his retreating back as he continued down the aisle of the plane without stopping to help. Had common courtesy gone to the dogs? The other passengers averted their eyes, clearly going for the "if I can't see it, it isn't happening" approach.

"Excuse me?" I called out loudly.

The guy looked over his shoulder, running his eyes over my legs before shrugging and continuing on. Cursing under my breath, I carelessly shoved everything back in my bag, feeling the elderly lady watching my every move like a hawk. Who did she think she was, an undercover air marshal?

"Is everything okay, ma'am?"

The flight attendant hovered as I put my bag away, no doubt waiting for me to cause a scene. The urge to yell and throw things held enormous appeal, especially knowing I had Mitsy to look forward to at the end of my flight, but I hadn't been that scrappy, trouble-causing kid for a long time, so I held onto my calm composure and replied, "Everything's fine, thank you."

The flight was quick. It felt like we'd only hit cruising altitude when we began making our descent into Sydney. Rather than get caught in the pushing and shoving of everyone trying to be first off the plane, I waited. When the aisle cleared, I removed my bag from above, slung my guitar case over my back, and left the plane.

Retrieving my phone, I switched it on as I walked. Henry sent me a message before I left letting me know his two friends, Travis and Casey, would be collecting me. From what I knew, the two were partners in Jamieson and Valentine Consulting, a firm that took care of the band's security. The message included a photo so I knew who to look for. I went to check the photo when another message flashed up on screen.

Flicking it open, I faltered and stopped suddenly. The carry-on bag in my hand fell at my feet. Someone swore as they nearly ran into me, keeping up their rant as they bypassed me and continued on. I ignored it all as I focused on my phone with disbelief.

It was a photo of Dalton in a compromising position, and by compromising, I meant clothing was optional. The girl wrapped around him, Selena, was a British model slash acquaintance slash tartmonkey, who had done the Italy job with us. She was also the one who sent the photo. There was no message attached. It wasn't necessary. A picture spoke a thousand words, and this one said, "Grace. You are a dumb chump. You are so chumpy, I have to send you photo evidence to rub this in your face because you're too blind to see it for yourself."

Suddenly John's overly enthusiastic character assassination of Dalton this morning became crystal clear.

He knew. He damn well knew and didn't say anything.

Hurt welled in my chest. Dalton might have been a douche, but John wasn't. I trusted him. He was the only friend I could be myself with, tell anything to, and know that he had my back without question. Why hadn't he had my back with this?

Anger built inside me like a tornado, overtaking the hurt and obliterating the calm composure I was so damn famous for.

There was only one thing to do.

Setting my jaw, I rage-dialled.

"Grace," John answered, his voice all warm and light as though he actually cared.

Asshole!

"Don't you Grace me, you bastard!" I shouted into the phone. This had been the biggest donkey's balls day ever, and damn if I wasn't going ram my wrath down his lying, two-faced throat.

"Ah hell," I heard him mutter.

Realising I was attracting an audience, airport security in particular, I lowered my voice and hissed, "How long have you known?"

He hesitated. Either he didn't want to say, or my sudden, uncharacteristic outburst had rendered him speechless. "A couple of days."

"You hesitated," I growled.

I heard him take a deep breath through the phone. "A couple of weeks."

"Two weeks!" I shrieked.

Airport security started towards me, obviously becoming aware of my emotional instability. Could they arrest you for that? One thing I knew for sure—I wasn't planning on finding out. With my guitar still slung over my back, I grabbed my bag off the floor and hustled towards the nearest restroom. Finding a vacant stall, I wedged my way inside and locked the door, breathing heavy from the sudden exertion.

"… you needed to know."

"What?" John had been talking the entire time I was making my escape and I'd missed his entire explanation.

"Your voice sounds tinny. Where are you?"

I set my guitar down against the wall and hung my bag on the hook of the door. "I'm barricaded in the airport toilet."

Oh God.

I was barricaded inside an airport toilet while my life collapsed around me like a house of cards and all I could feel was relief.

Amidst the odour of urine and lavender-scented deodoriser, I realised I wasn't even angry at Dalton. Knowing he'd cheated wasn't a burning hot poker to the heart. Okay. Scratch that. I wanted to rip his philandering dick off. But it was anger at myself that overshadowed the need to start tearing appendage's from Dalton's perfectly muscled, lying, cheating body.

I wasn't the person I wanted to be, and this wasn't the life I wanted, so why was I still living it?

I paused. Was it really that easy?

If so, why hadn't I done this earlier? I needed to get with program. I also needed to boot Dalton from my life. Modelling was something I'd never wanted to do. Living out of suitcases and different cities was lonely. I couldn't even comfort my loneliness with excessive booze or chocolate, because gaining a pound meant getting fired.

Being able to leave all that behind to play a guitar was like some … some unforeseen liberation. The opportunity to become emancipated from everything that made me who I was had just been served up on a silver platter and I wanted it.

"What?" John barked in my ear. "You're barricaded in an airport toilet?

Why?"

I want to be the girl I was supposed to be. I want to live life like my mother did. I want to… to…

"I want to eat," I hissed into the phone.

"You're barricaded in the airport toilet because you want to eat?"

I rolled my eyes. "Now's not the time to be ridiculous, John. This is serious. And I'm trapped in here because airport security was giving me funny looks."

"Funny as in har har, or funny as in this girl's on crack?"

"It doesn't matter, John." I huffed impatiently. "What matters is that I trusted you to be my friend and you didn't tell me about Dalton. I found out through Selena who had the bad taste to send me a photo. Oh God, I'm such a chump!"

"She did that? Fuckin' bitch." I heard him light a cigarette and exhale a plume of smoke. "I won't be doing a shoot with her ever again."

John was a hot commodity in the fashion industry. Anyone he photographed hit instant fame. His declaration meant bad news for Selena but feeling sorry for her was a bit of a stretch right now. "At least I know! Were you ever going to say anything, John?"

"Grace," John said so softly I wanted to weep. "Remember what happened just ten days ago?"

"Don't." My voice cracked on the single word because I did remember. And damn him for reminding me.

"It wasn't the right time to say anything."

"It's never a good time to share bad shit, right? But you know what? This is my reason to say fuck everything. Fuck the money and the shallow bitches, and Dalton, and my whole entire life. Fuck it all, John. I don't care anymore. Not about any of it. This is my life. I'm not going to sit back and let it kick me in the goddamn face when I've not even had a chance to live it how I want to. I'm going to fight for it."

"Holy shit!" he exclaimed. "I'm on the next flight out."

"No." I banged my fist against the toilet door for emphasis, feeling it shudder ominously beneath my unwarranted assault. "I'm not some crazy bitch gone rogue that needs restraints and white jackets. You know me, John. This has been a long time coming."

"And you choose now to have your emotional emancipation? Did they ring you again?"

"No."

I heard him sigh. "Jesus, Grace."

Flicking my wrist, I checked the time on my watch. Travis and Casey would be out there waiting, probably wondering if I'd missed my flight. "I should go."

"Are you sure you don't want me there?"

"I'm sure."

After assuring John I'd call him later that night, I hung up the phone and stared at the back of the toilet door. My eyes burned but I didn't let myself cry.

I locked my jaw and breathed deep as I blinked them back.

The long drawn out squeak from the restroom door opening interrupted my pep talk. The sound of boots was heavy and I jolted when someone rapped smartly on the toilet door I was barricaded behind.

"Ma'am? Airport security. Can you step out of the toilet please?"

I tensed. What the hell? Were they really going to call me out for disturbing the peace? Did they have nothing better to do?

"Just a minute," I called out, tucking my phone back into bag.

"Now, ma'am." Her tone was firm, indicating if I didn't open the door and step out immediately, she would storm it like a one-woman SWAT team. In this tiny space, all that would achieve was the door slamming in my face.

Not relishing the idea of a bloody nose or black eye, I unlatched the lock and opened it. My eyes stared at her shiny boots, following the starched uniform upwards to the dark hair pulled back into a bun so severe it only emphasised her narrowed eyes. She stood directly in front of me, barring my way out.

"Is there a problem?"

"Yes there is." She took one precise step backwards. "Please step outside of the toilet stall. We've been informed you may be carrying drugs. You'll need to come with me so we can arrange a search of your person and all your items."

Drugs? My mouth opened and closed. My person? Did she mean a strip search? Surely this was some kind of joke?

The restroom door opened again. This time there was no drawn out, sinister squeak. It banged open with purpose, making me flinch.

"Grace, baby?" The words were spoken casually yet the deep voice rumbled through the confined area, setting off shivers across my skin.

My eyes shifted from the current threat to the strange man suddenly invading the female restroom. I blinked. Flirty blue eyes, clear as a luminous crystal, raked me over in a way that suggested he knew me. Intimately. For a split second, I wished it were true. In my line of work I saw pretty boys every day, but this guy oozed masculinity in a way they never could. His dirty, dark blond hair was casually windblown, not carefully and deliberately mussed like the male models I worked with. His shirt and jeans were worn and faded, comfortable, yet easily emphasised the wide chest and biceps thick with muscle.

With his full lips, straight nose, and firm, stubbled jaw, he bordered somewhere between rugged man and pretty boy. It was quite a feat. Unfortunately, he appeared on the verge of insanity because I'd never met him in my life.

I opened my mouth, prepared to tell him I was no one's baby and he could shove that endearment up his clacker, when he shot me a warning glance. The sharp flash of intelligence skewered me before the lazy, amused glint returned to his eyes. "There you are. I was getting worried."

"Casey!" The security guard grinned, startling me with her sudden friendly demeanour.

Casey? I mouthed, looking between the two as I tried to make sense of the situation.

He returned her grin, dimples popping as he turned those flirty eyes on her like he knew her too. "Helen. How's the move from Bankstown Police treating you?"

Helen smoothed a hand over her tidy hairstyle, ensuring no strands dared stray from formation and then shrugged. "It's a paycheque. How are things with you cowboys over at Jamieson and Valentine Consulting? Haven't rolled any cars today?" She laughed loud and hard.

My brows flew up. Cowboys? Jamieson and Valentine Consulting? Rolled cars?

Smart enough to put two and two together, I realised this must be the Casey that was here with Travis to collect me and here I was, hiding in the restroom like the guilty drug runner I was accused of being. My face burned with embarrassment.

Casey shrugged, keeping his smile as he said, "Can't complain and not yet, but the day's still young."

She laughed. The sound was so forceful you'd think it was the funniest thing she'd ever heard. After ending it with an awkward wheeze, she nodded at me. "She's with you?"

He met my eyes briefly, the corners of his lips curving in a sexy smirk before he looked back at the security guard. "She's with me alright. Is there a problem?"

She paused for a moment and I wanted to slap her for accusing me of carrying drugs. "No problem. We received notification that your young lady might've been carrying drugs on her flight but we must've been mistaken. We know you boys don't tolerate that shit."

With a wink, Helen slapped him on the back as she strode out of the restroom, pausing only to say, "You two take care now," and she was gone. My jaw hit the floor. She was letting me go on his word alone?

Before I could speak, my wrist was grabbed in a vice and I was manhandled from the restroom and shoved against the wall behind me. The sudden assault made my lungs burn and my pulse race in panic. I flattened my palms against his muscular chest and shoved, but he didn't budge. The man was made of goddamn steel and damn, he was big.

"If you don't let me go," I growled with menace, "I'm going to … to …" What, call security? Jesus. Somehow I'd gone from the frying pan into the fire.

Think, Grace. You need an exit strategy.

Casey pressed himself against me, wedging a firm thigh between my legs, effectively shutting down my struggles. The heat of his body was intense, and I felt sweat break out on my brow. Swallowing hard, I scrambled for my inner fearlessness and looked into his beautiful face. It was only inches from mine, his flirty eyes now flat and hard. He glared at me. It was so harsh you'd think I'd just punted a puppy across the room.

"You bitch," he ground out.

Bitch? Me? This man had me a breath away from losing my shit. I didn't know whether I should just bite him or scream for help. Instead, I paused my struggles and narrowed my eyes, returning his glare with one so almighty it should've ruptured his veins. John would've been proud. "You asshole!"

Chapter Five
CASEY

"I'm the asshole?" I growled.

The smell of honey and vanilla drifted from her hair, invading my senses as she struggled to get loose. To my horror, the sweet scent and the press of her tits against my chest had my cock responding, waking up with a perkiness that would soon be obvious. Cursing silently, I shifted my hips backward.

She glanced down at the bulge in my jeans before her wide eyes met mine. "You pervert!" she hissed. "Is this how you get off? Cornering innocent women inside airport toilets and rubbing all over them?"

"Stop moving," I ordered harshly and took a small step back without loosening my hold. Grace was right. I felt like a damn pervert. "I just saved your ass from getting arrested for carrying drugs, dammit. Travis and I were supposed to be picking you up, but I'm considering telling everyone you never arrived and sending you back home. We don't want your kind hanging around."

"My kind? My kind?" Grace shot me a glare, her narrowed eyes darkening to rival the deep blue depths of the ocean. "Who the hell do you think you are? Batman? I hate to be the one to disillusion you, but this is not Gotham City, and no one appreciates your misguided vigilante type justice, least of all me. I am not carrying drugs, you idiot. You can search my bags if you don't believe me. Hell, you can have my bags. I'm so freaking done with this day I don't even care anymore!"

Travis appeared beside me, scratching the back of his head as he assessed the situation.

Nostrils flaring in anger, Grace cast him a quick glance and her brow arched sardonically. "Robin, I presume?"

I shook my head, cursing at myself. I should have been prepared for this, despite my day starting off none too badly.

I'd only just arrived at Jared and Evie's house earlier for their Sunday barbecue before I was back in the car with Travis and on our way here to the airport. Frog, the bass guitarist with Evie's band, had been in a car accident that morning. The outcome was a broken arm. With the band playing at the awards ceremony later tonight, it wasn't looking good for them. Mac had been frothing at the mouth from stress, Quinn looked ready to pass out, and Evie was greener than she was yesterday.

Arriving to the chaos had come as no surprise. The Jamieson and Valentine clan might have been my family, and don't get me wrong, when everything was good with them, it was like the stars aligned and shimmery fairy dust fell from the heavens, but when it went to shit, it went there via the seventh circle of Hell.

Taking that into consideration, offering to collect their replacement guitarist from the airport with Travis had seemed like a good idea, until Travis opened his mouth about last night.

"You and Morgan?"

I shook my head in answer, focusing my attention on driving rather than explaining myself.

"Was she the one that went home with you on Friday night? You're seeing her now?"

"Calm the fuck down, Trav." Stopping at a red light, I turned to face him. "If we're going to have a gossip session about my night out, maybe we should start with the outfit I chose first before discussing whether I put out or not."

The light turned green and I accelerated, satisfied when the small burst of speed left the traffic behind me scrambling to catch up. The deflection would only work for so long. Travis and Coby had seen Morgan last night when I answered the door. The suggestive gleam in her eye and the overexposure of skin left no doubt to her intentions. Between that and the damn sex shop bag on the counter, it was obvious I'd been on board with those intentions.

"So?" Travis waved his hand. "What did you wear then?"

Smug sonofabitch.

"Fine." My hands tightened on the steering wheel as I hit Sydney's M1 freeway and opened the car up. "I fucked her, okay? I may plan on doing it again. Do I need to check every potential fuck with you first and get your approval in duplicate?"

"You know what?" Travis turned in his seat to glare at me. "Yes. You fucking do if you're gonna pull shit like this. We have contracts with the government that includes the damn Sydney police. Our firm doesn't need you going and poking your cock into the middle of all that. There is no doubt we will be dealing with her in an official capacity at some stage, and if she gets your customary brush-off, how are we supposed to trust her to have our backs? What is it, Casey, you like her that much she's worth that kind of hit?"

Travis took a deep breath. He sat there fuming in the passenger seat, waiting for my answer as I navigated through traffic and took the airport exit off the motorway. I didn't have one. Well, not one that wouldn't give away my intentions, so I kept my mouth shut.

"If you're just looking to get laid, find someone else," he added, unwilling to leave it alone.

Reaching the domestic terminal of Sydney airport, I found a spot and parked the car. Turning off the ignition, I sat back in my seat and took a deep breath as I stared out the windshield. Travellers moved at a rapid pace, wheeling their suitcases between cars and over the pedestrian crossings.

"I'm not just looking to get laid. That's the problem."

Travis furrowed his brow. "I don't get it."

Yanking the keys, I got out of the car. Travis followed and I beeped the locks, shoving the keys in my jeans' pocket. "She works cybercrime now," I reminded him as we strode towards the building entrance. "You know how closed off those tech cops are."

After a moment, he mumbled, "Ah hell. You think by fucking her, she might be willing to instigate a search for the wiped information."

"No one else will do it," I bitched. "As far as everyone else is concerned, the case was closed and the missing files are just one of those things that happen."

The pileup of cars waiting for pedestrians to cross was long. We both jogged over the crossing and towards the front doors. They whooshed open automatically, emitting cool air as we strode inside.

"Let it go, Casey. It's in the past. You can't change it or fix it, and getting Morgan involved is going to make it all worse."

Anger burned in my chest. I grabbed his bicep, effectively halting him, and looked him in the eye. "Fuck you, Trav." My jaw ticked as I fought to lock the resentment down. "It's not that simple. How can I let go when I've lost everything already? If I had answers, then maybe I …"

I, what? Could move on? Forgive myself?

"You could what?"

I shook my head and started walking again. "Let's just collect whoever the hell it is we're here to collect, okay?"

In tense silence, we arrived at the gate and waited as passengers started flowing out. That was when I saw her walking directly towards us, a guitar case slung casually over her back.

"Jesus," I breathed, standing beside Travis as I took in the deep red tangle of hair flowing down her back and colourful tattoo that wound around the length of her bare arm and shoulder. Tiny black leather shorts displayed long slender legs that strode towards us with purpose. The blood in my veins heated as I fixed on her. My mind immediately had me bending her over from behind, pulling on that wild mass of hair, and yanking her head back as I thrust inside her, over and over. "Do you think that's her?"

Travis checked the photo Quinn messaged through to his phone so we'd recognise who we were collecting. "I think so."

She appeared oblivious to the people craning their necks to get a second glimpse of her, absorbed in her phone as her finger scrolled down its screen. For a second she glanced up and it was like getting punched in the gut. The girl wasn't just beautiful—she was shock and awe. Her eyes locked on mine for a split second. They were a wild, stormy blue, and immediately I imagined her on her knees, those wide eyes staring up at me as I fucked her mouth.

Who was I kidding? I'd have had her any which way. All I needed was a plan on how to go about it.

I glanced at Travis. "Who is she?"

"Henry's sister apparently."

Henry wasn't just lead guitarist for Jamieson, he was a friend. That instantly turned her from a quick fuck into a complication. Hell hath no fury like a brother protecting the virtue of his little sister. He would hack off my balls with a rusty spoon.

Morgan, Morgan, Morgan, I silently chanted, reminding myself that I had no business building a harem, but my eyes were locked on her and wouldn't budge. "What did Quinn say her name was?"

Travis checked his phone again. "Grace."

Grace was … suddenly shouting into her phone. Her bag dropped at her feet as hurt and anger collided violently in her eyes. The abrupt disturbance began attracting attention. The general public began giving her a wide berth as they moved past. I heard her shriek "two weeks" into the phone, or it could've been "blue cheeks" for all I knew—we weren't standing that close. She took in the airport at a glance and in an unpredictable turn of events, she seized her bag and made a rapid exit. Airport security moved in quickly, following her fleeing form.

My mouth fell open as the scene unfolded before us. "What the fuck was that?"

Travis shot me a look of wide-eyed disbelief. "I have no idea."

Grace disappeared inside the female restroom, the door banging shut in her wake. I was pretty sure I recognised the female security guard who was speaking on her radio nearby. After a minute, she followed Grace inside.

"One day. Just one fucking day without a drama. Is it too much to ask?" I heard Travis mumble.

I folded my arms. "You better go after her."

He raised his brows and mirrored my actions, creating a standoff. "No way. You go."

"Rock, paper, scissors?"

Travis scowled. "Hell no. You cheat."

"Cheat?" My voice pitched a little high and I cleared my throat. "How the fuck can I cheat? It's not like I can read your mind, Travis. Stop being a little bitch and go get her."

"A little bitch? You're kidding, right? I married Quinn, for fuck's sake. Mac is my baby sister. Evie is my sister-in-law. I live this drama every damn day. If you were any kind of friend—"

I held up a hand. "Fine. Just … fine."

Leaving Travis behind, I headed for the restroom. Reaching the door, I caught the mention of drugs and anger slammed into me. Drugs? Are you kidding me? That was bad enough, but bringing it into the Valentine and Jamieson family? That put her a little lower than the crust of the earth in my estimation. I pushed open the door with a resounding bang. I didn't care if she was Henry's sister or the goddamn Queen. I wanted to shove her on the next plane back to Melbourne.

Schooling my white hot anger into a flirty grin, I dealt promptly with the situation, but after the security guard left, the fury bubbled over until I found myself pinning Grace against the wall. Her stormy eyes were furious as she swore at me.

"What the hell's going on?" Travis questioned after she just finished giving her Batman spiel.

Letting go, I stepped away from Grace. She adjusted her clothes with short, sharp movements before stooping to collect her bag and guitar. "You tell me. I'm here because my brother needs me, but I wasn't aware the Dynamic Duo was going to lay out the welcome mat in such a violent and dazzling display. If you'll both excuse me …"

She brushed past the both of us before pausing. Turning slightly, she added, "I think it might be safer if I just get a cab to Henry's place," before spinning on her heel and walking away.

"What the hell did you do?"

I dragged my eyes from Grace's retreating form and met the accusatory glare of Travis. "Airport security said she was carrying drugs, Trav. Am I supposed to just let that slide?"

"Was she?"

"Was she what?"

Travis shook his head. "Carrying drugs, dammit."

I paused. Taking a deep breath, I let the burn of anger cool off. With it came the image of righteous indignation on Grace's face, and the feel of her smooth, warm skin beneath my palms. Maybe I acted rashly, but the way my body responded so quickly just by looking at her pissed me off. The last thing I needed right now was a hard-on for Grace when I needed to stay focused on Morgan. "She was about to get taken away and searched before I intercepted, so I uh, don't know."

"You don't know?" he ground out. "This is Henry's sister, Casey. You really think she's some kind of junkie? Did she look like she was cracked out on meth to you? It's obviously some kind of mistake, one you should've recognised before you went all Batman over her just like she accused you of. What the hell is with you lately?"

Without waiting for an answer, he called out, "Grace, wait!"

She spun around with raised brows, walking backwards—no doubt in a hurry to get as far from me as possible. "Look. We're sorry, okay? How about I give you a ride back to Henry's and we can send Casey home in a cab?"

"It's my car, asshole," I muttered.

"Shut up," he snapped.

Pausing, Grace spared another glare in my direction before her face lit up in what I could only conclude was a look of glee. It would've made me nervous if I wasn't so focused on her glossy lips. Remembering the sweet scent of honey, I wondered what they would taste like if I licked them.

"Actually, that's not necessary," she replied.

My eyes lowered as she started walking towards us again. It was impossible not to. Jared might've been a boob man, and Travis had an odd quirk for the naked lines of Quinn's back, but I was all about the legs, and this girl was born with stilts.

Hell.

"I'll take you up on your offer, but there's no need for Casey to catch a cab. Actually..." she turned her considering gaze on me, unholy glee lingering in her eyes "...there's something you can do for me if you wouldn't mind?"

Travis cleared his throat pointedly.

Folding my arms, my blue eyes narrowed as I offered Grace a cool smile. "Sure. What do you need?"

She grinned. "I need you to go to the Qantas freight terminal for me."

"You have freight?"

Grace shrugged. "If you could call Mitsy 'freight,' then yes, I do."

Travis tilted his head and asked the all-important question. "What's Mitsy?"

"A dog."

My brows flew up. "You brought a dog with you?"

"Yes. A dog. They're common as pets, you know? Never had a pet before, Casey? Considering your profession, you probably prefer the company of bats, right?"

Travis choked on a laugh beside me. Prick. If he told Grace the only pet I'd ever owned was a frog called Batman when I was eight years old, I'd strangle him right there in the damn airport.

I'd caught the frog down the backyard of our house where I used to watch the tadpoles in the dirty creek. I always went there to escape when my father was having one of his rages. I had to sneak the damn thing inside because I wasn't allowed pets. I set up him with rocks and water in an old fish tank I'd found in the garage, putting it out of sight behind the desk in my room.

It had only been a week when late one night his croaks boomed through the quiet house like thunder, alerting my father to his presence. He stormed into my room shoving the door open so hard it banged against the wall. Batman flinched, going quiet. He knew something bad was going down. Animals were masters at sensing hostility.

Horror knotted my belly when my father grabbed my beloved pet, threw him on the floor, and crushed him beneath his boot. I remember howling so loud he reached over and clipped me across the face. The blow packed enough force for a bone to crack in my jaw. Dazed, I puked on the floor, and after growling at me to clean up the mess, he left the room, slamming the door behind him. Tears blurred my eyes when I collected the frog's lifeless body off the floor and took him outside. Even now I couldn't erase the sound of Batman's bones crunching beneath my father's boots.

"I've had a pet before," I muttered through gritted teeth.

"Good," she replied. "Then Mitsy should be no trouble for you."

Chapter Six
GRACE

"So you play in a band back home, Grace?" Travis was half twisted in the front passenger seat of Casey's car, questioning me on the ride to the duplex where Henry lived.

The car was a Corvette Stingray in spectacular condition. I'd watched Gone in 60 Seconds enough times to know this was Casey's unicorn car. The tyres were wide with thick tread that screamed "mess with me and I will mow you down like a motherfucker." Not a single scratch or dent marred the gleaming gunmetal grey paint job, and despite the vintage model, the interior smelled like new leather. Just sitting in the back seat had my insides fizzing like I'd overdosed on champagne.

"Not at all. I haven't played for years. Not since before Henry moved in with Evie and started uni," I replied distractedly as Mitsy chewed savagely on the corner of the back seat. I winced at the sacrilege. I didn't need to know Casey to know he would shit a brick when he saw the damage. Still. The man had it coming—shoving me up against the wall the way he did and accusing me of being some crack whore. I bit the insides of my cheeks as I left the dog to it. Who knew Dalton's tiny furbeast would come in so handy? Karma was a bitch called Mitsy, I thought with an audible snort. Feeling Casey's gaze on me in the rearview mirror, I schooled my features.

To say he was unimpressed with collecting the dog was saying the ocean was a little bit wet. He'd backed up a step when the freight attendant brought

Mitsy to the counter in the little dog carrier and handed it over with obvious relief. The damn dog hadn't appreciated the flight, as evidenced by the bared teeth locked on the cage door and the pile of puke near his front paws. It had almost been worth bringing him to see the look of horror on Casey's face. Mitsy, for some unexplainable reason, had barked excitedly when I came into view.

"This yapfest is yours?" Casey turned raised brows on me with disgust. "With a name like Mitsy, I should've known," he muttered under his breath, because yeah, if he had a dog, it would no doubt be some badass pit bull named 50cent. Wanker. I didn't tell him the dog wasn't mine for long if I could help it. This partnership was temporary. As soon as Dalton set down on Australian soil, it would be sayonara Mitsy.

"You have a problem, Casey? Want to search his cage and do a pat down for contraband? I hear up the ass is the best place to hide things," I pointed out helpfully. "Perhaps you should start there."

Travis choked from somewhere on my left and Casey scowled. "No problem, Slim," he replied, taking a firm grasp on the cage as Mitsy growled in warning. "Seems like your type of dog."

"My type? Wow." I raised my brows, choosing to ignore the insulting nickname he bestowed with such originality. "You're pretty big on pigeonholing people. That just smacks of deep-seated issues. What's yours?"

"What's my what?" he asked as we began the trek to the carpark, Travis kindly wheeling my suitcase for me as Casey led the way.

"What's your issue?"

"My issue?" he retorted, his tone implying that I was sorely mistaken and it was me with the issue.

Travis ping-ponged his gaze between the both of us with an amused glint in his green eyes. Ignoring it, I replied, "Yeah. Your issue."

Casey shrugged, his muscular shoulders tightening beneath his worn shirt. I fought not to stare. No man had the right to look as good as he did and turn out to be an asshole. The fact that I wanted to run my hands over that smooth, golden skin was like the universe playing a cruel joke. "No issue."

But something flashed across his face before it was hidden quickly. If I had to name it I'd say his pretty blue eyes looked haunted. Just like they did when I mentioned him having pets. Perhaps he once had a cat that got run over when he was little? My heart filled with an unexpected surge of tenderness towards him.

"You're just obviously high-maintenance," he added as we crossed the road and began weaving through parked cars. "Like your dog."

I beat back the tender feeling with a big, baseball bat, bruising it into submission. The last thing I needed was to go getting a ladyboner over an antagonistic hero on a bender for justice.

"Screw you, Casey," I hissed as we stopped in front of the magnificent car that I wanted to kick with the heel of my shiny black boot. "Oh wait. That must be your problem, right? You're all uptight because who wants to fuck a douchebag?"

Travis shouted with laughter, stowing my luggage as I released Mitsy from his little prison and clipped his leash on with haste. As a final insult, the dog cocked his furry little leg, displaying his ample appendage as he pissed all over Casey's motherfucker tyres.

"Dude," Travis declared as they both eyed the dog like the menace to society that he was. "You called a male dog 'Mitsy?'"

Now here we were, on our way to Henry's so the man could dump me and run. He was quiet, his temper seeming to have cooled right off, leaving him calm. It was almost unnatural and I found I didn't like it. If this had been my car and a dog like Mitsy emptied his bladder all over it, I would've made them walk home.

"So Henry's told me you're a pretty big deal in the world of modelling. How long have you been doing that for?" Travis asked.

"Since I was fourteen."

"Fourteen?" he echoed, looking unimpressed. "That's a bit young, isn't it?"

"It is," I told him honestly. Missing out on normal teenage years and life at home had been lonely, though I suspect his expression related more to the exploitation of young girls in an adult profession. "But I got to travel the world and meet a lot of amazing people," I added, as if that somehow made up for it.

Casey glanced at me through the rearview mirror. "So you're an international model then, huh?"

I cocked my head, unable to avoid one last dig. "Sorry to disappoint you, Casey, but international model isn't a euphemism for international drug runner and crack whore."

Casey's mouth fell open. "If you hadn't—"

Travis cut him off. "Henry must be proud of you, huh?"

Swallowing the sudden lump in my throat, I stared out the car window. "I wouldn't know," I said softly.

Travis's phone rang then, thankfully interrupting the conversation. He answered it and I tuned the call out, instead thinking of my brother. What had I gotten myself into, agreeing to spend weeks with a whole bunch of people I didn't know? A sudden ache of loneliness welled in my chest. I fought the urge to message John and tell him that I needed him here to hold my hand.

"Grace?" Casey spoke quietly.

I glanced up, meeting his eyes in the rearview mirror. "What?"

His eyes flicked to the road briefly before returning to the mirror. He shook his head, dismissing me. "Nothing."

Soon after, we pulled up to the huge duplex where Henry lived. There was a mammoth security gate out front with black cameras trained on the drive like scary sentinels. I concluded the high brick fence was new going by the dug out turf bordering along the edges. There was no doubt fame had stripped their anonymity. It had probably resulted in rabid fans camping out on their doorstep until better security measures were put in place.

As though Casey's car had just said "open sesame," the gates began opening, allowing us through the drive. The amount of parked cars announced it as a current hive of activity. They ranged from a huge blue Hilux to a gleaming black Porsche and a savage looking Subaru.

Travis and Casey exited the car, but my confidence gasped its last breath like a rapidly deflating balloon. I went for the door handle but my hand wouldn't move. What if I let Henry down? What if—

My phone rang, cutting off my meltdown.

Digging through my bag, I pulled it out and checked the screen.

Shit.

Suddenly the urge to projectile puke all over the interior of Casey's unicorn car overwhelmed me.

Breathe. Breathe. Breathe.

My glance fell on Mitsy chewing the interior with his inherent ferocity. He had bigger balls than I did. The tough little furbeast could probably teach me a thing or two.

With a churning stomach, I hit the answer key and put the phone to my ear. "H-hello?"

"Grace," came the firm male voice on the other line.

"Yes?" I whispered.

"You know we've been trying to reach you for two weeks now."

"I-I know. I just … I'm sorry, but—"

"Did you receive the package we sent you?"

"Yes," I whispered repetitively. My brain couldn't seem to grasp much more out of the English language than a simple word.

When the call ended, I threw the phone back in my bag like it was viper about to bite my face off. Oh God. Why did I have to answer?

Stupid, stupid girl.

The passenger door closest to Mitsy flew open and Travis ducked his head. "Coming?" His eyes widened in panic as they fell on the mutilated seat. Mitsy must have felt the sudden vibe of terror because he growled ominously.

"You're dead," Travis said. "You know that, right? It was nice knowing you, Grace, and it was a privilege to have you share your last moments with me."

I fought the urge to laugh hysterically. It was quite possible my life was forfeited already anyway. The thought made me gag, literally, and Travis's eyes widened further. "You okay?"

"Absolutely," I muttered on a heave. Knowing I needed to pick my battles meant Casey was priority threat number one. I ran my eyes over Travis's thickly muscled, six-foot-three frame with hope. "You're a big dude, Travis. You can take him in a fight, can't you?"

Travis shook his head. "These muscles are for display purposes only."

"Har har. Thanks for noth—"

I flinched wildly when a loud rap came on the car window next to me and my head bumped the roof of the car. "You coming in, Slim, or are you going to sit in my car all day talking to yourself?"

"Go," Travis whispered with sudden urgency. "I got this." He shut the door, offered a quick thumbs up, and walked around the back of the car. "Oh shit," he said loudly. "Is that a scratch on the back of Marjorie?"

"What the fuck?" Casey squawked before disappearing from view. Marjorie? The big badass car with the massive, motherfucker tyres was called Marjorie? "The eighteen hundreds called, Casey, they want their name back," I mumbled under my breath.

Realising I had only a short window of time to escape, I shouldered my bag and put Mitsy in a stranglehold. Bracing myself, I pushed the car door open and got out, shutting it quickly behind me. I was setting Mitsy on the grass when they concluded the potential scratch was simply a false alarm and returned to my side. I flashed Travis a grateful smile. He returned it before humming the death march as he wheeled my suitcase up the driveway.

My already shot nerves skyrocketed. I was sure the damage was easily fixed. I'd simply offer to pay for it if I ever saw the man again, which wasn't likely. The thought calmed me as I took in the exterior of the duplex. What hit me first was its inviting charm. In a tree-lined street, the duplex sat harmless and unobtrusive. A shared timber porch between both front doors ran along the front. The weatherboard was painted a deep, rich stone colour with white trim, and lush, bright green hedges lined the front gardens. It was obvious that warmth and happiness resided within, and it beckoned me like a thickly frosted cupcake with chocolate sprinkles.

I hesitated.

"You going to move or are you waiting for me to carry you in?"

Turning to Casey, I delivered my menacing threat with a sweet voice. "You even think about carrying me, or touching me, or even breathing in the same airspace as me, I'll punch you so hard you'll be spitting teeth for a week."

As though I'd just issued a challenge, Casey's lips curved suggestively, causing my pulse to spike. The smile was delivered casually, but the sex appeal hit like a tsunami obliterating everything in its path. He obviously assumed my threat carried no substance, which was unfortunately true. I'd never punched anyone in my life, but if there was ever an opportunity to rectify my non-violent status, this would be it.

His hand started moving towards my hip. My eyes narrowed. "Don't even."
He did.

With an insolent grin, Casey splayed his big palm over my hip. Not stopping there, it travelled around to the small of my back. I froze at the audacity, my skin tracking his touch as his hand slid further down, covering my ass. My heart felt ready to thump from my chest at the intimate caress.

"Get your hand off me," I hissed.

But he didn't heed my warning. Standing at the front driveway of Henry's duplex, Casey brazenly squeezed my ass.

"What would you do if I squeezed your ass?"

"You already did," I ground out, standing stiffly as the warmth of his palm burned right through to my skin.

I held my breath when he leaned in and bit my earlobe before trailing his tongue over it to soothe the sharp sting.

"Oops," he replied with a throaty whisper in my ear. "My bad."

Heat throbbed deliciously between my thighs, leaving no doubt it was Casey's intention to humiliate me by getting me hot for him. It worked, and I hated that it worked. My situation had left me emotionally vulnerable, I reminded myself. Casey could possibly be a sexy distraction, but right now I needed someone who cared, and he was definitely not that person.

When I went stiff and silent, he pulled back, his brows drawn together as he looked at me.

"Slim?" he questioned, his fierce blue eyes softening slightly.

Damn. The sudden concern he showed was too much. It made my eyes burn. Now I'd done the unthinkable in warfare and exposed my weak link.

Retreat, Grace, retreat!

"Oh God," I mumbled hoarsely, averting my eyes and blinking rapidly. "I need to go. I have to—"

"Grace?" Henry appeared at the front door, a grin lighting up his face.

I shoved Casey away with superhuman strength. You know the kind you got when your adrenaline hit hyperdrive like you were facing down a bear? That was how desperately I wanted Casey out of my space. My eyes must have communicated a trapped wild animal, because he actually backed up a step.

Feeling emboldened, I muttered harshly, "Don't ever do that again or I'll … I'll …" You'll what? I glanced at Marjorie, Casey's obvious Achilles heel. "I'll scratch your car."

Henry wrapped me in a hug before Casey could reply. I buried my head in his neck as he squeezed me tight.

"Gracie Bean," he whispered.

My eyes filled at being held by my big brother. "Henry Bear."

He pulled back, looking me over. Henry hadn't changed at all. His eyes were still as blue as the sky and his white blond hair was still thick with a slight curl, but more styled now than I remembered. The faint scar on his chin was still there from when we were little. I was seven and Henry nine when we decided that jumping out his two-storey bedroom window and onto the trampoline would increase our bounce ratio. That had been during my aspirations of being a professional trampolinist and competing in the Olympics. Being the eldest, Henry had insisted on going first. Hitting the mat feet first, he bounced up in the air, flailed wildly, and flew off the other side, landing on the gravelled pathway that lined our fence. Dad had been out at the time, and by that stage mum's health had been on the decline. With blood pouring down Henry's chin, she bundled me, Henry, and the twins in the car and raced off to Emergency. They simply cleaned it out, glued his chin back together, and sent us home. Dad dismantled the trampoline the next day. I watched on, my dream of Olympic glory crushed.

I brushed my thumb over the pale scar. "It's still there."

Henry grinned. "I like it. It reminds me of the fun we used to have. Besides, chicks dig scars."

"They do, do they? Getting attacked by a trampoline is sexy now?"

"Come on, Grace. I don't tell them it was from a trampolining incident." Henry turned his grin on Casey, telling him the story. "I was grounded for two weeks after that," he added.

Casey laughed, turning amused eyes my way before asking Henry, "Grace get you into lots of trouble when you were little, did she?"

"Loads," he replied as they started towards the front door. I followed behind as Henry began another story, throwing me under the bus and at the same time bringing on a wave of nostalgia.

We'd been a tight family unit once, but we were all scattered to the four winds now. I wasn't sure our family would ever be what it used to be, but Henry looked happy. He didn't need me stampeding like an elephant through all that happiness and ruining it for him. I would simply stay a few weeks, fill in for whatever live commitments the band required during that time, and then leave with hopefully less fanfare than when I arrived.

Chapter Seven
GRACE

As we reached the front door, Casey and Henry paused to finish their conversation. While my brother spoke, I peeked a glance at Casey. His lids were lowered as he focused on my mouth. My body responded with an answering wave of heat, and when he noticed my flushed face, he grinned, his dimples popping in a display of pure, male perfection. I pretended not to notice, stepping away as I feigned interest in the shrubbery. Mitsy was only too happy with the sudden change of direction, making a conscious effort to cock his leg over several of the plants lining the front garden.

Sneaking another glance, I realised he was watching with an amused expression until Henry distracted him with a question. He gave me his back as he answered, lifting his arm to rub tiredly at his neck. The movement made his shirt ride up, drawing my eyes to the strip of tanned skin just above his ass—his toned, muscular ass. Realising I was staring, I pulled a face at his back which was more immature than I cared to admit, but it made me feel infinitely better.

When Mitsy finished marking his territory, we returned to Henry's side in time for Casey to offer a quick goodbye. He had the nerve to wink when my brother wasn't looking before he disappeared down the drive. No doubt he was in a hurry to leave me behind and get back to his underground lair. I told myself I was relieved to watch him go. There was no doubt that Casey made me tense.

Once inside the duplex, Mitsy introduced himself properly to Henry by baring his teeth. Henry took him in with a wide-eyed caution I thought was wise. "I didn't know you had a dog, Grace."

I tugged on the leash, creating a safe distance between the two of them. "He's a new addition."

Somewhere along the drive here I'd decided that Dalton wasn't getting the dog back. Mitsy had proved his worth and didn't deserve a philanderer taking care of him. The ballsy little animal acted like he could take on Cujo and win. It showed an admirable spirit that someone like Dalton would only crush. The fact that he'd pissed all over Casey's motherfucker tyres and then gouged a hole in the back seat probably helped in making the decision. Just a couple of dog training classes to curb some of the more offensive behaviour, and Mitsy and I would make a good team.

"Umm … okay. Cool dog. He's really uh, white."

"Thanks."

After setting a bowl of water and doggy treat out on the back deck, we left Mitsy to get acquainted with the backyard so Henry could introduce me to the band.

Returning to the living room, I met the bass guitarist I was temporarily replacing first. Frog had dark silky hair, hazel eyes, and olive skin. A tattoo sleeve covered his right arm, but I couldn't tell with his left; it appeared bandaged from his hand upwards and rested in a sling.

"Ouch." I winced sympathetically.

"Dude." Frog looked from me to Henry. "I finally get to meet your sister." Henry folded his arms and Frog grinned, looking back at me and holding out his good hand. I took it in mine as he said, "Nice to meet you, Grace. I'd say it was unfortunate circumstances, but frankly, if breaking my arm is what it took to get you here, then I'd have done it a lot sooner."

I laughed, but when his expression remained serious, I cleared my throat and replied, "Nice to meet you too, Frog. I'm sorry about your arm."

He shrugged. "Shit happens."

There was an awkward moment where I tugged at my hand and he didn't let go.

"Let go," Henry told him, and Frog smirked, giving my hand a squeeze. Henry gave the small of my back a quick shove, propelling me away from Frog and breaking the connection.

Next was Cooper, the band's keyboardist. "Brothers?" I asked, looking between him and Frog. Their colouring was similar, but Cooper's eyes were dark brown, bordering on black.

"No, but we can be if you're into that kind of—"

"Cooper!" Henry snapped.

He gave Henry a look of wide-eyed innocence and something pinged in my memory. "Have we met before?"

"I don't think so." Cooper ran his gaze over me, his brows drawing together as he cocked his head. "I would definitely remember you." He glanced quickly at Henry and Frog before stepping in close, his chest almost brushing mine. Leaning in, he lowered his voice as he spoke in my ear. "Uh, was that a line? Because if so, that's fucking awesome. I live just next door you know, but I can give you my number."

"Oh," I murmured, biting the insides of my cheeks so I wouldn't laugh. He stepped back, meeting my eyes with a knowing grin.

"What did he say?" Henry demanded.

"He uh …" Cooper shook his head at me quickly. The action made me realise Cooper was familiar because he looked like a model I'd worked with a long time ago. Clearing my throat, I replied, "Nothing."

Frog snorted, tucking a lock of dark hair behind his ear. It looked like he was trying to keep it tied back at the nape of his neck, but it wasn't quite long enough and kept falling in his face.

"Well, it's nice to meet you, Cooper."

"Gracie Bean!" A loud feminine squeal and the sound of stomping heels rapidly climbing the basement stairs cut through the chatter. Moments later, I was smothered by Henry's best friend and the band's lead singer. "It's been years!"

"Evie," I choked out as she squeezed me hard.

She pulled back, her chocolate brown eyes widening as she ran her fingers over the tattoo covering my arm and shoulder. "What's this? Never mind. We've got time to catch up later." She turned to Mac. "You remember Mac, don't you? Our band manager?"

I nodded as Mac took her turn giving me a hug. Mac had beautiful green eyes, blond hair, and a take no prisoner's attitude.

"I owe you big for this, okay?" she informed me as she took a step back, smoothing her gleaming waves of golden hair. "Whatever you want—shoes, a new gun, my firstborn child, it's yours. Just promise me you'll stay until Frog's well enough to play again."

I agreed, administering my promise to Mac in triplicate. Apparently that was the right thing to say if the smiles and matching expressions of relief were anything to go by.

Henry took my hand and gave me a quick tour of the duplex. Downstairs was an open-plan kitchen, living, and dining room, along with the laundry and study. After leading me upstairs, I realised it only had one bathroom, which didn't just surprise me, it reminded me that my brother was a shower hog. Years of Henry's monopolisation had made the bathroom a hot commodity growing up in our house, but I wasn't worried. I considered myself a veteran of Henry's antics. I had that particular issue covered.

Henry raised his brows at my smug grin. "What?"

"Nothing," I murmured.

With a shrug, he showed me Mac's room and then his. My wide eyes took in the pink coverlet on his bed. "Henry, you have pink sheets, and they're not just pink, they're trimmed in lace. And pretty."

"I know. They were Quinn's sheets from when she used to live here. I stole them when she moved out."

"You stole pink sheets?"

"Yep." He folded his arms, nodding as we both stared at the girly display. "They're really soft, and when you lie on the bed and close your eyes, you don't notice the colour."

The guest room—the room I would be staying in—was next. It was modern and pretty with a decent size walk-in wardrobe. The bed was a vintage-inspired black metal frame with fluffy white bedding. The matching black bedside tables were also vintage in distressed timber with pretty lamps sitting on top. My suitcase sat by the door and someone had rested my guitar case up against the wall.

"Is this okay?" he asked, opening the blinds to slight views of Bondi Beach.

Walking over to Henry, I slid the window open. Breathing in the fresh scent of salty ocean air, my body felt suddenly lighter. My problems were far away in Melbourne, and Italy if I factored in my boyfriend as a problem—which he wasn't. A simple phone call telling Dalton we were over shouldn't come as a surprise to him, and I could take care of that tomorrow. Jemima would reschedule all my current commitments, leaving me with nothing to do but play guitar and plan my new future. All I had to do was make sure Henry was kept out of the loop, which wouldn't be hard. I didn't bring anything incriminating with me except for my phone, and there was no reason for him to be snooping through any of the messages on there.

I turned, giving Henry a grin. "It's perfect."

I flopped down on the bed, scooting over to make room for Henry when he did the same. He tucked his hands behind his head and stared at the ceiling. "It's good to have you here, Gracie Bean."

I mimicked his actions. "It's good to be here."

He turned his head to look at me, meeting my eyes. "But?" he prompted, sensing my hesitation.

I grimaced. "It's been a long time since I picked up a guitar." Henry had always been the musical talent, not me. When mum was sick, he would sit on the floor of his room plucking the strings like it gave him peace. Then his best friend, Evie, came along with her rich voice like melted butter, and the music they created together was more than special, it was fucking incredible. "Back when we were young my fingers could walk the walk, but now I don't even know if they can talk the talk."

Tonight I would be standing up in front of thousands, not including the televised audience, and I didn't want to fail spectacularly and damage Jamieson's reputation as one of the hottest live Australian acts of the decade.

"You could've just hired a professional, Henry. Why me?"

"Because I miss you, Grace." His eyes skimmed over me sadly, taking in the makeup, tattoos and deep, dark hair that used to be a light golden brown. I knew I looked nothing like I used to, but that was how the industry worked. Changing your look on a regular basis kept you fresh and in demand. "You might be my sister, but I don't know who you are anymore. I don't know anything about you. Hell, I didn't even know you had a dog. It sucks that Frog broke his arm, but what he said was right. If that's what it took to get you here, then I'd have broken it myself. Well, maybe not, but you get the point. You're not here just to fill Frog's place—because as you said, we could've hired a professional—you're here because I want my sister back. Is that okay? I don't care if you play like a cat on crack. I just care that you're here."

I grabbed blindly for his hand and gave it a squeeze. "I miss you too, Henry. This wasn't how I imagined the two of us would end up, but life just got in the way."

Henry let go of my hand. Swallowing hard, he averted his face as he sat up. "Fuck that," he muttered.

"Henry—"

"Don't." He got to his feet and walked to the window. After a moment, he spun around and there was anger in his eyes, a hardness that I'd never seen before. "Life doesn't just get in the way. It plays out based on the choices we make, and you chose to leave us. I'm still so fucking mad at you for that." I sat up, my heart aching at the pain in his voice. "You know why mum always tolerated your crap when we were little? Because you were so fucking full of life that whenever you got in trouble, the light would literally fade from your eyes and it was like … I don't know, crushing a butterfly or something. No one could bear to do it. When mum got sick, it was you that held us together. You. You were that shining beacon of light just like she was, and when our family fell apart after losing her you were never there to see it, because somewhere along the way we lost you too." He paused, taking a deep breath. "I never saw that light in your eyes return, Grace, and when I look at you…" tears filled his eyes "…it's still not there."

I swallowed the lump in my throat and stared at the floor. I had no idea the choices I'd made had torn such a huge, gaping hole in our family.

"Say something, Grace," he whispered hoarsely.

I shook my head, choking on a sob. "I'm sorry. I'm so sorry I wasn't there, Henry."

"Why?" he cried out. "Why weren't you there? Was your modelling career that much more important to you than we were?"

"Of course not." But it was too late for explanations. Far too late to go back to how we used to be, and the thought made hurt well inside me until I ached from it.

"Then what?"

"Let it go, Henry," I pleaded. "Please? I'm here now. I'm here and I won't let you down, okay?"

"Jesus, Grace." Henry rubbed at his eyes. After a brief moment he walked over to me. Crouching so we were eye level, he rested his hands on my knees. "I didn't mean to get into this. The past is in the past, it's just … having you here, I didn't realise I was still so angry. All the hurt just came flooding back like it never left. You know I love you, right? You're my little sister. I'll always love you, no matter what."

I exhaled a shaky breath at the intense sincerity in his pretty blue eyes. "Promise?"

"Of course I promise." He cocked his head, his brows drawing together. "Why? Has something happened I should know about?"

"No," I lied, and my heart broke. "Everything's fine."

After taking a few minutes to freshen up and compose myself, Henry led me down to the basement so they could start on teaching me the song. Being underground, the whole area was windowless, but the space was large enough not to induce a claustrophobic attack. The soundproofed walls featured big black and white prints of Jamieson playing at live venues, and the room was filled with their equipment: drums, amplifiers, guitars, and microphones on stands. Evie and Cooper fiddled with dials and sound on the keyboard while Frog sat on a nearby amplifier offering suggestions. Cables snaked all over the floor, leading behind a worn, comfortable couch where Mac stood talking to a guy I recognised as Jake Romero, the band's drummer. His size was intimidating. A fitted tee shirt emphasised wide muscular shoulders and thick biceps covered with tattoos. His golden brown hair was shorn in a simple buzz cut and eyes the colour of single malt scotch were busy glaring at something Mac said.

"What was I supposed to do?" he replied, his voice raised in anger as Henry led us over to introduce me. "You pushed and you pushed, just like you always do, but in the end you got what you wanted, didn't you?"

The guy looked like he wanted to rip someone's face off. Not wanting to get caught in the crossfire, I tugged at Henry's hand but he wouldn't let go.

"Don't deny you got what you wanted too, Jake, so fuck you," she hissed.

"Too late!" he shouted. "You already did."

Everyone froze, including Henry and I. The sudden silence was thick with tension and everyone looked to Mac, appearing breathless as they waited for her to say something.

"I don't have time for this. I have work to do." Spinning on her heel, Mac disappeared up the stairs, her shoes clicking loudly on each step as everyone watched in silence.

"Dammit," Jake muttered, brushing a hand over his buzzed hair before dropping it to his side in defeat.

Cooper's grin encompassed the room when Jake angrily flung his set of drum sticks on the couch and disappeared up the stairs after her.

"You all owe me ten bucks," he crowed with glee.

"So that was Jake," Henry informed me, pulling his wallet from his back pocket as money began changing hands. The swift transaction was peppered with a few grumbles and two unsavoury threats that alluded to Cooper's lack of morals.

I raised my brows. "He seems … nice."

"Sure he is," Frog agreed and held his bass guitar out towards me. "Here, Grace. You can play my guitar. It's tuned and ready to go."

"Bet that's not all that's tuned and ready to go," I heard Cooper mutter as I took hold of the gleaming black and silver guitar, testing the weight in my hands. It was heavier than mine and likely a thousand times more expensive.

"Flip it over," he told me.

Doing as he said, I turned it over in my hands and saw flowing script on the back that read: Live hard, fuck hard, play hard. I grinned at Frog as I lifted the strap over my shoulder and settled the guitar in my hands. "That's your motto, is it?"

"Yep." He returned my grin and reached for the button on his jeans, saying, "I've got it tattooed across my lower abs. Wanna see?"

Two hours later and I was confident enough with the song to know I wasn't going to embarrass both the band and myself. After a quick shower, my hair and makeup was done courtesy of a stylist Mac arranged to come to the duplex. I was given dark smoky eyes, glossy coral lips, and my hair styled in loose, textured waves. Returning to my room in a cotton dressing gown, I noticed my suitcase had been ransacked and an outfit was laid out on the bed—my black leather bustier and a pair of royal blue pants that flared at the hip and tapered at the ankle.

"Jesus, Grace." Mac said from behind, startling me. She waved her hand towards my things. "Your clothes. Gorgeous. I took the liberty of getting your outfit together and ironing your pants. Hurry up and get dressed because we have to motor. Sing out when you're ready and I'll come in and do the zipper up on your bustier, okay?"

"Wait!" I called when she was halfway out the door.

She paused.

"You and Jake. Is everything okay?"

She opened her mouth, ready to say something before snapping it shut. "Everything's fine," she told me, and when she left, I wondered if I sounded more convincing when I lied about the same thing to Henry just hours earlier.

Taking off my cotton robe, I pulled on my pants and buckled up the black, diamante stilettos. I was just sliding the bustier down and settling it in place when a tap came at the door.

"Just in time. I'm ready to go. Can you get the zipper?"

My hair was swept gently aside, baring my back. Warm, rough fingertips trailed gently down my spine, making me shiver. "You smell like honey, Slim," came the hoarse voice in my ear.

I spun around, suddenly breathless. "Casey." The hasty movement made my unzipped bustier slide down. I grappled with it, holding it in place with my hands, as he stood there and watched. "What are you doing in here?"

Casey gave an unconcerned shrug like he had all the time in the world, which was convenient, because right then I needed all the time in the world just to take him in.

He'd changed from his worn jeans into a suit—navy silk with a crisp white shirt. The fitted cut made it obvious the suit was tailored specifically for him, and the open collar gave a tantalising glimpse of tanned, muscled chest. He was … Good Lord, he was beautiful.

Breathe, Grace, I had to remind myself. This man is not your friend.

"Get out," I snapped.

"And miss seeing you half dressed? I think not." He tilted his head, cocky grin in place as I wrestled with the back of the zipper trying to do it up myself. "Can I do that for you?"

Nothing good could come out of him doing anything for me, or to me, for that matter. From the minute I'd set foot on Sydney soil, I'd lost all sense of emotional composure around the man. He was a menace to my mental health. "No."

"No?" He leaned casually against the wall and folded his arms.

"Grace!" Henry shouted from downstairs. "The limo's here!"

"Where's Mac?" I called back.

"She's already in the car. We're waiting for you!"

Goddammit.

"Well," Casey drawled, inspecting his fingernails calmly. "Looks like you're in a bit of pickle there, Slim. Everyone's waiting for you, but don't worry, I've got an idea." A smirk spread slowly across his face, and I felt the urge to slap it off. "How about asking me nicely to do your zipper? I think I'll like hearing a please and thank you from those pretty lips of yours."

Anger made my stomach churn, and the fact that I couldn't remember the last time I ate only made it worse. "I'd rather eat dirt," I hissed. Holding my bustier in place with one hand, I grabbed my bag with the other. Asshole! I'd just get Henry to do the damn zipper and be done with it. Straightening my shoulders, I made for the door, doing my best to escape with dignity and failing in a spectacular fashion.

Casey's arm snapped out, grabbing my wrist. "Wait."

I tugged, but his strength was superhuman, reminding me of his earlier assault at the airport. "Oh, okay. We're doing this again." I rolled my eyes as he dragged me unwillingly towards him.

The subtle scent of his aftershave hit me and I recognised the warm, woodsy tone of Bvlgari Man instantly. It suited him perfectly, and I wondered if it was something he'd purchased himself or was bought for him. Then I wondered why the hell I was wondering something like that.

I made a show of looking at my watch. "Make your lecture quick this time. Everyone's waiting remember?"

Casey's chuckle came deep from his chest, surprising me. I met his amused eyes, falling in love with the clear, pretty blue colour. "This is funny now?"

"Will you let me speak?"

"Grace!" Henry yelled.

"Be right there!" I yelled back.

"Slim," Casey murmured, and his thumb started rubbing the inside of my wrist. The touch was both soothing and sensual. I repressed a visible shiver. "I'm sorry."

"Sorry?"

He nodded. "For today. For jumping to conclusions. I have some stuff going on and it's made me a bit …"

"Of a loose cannon? A Batman wannabe? An irrational vigilante?" I supplied.

Amusement returned to his eyes as his hand started sliding up my arm, the rough callouses of his palm scraping my skin. Reaching halfway, his thumb started rubbing again—this time the inside crease of my elbow. My breathing escalated along with the sensual touch.

"I was going to say a bit stressed."

"That's you a bit stressed?" I tugged my arm from his grip and this time he let go. "God help the universe then if you have a major meltdown. Planets will get thrown out of alignment. Stars will collide. Perhaps an asteroid will change trajectory towards Earth." A look of mock horror crossed my face. "You would go down in infamy as the sole man responsible for Armageddon."

Casey laughed and dimples popped on his cheeks, morphing the man from beautiful to adorable. A kitten with a ball of yarn had nothing on Casey when he was laughing. I stood there for a moment staring in wonder.

"I think we should call a ceasefire, don't you? I shouldn't have made assumptions about you, and I shouldn't have lost my temper. I just …" Casey looked away, sliding his hands into his pockets. It was an oddly vulnerable move. I had the urge to reach out and cup his face, forcing him to look at me so I could see into his eyes. I'd never felt that with any other man before—so much irritation along with intrigue and an overwhelming craving to touch.

"You just what?"

He looked at me then, but his eyes were clear, giving me nothing. "A shitty day, Slim. That's all. I just had a shitty day." He stepped closer but didn't get in my face like he had earlier. Instead, he cocked his head, waiting. "So will you accept my apology and let me do your zipper?"

I relaxed a little until I remembered Mitsy and his annihilation of Casey's car. I had to accept his apology or appear churlish, but damn, when he saw the torn interior—because there was no quick fix for the damage I'd allowed Mitsy to inflict—all bets would be off. The ceasefire would cease.

Travis was right. I was a dead woman walking. My panic must have been obvious because his brows drew together.

"Slim?"

"Grace!" Henry yelled again. It was followed by the sound of feet stomping up the stairs.

"Accept," I blurted out. "I accept."

"Good. Turn around."

I gave him my back. This time he took care not to touch my skin but the time it took for my zipper to slide upwards felt like minutes. I turned back around to Casey grinning.

"Let's start again." He held out his hand. I looked at it dumbly before meeting his crinkled eyes. "My name's Casey Daniels, but you can call me Batman if you like. I've been assigned as your personal security for tonight's proceedings."

Chapter Eight
CASEY

Grace looked at me like I just announced I was here to harvest her kidneys. Did no one mention Jamieson and Valentine Consulting handled all the security for the band? After a brief pause, she took my hand in hers. I closed my fingers around it feeling it disappear in mine.

"Grace Paterson," she replied, "but you can call me Grace if you like. I've been assigned as the bass guitarist for tonight's proceedings."

My eyes raked the length of her as I shook her hand. Grace was tall and slender, not curvy like the girls I usually went for, but the black top thing she wore was hot. It drew my eye to the creamy swell that rose out the top in two delicious handfuls.

She cleared her throat and my lips curved as I diverted my attention back to her face. I let go of her hand and nodded towards the bedroom door. "Shall we go?"

"Grace?" Henry arrived at the top of the stairs, his brows drawn impatiently. "You ready?"

"Sure am," she replied.

"Good. Go wait in the limo, will you?" He shifted out of the way, bringing him further into the room so she could get by. "I just need to speak to Casey for a second."

"Um, okay." Grace glanced at me quickly before she left, a question in her eyes.

The minute she was out of earshot, Henry spoke, his eyes turning hard. It didn't surprise me. There was no way Henry could have missed the way I'd been looking at Grace like I wanted to eat her alive, but looking away proved difficult. Henry's sister wasn't just as shock and awe like I originally thought. She was sassy with an underlying hint of sweet and had a backbone that made her nobody's pushover. I fucking loved that.

"Don't, Casey. Whatever you're doing, or thinking of doing, don't. Grace is my sister, you asshole, and every time some female gets caught up in all your Jamieson and Valentine bullshit, they end up getting maimed or shot. That is not going to happen to Grace. I fucking mean it. Got me?"

I stiffened as he jabbed his finger in my chest, insulted he would think I'd deliberately get Grace caught in the middle of a life-threatening drama. "You need to calm down, mate. I've known your sister for mere hours and already you have me getting her shot?"

Knowing we were on a tight schedule, Henry started down the stairs, over his shoulder, saying, "I know you, Casey, just like I know Jared, and just like I know Travis. Mere hours is all it takes."

"I understand you're her brother, Henry, and you're gonna worry no matter what I say," I told him as I followed behind, "but you can relax. I'm covering her security personally tonight, and I have no intention of letting anything happen to her, okay?"

Reaching the door, I opened it letting Henry step out before locking it behind us. "It's not everyone else I'm worried about, Casey. It's you."

My brows flew up. "You're kidding, right?" I glanced sideways at him as we walked towards the limousine. It was parked by the kerb, the door open and the driver standing patiently as he waited for us to get in. "Your sister is going to be keeping company with Mac and Evie, and Quinn too, and you're worried about me?"

Henry paused before reaching the door, and I stopped with him. He rubbed at his brow before his arm fell limply by his side. "I respect you, Casey, and consider you a good mate, but the fact is, your friends have set some kind of dangerous precedent. I don't want her getting caught up in anything—you included. Grace and I haven't been close for a long time and I'm trying to rectify that while she's here, so after tonight I think it's best if you stay away."

My hands clenched into fists. While I couldn't blame him for his words— big brothers were supposed to look out for their siblings—I couldn't deny the hurt they caused. I also couldn't deny what the ramifications would be if I allowed myself to feel more for Grace than I should.

"Of course," I said flatly.

Henry nodded. "Good."

I jerked my chin at the car. "Let's go."

We both climbed in, the door shutting swiftly behind us. Being the security for Grace tonight, the seat beside her was kept free for me to sit next to her. I didn't look at her as I sat down. Instead, I kept my gaze on the window as the car pulled away from the kerb and headed towards the venue. I felt her yawn beside me, her bare shoulder brushing against the sleeve of my jacket as she exhaled audibly.

"Tired?" I murmured, glancing her way.

"Mmm," she replied, her lids lowered sleepily. Damn, was that how she looked waking up in the morning? I could already see her hair mussed, the creamy skin of her body folded between the rich navy sheets on my bed. I shifted in my seat, feeling the need to adjust my cock in my pants. "It's been a rough day."

I grimaced, knowing I played a part in that. Leaning in so no one would hear, I asked softly, "I didn't hurt you, did I?"

Grace turned her head and because I was already close, we almost bumped noses. Everything else faded as I lingered for a moment, taking in her scent and feeling it stir my blood. All I had to do was tilt my head and my lips would be on hers. I think it's best if you stay away. Feeling Henry watching, I pulled back, reminding myself that tonight was about work.

"No," she whispered. "But you did manage to surprise the crap out of me and piss me off at the same time. That's quite impressive for a first day."

I chuckled quietly and she gave a long, suffering sigh, rolling her eyes before turning her attention to the passing scenery.

"Slim?"

Her gaze returned to mine.

"Any idea why airport security might think you were carrying drugs?"

I watched her face carefully as I delivered my question. Her blue eyes turned stormy and I felt our tentative truce waver, yet her expression gave me no answers. "No, Casey. No idea." Her voice was sharp and her brows drew together. "Why? Do you?"

"No." It could only have come from them seeing something in her luggage or someone tipping them off. The fact that she was candid about us checking her bags led me to believe she was being honest, which meant the likelihood that someone had it in for her was high. "But I can find out."

"You can?"

I shrugged. "I know some people."

Her lips curved. "Oh you do, do you?"

"It's Monday tomorrow. I'll be in the office so I'll look into it." My hand started reaching for her leg, ready to slide it down her thigh in a reassuring gesture. Hell. Letting out a pent-up breath, I pulled back, resting my hand on my knee and thrumming my fingers instead.

Grace raised an eyebrow. "What does looking into it involve?"

"Just a couple of phone calls, Slim. That's all."

"You know, I really appreciate your offer," she said, her words seeming heartfelt, "but then I'd owe you one, wouldn't I?"

I couldn't help the wicked grin at the thought of Grace owing me one. After tonight, I was supposed to be keeping my distance—meaning the likelihood of collecting was lower than zero—but the thought of teasing her anyway was too delicious to ignore. "You read my mind." My gaze fell to her lush, glossy lips, and the sudden craving to taste them hit me hard. "I don't even have to think about how you can repay me. I already know."

I breathed in the clean scent of soap from her bare shoulders as she leaned towards me. "And?"

"I want a kiss," I told her quietly.

"A kiss?"

Grace said the word so loud she may as well have shouted it. The chatter surrounding us in the limousine died off abruptly and Henry was now looking at me with an accusatory glare.

Travis leaned around Quinn to look at the both of us. "Sounds like your conversation is way more interesting than ours, Casey."

Shifting in my seat, I cleared my throat. "We were just discussing the band, Kiss. Grace was telling me they sing one of her favourite songs."

"Oh yeah?" Frog perked up in his seat next to Henry, who still wasn't looking any happier. "Which one?"

Fuck. Think, idiot!

"I was made for lovin' you," I replied quickly. It was the only song that came to mind quick enough.

"Kiss songs are so awesome to play," Cooper added. "We should try playing that one during a session next week."

The chatter picked up again as Grace chuckled beside me. The husky sound had my pulse thumping. "Smooth, Casey," she whispered.

I winked. "Thanks." Checking to make sure we were no longer the focus of everyone's attention, I said, "So how 'bout it?"

"How 'bout it? Wow. What an irresistible offer." She tapped a finger against her lips, pretending to think about it. "But I'm going to have to decline."

"So that's a no then?"

"Yes."

"Yes it's a no to the kiss, or yes you've changed your mind?" Grace shook her head, clearly exasperated. I grinned. Pressing in close, I whispered in her ear, "Are you sure, Grace? Because I didn't say where I wanted to kiss you." I glanced meaningfully between her thighs before meeting her eyes. "And I'm good with my tongue."

A whimper escaped her lips and the soft sound had my cock throbbing in my pants. My teasing had backfired on me in the worst way. I sat back in my seat, creating some much needed distance.

"It's still a no." Her voice was a rasp as she rubbed her palms along her pants in a nervous gesture.

I reached for her hand and once again had to restrain myself. Why wasn't

I able to keep my hands to myself whenever she was near? My lack of control was embarrassing.

"Grace?"

She looked at me and I saw the desire I felt reflected back at me in her eyes. The knowledge that her attraction was as strong as mine didn't help with my restraint. In lieu of asking the driver to pull over so I could get some much needed air, I forced myself to focus on the issue at hand. Someone had made the accusation about Grace carrying drugs. Maybe it was nothing, but it could've been something and was worth checking into.

"I'll look into it, okay? You won't owe me one. After my actions today, I think we can consider ourselves even." I held out my hand. "Now give me your phone."

"My phone?"

"I'm in charge of your protection tonight," I explained patiently as she dug through her bag. "That means you need my number. I figure tonight's event should be pretty safe, but stick close anyway. If we get separated you call me, got it?"

Locating her phone, she put it in my hand. I started tapping in my contact information.

"Do I even need security tonight?" she asked.

I glanced at Mac, recalling the image of her beaten body after being kidnapped by Jimmy; then Evie when I arrived on the scene after she'd been shot—blood spatter covering every surface; and Quinn, taken by Luca Zampetti and almost dying in a horrific car accident. Each incident was enough to induce a heart attack. Even now I had the urge to rub my chest from the rawness the images evoked. Trouble had always been hot on their heels and instead of them doing what they were told, they always took matters into their own hands.

I brought my eyes back to Grace. Henry's sister didn't seem like the type of female to be an exception to that particular rule. "Yes. You do."

A surge of satisfaction ran through me as she shrugged, appearing to give in on the issue. I already had Grace's number stored, it was provided in the security brief, but I sent myself a message from her phone anyway to confirm I had the number correct. Done, I handed the phone back. It started ringing before she could take it, the name "Dalton" coming up on the screen. Her brows drew tight, indicating annoyance as she grabbed for it.

"Who's Dalton?" I asked, wanting to know who the other man in her life was that pissed her off as much as I did. Frankly, I would've been shocked if she answered me. It was none of my business who Dalton was, but when she cursed under her breath, I didn't let go of her phone.

"He's no one," she replied, not looking at me as she tried tugging it from my grasp.

The phone rang out so I let her have it, but as soon as it stopped ringing, it started again. I watched as she hit the decline button on the screen and put it away. The muffled sound of it ringing again set my teeth on edge. Three times in a row wasn't no one. "You gonna answer it?"

"No," Grace replied, her voice sharp. She dug her hand through her bag and after a brief moment, the ringing stopped again.

When it started for the fourth time, I growled, "Are you fucking kidding me?" Snatching her bag, I found the offending phone, checked the screen and looked at Grace. "Who's Dalton, Slim?"

Her nostrils flared ominously, but the anger was countered by the sudden sheen of tears in her eyes. "He's no one, Casey."

No one, my fucking ass. I held up the phone in my palm. "So if he's no one, you won't mind me answering the phone and telling him to stop calling you, right?"

"Answer that and I'll …"

My brow arched sardonically. "You'll what, scratch my car? Punch me so hard I'll be spitting teeth for a week? Enough with the empty threats, Grace, unless you actually plan on following through."

"We're here!" Mac barked, interrupting our standoff.

I dragged my eyes from Grace's stormy blue ones and glanced out the window. We were running behind, making us the last in a long line of limousines. The red carpet leading into Sydney's The Star hotel where the event centre was located was starting to empty. Good. It made my job that much easier.

Grace snatched the phone from my hands, switched it off quickly, and dumped it in her bag. Did she not hear the part where I told her we needed to keep the lines of communication open?

"Turn your phone back on," I ordered. "If something happens, I need to be able to contact you."

"What could possibly happen?"

As the car pulled smoothly to the kerb, a suited man stepped forward and opened the door. Everyone started piling out, Grace and I going last. I put a hand on her arm, halting her so I could go first. Press flashbulbs were going crazy as they photographed Jamieson's arrival. Evie's name was called out several times as they started making their way inside. Turning, I ducked my head and held out my hand, grateful when Grace slid her palm easily in mine. I clasped it tight and helped her from the car. She stepped out elegantly, as though she'd done this a thousand times before. Sweeping by me, she hissed from the corner of her mouth, "And something you should know … I don't deal in empty threats."

What looked suspiciously like guilt flashed across her face before it was hidden. My eyes narrowed. "What did you do?"

Someone from the press gallery called out, "Hey! It's Grace Paterson! Grace! Over here!"

A wide grin spread across her face as she let go of my hand and continued forward. "Nothing."

"This way, Grace!"

Grace gave a brief wave and a smile to the crowd and my body tensed. The attention she was getting made it obvious she wasn't just a model—she was a fucking famous one. The hastily pulled together brief I reviewed this afternoon since leaving Grace had indicated she was well-known, but this was a whole other level of attention. I stalked forward, keeping close to her side as I eyed the press with an alert gaze.

"Who designed your outfit, Grace?" someone yelled.

"Grace! Over here!"

Jesus. It was a fucking circus.

Grace stepped closer to the crowding photographers and microphones as she smiled for photos and answered questions. I stepped with her, staying close.

"Grace! Where's Dalton tonight? Are the rumours of him and British model Selena true?"

Grace paled, her confident demeanour faltering, and I wanted to growl at their probing questions. I slipped my hand in hers and gave it a reassuring squeeze.

"Is this your new boyfriend?" someone called out.

Cameras turned my way. Their flash caused white spots to dance in front of my eyes. I had to blink to clear my vision.

"No comment," I barked and dragged her away from every last one of them, moving her swiftly up the red carpet.

Fucking vultures.

As we slipped inside and joined the rest of the crew, I felt rather than heard her sigh of relief. "You okay, Slim?"

"Of course." She smiled the same smile she gave all those photographers and reporters out there—smooth and practiced. I found I didn't like her using it on me.

"So … Dalton, huh?"

Chapter Nine
GRACE

"**S**o … Dalton, huh?"

Last night's events filtered through my mind as I lay tangled in my sheets. Morning sunshine seeped through the blinds, doing its best to entice me out of my bed and failing miserably. It was—I sat up and checked the time on my phone—almost midday already. That meant I'd slept ten hours straight.

I flopped back on my pillow, dragging out a long yawn that ended with a squeal and a stretch.

"So … Dalton, huh?"

"Arrrghhhh!" I growled and punched my pillow. Get out of my head! Cocky bastard.

Straight after posing that leading question last night, the attendant arrived to usher us to our table, thus saving me from answering. Casey had placed his hand on the small of my back, hovering close as we were led through crowds of people taking their seats. Thinking back, the gesture hadn't irritated me like I would've thought. The warm flutters in my belly told me I liked it. More than a little. Dalton had never been solicitous that way, but he'd also never forcefully pinned me against the wall and called me a bitch either.

After sitting down at our designated table, Henry on my left and Casey on my right, an attending waiter poured iced water into our glasses and took beverage orders. Five minutes later, the lights dimmed and the host walked on stage. The lighting turned blue and purple and a bright spotlight hit the clear perspex podium where he began his opening speech. Henry began drumming his fingers on the table, so clearly nervous that my heart did a little flip for him. I grabbed his hand in mine, stilling it. He looked at me and smiled. The gesture was obviously meant to reassure me he was fine, but it came off more like a grimace.

Leaning in so he could hear, I said, "Chill, Henry Bear. I want to say I can't believe you're here, playing at such a huge event, but I can." My chest swelled with pride for my brother. "Thank you for including me. For having me here. Watching you play this afternoon was incredible, seeing how all your talent and hard work has paid off." I gave his hand a squeeze before letting go. "You've got this."

Quinn cleared her throat from the seat on the other side of Henry. She inclined her head around him so she looked directly at me. "Did you just say 'you've got this?' Because really, it sounded like you did, and whenever anyone says that it makes me nervous."

My brows flew up. "Oh. Um …"

"Nervous?" Travis laughed from his seat beside Quinn. "Don't you mean aggressive? Because someone saying that is usually preceded by you throwing a chair."

The entire table erupted in laughter, but I didn't quite get the joke, and Quinn was the only other person besides me who wasn't joining in. In fact, she was sitting there with pursed lips. "Perhaps next time I'll just try the direct approach that Mac usually favours."

Casey tensed beside me and Travis's sharp green eyes turned flat and hard as he glared at his wife, making me wonder what that approach was. "You'll do no such thing."

The abrupt change in Travis from relaxed to something so incredibly fierce and primal left me dazed. He'd been the epitome of cool since the moment I met him—until now. Quinn raised her brows coolly as I watched the exchange with wide eyes.

"And there'll be no next time," he added, kicking back in his chair and folding his arms.

"Rein in your man, Quinn," Mac commanded. "He's getting out of control."

Travis turned his glare on his sister. "Are you kidding me?"

Leaning close to Henry, I whispered, "What's the Mac approach?"

"Guns," he replied with a shake of his head.

"Guns?" I repeated, not quite sure I heard him right.

"Tell you later," he muttered as everyone started weighing in with an opinion. Voices were getting loud enough for surrounding guests to turn in their seats. Seeing Casey reach for my bag from my peripheral vision distracted me from the escalating altercation. I gave him my full attention. "What are you doing?"

Ignoring me, he rummaged through the contents. I only had a moment to cringe at the thought of a close encounter of the tampon kind before he plucked out my phone and proceeded to switch it on. The screen came to life, prompting my four-digit passcode.

Casey's finger hovered over the keypad. "What's the code, Slim?"

"I'm going to tell you because …?"

He rubbed his hand over his smoothly shaven jaw. My eyes tracked the movement and I realised I wanted the stubble back. It took the edge off his beauty, giving him that rough just-rolled-out-of-bed look. Conscious of the fact I'd been staring at his jaw for longer than a mere glance, I flicked my eyes upwards and found him watching me. He crooked his finger.

"What?" I blurted out.

Casey simply cocked his head in reply and waited.

What game was he playing now? Keeping up proved almost impossible. Exhaling in a huff, I leaned in, saying a little more quietly, "What?"

"You're going to tell me because I take my job seriously," he replied softly. "Because Jamieson is paying our firm to provide security, and I happen to think they deserve more than a half-assed job. Because I'm trained to keep you safe. Because a seemingly harmless situation can escalate in a matter of moments and you might need me." His lips brushed my ear as he spoke, sending waves of heat through my body and setting off an ache between my thighs. I held back a moan. Why did our every interaction always result in such excessive levels of proximity? It kept throwing my composure off course. "Are those enough reasons for you, Slim…" he pulled back to meet my eyes "…or do you need more?"

I opened my mouth to reply and realised I had nothing. Casey was right, and interfering in the way he did his job would only be immature on my part. It was just … switching on my phone meant dealing with Dalton, and I couldn't do it. Not tonight. The whole mess was too raw.

"You're right." Staring down at my hands, I realised they were shaking. I clenched my fists. "Dalton is my … was," I corrected, "my boyfriend. He did something really shitty and I'm just not ready to deal with it, or him, just yet."

"What did he do?"

I shook my head and turned my attention to the stage, indicating I wasn't going to talk about it. Someone was halfway through singing a song on stage and I blinked with surprise. I hadn't noticed anything outside of Casey.

From the corner of my eye, I saw him unlock the screen of my phone, bringing up the passcode prompt again. He jabbed in a sequence of numbers and my phone came to life.

My mouth fell open. "How did you …?"

"The year you were born. It was included in your security brief. You shouldn't make it so easy." He stood abruptly, my phone in one hand and holding out his other. "Let's go."

"Go?" I felt like I'd missed a few steps in the conversation. And they had a security brief on me? I was mentally trying to backtrack when he took hold of my elbow and hauled me up. I stumbled a little at his haste.

"Grace needs the restroom," he told the table. "We'll be back."

Henry's shout broke my reverie of last night, making me aware I was clutching the pillow to my chest and rubbing my legs together to ease the ache still there. Grabbing for the sheets that pooled around my bare thighs, I dragged them up and over my head. My brother sounded angry and it was far too early for confrontation of any kind. His shout was accompanied by a fist pounding on my bedroom door and ended with the ominous, "Grace! You better be decent because I'm coming in to kill you!"

The door flung open. I couldn't see it, but I could hear the sudden whoosh, followed by a clang where it caught the doorstop. A giggle bubbled out of me.

"Grace. This isn't funny. Where are they?"

"No idea what you're talking about," I replied from beneath the sheets.

I squealed when they were ripped away from me. Brushing hair off my face, I watched as they sailed across the room, landing on the floor in a crumpled heap, before returning my attention to Henry.

He stood over me in his sleep shorts—chest heaving and hands on his hips. It felt just like old times. The fact that his next words mentioned the exact same thing only warmed my heart a little. "Jesus, Grace. This is just like old times. I thought having you here would be a great opportunity to get to know you again, but really, you haven't changed at all, have you?"

Mac stumbled in behind Henry, scratching at her head and scowling. "What's with all the noise?" She blinked a couple of times as she looked between Henry and me. Suddenly her eyes went wide, comprehension dawning that Henry wasn't hogging the shower this morning. She shot out of my room like she was Road Runner and Wile E. Coyote was on her ass. The sound of the bathroom door slamming shut echoed down the hall.

Henry's lips twitched.

Moments later, Mac came storming back into my room, placing her hands on her hips. "Alright. Listen up, because I'm only going to ask this once. Where are the fucking shower taps?"

I bit my lip, grinning at my victory.

Henry threw up his hands. "They could be anywhere." Turning for the door, he grumbled, "I'm going to find some pliers." He loved his long morning showers and was clearly prepared to do anything to get his fix.

When he disappeared out the door, Mac turned to me, her mouth open in what looked like wonder. "You stole the shower taps?"

My response was another grin. I slid out of bed, my feet hitting plush cream carpet. Crouching down, I lifted my mattress, showing her the taps that I'd wedged underneath.

"When did you do that?"

"Last night," I replied, smug. "When you were all stumbling to bed. It only took a minute." Reaching in, I grabbed them and held them out to her. "Here. You can go first if you like?"

"You …" Mac looked from the taps in my outstretched hands to my face. "Teach me," she breathed as she took them, clutching them to her chest like a pair of Manolo Blahniks. "I need to know all your tricks."

I flopped back on the bed. "I have a few more up my sleeve. Henry will soon regret asking me to stay."

"Rubbish. Henry needs you here keeping him on his toes." Mac shuffled over and sat down beside me. "I'll be honest with you, Grace. I feel like he's slowly losing his way. Like the bigger the band is getting, the more he's withdrawing. I don't know why. I can't put my finger on what it is, and I admit we've all been so busy I've let it slide hoping something would change, but it hasn't. That was why I jumped all over the idea of having you here. I'm not good at all those bullshit heart-to-heart talks. Maybe you can do what I can't."

"Oh." I exhaled at Mac's admission. It felt strange that I had no clue what was going on in his life. "I honestly don't know, Mac. I'll talk to him while I'm here."

"Thanks, Grace." She patted my leg before getting to her feet. "I better get in the shower before Henry finds those pliers."

Mac left the room and I picked up my crumpled pile of sheets off the floor. Shaking them out, I put them back on the bed and crawled back underneath them, planning to doze while Mac was in the shower. As soon as I closed my eyes I saw Casey, anger making his eyes sharp as he led me from our table last night. His big, warm palm clutched me to him as we wound our way through tables before eventually ending up in some dingy, badly lit corridor.

"I'll get you back for this when you least expect it, Beanhead," Henry growled, once again interrupting my reverie of last night.

"Uh oh." I whipped the covers off my face, hair falling in my eyes as I gave Henry a look of mock fear, his empty hands evidence that he had no luck finding a pair of pliers. "I know you mean business when you resort to nasty name calling. I'm scared."

He flopped on the bed beside me as the tinkling sound of water came from the shower. Mac had obviously screwed the taps back on and was taking advantage of Henry's unexpected misfortune. "You mock me, Grace, but this is war now, you understand." Lifting the sheets, he crawled underneath and pulled them up over his chest.

Thinking of Mac's plea to "teach her," I laughed. "You know what they say. The best weapon against an enemy is another enemy. I think it's pretty obvious I got that covered."

"Yeah?" Henry raised his brows. "You know what else they say? Sometimes we need to lose the small battles in order to win the war."

My breath hitched because Henry's words reminded me my own war was coming and I'd be fighting it alone. Knowing he was watching me, I forced a smile. "That's a good one, Henry."

He grinned. "I thought so." After a quiet moment, Henry yawned and said, "You did good last night. You only stumbled over a few chords and no one noticed. "Wild heart" was probably one of our most complicated songs, so if you can master that in one afternoon, the rest should be a piece of cake. We'll practice every day, starting with the set list for this coming weekend."

"Today too?"

"No. Mondays and Tuesdays are usually our days off from everything, but with Frog out of action, we'll start rehearsing Tuesdays so we can get you up to date on the songs."

"Sounds good." When I realised I couldn't hear the shower running anymore, I began inching unobtrusively off the bed. "Oh hey, I wanted to ask, the big, blue Hilux I saw in the drive yesterday … that's Evie's car, right?"

"Yeah, why?"

I feigned a stretch. It gave me a credible excuse for gaining a better position to beat Henry for the bathroom. "I wanted to buy a bicycle." That was a total lie but the idea was to distract him with conversation. "I thought it would be a cool way to exercise and I could ride to the beach and stuff. I can't do that from my inner city apartment in Melbourne. I'd get mowed down by cars."

"That sounds good, Grace. I'll give you her number if you don't have it and you can call her this morning. I don't think she's doing anything today."

"Thanks, Henry."

The sound of the bathroom door opening was loud. Henry leaped into action, bounding off the bed with legs like springs. Damn him. He'd always been quicker than me, hence having to resort to more subtle ways of subterfuge when we were growing up.

Mac strolled into my room in a short satin robe with her wet hair wrapped up in a towel. Henry paused, his eyes narrowing as he took in the shower taps in her hand. She tossed them towards me with a wink. "Shower's all yours, Grace."

I caught them at the same time my phone beeped a message from the bedside table. Sliding on a pair of black-framed reading glasses, I hugged the taps to my chest and picked up the phone with my free hand. The screen highlighted a message originating from Batman. Considering I wasn't acquainted with the real Bruce Wayne, it knew it could only be his imposter.

I swiped the screen, squinting a little because there were two deep cracks in it, and read the message.

Sorry about last night, Slim.

Damn straight he should be sorry after—

"Who the fuck is Batman and why is he sorry about last night?"

"Huh?" I glanced up at Henry's livid tone, realising he was reading over my shoulder. I moved the phone away from his prying eyes.

"That's not from Casey, is it?"

My brows flew up. "How did you know it was Casey?"

"Slim. He's the only one I've heard call you that." Henry set his jaw. "Stay away from him, Grace."

I suspected Henry's warning stemmed from Casey's volatile behaviour so I didn't question it. Standing up, I replied with, "Whatever you say, Henry," as I headed for the bathroom with the shower taps.

Chapter Ten
CASEY

After messaging Grace, I pocketed my phone and walked through the entrance of our Darlinghurst office. It was late. Midday already. I was usually the only partner who worked Mondays, but if I did security on a Sunday night, which wasn't often, I usually slept in and only worked half a day.

Today I hadn't slept in at all, yet I was late anyway. I'd woken at five a.m. with morning wood that was painful. Knowing it wouldn't go away, I pushed my boxer-briefs down and wrapped a fist around my hard cock, giving a couple of hard, purposeful tugs.

Wild, stormy eyes flooded my mind, forcing a rush of blood that had my hips arching upwards. I groaned audibly as my fist moved up and down, stroking in rough movements that I knew would get me off quickly. My thumb slipped over the head, imagining it was Grace touching me, her tits brushing against my legs as she gripped me with firm hands. My stroke sped up at the image of me gripping her dark tangle of hair in my fist, forcing her head back to look at me while I thrust in and out of that smart, luscious mouth of hers.

There was no denying I wanted my hands all over her. Just the simple thought of trailing my fingers over her belly, down between her thighs, and inside made my pulse leap. Even better was imagining my mouth between her thighs, tasting her on my tongue as I rubbed it over her clit while she whimpered and clawed at my hair. The thought of her coming against my tongue was enough to set off my own orgasm. My cock pulsed heavily and my balls grew tight as I moaned, my fist pumping as I shot all over my belly.

I lay on my back for a few minutes, catching my breath before I got up and walked naked to the bathroom to clean up. After wiping off my stomach, I brushed my teeth and washed my face to wake myself up. Done, I decided to head out for an early morning surf. The air was cool and the morning dark when I padded out to the back deck. I pulled my wetsuit from the little outdoor clothesline and tugged it up my legs, leaving the top half hanging around my waist as I grabbed my board and headed out for a surf.

The ocean was smooth like glass, which meant only the diehard surfers were out. Plunging into the icy water jumpstarted my system. The days I didn't get to the beach in the morning were the ones where I felt sluggish and tired. Paddling past the breakers, I reached the other surfers and sat up. A few short nods were enough to acknowledge those I knew. We all sat quietly, taking in the sunrise as we drifted gently on the tide. The only sound was the lapping water and a few lone seagulls as my mind wandered back to Grace and last night.

"You're right," she told me. My eyes fell to her fisted hands and I realised she was distressed. "Dalton is my … was," she corrected, "my boyfriend. He did something really shitty and I'm just not ready to deal with it, or him, just yet."

"Grace! Where's Dalton tonight? Are the rumours of him and British model Selena true? Is this your new boyfriend?" I shook my head, cursing under my breath. Her sudden change in demeanour made it clear these so-called rumours held a grain of truth. Had Dalton cheated on her? Clenching my jaw, I unlocked the screen of Grace's phone and jabbed in the year of her birth, unsurprised when I received immediate access. Let him ring. I'll deal with him instead.

But first things first, Grace needed to tell me what was going on. Not wanting to have the conversation in a public arena, I pocketed Grace's phone and pretty much dragged her from the table. Having already memorised the building layout from the brief, I led her straight to the nearest quiet corridor.

Spinning her around, I let go. She was panting a little and my eyes fell to her chest. Even with anger stirring my blood, so did the lust.

"Dammit," I growled, needing to let go of the attraction but not knowing how. I cracked my knuckles a couple of times. Grace winced at the sound so I folded my arms instead. "What did Dalton do, Grace?"

She lifted her chin. "It's really none of your business, is it?"

I stared at the floor intently, arms still folded as I nodded in agreement. Of course it was none of my business, but that wasn't going to stop me from digging for answers. "Did he hurt you?"

"So what if he did? Why do you even care? We hardly know each other."

That was a good question. I wish I knew how to answer it.

Grace's phone started ringing in my back pocket. Satisfaction ran through my veins when I pulled it out and saw Dalton's name on the screen.

Her eyes fell to the phone. "Don't you even— Goddammit, Casey!" she yelled when I tapped the accept button and put the phone to my ear.

"Grace! Thank God!" came the male voice in my ear. Grace froze. Her eyes locked on mine and all I could see was hurt. It fed the anger burning in my chest knowing this man put that look on her face. "You haven't been answering your phone."

"Is this Dalton?" I asked.

There was a pause. "Who the fuck is this?"

"That's not your concern," I replied as I held Grace's eyes with mine. Our contact proved impossible to break. "What is your concern is what I'll do to you if you keep calling Grace. She doesn't want to talk to you."

"What the … Are you fucking kidding me? Put Grace on the phone. Now!" he demanded.

Grace backed up a step, her wide eyes frantic as she shook her head. "I said I wasn't ready to talk to him!"

"Is that her? Grace!" Dalton yelled.

I shook my head. "She doesn't want to talk to you, mate, so stop bothering her."

"She's my fucking girlfriend, mate. It's not harassment if all I want to do is talk to her on the phone. Is this about Selena?"

There was a pause when I didn't answer the question.

"Goddammit. It is, isn't it? I wouldn't have fucked her if Grace wasn't such a cold bitch."

Grace flinched, obviously hearing his loud words in the quiet corridor. She flushed, soft colour slowly rising in her face before she turned away, hugging her body with obvious embarrassment.

Sonofabitch! My hand gripped the phone so tight it should've pulverised into dust. Did he not even know his own girlfriend? In a short space of time, I'd already seen Grace passionate, fiery, funny, and considerate. The one thing she hadn't been was cold. The fucktard must be living in a parallel dimension.

"If that's what you think," I bit out, "then you don't really know Grace at all, do you?"

"You obviously haven't fucked her then. Put her on the—"

I cut him off, furious. "You useless sonofabitch! Dial this number one more time and I'll make you wish you'd never been born." Simply hanging up the phone wasn't enough so I hurled it at the wall in a fit of temper. It didn't feel as good as what punching Dalton in the face would have. There was no satisfaction in one-sided violence against inanimate objects.

The screen cracked on impact before it fell to the ground. Grace knelt, letting out a sob as she grabbed for it.

Only then did it register that I'd just thrown her phone, not my own. I opened my mouth but nothing came out.

She stood up, facing me, and her eyes were wild so I backed up a step. "Are you happy now!" she cried and shoved me in the chest with both hands. "You couldn't let me handle it, could you? You've just gone and made everything worse! Arrghhhh!" Grace threw up her hands, giving me the distinct impression that I'd fucked up. Again. What the hell was wrong with me? "Just stay away from me," she hissed, pointing a finger in my face. "After tonight, I want to forget you even exist."

She slid the damaged phone in the pocket of her pretty blue pants and stormed off down the corridor. "Grace!" I called after her. "I'm sorry!" Without turning around, she flipped me off as she kept walking. Seeing her do that made me want to call her back and kiss her until neither of us could breathe. It took me a minute to realise she was heading in the wrong direction. "Grace!" She gave no indication she'd heard me. "You're going the wrong way."

After pausing for a long moment, she spun around, nostrils flaring as she stalked back towards me. My pulse sped up with every step she took. If I kissed her right now, she'd probably throw that punch she threatened me with earlier. I had to press my lips together when the thought made me grin.

Grace looked at me like I'd lost my mind. "This is funny to you?"

"No! Slim …" I reached for her.

She flinched. "Don't touch me. Don't talk to me either. Just get me the hell out of this maze and back to the table."

I winced at the recollection as I floated gently on my board. True to her word, Grace pretty much ignored me the rest of the night. When asked what happened to her phone, she simply said she dropped it, knowing that disclosing what really happened would only invite further questions.

Resolving to hit the shops this morning and buy her a new one, I lay down on my board and began the paddle back to shore.

"Later, Boyd!" I called out, offering a brief salute to the surfer closest to me in the water.

"Daniels." The guy gave a short nod before returning his gaze back to the horizon. Jack Boyd was out every morning, frequenting the same surf spots I did. He seemed like a bit of a loner and I'm pretty sure I heard it mentioned he was going through a divorce. The guy seemed too young, but I guess relationship difficulties didn't discriminate based on age.

After riding the waves to shore, I undid the leg rope and jogged up the soft sand with my board. Tugging my wetsuit down halfway, I rinsed quickly under the outdoor shower, shivering as I got rid of the excess sand. Wrapping a towel around my waist, I peeled off the bottom half of my wetsuit and headed back to the car.

By the time I got home, took a hot shower, and caught up on all the shopping I needed to do, it was midday when I arrived for work.

Having messaged Grace, I walked through to the outer office where my assistant, Tim, was talking on the phone with his back turned.

"I want to do bad things with his boy parts," I heard him hiss into the line, obviously not realising he was no longer alone. I bit the insides of my cheeks to hold back the laugh. "Are you kidding me? I would suck him so hard my eyeballs would literally pop right out of my head." Tim paused, listening as someone on the other end spoke, before replying, "It does not make me a vampire, you ho." Relaxing back in his chair, Tim laughed and started spinning around lazily. "You're just a jealous bitch, Mac. I bet you wish you were the one working for—" Spying me walking through, he froze before hurriedly turning back to his desk and clearing his throat. "Thank you. I'll make sure he returns your call," he said into the phone and hung up. The phone started ringing again immediately and Tim ignored it, his hands twitching nervously.

"Morning, Casey," he said, and began brushing at an imaginary piece of lint on his pants.

"Tim." I gave him a nod as I passed through his outer office and into mine.

"Back the truck up," he commanded, suddenly on full alert as he eyed the bags in my hand. "You went shopping?"

I turned, arching a brow as I walked backwards into my office. "Is that a problem or should I have cleared it with you first?"

He muttered something I didn't catch. I dumped the bags near one of the cabinets by my desk and sat down, noting the cup of piss-weak coffee sitting on a coaster by my laptop. Fuck it. This ridiculous feud Tim had going on with the local barista had to stop. I vowed to go down there myself and sort it out. Just not today. Today was Monday, and Mondays were right up there with boy bands—an unbearable phenomena that kept recurring no matter how fucking horrible they were.

Flipping open the screen, I fired up my laptop. I had a routine. My week would start with me unlocking the bottom drawer of my desk and pulling out the old, worn file. I would review it carefully like I always did. Then I would find nothing new and hide the file away again with a lump in my throat I could never swallow down. Frustration would grind my bones until it made me ache. And then I would begin my week, hurting just a little more than the week before.

Today was no different, but the possibility of getting answers via Morgan firmed my resolve. Just as I reached for the locked drawer, Tim barged in, pausing just long enough to strip all the clothes from my body with his eyes.

That was Tim's morning routine. I was left feeling naked as he marched into my office with an ominous pile of files. His other hand held a bunch of phone messages. He dumped the files on my desk and handed me the messages one by one as he recounted them.

"Richard. Penrith Police. He wants you to call first thing."

He handed me the second.

"Carol." I raised my brows at that one. Carol was our office administrator and supposed to start annual leave today. "Her cruise ship leaves in an hour. She wants you to call before then. She's worried about not getting reception once they leave."

He handed me the next one, bristling with irritation. "Morgan. She wouldn't say what it was in relation to despite me asking her. Twice." I held my hand out for the message, raising my brows when he didn't let go. "Who's Morgan?"

I shrugged. "She was at the Florence Bar on Friday night."

Tim sniffed as my phone beeped an incoming message. I picked it up, unable to hide the grin when I saw Grace on the screen. Opening the text, I read it silently, my grin turning into a chuckle.

You can shove your apology up your ass.

I quickly hit reply and tapped out a new message. Ouch. Sounds kinky. Got you a new phone.

"Who's Grace?" Tim asked, peering at my phone. "And why's she talking about your ass?" His eyes went wide. "Wait! This isn't Grace Grace, is it? Henry's Grace? His sister, Grace?"

I tossed my phone back on the desk and snatched the message from Morgan out of Tim's hand, replying, "Yep," as I read his neat scrawl. Putting the message aside, I went back to my laptop. "Anything else?" I asked Tim's hovering form.

"No, no." He backed away. "I've got some calls to make. Those reports from Friday are in the files on your desk."

"Oh, Tim?" I called out before he disappeared. "Can you get Frank to find the contact information for Helen who used to work at Bankstown Police? Tell him she's working airport security over at Sydney Domestic now." Frank ran our control room upstairs and usually handled all our operations behind the scenes as well as ferreting out information that wasn't public record. He was good at finding out what you needed to know without asking questions.

"Helen?" His voice sounded faint. "You've had a busy weekend."

I schooled my features, not wishing to instigate one of those office gossip sessions Tim excelled in. Having my balls waxed was less painful. "And now it's Monday, and some of us have work to do," I pointed out.

He left as another message from Grace beeped through on my phone.

You can stick the new phone in the same place as your apology.

My lips curved as I sent off another reply. Do you have a fetish for my ass? You keep mentioning it.

Despite Henry's warning, Grace was proving addictive. When no immediate response came through, I tried putting her from my mind and focused on working through the draft reports Tim left for me. I stopped after an hour, my growling stomach reminding me I hadn't eaten breakfast. Sitting back in my chair, I stretched before picking up my phone and checking the screen. Another message sat there from Grace. Maybe because you're always talking out of it.

I laughed out loud and Tim appeared in my office. "Having fun on a Monday, Casey? That's not like you." His eyes fell to the phone in my hand and his brows raised inquisitively. "Grace again?"

"Need something, Tim?" I asked mildly as I tapped out another message. Seems there's too much talk about my ass and not enough about yours.

"It's lunch time," he announced as I put my phone back on the desk. "Want me to grab you something?"

Mondays were officially declared 'Fast Food Mondays' in our office. With Jared not working, it was the safest day of the week to indulge without getting chewed out, no pun intended. The man was a health food Nazi and I didn't need someone telling me what I could and couldn't eat. I might've appreciated the whole my body is a temple thing, but too much clean living was bad for your health.

"Great. Can you get me—"

"A burger with the works and a brownie," he replied, fussing at his hair so it sat just so. At my raised eyebrows, he added, "You went for a surf this morning, right? That always makes you hungry, but you went shopping straight after, which means you probably didn't take the time to eat. You've also got that little fucking hell, it's Monday furrow in your brow going on, which means you need sugar if I'm going to put up with you this afternoon."

As soon as Tim left the office, I picked up the phone and dialled Morgan. She answered after several rings, sounding breathless.

"Bad time?" I asked, hearing loud voices in the background.

"No! Just … hang on." The sound of footsteps came through the line, followed by muffled quiet before she came back on the line. "I'm at work and it's a little crazy today."

I tapped a pen impatiently on my desk before stilling the movement. Keeping my voice low, I asked, "Settling in okay over there?"

"I think so. I'm learning off a great partner, but he's giving me all the grunt work. I was expecting it, but it kinda sucks."

I laughed. "Yeah I remember all about being a rookie. I don't miss it."

She sighed. "So … I was wondering if you were free Thursday night? We could go to the cinema. There's a couple of good movies out I've been wanting to see."

"Great. Sure thing."

"So … should I message you the time and then meet you there?"

My gut feeling was busy telling me this was all wrong. Ignoring it, I replied,

"This is a date, right? So I'll pick you up, okay?"

"I'd like that," she replied with warmth in her voice. "I'll message you my address."

"I'll look forward to hearing from you." I checked my watch. "You must be a busy girl, so I'll let you go. Talk soon, okay?"

"You got that right. Later, Casey."

"Later," I replied and hung up.

After eating lunch and putting in another solid hour on paperwork, I pushed it all to the side. Tim never made mistakes and these were filled with too many to count. Pushing back my chair, I picked up the files and headed for his outer office.

"What are these, Tim?"

He took the reports, flicking through all the sections I'd highlighted and frowning. "Crap," he muttered, his eyes suddenly filling with tears. "These are a mess."

Shit.

I backed up a step.

"It's just …" Tim took a sudden turn for the worse, drawing a deep, shaky breath that made me nervous. "Dean and I broke up over the weekend," he choked out. "He accused me of having a thing for Jean and, well, someone else." Tim cleared his throat. "He says I'm not focused on us and that I need to grow up. I'm sorry," he added, slumping a little. "I thought coming into work would be a good distraction. I should've stayed home."

"Jean?"

"You know, the barista?" he replied impatiently.

No, I didn't know the barista's name was Jean, but there you go. The barista was ruining my day by proxy once again. First with bad coffee, and now this. Tim was a flirt. This was not news. He and Dean broke up over the issue more times than I could count, but Dean needed to learn that Tim was Tim, and he didn't have to change his spots for anyone. It meant the time had come to intervene. "And do you?"

"Do I what?"

"Have a thing for Jean?"

"No!" he cried out. After a pause, he added, "Well, maybe. But just because the guy's hot doesn't mean I'm trying to get in his pants. I love Dean!"

I sighed internally and folded my arms. Fuck Mondays. Fuck them upside down, left, right, sideways, and every which way. "Do you want me to punch him?"

Tim looked me over and visibly shivered. "Yes!" Then he covered his face with his hands. "God, what am I saying? No! I don't want you to punch him, but uh, thanks. Violence is not my thing."

"Oh, okay." I pretended to nod thoughtfully. "So that guy I saw watching the MMA on YouTube the other day was your alter ego?"

"Yes." He nodded along with me. "It must have been."

"You want to take the afternoon off, Tim?"

"No!" He shook his head, his eyes once again filling with tears. He dashed away one that spilled over. Reaching for a tissue, I offered it towards him but rather than using it, he began shredding it into little pieces. "He isn't working today. He said he was going to pack some stuff and stay at his brother's place for a few days."

My phone buzzed in the background. "You should get that," Tim told me. "I'll ring Mac. Maybe I can stay at the duplex for a couple of days. I can't face going home without Dean there."

"You can't stay there. Grace is using their guest room." Tim chewed on his fingernail and gave me a hopeful expression. After a few beats of silence, I yielded far too easily to his puppy dog eyes. "Fine. You can stay at the loft. But don't leave your million and one products all over the bathroom like you did the last time you crashed our pad. I couldn't find the basin beneath all your crap. And you can't have Coby's bed this time. You have to take the couch." Coby had been out of town the last time Tim and Dean had a falling out. I'd let Tim take over his room for three days. Coby was pissed when he found out. Well, maybe a bit more than pissed. The man had developed a nasty eye twitch on hearing where Tim and Dean's reconciliation had taken place. It took weeks and the purchase of a new mattress for him to get over it. I narrowed my eyes in warning. "No sex on the couch." I liked my couch and its well-worn groove. I didn't want a new one. "Or anywhere else," I added.

"No sex on the couch!" he repeated and picked up the phone to ring whoever the hell it was he rang when this shit happened. "Thanks, Casey!" he called out as I returned to my desk.

"Don't thank me yet," I replied dryly, picking up my own phone to make a call. "You're gonna be the one to tell Coby."

After several rings, the call went to voicemail. "Hi, this is Dean. Leave a message."

After the beep, I replied, "Dean, this is Casey. We need to talk." After hanging up, I read the new message from Grace that was waiting on my phone.

You should stop messaging me.

You're right, I tapped out. I should ring you instead.

Chapter Eleven
GRACE

It was late Wednesday night when Casey rang. Two long days of band rehearsals had wiped me out. After going to bed early, I was twisted in a pile of blankets and sleeping like the dead when Lily Allen's "Fuck You" screeched loudly through the quiet duplex. Dragged reluctantly into consciousness, I scrambled for the phone off the bedside table and answered with a bleary, "'Lo?"

"Slim," came Casey's own sleep-rough voice. "Did I wake you?"

Brushing a tangled lock of hair from my face, I took the phone away from my ear to inspect the time. "Casey?" My own voice sounded just as rough when I spoke his name. "It's midnight so yeah, you woke me. Is something wrong?"

"No, but I spoke to Helen over at the airport today. I wanted to tell you." I heard the sound of rustling sheets as I struggled to wake up and failed. Closing my eyes, I started drifting off while I waited. "You there?"

"Mmm hmm," I mumbled, the phone starting to slide from my ear.

"Jesus."

"What?" I breathed. Rolling to my side, I put my phone on the bed so I could lie on it and keep both hands free. Then I grabbed a pillow and closed my eyes again, hugging it close.

"You're sexy when you're half asleep, Slim."

"I'm not," I mumbled, barely even able to process what he was saying.

"Can't take a compliment?"

Even though he couldn't see me, I rolled my eyes. I'd never tried that manoeuvre with my eyes closed before. It actually made my eyeballs ache a little bit. Letting go of my pillow, I picked up my phone, snapped a quick photo and sent it to him. "There. Submitting exhibit A into evidence."

There was a pause before I heard his soft chuckle.

"It's supposed to show you how unsexy I am when I'm half asleep, Casey. It's not supposed to be funny," I mumbled.

There was brief pause before my phone beeped an incoming message. Looking at the bright light of my screen made my eyes ache all over again. I opened the message to a photo of Casey that made my heart thump. Despite the cracked screen, I could still see his face. He was lying on a pillow so he must have been in bed too. He looked tired. His hair was mussed, eyes red, and his jaw covered in scruff. I wanted to bury my face in the spot where his neck met his bare shoulder and just breathe him in.

I put the phone back to my ear and whispered softly, "Casey."

"Grace," he whispered back.

I performed the 'lying on my phone and hugging my pillow' manoeuvre again and closed my eyes. Only now all I could see was Casey's face and how worn-out he looked, and for some reason that made me want to hug him instead of being pissed off at him like I should. "So what did Helen say?"

"She said the old lady sitting beside you on the flight gave them the information. Apparently she flies to Sydney regularly to visit her daughter and every other month she makes a delusional complaint. They tend not to take her too seriously."

"Oh."

"Oh?"

"All that drama over nothing." Though I knew why she might think me suspicious when I remembered the vitamins in my handbag. I'd accidently smashed the bottle and put the pills in a plastic packet. She must have seen them when my handbag was knocked on the floor and everything fell out. Still, making the leap to drug carrier was a stretch. "That little old lady has a lot to answer for," I told Casey.

"Agreed. I think she's probably watched Miami Vice one too many times," Casey replied. His voice was still low and gruff. I started drifting off at the hypnotic sound. "You there?"

"Mmm," I mumbled.

"I was thinking … Maybe we should start again."

"Again?"

"Yeah, again."

How many do-overs could you have before it got ridiculous? It was already feeling ridiculous, and maybe a tiny bit adorable. Perhaps Casey was right though. Starting again was probably a good idea. I could hold that to him when he eventually saw his shredded backseat. I could claim we'd started over therefore everything that happened before that point in time didn't exist. "'Kay," I agreed, impressed by such logical thinking on my part while still half asleep.

"I'll go first, okay?"

"'Kay."

"My name's Casey Daniels," he began and God, his voice was sexy. If I lay there long enough while listening to that deep, husky timbre, I would have an orgasm. I squished my pillow a little tighter, tempted by the idea of testing that particular theory. "Apparently, I'm addicted to fucking up on a regular basis. It's been…" there was a pause "…three days and four hours since my last douche move."

I giggled sleepily.

Douche move was right. The man had spoken to Dalton when I asked him not to and then finished the conversation by breaking my phone. Casey had issues. Big ones if you took his vigilante tendencies into consideration. I'd tried to stay pissed at him, I really did, but anger had taken a backseat to humiliation after Dalton's cold bitch comment. He'd said that to Casey. I'd wanted to curl into the corner and rock for a while after that. Unfortunately, there hadn't been time for such an emotional indulgence. The best I could manage was to ignore the man for the rest of the night, hiding the hurt and embarrassment behind a mask of indifference.

Talking to Casey should have brought that humiliation flooding back to the surface, but it wasn't there. Maybe because he was talking to me like I was a real person, not someone who was there to make money, or do someone a favour, or be used as an accessory to whatever event was on that weekend. Casey had stripped away my emotional composure in no time at all and refused to give it back. I liked that he made me feel. I liked him.

"Slim?" he prompted.

"My name's Grace Paterson," I began. "I used to date a douchebag. Apparently, someone told him if he called me again, he would wish he'd never been born. It's been…" I paused "…just over three days and four hours since he rang me last."

"I'm sorry," he said softly.

"Hey. We're starting over remember? That means a clean slate. Technically you can't apologise if we only just met," I pointed out.

"Do you think we'll do a better job this time?"

My stomach growled, reminding me what little I ate at dinner had long since burned off. "Of what?" I asked, picking up the phone and holding it to my ear as I slid out of bed.

"Our do-over."

"That depends," I replied, padding down the stairs in nothing but a singlet and panties. It must have been only a quarter moon because it was so dark I could barely see.

"On what?" he asked as I used my free hand to trail along the wall, feeling my way as I took each step with caution. Late night tumbles down stairs rarely ended well, and with Casey on the phone, it could only end in embarrassment.

"On the potential for future douche moves and interference by ex-douchebags," I answered, arriving safely in the kitchen.

A deep chuckle came through the phone. "That's a lot of big words for someone who's half asleep."

"Douche is a big word?" I scoffed as I flicked on the electric kettle. A cup of tea would settle the ache of hunger in my belly. "And I'm awake now, thanks to you," I told him, turning around to open the fridge and get the milk.

"I heard the fridge," he told me as I slammed it shut. "Are you having a late-night binge?"

"I wish," I muttered as I turned and grabbed a teaspoon from the cutlery drawer.

"You should eat if you're hungry."

I leaned against the kitchen counter while I waited for the kettle to boil. "The industry I work in doesn't allow for that kind of luxury, Casey."

There was a pause. "Then you should quit. No amount of money is worth starving yourself."

Thinking of what that amount of money had done to pay medical bills, tuition for my brother and sisters, and give them a future, I couldn't agree. If I had to do it all over again, I wouldn't change a thing. "You're wrong," I told him around the lump in my throat. "You're dead wrong, Casey."

"I'm wrong? Really?" His voice turned hard. "I'm disappointed you put money above all else, Slim. I didn't realise you were so superficial."

"You asshole!" Hurt welled in my chest. "What gives you the right to sit in judgement of me? You know nothing about me and my life. You know what? Fuck you. This whole do-over was a mistake."

"Touchy subject, huh?"

"Arrghhhh!" I tossed the teaspoon at the sink. The resulting clank was loud in the quiet kitchen.

"Shit. Slim." Casey exhaled sharply. "You're right. I don't know anything about you and your life. You want to hear what I do know?"

I wanted to tell him to shove what he knew up his ass, along with his apology and the new phone, and despite the anger, I almost laughed, thinking it was getting crowded in there, but he continued before I got a word out.

"What I do know is that you have an issue with food. If the amount you ate at dinner on Sunday night was normal for you, then I have no idea how you find the energy to get up each day. I know you get photographed for a living. I googled and saw pictures of you that took my breath away. I know that when your older brother needed you, you dropped everything in an instant to be there for him. I know you're good at making threats but your follow-up could probably do with some work. You have a soft spot for aggressive little dogs that nobody else wants. You're crazy beautiful when you're angry—your eyes become like some wild, windswept ocean that a man could drown in and die happy. I know that nothing is sexier than you half asleep in bed, and after seeing your photo message without all that makeup on your face…" there was a pause before his voice got huskier "…I now know you have a sprinkling of freckles across your nose that I have a desperate urge to kiss."

Dazed, I slid slowly down the kitchen cabinets as he spoke. How could he do that—piss me off and make my body melt into a puddle on the floor at the same time? I barely knew him.

"There's something else I know," he continued. "Somehow, somewhere along the way, something happened to make you think your self-worth was based only on how much money you earned."

"No." My voice came out hoarse so I cleared my throat. "Maybe when I was younger I felt that way, but not anymore." I'd made the declaration on the phone to John that my new life started now. I had all intentions of following through. I wasn't going to feel sorry for myself or sorry for the choices I made. I was just going to start making those choices for me now rather than everyone else.

"What happened when you were younger?"

I moved my hand away from my mouth when I realised I was chewing my thumbnail. "You heard some of Henry's stories. That was me all the time. I was a difficult child."

The light flicked on, flooding the dark kitchen into brightness. I hissed and burrowed my face into my knees. I tried opening my eyes against the blinding glare and failed. Covering them instead, I peeked through my fingers to find Henry standing in the kitchen. The left side of his hair was sticking up and pillow creases lined his cheek.

"Grace?" His brows were raised as he stood looking down at me. "What are you doing?"

Casey was silent on the line while Henry spoke.

"I'm trying to make a cup of tea."

He paused. "In the dark while sitting on the kitchen floor?"

Henry sounded incredulous, as though such a feat was impossible to perform. "You think it can't be done?" Casey's laugh came through the phone. "Stop laughing," I told him.

Henry shuffled over to the sink and filled a glass with tap water. He turned around eyeing me as he took a sip. "Who's on the phone?"

I opened my mouth to answer when Casey said quickly, "Don't say it's me."

"What? Why?"

"Grace?" Henry prompted.

"Just a friend," I told him as I pushed up off the floor.

"Am I being friend-zoned?" Casey sounded annoyed.

"Seriously?" Shifting the phone from one ear to the other, I dusted off my hands. "You know that term was created by men with overinflated egos who, for some unfathomable reason, can't understand why a girl doesn't want to have sex with them."

Henry's hand jerked, spilling water down his chest. His brows rose at me inquisitively as he wiped himself dry with the tea towel.

I rolled my eyes. After saying goodnight to my brother, I left him to his water and headed back to my room.

"You're getting ahead of yourself, Slim," I was told as I made my way back up the stairs. I could hear the smirk in Casey's voice. It was louder than my growling stomach after being denied sustenance. "I haven't mentioned the possibility of us getting naked together."

"Oh, of course. Because that whole I didn't say where I wanted to kiss you thing in the limo had nothing to do with getting naked."

"That's right." Casey's voice deepened. "You don't need to get naked for that. All I need to do is kneel between your thighs and slip your panties to the side."

Heat.

Waves of it slammed my body until I was on fire. Damn him. I climbed back under the sheets and buried my face under the pillow, as if hiding would somehow cool me off. It was either that or slip my hand beneath my panties to ease the ache.

"Grace?"

"I'm here," I replied breathlessly from beneath the pillow. "Is this phone sex now? Because I'm not having phone sex with someone I barely know. In fact, I've never had phone sex. With anyone. Ever."

Casey's voice perked up. "Really?"

I groaned. Why did I just say that?

"We should get to know each other better."

I pushed the pillow off my face and filled my lungs with air. "Now? I need sleep. And why couldn't I tell Henry it was you on the phone?"

"So we're putting the whole phone sex thing on ice?"

"Casey! What's going on with you and Henry? The other day you seemed like friends. Now I'm not supposed to be talking to you on the phone?"

Casey sighed. "He doesn't want me seeing you."

"He might have mentioned that," I admitted. "But he didn't say why."

"You want the long story or the short story?"

"It's late," I mumbled, feeling drowsy again now that I was back in bed. "Give me the short story."

"He thinks I'm going to get you hurt."

Henry was playing the big brother card? I mulled that over in my head, unsure of how it made me feel. "Why would you get me hurt, Casey?"

"Telling you why is the long story."

I suddenly decided I wanted the long story. And more of Casey. "We're having a barbecue here tomorrow night. You should come. You can tell me the

long story."
    "Tomorrow night? Thursday night?"
    "Yes," I replied decisively. "Thursday night."

Chapter Twelve
CASEY

"Are you sure about this, Casey?" Tim yelled through the bathroom door. Having just showered, I had a towel wrapped around my hips as I shaved in preparation for tonight's date with Morgan.

"Sure about what?" I called back.

"About tonight."

I leaned close to the mirror, swiping the razor down the left side of my jaw. "What are you talking about?" I asked, pulling back and rinsing the blade in the sink. "It's just a date, Tim. I'm not asking her to marry me."

"What about Grace?" he asked as I leaned in again.

I paused, the razor hovering near my chin. Yeah, idiot. What about Grace?

Grace had surprised me with her invitation. I almost blew off my date with Morgan and said yes. Somewhere in the middle of our phone conversation, my heart had tripped over and hadn't recovered its normal beat since. I liked it. I liked her. So much that I wanted more nights on the phone like last night. Listening to her laugh in that husky voice made my cock ache in the best possible way.

Walking over to the bathroom door, I opened it and looked at Tim. He ran his eyes over me and blinked. After clearing his throat, his gaze fixated on my chest.

"Tim?" I barked to get his attention.

His gaze moved to my jaw and he huskily said, "You … ah … missed a spot."

I stalked back to the basin. Picking up the small towel resting nearby, I scrubbed it over my face. I turned back to Tim as I tossed the towel in the general direction of the sink. "What do you mean 'what about Grace?' What do you know?"

Tim suddenly looked everywhere but at me.

I arched a brow, waiting silently. Tim hated silence. It made him twitchy and more willing to talk.

"Don't do that."

"Do what?"

"That brow thing."

With a roll of my eyes, I folded my arms impatiently.

His eyes widened on my biceps. "Don't do that either."

"What the fuck, Tim. You're gonna make me late. Just spit out whatever it is you know so I can get going, okay?"

"I heard you on the phone with Grace last night," he blurted out.

My eyes narrowed, annoyed that my private conversation hadn't been so private after all. "You were listening?" Unfolding my arms, I stalked past him and into my room to get dressed.

Tim followed behind. "Not exactly. I mean, I'm staying on your couch. Its general location isn't far from your bedroom. It's not that I heard your exact conversation, but I heard your tone. It was low and flirty. And you were talking for well over an hour. You! Jesus, Casey, you're one hell of a charming bastard, but when faced with a dreaded phone conversation, you turn into a boring mute."

Tim kept up his verbal diarrhoea as I walked to my dresser. Knowing we were only going to the movies and not somewhere upscale, I yanked a casual black shirt from the drawer and went to tug it on. It was snatched from my hands.

"Not that one," I was told when he took a breath. Tim folded it carefully and put it back in the drawer. He pulled out my vintage blue and black Sex Pistols shirt. "This one." He held it out to me. "It's way sexy."

I took it without comment, shrugging it on and smoothing a hand down my chest. The fit was a little more snug than I remember it being. "It's not too tight?"

Tim paused, appearing taken aback at the question. "You're kidding, right? With your body? There's no such thing as too tight."

I rolled my eyes as I rummaged in the next drawer down for a clean pair of jeans. "I'm your boss, Tim."

"And your point is? I've seen you naked." My eyes went wide as I stopped to look at him. "Almost," he amended. "I mean, those running shorts you wear? You may as well be."

I shook my head as I yanked open another drawer in the hunt for clean jeans. He watched me for a moment.

"So you're sure about tonight then?"

"Yes!" I reiterated, annoyance clear in my tone. Tim was like a dog with a bone.

"It's just … I know you don't get by on flirtation alone," he told me. "But I've never known you to play more than one girl at a time. All of a sudden you're dating Morgan and what, keeping Henry's sister on the side? It's obvious you like Grace," he said loudly when I starting shaking my head. "Well, it is to me anyway. So what I don't get is, why is Morgan in the picture?"

Finding a pair of jeans, I shook them out, ready to put them on. Lifting my chin at the door pointedly, I said, "You mind?"

"You're not a player, Casey."

I shrugged off the disappointment in Tim's voice and forced a cocky grin. "Don't hate the player, hate the game," I told him with a wink.

With a loud huff, he spun on his heel, leaving me to finish getting dressed. After tugging on my jeans, I sank to the edge of the bed. I needed a drink. Something strong.

After, I promised myself. Then you can self-medicate the haemorrhage so it stops hurting for a little while.

As promised, midnight saw me sitting on the couch in the dark. A half-empty bottle of scotch sat next to an empty glass on the coffee table in front of me. It was quiet with Tim and Coby still out at the barbecue. Too quiet. I needed noise. Something to distract my mind from Grace. From the fact that just thinking of her made breathing difficult.

This is how obsession starts, Casey. With alcohol and some girl you see every time you close your eyes.

I poured another glass and stretched out, my head tipping back against the couch as the scotch slid down my throat. The gratifying burn of alcohol drew me a little further from reality as I reflected on my date with Morgan. It had upped the complication factor of my life for the sole reason it meant seeing her again. Sitting in a movie hadn't been the best place to hold a conversation, so I'd taken her to Kingsley's on the wharf for a late dinner. I didn't discuss specific details with her. I kept my questions indirect, knowing her natural detective curiosity would pave the way.

"I have a case I've been puzzling out for a long time," I'd mentioned offhandedly.

Her eyebrows had risen in interest. "Yeah? What case?"

I shrugged, my gaze shifting from her to the outside view when I felt the familiar burn in my eyes. "An old homicide. I was given informal permission to look into the case."

She nodded thoughtfully, not even questioning my clearance, or lack thereof in this instance. "You want me to run my eye over what you have? Sometimes a fresh eye can help."

"It's not fresh eyes I need, but information. I don't think I have all of it. Actually, I know I don't have all of it. The files aren't in the system or in archives."

I searched her face, trying to read her reaction to my words. The waiter chose that moment to stop by. Morgan held out her glass when he offered a refill. When he disappeared, she smiled slowly as she swirled the wine in her glass.

Her voice turned husky. "Maybe I can help. We can get together on the weekend and go from there?"

My lips curved.

Bingo.

After leaving the restaurant, she grabbed my shirt and pulled me close, plastering her lips on mine. I responded automatically, willing myself to feel something, a twitch of my cock at the least, but I got nothing.

Morgan broke away and licked her lips before smiling suggestively. "Come back to my place?"

I couldn't believe the timing of her phone ringing before I could reply. She answered it and after a quick conversation, hung up with a grimace. "I have to go," she said irritably.

I was too busy welcoming the sudden reprieve to question the phone call and subsequent mood change. "Can I drive you home?"

"Actually, I think I'll just get a cab," she told me, her expression pained.

"Everything okay?"

Morgan fumbled with her phone, tapping out a message. "Yeah." She sighed. "Just a big brother who keeps interfering in my shit. He's just turned up at my place. He wants to see me and God forbid I don't do what the fuck he says."

I stepped up to the kerb and hailed her a cab. "Sounds like an asshole," I said to her over my shoulder. I didn't want to interfere, but if he was the type of asshole that got violent, then I should at least make sure she was okay. "Sure you don't want me to take you home?"

"Uh, no. I'm good."

I opened the car door for her and after hopping in, Morgan wound down the window so I leaned in.

Meeting my eyes, she said, "Call me, okay? We'll set something up for the weekend. I can't wait to get my hands on you again."

I could wait and it should've surprised me. Morgan was hot, and I was never one to turn down a good fuck. But that was before Grace. It seemed the only woman I wanted right now was her.

After quickly pressing her lips against mine again, Morgan gave the driver her address. I waved briefly before walking the few blocks home to my loft. I needed that drink I'd promised myself.

Leaning forward on the couch, I tugged my phone from my pocket before sitting back. Scrolling down the contacts, I found Grace and dialled. Putting the phone to my ear, I waited, wanting to hear her voice and feeling like an asshole because I had no right to want it.

"Batman!" she answered, sounding drunk and happy.

"Hey, Slim," I murmured, feeling better already. "How's your night going?"

"Oh God. So good, but it just went downhill really fast," she slurred.

Before I could reply, a bloodcurdling scream pierced my ear through the phone, causing my heart to thump in panic. "Grace?" I shot to my feet. "Grace? Are you there?"

"Oh God," she moaned. "It's getting worse."

"Are you okay?" I asked, my tone urgent.

"No," she whispered in the phone. "I'll never be okay again. Ever. Never ever in my whole life. I'm gonna be—"

I heard her gag.

"Do you need me there?" I was already reaching for keys and shoes and when I heard another shrill scream, I said in the phone, "I'm on my way."

I stumbled over the coffee table when the floor shifted under my feet. There was no way I could drive.

Fucking hell.

"Hang on. I can't hear you." Loud drunken laughter boomed in the background and my panic eased a little. The noise decreased as though she was walking away. "Are you there?" she whispered.

"Yes, I'm here."

"They're making me watch Wolf Creek, Casey. I don't know why they would do this. Somehow we got talking about horror movies and Evie said it was the most terrifying movie of all time, so naturally I was an idiot and told everyone I'd never seen it. Have you seen it?" she asked and then continued before I could tell her there was no fucking way you'd get me watching that shit. "It's his laugh," she hissed. "His horrible, creepy-ass laugh. It's more terrifying than zombies chewing off all your body parts, or … or … falling out of a shuttle and floating off into space."

I pressed my lips together, laughter rumbling in my chest while I listened to her drunken chatter. She stopped suddenly and whispered my name.

"Mmm?" I replied.

"You should've come. You could've been here right now, doing that thing you said you wanted to do. You know, the thing you said I didn't even have to get naked for. How do you make me want you so much?" Her voice cracked and the sound resonated straight to my heart.

"Ahh hell," I rasped. I was fully hard just thinking about it. Reaching down, I adjusted my cock in my jeans, giving it a quick squeeze. I knew I'd come easily if I sat on the phone and detailed all the things I wanted to do to her.

"I wanted to see you, Casey. I want to see you."

I closed my eyes, swallowing hard. "You mean … like a date?"

A feeling of utter shame hit me. Dating both Grace and Morgan would be something no do-over would fix. Trust was something special, and after Dalton, Grace needed trust, not some stupid prick who'd only fuck up her life more.

"No!" Grace blurted out. "Not a date. I mean, like …" She paused. "I don't know. I just want to see you."

"Grace," I muttered hoarsely.

"Just … let's be friends," she announced decisively. "You know, buddies, pals, mates. We can draw a line. No talking about kissing, or sexing. Sexting," she corrected with a slight slur and a hiccup. "Or whatever the hell you call it. What do you do with your buddies, Casey?"

Definitely not the things I want to do with you.

I cleared my throat. "Most times we just catch up for a drink, but we do other stuff, like paintball, or the shooting range, surfing—"

"Surfing! Let's do that. I can do that. Saturday morning?"

"Ahh, okay," I agreed slowly, my mind still trying to catch up with the whole idea of being Grace's buddy. "It's best to go early though. How about Bondi at six?"

Grace's answer was a light snore into the phone.

"Grace?"

Nothing.

A smile crept slowly across my face.

"Sweet dreams, Slim," I whispered softly before hitting the end call button on my phone, wondering if she would even remember the conversation in the morning.

Chapter Thirteen
CASEY

I crouched in the sand, putting on the leg rope from my board, when I heard a hoarse, croaky mumble from behind say, "It's early."

A cool, blustery wind ruffled my hair as I stood and turned. "You're here," I said to Grace, recognising that familiar breathlessness when I looked at her.

Her hair was loose, hanging down her back in messy waves. It was obvious she'd just rolled out of bed and walked straight out the door because one side stuck out in a big, frizzy tangle. She was wearing a full body wetsuit. It looked brand new, but the board she carried under her arm didn't. It looked like Henry's board. I wondered if he knew Grace and I were now buddies.

She looked at me through puffy eyes that were mere slits. "You said Bondi at six, right?"

I grinned, thinking of her sweet little snore through the phone after passing out. "Didn't think you heard me."

"Yeah, well. I have this really bad habit of remembering everything when I'm drunk. Particularly stuff that's best left forgotten."

Grace jammed her board in the sand so it stood upright. With hands on her hips, she averted her face to assess the horizon but I still caught the flush climbing her neck. I knew then what she was remembering and my grin turned into a full-blown chuckle.

"Well if you change your mind about me doing that thing, you know the thing I said you didn't even have to get naked for, just say the word, buddy."

"Shut up, Casey," she ordered and accompanied her words with a punch to my arm. She looked pretty pleased with herself, but the effort was pathetic.

I laughed at her. "Seriously, Slim. No buddy of mine would ever punch like a pussy. You want me to help you work on that?"

"You're making a mockery of my good intentions," she complained. "I'm taking back the whole buddy thing, but if you want to go ahead and teach me how to throw a punch that will take you out, then sign me the fuck up."

"You want me to sign you up for full-contact sports, Slim?" I took a step closer until I was in her personal space. A gust of wind blew up and her hair fluttered in the breeze. Tendrils of it tickled my skin, covering me in goose bumps. "Because that sounds hot as fuck."

"Is everything a sexual innuendo with you, Casey?"

"Not usually," I admitted with a grin. "You seem to bring it out in me."

Grace rolled her eyes as she crouched down and began fastening her leg rope. A small furrow creased her brow as she concentrated on her task. "Maybe that's something I can help you work on."

"Buddies for five minutes and already you're trying to change me," I joked, watching as she fussed with the Velcro strap. It looked a little loose, so I crouched down. "Let me."

I pushed her hands out of the way and she stood up, watching as I took over. A quick examination told me it was worn and the seam had a slight tear. Even if the actual surfboard was in good nick, straps needed regular replacement.

"You need to get a new one of these," I cautioned, doing up the strap as tight as possible. The last thing we needed was for her board to cut loose on a wave and bean some surfer. "You can surf, right?"

"Of course I can," she replied, watching as I smoothed the Velcro fastening in place. "Well, it's been a while," she admitted. "I haven't surfed since I was young, but it's just like riding a bike."

I glanced up at her, eyes wide with disbelief. "Who the fuck told you that? Humpty Dumpty?"

Grace looked genuinely puzzled. "What's Humpty Dumpty got to do with surfing?"

"Nothing. That's my point."

She snorted as I finished fixing her strap. Throwing caution to the wind, I ran my hand up the inside of her leg, my palm grazing along her inner thigh as I stood.

Grace tipped her head back a little when I reached full height, her lids lowering lazily as she met my eyes. She placed her palm flat on my bare chest, running it slowly up smooth skin until it slid around the nape of my neck. She used it to tug me closer. My breath caught when it brought her lips close to mine.

"Casey?" she breathed.

The part of my brain directly connected to my cock took over the second her palm touched my bare chest. I ran my tongue over my lips, a split second away from crushing my mouth down on hers. "Mmm?"

Her lips curved and her hand shifted, smacking me gently on cheek. "Let's go, buddy."

Grace grabbed her board from the sand and started down the beach, laughter trailing behind her. Quickly tugging on the top half of my wetsuit, I picked up my own board and jogged after her, calling out, "You're a tease, Slim!"

Her eyes were wide with amazement when she spun around, walking backwards into the cold ocean. "I'm a tease? Me? Who was the one running their hand up my leg just before?" She snorted.

The sound was inelegant and utterly adorable. Between that and her bed hair, it was obvious she wasn't out to impress anyone, least of all me. It only made my heart thump all the more. Compared to all the calculated seductions I'd experienced in the past, the beautiful girl who was busy laughing at me as she ran into the surf was like a breath of fresh air.

Cool, salty water rushed up and over my feet as I followed her into the ocean. I kept a watchful eye on her as we headed out past the breakers, relaxing slightly when it appeared she could hold her own on a board.

Reaching the rolling swell, we both sat up.

"You did good," I told her, wiping the water from my face.

She nodded and grinned. "I know."

I lifted my chin at some good waves already starting to roll in. "Ladies first," I told her.

Grace caught the wave, getting to her feet on the first try, but she came off just a second later. The second time around she did worse, rather than better.

I laughed when she reached my side after wiping out on the third. "Just like riding a bike, huh?"

She flicked water at me, hitting me in the face.

"Hey!"

I paddled a little closer until we were sitting side by side, both facing the bright orange glow of the horizon. "So tell me how this buddy thing is supposed to work."

"Honestly? I don't know." Grace brushed a wet strand of hair off her face. After a minute, she shrugged but there was something behind the casual gesture that looked suspiciously like hurt.

After thinking about it for a moment, I wasn't sure I could be just a friend, not unless it somehow ended with me buried inside her. I hadn't even taken her whole buddy request seriously until now. How was it possible to be buddies with the star attraction of your mental spank bank? Just breathing the same air made my cock hard enough to pound nails. Was she supposed to just ignore the huge tent in my pants while we sat around watching chick flicks together, eating chocolate and doing each other's hair? Then there was the whole matter of her brother and his I think it's best if you stay away speech.

"What about Henry?" I asked. "He doesn't want me anywhere near you. Are you doing this just because he doesn't want you to?"

"No! Of course I'm not."

"Then why?" I pushed her when I should've let it go. I didn't know why. Maybe it was because I didn't want to be alone in this attraction. I wanted to know she was right there with me. I wanted her to admit she wanted more than being just buddies, which was fucked up because even if she did, we couldn't do anything about it anyway.

"Because you can never have enough friends, right?"

Her words were a deflection. Reaching over, I grabbed hold of her board and dragged her closer towards me. "Grace?"

She grimaced. "It's too early in the morning for confessions or deep conversation."

"Humour me."

"Okay." Grace leaned over, grabbing the edges of her board when a big wave rocked us. "But on the condition you share something too. Being buddies doesn't work if it's all one sided."

"Sure," I agreed. "And afterwards we'll sit here on our boards holding hands and sing Kumbaya."

Grace laughed and flicked me with water again. "You're an ass!"

"You're only just finding that out? Why would you want to be friends with someone you barely know?"

"You're right."

I grinned. "Say that again."

Grace rolled her eyes. "I meant you're right as in I barely know you. So give me a story. Something about your past that gives me insight into what made you the ass you are today."

The smile slid from my face. Grace had spoken with amusement dancing in her eyes but there was nothing amusing about my past. I didn't have any happy or funny stories, or even bittersweet ones. Hell, I didn't have any sad stories either. Mine were all just either pitiful or a goddamn tragedy. I didn't want to share any of that with Grace. What was the point? Sharing it wasn't going to change anything.

"My past?" I forced a grin. "Is this your roundabout way of asking me how many women I've slept with? Because you don't need to worry. I've always kept it wrapped."

"Hey!" Grace exclaimed. Reaching over, she poked me in the ribs. "What the hell was that?"

"What was what?" I asked, jerking backwards. My board rocked violently in the swell building beneath us. I hadn't noticed the breeze picking up and the size of the set on the horizon reflected it. Some big waves were coming.

"That bullshit line you just gave me," she replied, her brows knitted in apparent irritation.

I tensed on my board, surprised she called me out on it when no one else ever did. "It wasn't a line," I said teasingly. "Practising safe sex is no joke."

"Don't deflect." Grace grabbed hold of her board as the first of the big incoming waves rocked us forcefully. "We're supposed to be buddies now. Buddies tell each other everything."

I arched a brow. "We are? And there are rules now?"

"Stop!" she shouted, her loud voice cutting through the peace of the morning. Nearby surfers glanced our way with either curiosity or annoyance. Or both. "It's too early for verbal warfare, Casey." She shook her head at me. "Coming here this morning was a mistake. I don't know what I was thinking. Trying to be friends with you is like trying to hug a cactus." Grace turned on her board and began paddling towards shore.

The further away she got, the bigger the ache in my chest grew.

"Grace?" I called out.

She paused mid paddle and glanced back at me, her stormy, blue eyes full of disappointment. I hated seeing her look at me like that. I'd disappointed enough people in my life to last a lifetime. But it was better that she kept her distance because it would only get worse. Grace might be the woman I wanted, but Morgan was the one I had to focus on right now.

"You're right," I told her. "I am an ass. I might want to fuck you, but it doesn't mean I want to be your friend."

Grace flinched. Actually flinched. The sight made my stomach churn. Christ, I was selfish prick. Rather than continuing to shore like I expected her to do, she turned on her board and sat up, cocking her head at me.

"You want to know why I wanted to be friends?" She clenched her jaw for a moment, looking out into the distance as though finding the words. "I've always been tall," she began, looking back at me. "Even as a child I hovered a full head over all my classmates at school. They would tease me—calling me beanpole or stretch. I even got Big Bird. None of it was terribly original, but it didn't have to be. The words were intended to hurt and I admit they did their job. One day, when I was about eight, I saw this dress in a shop window and it took my breath away. It was something you'd imagine Tinkerbell wearing. It had dainty pink butterfly wings that glittered under the light. The skirt was tulle and looked like a big cloud of fairy floss." A wave rocked her board and she paused to wipe the water from her face. I wanted to grin at the thought of a young Grace in that over the top dress, but instead I remained still, intent on hearing the small piece of her past.

"I looked at that dress," she continued, "and I knew, I knew, that if I wore that dress, the kids at school wouldn't see how tall I was, they'd only see someone they wanted to be friends with. But Mum said the dress was more than we could afford. So the very next day I painted a huge rainbow in my bedroom. It covered almost the entire wall and some of the carpet. The colours all ran into each other until it looked mostly brown. It was really, really ugly but I did it because I was convinced that when I woke up in the morning there would be a pot of gold at the end of it. I was going to give the gold to Mum so she could use it to buy my dress. But when I woke up, there was nothing underneath my hideous brown rainbow. I cried for two days. On the third day, Dad caved and bought me the damn dress." Grace laughed but her eyes were wet with tears. "I was so excited I wore it that Sunday to our school fete where this boy, Alan, stood on the end of it and tore half of the skirt away. Mum mended it, but I refused to wear it anymore when I realised that no one wanted to be friends with the beanpole, even if she was wearing a pretty dress."

She drew a deep breath and shook her head. "Looking back, I can see how ridiculous it was. It didn't matter if I was tall or short, or skinny or overweight, if I wore the damn dress or a brown sack. Changing what I looked like wouldn't give me friends. They had to want to be your friend—enough that they didn't care what you looked like, or who you knew, or what you could do for them. They just wanted to be your friend because they liked who you were on the inside."

I sat quietly on my board staring at Grace, suddenly wanting to punch the whole world for making a little girl feel like she wasn't good enough. Then I wanted to punch myself because I'd just gone and done the same thing.

"I'm not really sure why I'm telling you this. Maybe because you remind me of those kids at school." She shrugged and started again for the beach.

"Grace!" I called out. "Grace, I'm sorry!" I knew she heard me but she continued on regardless, paddling hard to ride the next wave to shore. "Shit. Just … fucking shit," I growled angrily and punched my fist through the water.

She disappeared quickly beyond the roll of the swell. A few more seconds and I saw her again. She was on her feet, riding the wave. I held my breath watching her. For five seconds she managed to keep her feet before she turned inwards and lost her balance. She went flying up in the air before tumbling beneath the power of the crushing wave. The force of her wipeout ripped the leg rope from her ankle and her board crashed down above her.

"Oh fuck," I breathed, my stomach tightening with dread as I waited for her to surface but she never did.

I paddled swiftly towards where she went down but there was no telling where the tide of the wave could have taken her.

"Grace!"

Nothing.

"Grace?" I yelled, panic making me dizzy. I did a complete one-eighty, casting my gaze across the ocean but she didn't fucking surface. She went down and never came up.

I caught Boyd paddling quickly towards me.

"Take my board!" I yelled at him. I caught his quick nod before I ripped off my leg rope and dove into the water. There was no telling where she was in all the whitewash, but I couldn't sit there waiting until I got a glimpse of her. The waves shoved me around carelessly and the salt water burned as I used my eyes and hands to try and locate her. When I ducked above the surface to see if she'd come up, Boyd yelled, "Over there!"

I followed the direction he was pointing and dove again, swimming underwater. Reaching out, I grabbed hold of a limb; I wasn't sure what limb it was, but I had a fucking hold of her and that was all that mattered. Pushing up off the ocean floor, I shot us both upwards. Breaking the surface, I was relieved to hear Grace drawing in huge gulps of air.

"Grace," I panted, wrapping myself around her until we were tangled together.

She twined her arms around my neck, her teeth chattering from the shock. I held on tight, not knowing whether I wanted to yell, cry, or puke. Maybe just doing all three at the same goddamn time would be more efficient.

"Fuck," I muttered, waiting for the emotional disparity to pass.

Boyd called my name. I turned my head, watching him paddle over with my board. "You guys okay?"

I pulled back a little to look at Grace. Ice-cold fear shot through me at the sight of the blood trickling down the side of her face. "Oh God, Grace, baby." I shifted, trying to get a better look. "You're bleeding."

A wave crashed into us and she started sliding from my grasp. "Don't let go," I ordered while I turned in the whitewash, loosening an arm from around her to take my board. "Thanks, mate," I told Boyd. "Goddamn leg rope snapped off."

"Nasty shit, dude." He lifted his chin towards the shore. "Go take care of your girl."

Boyd gave a casual salute before paddling away. I nudged Grace towards the board before the next wave could hit. "Hop on."

She climbed on, straddling my board without a word. Only once she was sitting safe did I realise my heart was hammering hard enough to beat out of my chest.

"I lost Henry's board," she said, holding a hand to the wound on her head with a wince.

"Who gives a shit about the damn board!" I swiped a hand across my face, looking up at her as I treaded water. "Jesus, fuck! Are you okay? That fucking strap. I shouldn't have let you on the damn board. Henry shouldn't have let you take the damn board."

"It's not a big deal, Casey. I'm barely even bleeding. I got beaned by a surfboard and got a little disoriented, that's all. I couldn't work out which way was up and every time I tried, another wave came and shoved me back down."

"Barely bleeding?" I growled as I climbed on the board behind her. It sunk low beneath the water's surface under our combined weight. "Look at this!" I pulled her hand away from her head. It was dripping blood, dammit. "That's barely bleeding to you?"

She yanked her hand from my grip and pressed it back against her head. "You're being irrational," I was told as I began the awkward paddle back to shore. "Head wounds always bleed like a bitch."

"Just keep pressure on it until we're back on dry land and I can have a proper look."

"Well, it's been fun," she said with sarcasm when we made it back to the beach. "We should definitely do this again."

"Yeah?" Reaching dry sand, I dumped my board and grabbed her wrist when she kept walking. She jerked backwards. "I thought you said you could surf. Some buddy you're turning out to be."

"I know!" Grace snapped her fingers. "We could have a buddy do-over. Oh wait." She shook her head in mock regret. "You don't want a friend. You just want a fuck."

"Grace," I growled.

She tugged her wrist free. I grabbed at it again and she squirmed from my grip. "Dammit, Grace. You're bleeding everywhere. Let me have a look. You're probably going to need stitches."

Grace started walking off. "Well then, I'll just call a friend," she said with a sneer, "to come help me."

Lunging forward, I grabbed both her shoulders in my hands and held on tight. "Stop it!" I shouted, my chest heaving as I fought to control my anger. "Okay? Just stop."

Her jaw locked and her nostrils flared as she glared at me, trapped in my hold. Swallowing, I forced calm and met her eyes. "Will you let me look?"

A beat of silence passed before she nodded stiffly.

I let go of her arms and reached for her scalp. I kept my movements gentle, not wanting to startle her into walking off again. The bleeding had slowed and she was right, the wound was minor, but it would need at least two stitches. I told her the verdict. "I'll take you to hospital. Emergency should be able to fix it up quickly."

"No." She pulled away. "I can take myself."

"I wasn't offering you a choice, Grace." I pointed towards the outdoor showers. "Go rinse off and meet me back at my car. I'll go have a quick look for Henry's board."

"Okay," she agreed quickly. Too quickly.

I paused, narrowing my eyes as I studied her. "Good."

Grace started off, walking in the complete opposite direction of my car and the outdoor showers. "Why do you have to be so damn difficult?" I yelled after her.

She did it again. She fucking flipped me off as she stalked away. The girl had an attitude bigger than the Grand Canyon and it only made me want her more.

I remember reading once that if you want something you've never had, then you've got to do something you've never done.

Screw Henry and Morgan and everything else. Screw the fallout. I'd worry about it another day because right then my care factor just went right out the window. I wanted Grace. It was that simple and that complicated. I wanted to laugh with her, get drunk with her, be buddies with her. I'd do whatever the fuck she wanted me to just so I could keep feeling the way I did when I was with her.

"You want something? Fine!" I shouted angrily at her retreating back. She stopped and turned around. Her eyes were cold as they stared at me, waiting. "I don't …" I swallowed, trying to get the words out past the lump in my throat. "I don't have any good stories."

"Casey—"

"Just let me try and think of one," I said over the top of her. "Please? Just …" I held up a hand and she pressed her lips together. "My brother, Kelly, he … Oh God." I exhaled shakily as she started back towards me. "His eighth birthday party. We never had parties. Dad didn't like people coming to our house. Mum used to sneak us out for ice cream on our birthday instead, but this one year Kelly got a party. Mum never said why so I have no idea why dad relented. Anyway, the party was a disaster. Mum did invitations for about thirty kids, including our neighbours, thinking only half of them would come, but they all turned up. So the house was full of screaming, hyper kids, our neighbours, and the neighbour's golden retriever. About halfway into the party a late afternoon thunderstorm hit. One of those wild ones with flash flooding and hail." I closed my eyes, remembering the sound of us kids yelling and laughing as we scrambled to catch all the icy pebbles while lightning cracked around us. "The power blacked out just when Mum was bringing out the cake, only for a minute, but when it come back on, the neighbour's dog was eating it. Dad lost his shit and started yelling and the dog got scared and pissed on him. I can't remember ever laughing so hard until I realised Kelly was crying."

I jolted, not realising Grace was standing there holding my hands until she squeezed them.

I squeezed back. "Dad … he …" I swallowed again, tasting bile, bitter in my throat. "Kelly slept in my bed that night and when we woke up, Mum had bruising on her throat, a swollen lip, and a split in her left brow. We never asked for another birthday party after that."

Grace cupped my face in her palms, forcing me to meet her eyes. They were filled with tears. I watched one spill over and fall down her cheek. "I'm sorry," I whispered, using my thumb to gently brush the tear away. "I guess that wasn't such a good story after all."

"Casey?" she breathed.

I looked into her eyes. "Yeah?"

"Kiss me, okay? Please. I need you to kiss me. Right now."

We stared at each other silently for a moment. There was no other sound around us apart from the waves breaking on the shore. Resting my hands on her hips, I leaned in close. Grace's eyes fluttered closed, her breath catching on a ragged moan when my mouth brushed softly against the corner of her lips.

"Is that okay?" I murmured.

"More, please," she whispered.

I closed my eyes, focusing on nothing else but the feel of her bottom lip when I took it between my teeth, nibbling gently until Grace parted her lips. My tongue swept inside her mouth and I groaned loudly, tasting salty ocean and sweet, sweet honey. Reaching up, I grabbed a fistful of her hair as she responded, mashing her lips against mine, deepening the kiss. Blood pumped through my veins until my cock ached from the intensity. Releasing her hair, my hands began moving over her, down her chest, over her hips, frustrated when all I got was wetsuit rather than bare skin.

I dragged my lips from hers, breathing harshly.

Her eyes were wide on mine, hands gripping my shoulders as if it was the only thing holding her up.

Be careful what you wish for, Casey, because once you get it, giving it back is gonna hurt like a motherfucker.

"Grace," I muttered hoarsely, suddenly feeling so hollow I ached from it because this was only going to end in hurt, but I felt helpless to stop it.

Chapter Fourteen
GRACE

"So then what happened?" John asked.

The late afternoon sun hit my bed, right across my eyes, so I shuffled until I was lying the other way. Mitsy growled when I got too close. Getting up, he stretched, circled three times, and curled back up on the bedspread, all the while giving me a dirty look. I bared my teeth at him and if dogs could roll their eyes, Mitsy was doing it right then.

"Grace?" John prompted.

"He took me to the hospital and I got two stitches in my scalp," I whispered quickly, mindful that Henry was a lurking ninja who had no qualms about eavesdropping on my phone conversations. He'd already done it twice in the past week. Once when I was talking to Casey, and the other when I finally forced myself to phone Dalton and have it out.

"Holy shit, Grace," John announced. It had taken two hours to complete the entire recount of events since my arrival in Sydney. "Your whole trip's been like The Hangover minus the bachelor party."

"I know," I replied, planting my feet on the wall above my pillows. I closed my eyes, remembering back a week ago to my surf with Casey and subsequent hospital visit.

I was sitting on the edge of the hospital bed, waiting to be seen by the doctor. Casey was on my right, leaning up against it as he stared at the floor.

"How long are you here for?" he asked me.

"I don't know. Eight weeks maybe, why?"

Casey exhaled sharply and ran a hand through his hair. "Then you go back to your life in Melbourne?"

"Yeah," I replied, feeling disheartened knowing what I was going back to. I wanted to stay but it wasn't possible and the reason for that was something I wasn't willing to share with anyone. Not even with Casey.

"So what was with that kiss then, Grace? You got pissed off when I said I wanted to fuck you and the next minute you're kissing me like you wanted me to. So much for buddies, huh?"

Ugh.

He was right. I was confusing the hell out of him. And myself.

I wanted him. There was nothing confusing about that part. But I didn't want to lead him on either. If we were going to act on this attraction, Casey needed to know it could only be temporary. I wouldn't drag him into the nightmare my life was about to become.

I cleared my throat, glancing at him sideways. "So I have a proposal for you."

He lifted his brows. "A proposal?"

"Hear me out," I began and ran sweaty palms down my bare thighs. I'd arrived at the beach in a wetsuit over my bikini, forgetting to bring something to change into after being in the water. Casey had loaned me a shirt from his car. After putting it on over my bikini, it reached mid-thigh and smelled like him. I was keeping it.

"Grace?" he prompted, making me realise I was staring at the wall.

"Eight weeks together and then I go home," I blurted out, making my proposal sound in no way appealing. Making it worse was that I was standing there like a drowned rat, my hair tangled, and dried blood all over my face. And that was after wiping out on Henry's board. Still. It wasn't like I could've added flashy disco lights and a seductive lap dance to go with it. The man was going to have to take me as he found me.

"What?" Casey pushed off of the bed so he could face me properly, his expression incredulous. "That is your proposal? You and I having sex together for the next eight weeks and then you leave?"

I shifted uncomfortably under his penetrative stare. "Well, it sounds a bit sordid when you put it that way."

"Grace." His lips twitched. "It is kinda sordid."

"I didn't mean for it just to be about sex," I explained, folding my arms defensively.

He unpeeled my arms and placed them around his waist, bringing us close together. "What did you mean then?"

"Well … we can do other stuff too, like spend time together."

His lips twitched again and I sighed because it was almost too sexy for my eyes to absorb. "Spend time together naked?"

"There is that," I replied, because Casey and naked went together like peas and corn or vodka and orange, but they also went together like cocaine and heroin—mixed together you've got a highly dangerous addiction and no hope of shaking it loose. It would so be worth it, I told myself. If I said no to a naked Casey, I may as well just go out into the yard, dig a nice big hole, and bury myself in it. "But it's not just that," I admitted. "I like being with you. I like that I can be myself with you."

"Even when I'm being an ass?"

I looked up to regret in his eyes. "Even then. Because at least you're honest about it."

His voice turned soft. "So I get you for eight weeks of whatever this is, and then I have to give you back?"

"After eight weeks, you'll be begging to give me back."

Casey took my face in his hands. He tipped my head back so I was looking at him properly, and then he brushed a kiss over my lips.

Drawing back slightly, his next words made my heart thump hard in my chest. "And what if I want to keep you?"

I closed my eyes because if I kept looking at him I'd tell him he could. "You can't. After eight weeks we both walk away, no questions asked." I opened my eyes. "And no one needs to know. No Henry, or Travis, or anyone. Just us, then we walk away."

"Is that what you want, Grace?"

"It is," I lied, because I wanted so much more.

"Why?"

"Why what?" I asked.

"Why is it goodbye, no questions asked?"

"Because we both have our own lives and questions just create unnecessary complications," I pointed out. "We should just keep this easy, right?"

"I must be losing my mind to actually be considering this," he muttered. I held my breath, waiting, and when his nod finally came after a full minute I was sure I'd turned blue. "Okay."

Was that it? Okay and he was mine for eight weeks? Would he walk away no questions asked? I had to be sure. No. I needed to be sure. "Promise me, Casey, that after eight weeks we both walk away."

His blue eyes turned sombre as he stared at me. Something about him right then looked so broken it almost hurt to see. It was the same look when he told me that heartbreaking story about his past. I couldn't have done anything else but kiss him, never wanting to see that look in his eyes ever again.

Then the look was wiped from his face. "Alright. I promise."

The doctor walked in, his eyes focused on a chart. Casey moved back to my side and picked up my hand, lacing our fingers together while the doctor flicked through the pages in front of him.

When he eventually looked up, his brown eyes were amused. "Grace Paterson?"

I cleared my throat. "Yes."

He waved the patient profile sheet I'd been required to complete in the waiting room. "You have an interesting occupation."

"I do?" Casey had completed the questionnaire for me when he saw me squinting at the page. Without my reading glasses, I could have been signing away my firstborn child for all I knew. My eyes narrowed on Casey before giving the doctor my full attention. "What exactly do I do, Doctor…" I glanced at his nametag "…Reed?"

"It says right here that you're a Surfboard Wrangler," he replied, sitting the chart on the bed and reaching for the stethoscope from his neck.

Casey snorted beside me, the bed shuddering under his silent chuckle. I jabbed him with my elbow when the doctor turned his back. He winked at me and grinned. I stared wordlessly. He was so beautiful I felt something inside my heart shift. Enough that I wanted to memorise every wild, crazy moment with him so that when I left, I could replay it on an endless loop.

"What?" he whispered, squeezing my hand, his lips still curved in a smile.

Whatever I'd felt for any other man in my past faded because I knew then that I was looking at the man who was going to break my heart. I opened my mouth to tell him the proposal was off, that I'd changed my mind, but when I opened my mouth, I couldn't form the words.

"Nothing," I replied.

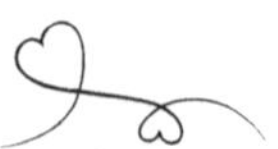

"John," I whispered, still mindful of Henry lurking as I finished my recount. "What the hell am I doing?"

"You're in a haze of lust, Grace. Just roll with it. Have sex with him a few times and it'll pass."

"You're wrong," I said with a roll of my eyes. Sometimes having a male best friend worked against you. I would seriously be questioning my morals if I took even half the advice John dished out.

He sounded confused. "You don't lust after him?"

"Don't get carried away. I just think that having sex a few times is going to make it worse. It's more than just lust for me and that makes this whole proposal idea really, really stupid."

"Is it more for him than that, too?"

"No!" I replied hastily, remembering Casey's words.

"I might want to fuck you, but it doesn't mean I want to be your friend."

I know he was only lashing out, saying the words to push me away. Getting guys to open up was difficult at the best of times, and Casey was a vault. But it didn't mean there wasn't a ring of truth to what he said. This proposal was about sex for Casey, nothing more. I was sure of it.

But he did share, said the niggling little voice in my head. When you were walking away from him at the beach, he dragged out that painful memory about his brother and shared it with you.

That's because I was injured, I replied defensively. He was trying to get me to go with him to Emergency because he felt bad about what he said.

Yeah, said the voice. Keep telling yourself that.

I will, thanks very much.

Whatever, the voice muttered.

"You there?"

"Yes," I replied, realising I'd gone silent while I had a conversation with myself.

"Have you even had sex with him?"

"No. It's been a whole week since the surfing incident and I haven't even seen him. We've talked on the phone every night though. For hours," I added.

If I had a female best friend, she'd be squealing right now and subjecting me to a detailed inquisition on what Casey and I talked about. I knew because I'd seen it happen in movies.

"That's nice," John replied.

I sighed and rolled over. Mitsy snarled at the move and retreated to my pillow, curling himself into a little white ball of fluff on top of it. "So back to my original question, what the hell am I doing?"

"We're back to this again? If you don't know that by now, then I agree, this proposal is stupid and so are you."

"Nice, John," I muttered. "Thanks for the pep talk."

"I'm a guy. We base pep talks on reality and logic."

"And what do women base pep talks on?" I dared to ask.

"Fantasy." John paused and I heard the flick of a lighter. "It's all about what you want to see, not what's right in front of you."

"This conversation is getting ridiculous," I told him.

"Agreed."

We finished up the phone call with shop talk, and then I hung up no better off than what I was before.

I stretched with a loud squeal and rolled back over, careful not to jostle a dozing Mitsy. It was Friday afternoon and with no live show for Jamieson happening until Sunday, I promptly fell asleep, the phone still clutched in my hand.

Minutes later I woke to something tickling my face. I swatted it away, murmuring irritably. When the tickling began the second time around, I was more alert. My eyes flew open. Henry hovered above me, a black permanent marker sitting ominously in his right hand. My eyes flared wide. "You didn't. Tell me you didn't, Henry."

He grinned and I wanted to smack it off his face. Repeatedly. Really, really hard. Preferably until he was unconscious. "Black's your colour, Gracie Bean."

I shoved him away as I leaped from the bed. Racing for the mirror on the back of the wardrobe door, I grabbed the handle and flung it open.

"Oh my God," I declared as I stared at my reflection in horror. A moustache and three quarters of a goatee had been drawn on my face. Henry obviously hadn't had time to finish before I woke up. It made me look like a serial killer.

"You ass!" I hissed and pegged the only thing at him I had handy—the new phone Casey gave me when we left the hospital on Saturday. It was supposed to bean Henry in the head, but he ducked and it sailed past, smacking into the wall behind him. The screen cracked on impact before falling harmlessly to the floor. "Oh great. Thanks, Henry," I said, my voice biting with sarcasm. "Now you broke my new bloody phone."

"I broke it?" he said, incredulous. "You threw it!"

"Arrrghhh!" I screamed wildly. Recognising my best battle cry, Henry spun around and ran for the door. I leaped on his back. I hoped my momentum would take him down, but he stayed steady on his feet. Grabbing fistfuls of hair, I yanked hard.

"Owww!" he howled and tried to loosen my grip with his hands. "Get … off …" he panted. When that didn't work, he took two steps back, slamming me into wall.

"Ooomphf." My head bounced off with a crack and we both slid to the floor.

Henry started crawling away, but I wasn't done so I grabbed at the back of his shirt. It ripped when he kept moving, the fabric tearing away from the ribbed neckline.

"My shirt!" he gasped and did some weird kind of tuck and roll.

I leaped on him again like a Terminator programmed to destroy or die trying. This time I grabbed the front of his shirt in my left hand. "You know what drawing on someone's face get's you, Henry?" I cocked back my right fist and glared. "Punched. Repeatedly."

The sound of someone clearing their throat was heard above the harsh sound of our breathing. We both froze and looked towards the door.

Casey stood there, leaning casually against the doorframe. He looked good enough to eat in a pair of expensive navy pants and a grey pinstripe shirt. The top two buttons were undone and the shirtsleeves rolled up, revealing tanned, muscular forearms. Dragging my gaze upwards, I saw eyes full of laughter.

"Casey," I breathed. Pushing away from Henry, I brushed the hair off my face in a casual gesture. "You uh, been there long?"

"Awhile," he told us, his eyes raking over me in a way that set a flush to my skin, "Everyone's downstairs and dinner's ready."

"Dinner?" I repeated stupidly. I tugged my tank top down where it had ridden up near my armpit, revealing the hot pink lace of my bra beneath.

"Yeah, everyone's here for Friday dinner. Didn't Mac tell you we were all coming?" he asked for Henry's benefit, because of course I knew. I'd only messaged Casey about it that morning but I didn't want to give us away. "Henry was sent upstairs to wake you."

I narrowed my eyes at Henry and his definition of 'waking' someone, silently informing him that this wasn't over. Aloud, I said, "Dinner's not until seven."

"It is seven," Henry told me. "You've been asleep for four hours."

"Oh." I blinked. "I guess I was tired."

All those late nights staying up talking with Casey. His lips pressed together in a smirk and I knew he was thinking the same thing.

I returned to the mirror before the two of us gave anything away to Henry, hoping my face didn't look as bad as it did when I first saw it.

It looked worse.

Between that and the stitches in my scalp, my head could officially be declared a warzone. It was lucky I was on a moratorium from modelling or I'd get fired.

"Rubbing alcohol," Mac declared, taking in my appearance at a glance as she walked the room. "That'll get it off."

"Really?" Casey raised his brows as the three of them stared at the half-assed goatee on my chin. "Let's fill in the rest first. See how it looks."

Henry weighed in. "Maybe we should we put it to a vote?"

Feeling the flush of embarrassment climb my cheeks, I replied, "I've got an idea. Why don't you all disappear so I can get changed and get this crap off my face."

Walking inside the wardrobe, I slammed the door shut behind me for good measure and flicked on the light. I didn't have any rubbing alcohol—I wasn't even sure what that was—but I had nail polish remover. Surely that was the same thing.

Rifling through my beauty case, I took out the little pink bottle and a cotton ball. Stepping up to the mirror, I wiped at the black scribble. The acetate in the remover left behind a slight burning sensation on my skin and made my eyes water, but I was relieved to see it coming away with some heavy duty pressure.

The wardrobe door opened suddenly and I stumbled back in surprise, the cotton ball hovering somewhere near my chin. "Casey."

I set the polish and cotton ball down when he shoved his way inside the little space, pushing me in farther with his bulk. He shut the door behind him and my pulse ramped up a notch.

"I told them I had to use the bathroom." His hands clamped hold of my hips and he yanked me against his body. "I thought about you all day."

I licked my lips. "All day?"

His eyes fell to my mouth and they burned. "All fucking day."

"Me too," I admitted.

There was a pause where I thought he was about to kiss me and didn't. "Grace," he began, his tone suddenly serious. "If we're going through with whatever this is we're doing, then I'm telling Henry that you and I are seeing each other."

"What?" Henry would have a stroke. "It's none of his business."

"It is his business," Casey argued. "You're his little sister."

"I'm also someone who's quite capable of making my own decisions. Henry's not. He thinks my life is going to turn into some Liam Neeson movie." That was no joke. Casey told me that his business partner and friend, Jared, had been involved in a case that got his sister, Mac, kidnapped and Evie shot. Then Travis got called in by the Federal Police to work a case that involved Jamieson's assistant manager, Quinn. She had a stepfather involved with the Sydney Zampetti crime ring, owing them money. They came after her and not for the money her stepfather owed like they all thought, but because Quinn's father was working undercover inside the crime ring. The Zampettis found out and she almost died. "I can take care of myself," I added stubbornly.

Casey didn't look reassured at my words. In fact, he drew back, creating a small amount of distance between us. I felt the loss like a physical ache. "You're asking me to lie to your brother, Slim. I don't like it. He's a good guy and a friend. I respect him."

"I'm not asking you to lie. I'm just saying we should keep this on the down low. Look, if you don't want to do this…" I folded my arms and tipped my chin in the direction of the wardrobe door, my internal voice screaming at me not to say the next words "…then just leave."

Casey's eyes locked on mine with enough intensity that I couldn't look away if I tried. "Is that what you want? For me to leave?"

Absolutely not. Hell to the no.

"Because I'm not leaving, Grace."

Oh thank God.

His hands clamped on my hips once again. They slid around to my ass, his fingers digging in as he pulled me against him. I flailed, forced to unfold my arms and grab on or lose my balance. "You're mine for however long we have left." He ducked his head and swiped his tongue along my lips. "We'll work it out, okay?"

Then his mouth was on mine, soft at first, until I parted my lips and let his tongue sweep inside. His mouth was hot and wet, his kiss hard and controlling. I whimpered at the force, at being shoved back against wall. My arms wound around his neck, my fingers sliding into his hair as he grabbed at my leg, lifting it up and wrapping it around his hip.

My breath hitched when his palm scraped along my outer thigh, sliding down until he was rubbing between my legs. I broke the kiss, throwing my head back and hitting the wall as I gasped in a lungful of air.

Casey groaned, his mouth and tongue biting and licking at my exposed neck. He ran his finger along the seam of my panties, and my clit pulsed desperately, urging him to touch me. Instead, he drew back and I wanted to cry.

"Grace," he panted and licked his lips as I regained both my feet. "You taste like … like … ethanol."

I laughed, reaching up to touch my chin where the permanent marker had been. "I guess I better have a quick shower."

Ten minutes later, clean and dressed in a short, stretchy black dress that showed off a mile of leg, I made my way down the stairs and onto the back deck. Everyone was already seated and eating. Indoor chairs had been dragged outside to cater for the numbers. I wedged myself into the only available space between Mac and Cooper and sat down.

"Here." Evie leaned over the table, thrusting a glass of wine at me from two places down.

"Thanks," I replied, a little breathless when I spotted Casey across the table from me, his eyes on my lips. I downed half the glass in record time, feeling the warmth of alcohol flood my system instantly.

Henry placed a plate of food in front of me before returning to his seat beside Casey. It was piled high with roasted chicken and hot chips. A drizzle of gravy was added as the final flourish. My stomach almost wept at the vision. I looked over at Henry with a furrowed brow as I set my glass down. "Where's the salad?"

Jared pointed his fork at me. "Exactly."

"Get a room you two if eating a bunch of lettuce gets you so hot," Evie bitched.

Jared arched a brow as he glanced at her belly. "That's my baby in there. I should get a say in what you feed it."

Evie, who'd announced her pregnancy just shy of two weeks ago, gasped. "You did not just say that."

Everyone at the table began weighing in with their opinion on what Evie should be eating. I cringed at somehow being the instigator. Mouthing a quick "Sorry," her way, I reached for my glass and downed the remaining contents quickly.

Cooper topped it up again without missing a beat.

I glanced sideways. "Are you trying to get me drunk?"

He leaned in, whispering, "Yes. Is it working? You seem a bit edgy."

That was because my body craved sex. Lots of it. With Casey. A quick check across the table found him watching our exchange intently.

Between the revolving front door of the duplex and his roommate, finding privacy was going to be more complex than long division. He would either have to climb a ladder to my window or sex was going to happen in the back of his car, and because he was yet to mention anything about the damaged backseat, that option was off the table. The man was either biding his time or he hadn't yet seen it. Considering I was still alive, I was voting for the latter, but it was only a matter of time.

Focusing on my plate, I picked up a piece of chicken and peeled the skin away. "Can you pass me a napkin?" I asked Mac on my left as I licked my finger.

My phone vibrated in the pocket of my dress as she handed it over. Pulling it out, I saw a text message from Casey. I glanced at him across the table, but he appeared in deep conversation with Travis. Swiping a finger across the cracked screen, I read the message.

Do that again.

Do what again? Lick my finger? I put my phone down, and after a quick glance around the table, I slid my finger in my mouth, sucking gently before dragging it slowly from between my lips. Finished with the slightly erotic display, I glanced over at Casey. His eyes were locked on my mouth, dark with hunger. Wincing slightly, he reached down and with a quick, casual movement, adjusted himself in his pants.

I quickly tapped out a return message.

Do that again.

He did.

After reading my reply, he actually reached down, cupped the bulge in his pants and squeezed. My entire body clenched at the sight, forcing a light sweat to break out across my brow. I reached for the wine Cooper poured, feeling the urge to rub the ice-cold glass soothingly across my forehead.

After downing another half glass, I set the wine down and caught Casey intent on his phone, his fingers tapping away.

This was sexting? How did people survive it?

Mac was talking to me when my phone eventually alerted the incoming message. After taking a bite of chicken, I picked it up and promptly began choking.

If my cock looks half as good as your finger did the way it slid in and out of your mouth, then I want in.

Mac pounded me on the back with surprising force while I choked and wheezed. Jesus. The message basically said blow me now, yet he'd managed to word in such a way that I was ready to get on my knees right then and there. I put my phone down to grab at the napkin Cooper waved in my face. Casey sat across from the table laughing at me while I dabbed at my watery eyes.

I narrowed my gaze on him with deliberate intent before putting down my napkin and tapping out another message.

You said you were good with your tongue, Casey. Prove it.

Travis was talking to him when he opened the message. I watched his eyes flare wide before he typed out a quick reply and pocketed his phone.

Upstairs. You've got five minutes.

I should've known better than to issue a challenge to Casey of all people. He was the type of man you saw running towards danger while everyone else ran in the opposite direction.

I utilised a good three minutes eating another piece of chicken, finishing off my wine, and getting caught in conversation with Cooper. I spent another minute wondering what the hell I'd gotten myself into. In the last minute left, I excused myself from the table and stood on unsteady legs. I glanced behind me as I walked inside. Casey was laughing at some comment Travis made that I didn't quite catch. His eyes met mine for a split second as he said something in reply, and they were on fire. That was all it took to know I'd never wanted anything more in my life than I wanted him right now.

No sooner had I closed the bedroom door behind me, it opened and Casey slipped inside. I barely had time to whisper, "This is crazy," before his mouth crashed down on mine. It wasn't a sweet kiss. It was hard and wild and almost painful. His hands gripped my shoulders, nudging me backwards until my knees hit the bed.

"We need to hurry," he muttered, and with a shove, I fell on the bed, crawling backwards to make room when he climbed on above me, wedging his hips between my legs and fusing his mouth to mine. He placed his palms on my outer thighs, pushing upwards until my dress bunched around my hips. Moving from my lips, he began licking and kissing his way along my neck.

I breathed in shallow pants as his hand found its way between my thighs. Using his thumb, he began stroking me over the thin, silky fabric.

He pulled back, breathing harshly, and hooked his thumbs in the waistband of my panties, yanking them down forcefully. Sitting back, he spread my legs, baring me to his gaze.

"That is the hottest motherfucking thing I've ever seen," he rasped. Moments later, I felt the warmth of his breath between my legs before he pressed his lips there, kissing me so lightly I wanted to scream with frustration. I bit my lip to keep from crying out when his tongue came out, licking me in one long, hot stroke.

"Casey," I moaned, my back arching off the bed from pleasure. "More, please."

"Whatever you say, baby," he murmured against me, and I could feel his chuckle.

I laughed breathlessly and it ended on a moan when he circled his tongue around my clit, rubbing and teasing me. My hands found the softness of his hair, and I scraped my nails gently through the strands.

"Don't stop," I panted, completely overwhelmed when he slid a finger inside me while still working me with his tongue.

"So hot," he groaned.

I couldn't remember this ever feeling so good. I'd never been one to let go during sex, but Casey kept up some kind of wild assault I couldn't fight. He slid another finger inside me and tingling pressure rose with mind blowing intensity. I held my breath, knowing I wasn't able to do anything with this man other than feel.

"Fuck … Grace …"

He sat back on his heels and grabbed at his belt buckle, undoing it swiftly. With a yank of his zipper, he shoved his pants halfway down his ass, releasing his erection. He took it in his hand and began stroking as he looked at me. "You're so beautiful. I want to jack off until I come all over you," he muttered.

I sat up, reaching for him, but he planted his free hand on my chest and shoved me back, working his erection as he pinned me to the bed. After a minute, his tongue found its way back between my legs.

"Casey …" I breathed, sinking back into the bed with a groan.

"I want to feel you come against my tongue."

There was no way I wasn't going to. His mouth was hot and wet, lapping at me with an unrestrained rhythm that would not let up. I watched his hips move against the bed. With his pants halfway down his hips, I could see his firm, muscular ass moving up and down as he rubbed his erection against the sheets. The sight of him getting himself off while his tongue teased and tasted me made me lose the last of my control. Panting, my head fell back as I tried drawing out the delicious tingles he stirred inside me but I couldn't. It rushed through me like a freight train and I came hard against his mouth. I knew he could feel it because he sucked hard at my clit, groaning as he ground his hips hard into the bed.

I tried not to cry out. My vision blurred and I bit down on my lip so hard it hurt. When the world came back into focus, Casey was sitting on his heels between my legs looking supremely satisfied, and so damn sexy.

"God," I moaned, blinking as reality returned.

He pressed a quick kiss to my inner thigh and winked. "You can call me Casey."

I groaned, laughing, and he grinned, dimples popping as he tucked himself back in his pants and yanked his zipper upwards. His eyes fell on the bedspread in front of him. "I came all over your sheets. I should probably be sorry about that but I'm not."

Neither was I. Casey was right. He really was good with his tongue. The next few weeks were going to kill me.

He slapped me lightly on the rump before I could form a coherent word of reply. "Get up, Slim. We need to get back downstairs. Quick. Before I get my second wind and decide to fuck you so hard, you scream my name loud enough for everyone in the whole damn house to hear."

Chapter Fifteen
CASEY

Subterfuge.

Casey 'Subterfuge' Daniels. That was a new low for me.

I sighed heavily at my desk on Monday morning, tossing my pen down with irritation. I wouldn't tolerate going behind Henry's back with Grace, so why was I doing it to Grace with Morgan?

Because you're a dumb prick, that's why.

Leaning forward, I tapped at my keyboard, googling the word as though I had nothing better to do.

Deceit used in order to achieve one's goal.

I laughed humourlessly because whatever my goal was supposed to be, I hadn't achieved it. I'd been avoiding Morgan and it had been over a week since I last got my hands on Grace. Getting a taste of her hadn't been anywhere near enough and that eight weeks had now dwindled to six. Why did time always move so damn fast?

Closing the Google tab, I called up Facebook instead, clicking on her page before I could stop myself. She hadn't updated it in a couple of days. Her last post was an update to her profile picture. It showed a photo of her and Henry, hugging close and smiling at the camera.

Picking up my phone, I sent her a message.

What are you doing today?

After hitting send, I realised I was a stalker now. I sat at my desk, stalking

Grace on a Monday morning. That was fucking sad. I was a sad, pathetic bastard. And a stalker.

"On the phone again?" Tim appeared in my office, holding aloft my customary Monday morning cup of piss-weak coffee.

"Really? You're investigative powers of deduction dazzle me," I replied dryly as he set the coffee on my desk.

I tucked my phone away, knowing I needed to get a hold of myself. Maybe getting a real coffee would go a long way towards achieving that. I got to my feet, snatched up the takeaway cup, and started for the door.

"Where are you going?" Tim called to my retreating back. "You've got a meeting with Frank in ten minutes."

Hell.

I'd forgotten about that.

Frank had resigned last week. The news was not unexpected. He'd been making noises about retiring for over a year now, yet every time he mentioned it we played deaf. Now my Monday was lined with screening potential new employees, and because Frank knew the job better than anyone, he was sitting in on them with me.

I waved the cup as I kept walking. "I'm going to sort out this problem with your barista, Tim. I can't function properly without decent coffee."

"Wait!" The sound of rapid footsteps came from behind me. "He's not my barista. You can't just—"

"Shit," I muttered when I tripped over a box in the front reception. I rescued the cup before it flew from my hands. Why, I don't know. It would have been better off smeared all over the sleek timber flooring. "What the hell is with all these boxes?" I asked no one in particular. Having come through the back entry from our underground car park, I'd completely missed seeing them earlier.

They were stacked precariously throughout the front entryway, creating a safety hazard for any sad, pathetic stalker bastard who happened to walk through.

"Um …"

I turned, directing my gaze on our receptionist, Alice. She'd taken over from Tim when he was promoted. She seemed a little too timid for the role in my opinion. No one else had agreed and when put to a vote, majority ruled.

"They um …"

"They …?" I prompted after a moment of silence.

Alice flushed. Seriously. Had she forgotten what she wanted to say in just a matter of moments?

"It's Jared's fault," Tim said from behind me, quick to cast blame on the situation.

I spun around, dismissing Alice. Tim's eyes flew up quickly. Was he staring at my ass? Goddamn, but this office was going to the dogs. "Why?"

"He worked all day Saturday clearing out all our old files from archives. I think he might be nesting."

My brow furrowed. "Nesting?"

Tim nodded. "Yes, nesting. You know, that thing people do when they have babies?"

I pinched the bridge of my nose with my thumb and forefinger, needing caffeine so desperately I wanted weep. "Do I look like I know anything about what people do when they have babies?" I asked irritably.

"Not really," Tim admitted, "but you do look like someone who knows a hell of a lot about what people do to make them."

"Amen," Alice muttered under her breath.

My brows flew up as I turned back to look at her. Did she just say Amen? "You know what?" I set the takeaway coffee cup on the reception counter and held my hands up in surrender. "Never mind the coffee. Let's just get rid of these damn boxes. We can't have them piled up here when we're trying to interview potential employees. Not only does it make us look like some half-assed operation, it's not safe."

"Where should we put them?" Tim asked as he stood staring at them, one hand on his hip, the other fussing with his hair.

Alice cleared her throat so I gave her my attention. "Document destruction."

I waited for her to supply more information but none was forthcoming. Should I ask to buy a vowel? "What about them?"

Tim spoke up. "They were supposed to stop by Saturday afternoon to collect them, but they never arrived."

"Has someone rung them?" I asked.

Tim started for his desk, saying, "I'll go do it now."

"No." Tim halted while I dug my car keys from my back pocket. "Alice, you ring them, tell them I'll take them over." I tossed the keys at Tim, who fumbled and dropped them. "Go unlock my car. I'll start bringing all the boxes out."

Tim started for the back entrance and Alice picked up the phone and started dialling.

"Fucking Mondays," I growled under my breath when I picked up the first box and followed Tim to the car park. He was unlocking my car when I arrived behind him. "How do you think Alice is going, really?" I asked. Tim was the one that trained her to take over his position. He would be honest if he thought she wasn't doing okay.

"She's amazing." He paused in the act of opening the rear passenger door. "Why? You're not going to fire her, are you?"

The odds of that were low. No one else seemed to have an issue with her. "No, but a receptionist is the face of the company. They're the ones who answer phones and greet clients. For someone who never speaks, I'm not sure if Alice is suited to that type of role."

With a shake of his head, Tim swung the back door wide. "I barely spoke to you for the entire first year I worked here, remember? She'll …"

"She'll what?" I prompted when he trailed off, his eyes wide on the backseat of my car. I looked from him to the seat. "What the fuck?" I breathed, the bottom falling out of my stomach. I dropped the box in my arms. It landed on my foot but I barely noticed as I stepped over it to get a better look at the … the … "What the fuck is that?"

Tim leaned in for a closer inspection, his shoulder jostling mine as we both stared at the torn and mangled leather. "It looks like some kind of … small animal has attacked your car."

I ran a hand over the shredded pieces of leather, feeling ready to puke. I'd spent years restoring this car. The backseat had been shipped from the States for the same price it cost to buy a small aeroplane. I looked at Tim. "You think an animal somehow infiltrated my car, climbed onto the backseat, and in a sudden fit of rage just …" I closed my eyes, swallowing. "Grace," I muttered.

"Grace? You think Grace chewed your backseat?"

Opening my eyes, I snatched the car keys from Tim's hand and started for the driver's side door. I jabbed a finger at Tim. "Ring all my appointments for today. Tell them I'll be late."

"How late?" he called as I swung the driver's door open and slid inside the car. I turned the key in the ignition, surprised I was even able to see it over the red haze of fury.

"However long it takes to kill someone and hide the body," I yelled as the engine came to life with a loud, throaty growl.

I pulled into the driveway of the duplex in record time. I could see Grace standing by the front door already. I didn't have much room in my schedule for a killing today so that made it convenient. I got out and slammed the door with force before whispering a silent apology to my car.

The sky was clear and the sun bright, warming an otherwise cool day as I strode up the drive. I ran my eyes over Grace when I got near, feeling that familiar pull in my groin as though she was a shining beacon and my cock had just seen the light.

Her skin glowed with a light sheen of sweat. A white tank top was plastered to her chest and a tiny pair of hot pink Adidas running shorts showcased her legs perfectly. They were the kind of shorts you knew were designed by a man because the little splits up the sides were more than just aerodynamic, they were a cocktease. Combine all that with her flushed cheeks, and Grace was the perfect combination of athleticism and raw, sweaty animal sex.

Focus, asshole! You're here to kill Grace, not fuck her.

I took a steadying breath and dragged my eyes away, letting them fall on the two guys standing on the timber porch facing her. I figured it must have been Rage Monday all round because Grace was ranting at them, her eyes flashing fire. My brows drew together, wondering what they'd done to incur her wrath. They had their backs to me, but that was enough for me to know I didn't recognise them. She obviously knew who they were or they wouldn't have been let inside the gates.

My eyes scanned guy number one. I didn't need to see his face to know he was a complete wankjob. His jeans weren't just tight, they were white for fuck's sake. I was sure his brown shoes had a heel on them, and the sides of his blond hair were buzzed with the top gelled in a pompadour. He was in complete contrast to guy number two who looked like he'd just rolled out of bed. A crumpled tee shirt, old ripped jeans, and a cigarette dangling from his right hand completed the look. He turned slightly and I got a glimpse of beard—like he'd not bothered shaving for a couple of weeks—and a pair of expensive aviators that were at odds with his whole don't-give-a-fuck appearance. I knew they were expensive because I had the exact same pair. I ripped mine away from my eyes, tucking them into the neckline of my shirt as I arrived at the little scene.

"Grace," I growled, interrupting her rant because I didn't have the time or the patience to wait for her to finish.

Three pairs of eyeballs shot my way, Grace's mouth falling open in surprise at finding me standing there. She must have been so focused on delivering her wrath that she hadn't seen me arrive.

I ignored the two guys, choosing to favour Grace with a hard glare instead. "I'm here to kill you. If you come quietly, I'll make it quick rather than drawing it out in a long, torturous process."

A wide range of emotions played across her face—confusion, indignation, dawning comprehension, and finally the one that damned her for the crime—guilt.

"Who the hell are you?" growled don't-give-a-fuck guy, turning to face me full-on in an aggressive stance. He flicked his sunglasses to the top of his head so his glower made more impact. I took in his features coolly—from the dark eyes and the prominent cheekbones, to the fat lip and graze above his right brow that announced him as trouble.

"Who the hell I am is none of your business," I retorted at the same time Grace began inching backwards. My hand snaked out and snatched her wrist without missing a beat, halting her. I had to forcibly stop my thumb from caressing the trail of veins where her pulse thumped erratically. There was a time and place for soothing, sensual gestures, and this wasn't it. "Going somewhere?" I asked through gritted teeth.

"Let go of her," bit out don't-give-a-fuck guy.

"John, it's okay. This is Casey," she said. The emphasis on my name and the exaggerated wide eyes she threw his way conveyed some silent form of communication.

John looked me up and down, a smirk forming on his lips while the blond guy stood quiet in the background, his arms folded. I knew then that this was her friend from Melbourne and that Grace had told him everything. That was awesome. Nothing like knowing another guy was all up in your business.

"If this is about the car," Grace said, trying to tug her hand free and failing, "you should know I had nothing to do with it. And you shouldn't let yourself get so angry or you'll have a heart attack. It is just a car after all," she added.

Her attempt at cooling the situation only served to further inflame it. Just a car? My mouth fell open as I stared at her, unable to even find the words to reply to such a reckless statement.

John's smirk turned into a full on grin. "That dog's going to get you killed, Grace."

"That's my fucking dog you're talking about and I want him back," the blond guy snapped, his face turning red as he took a step closer to Grace.

I dropped her wrist instantly and turned to face the blond guy who I hadn't heard speak until now. Hands fisted, my eyes flared wide before narrowing. "You're Dalton?"

"I am," he confirmed, lifting his chin as if to say what of it?

Someone had done a real number on him. In contrast to his careful outfit and hair, his face looked like someone had pounded him to the ground. I barely saw it. All I could see was an idiot who shopped his dick around on the best thing that ever happened to him.

Before he could take another breath, my hands gripped his precious shirt and his back slammed against the front wall of the duplex. The white-painted weatherboard shuddered under the force of the impact.

"Casey!" Grace shouted.

"What the fuck," Dalton grunted. He shoved back, but whatever muscle he had under his clothes must have been for show because I didn't budge.

I cocked my head at him as he panted and squirmed underneath my grip. "First, I'm going finish the job someone started on your face. Then we're going to have a chat."

"I did that," John said from behind me, sounding pleased with his handiwork.

It explained the graze and split lip. Dalton must've taken John by surprise to get that in because Grace's friend was no lightweight. And while it was good to know he had her back, judging by the attitude just thrown at Grace, Dalton still hadn't learned his lesson. "But you didn't finish the job."

John's brows flew up. "I didn't?"

"He's still breathing," I growled aggressively.

If Travis could see me right now he'd piss himself laughing. I admit I was laying it on pretty thick, but the guy was a cockroach.

I pinned my forearm across his neck, pressing down on his windpipe, and glared right in his face. Dalton looked ready to shit his pretty white pants and I had to forcibly swallow the laugh bubbling up inside me. Was this guy for real? What a pussy.

"Go ahead," Dalton wheezed, his face turning red as he tried his best to glare at me with contempt. Too bad it failed because he was busy choking. "I'll have you arrested for assault just like I did with John."

"He had you arrested?" Grace shrieked at John from somewhere to the right of me. I turned my head in time to catch her wild stormy eyes hit Dalton. "I'm going to kill you myself," she snapped. "Casey, step aside."

I ignored her crazy demand and laughed at Dalton. "Looks like there's a line of people itching to get their fist in your face. Maybe I should call Henry out here," I told him, even though I figured Henry either wasn't here or was passed out upstairs to have missed all the commotion. "I'm sure he'd like a turn."

"Fuck … you …" Dalton gasped.

"No!" I bit out. I took my forearm off his windpipe. He only had a second to suck in a breath before I jerked him forward and slammed him back against the wall. His head snapped backwards with a satisfying crack. "Fuck you, Dalton." The phone in my pocket rang and I ignored it. "You need to learn some fucking respect. Maybe you do things differently where you're from, but here, we don't step out on our women and we don't take kindly to those who do. Grace must've thought you were something special to keep you around, but newsflash, bud, she is so far outta your fucking league she may as well be in the stars. Sucks for you that she moved on so easy, because she's moving on with me. Grace might be outta my league too, but I'm not going to fuck it up like you did because I'm smarter than you. I don't know why you're here, but I want you gone. So here's what's going to happen." I grabbed his shirt and leaned right into his face, ignoring everyone behind me. "You're going to turn around and leave. You're not going to talk to Grace. You're not even going to look at her. You don't get to take Mitsy with you either because you don't deserve that crazy little piece of shit dog that Grace has somehow come to love. If you don't, I'll personally make sure you're breathing through a tube for the rest of your life."

I yanked him off the wall and spun him around.

"Seriously?" he snapped, and then he did exactly what I told him not to do. He looked at Grace, who stood there with her mouth open, her eyes on me and her expression dazed. "You're moving on with this Neanderthal?"

My arm cocked back and my fist hit his face before he could blink.

"Ooowww!" he cried, stumbling backwards.

I sucked in a breath because damn, that felt good.

"You heard the man," John warned, stepping up beside me. "Fuck off."

Dalton skewered John with sneering glare. "You always had your nose in Grace's business. It wouldn't have surprised me if you were fucking her while we were together."

Grace hissed and suddenly launched herself in the air like a cat, her aim true as she landed on Dalton. They both crashed to the ground in a pile of limbs and loud grunts. It took both John and I to pull her off him. I took hold of Grace, trying to calm her down.

"I am calm!" she shouted, slapping at my hands while John dragged Dalton to his feet and shoved him down the drive.

"Mate, good luck with your career," John called out to his back. "It's who you know in this industry and unfortunately for you, I know a lot of people. You'll be lucky to be doing Best and Less catalogues after this."

Dalton shot him the finger but he kept walking, mumbling something about us all being crazy. Satisfied he was actually leaving, I regrouped, remembering my reason for being here. Grace and the killing. She was obviously remembering the same thing because she started inching unobtrusively away again.

"Grace," I said warningly.

"Seriously!" She threw up her hands, exasperated. "It's just a little scratch in the leather. Get over it already!"

"A scratch? A fucking scratch?" I pointed at my car. "The seat is completely mangled!" I yelled. My phone started ringing in my back pocket again, and again I ignored it. "I've given years of my life restoring that car. I love that car. Do you know how much money I spent having that seat shipped from the States?" I spouted off the astronomical figure and even John flinched. Grace paled as my phone started ringing for the third time.

"Hell," I muttered.

"So I'll get you a new one," she replied as I tugged my phone out and checked the display. Tim. I exhaled sharply. "Just tell me where you bought it."

John shook his head, obviously knowing something about cars because he replied, "It's not like buying a litre of milk from the corner store," as I answered the call.

"Casey. Your first interview is here," Tim hissed into my ear.

I turned my back on an arguing John and Grace and walked to the end of the porch so I could hear him better. "I told you to put all my appointments back."

"I did, but I couldn't get hold of the first one. He just arrived."

"Remind me who the first one is again?"

"Jesus, Casey. It's Seth."

My brow furrowed. He made it sound like I was supposed to know who the fuck Seth was. "Seth who?"

"Seth McKinnon. Quinn's father."

"Oh shit," I mumbled for the thousandth time that morning. Seth was Travis's father-in-law and a recently retired agent with the Australian Federal Police. He'd only just returned from a one-year undercover stint before handing in his badge. The problem with taking him on at our firm was the bad blood between him and Travis. Travis had punched Seth in the face at the time of

Quinn's abduction by the Zampettis. It was a story we brought up at every possible occasion because it was fucking funny. What wasn't funny was being late for his interview. Travis would have a hernia if he found out I was making his life that much harder. "Tell him I've been held up and I'll be there in twenty minutes."

"Okay. I'll go get him coffee and a danish."

"No!" I yelled and then lowered my voice. "For the love of … We want to hire him, not run him off. Send Alice."

"I can't because Alice will give Jean a tip and he—"

"Tim," I growled.

"I'll work something out," he whispered quickly and hung up the phone.

I stalked back and interrupted with an "excuse us" to John and grabbed Grace by the wrist without stopping. Slapping my palm on the front door, I shoved it open, dragging Grace past a startled looking Mac on the couch, a growling Mitsy on his fluffy blue doggy bed in the corner, and Cooper with his head half stuck in the fridge, and up the stairs.

"Casey," she panted when we reached the top. Her chest was heaving up and down from the sudden exertion, distracting me. "What are you doing?"

I shook my head, clearing it. "I'm going to punish you," I enlightened her, feeling angry all over again. "And when I'm done, your ass is going to be so sore you'll never treat someone else's property with such disrespect again."

She jabbed a finger in my chest and my eyes narrowed. "You touch me and I'll—"

I cocked a brow. "You'll what?"

Grace paused, her eyes beginning to look suspiciously wet. She blinked and then went in a completely different direction. "You don't step out on women?"

I paused, completely thrown. Wasn't I about to do that to Grace with Morgan?

No, of course I wasn't. When push came to shove, I knew there wasn't a chance in hell I'd voluntarily touch another woman now that Grace and I were officially together, no matter how temporary it might be.

"No," I told her. "I don't."

She nodded carefully, deep in thought before she spoke again. "And I'm … ah … moving on with you?"

"Hell yeah, you are."

Then another pause and this time her voice was soft when she spoke. "You think I'm out of your league?"

My voice softened in response. "Yeah."

"Thank you."

"Thank you?" I echoed.

"For what you said to Dalton. For not bringing up the whole cold bitch thing because that would have been awkward—"

"And unnecessary," I added.

"I was handling it though, before you arrived."

My lips twitched. "Of course you were."

Grace nodded, satisfied with my response, and it was then that I realised we were in her bedroom. Alone. Grace must have been on my wavelength because she bit down on her lip as she stared at me with silent intent.

"Goddamn," I growled, because there would be no punishment today.

Taking her hand, I pulled her inside the walk-in wardrobe and shut the door behind us. "This is crazy," she breathed. "I can't even be around you for a minute without thinking dirty thoughts."

"Stop talking," I ordered and slammed my mouth down on hers before she could speak again.

My cock started hardening the instant I thrust my tongue in her mouth and got a taste. She responded violently, grabbing at the belt of my pants with rough, urgent movements. I tilted my hips back while I kissed her, giving her easier access. She took it, yanking down my zipper and slipping her hands inside my boxer-briefs. I groaned deep in her mouth when they wrapped around my cock, feeling an ache of relief at her touch.

Grace pulled off my mouth with a gasp when I grabbed at her shorts and shoved them down hard and fast.

Straightening back up, I slid my hand inside her panties, skimming through all that delicious wetness until my finger was inside her. My body shuddered as she squeezed around it.

"Casey!" she cried out when I began to fuck her with it.

There was no finesse to my movements. I was too turned on and she made sexy moans in my ear that only intensified my lack of control. Her hand tightened on my erection and her other one slid around my neck and up into my hair, grabbing and pulling at it as she jacked me off.

"Christ," I panted, in between nibbling her ear and sucking on her neck. "I need my cock in you so bad."

Finding her lips again, I kissed her, my entire body screaming for release as she fisted me hard and fast. I thrust my cock into her hand, adding more friction.

"Grace?"

We both froze at the sound of Henry's voice, my finger stilling inside her and her hand freezing on my erection. I gritted my teeth with frustration.

"Oh shit," she breathed.

Oh shit was right. I know I was all for telling Henry we were seeing each other, but catching us like this wasn't how I'd planned on going about it.

I shoved away from her quickly, snatching my hand from her panties. I felt the loss when her hand let go of my cock as we both began putting ourselves back together. Grace tugged up her shorts and started smoothing her hair haphazardly while I tucked my hard, aching cock back in my pants. After smoothing my shirt, I buttoned my pants and yanked up the zipper.

"Slim," I whispered, trying to get her attention.

"Fuck, fuck, fuck," she chanted.

"Grace?" Henry called again, his voice sounding closer. My heart pounded at the possibly of getting caught. Grace's brother would rip my nuts clean off.

Grabbing her shoulders, I faced Grace towards the mirror so she could see her reflection. Her hair was wild, her tank top all twisted. Beard burn covered half her face because I hadn't shaved this morning, and red marks dotted her neck where I'd sucked on it.

"We're done for," she hissed to my reflection in the mirror. With a final attempt at smoothing her hair, she ordered me to wait there before disappearing out the door and shutting it smartly behind her.

"What were you doing in there?" I heard Henry ask.

"I was looking for something."

"Oh." There was pause, and then, "What happened to your face?"

"Nothing. I've just been out running," she replied, her voice a touch too casual. "Why?"

"Because you look like you've just had wild sex."

I bit back a groan. We would've been having it right now if it wasn't for your timely interruption, I told him silently. Thanks for the cock-block, man.

"Don't be ridiculous. Who would I possibly be having sex with? I was out running and fell in some shrubbery."

I heard him laugh at the same time I smothered my own.

"You could be a bit more sympathetic," she snapped irritably. Grace was getting completely caught up in her little tale as though she believed it herself. My lips twitched because she was fucking adorable. "I even twisted my ankle."

No! She did not just say that. I hoped she knew that she was now going to have to fake that injury for the rest of the week. I glanced at my watch.

Shit.

I pulled out my phone and sent Tim a quick message to say I'd be another twenty minutes before setting the ring tone to silent.

"Have you seen Casey?"

She's seen a lot more of me than you'd like, Henry.

"No, why?"

"Because his car's out the front but I didn't see him anywhere."

"He's in the bathroom." That came from Mac, which meant she was on to us. Shrewd bitch, I thought affectionately. That woman didn't miss a single thing. I owed her for having my back on this. "Henry, have you got a sec? I need you to check something on that new contract I was reading. From what I can see, it sounds like they're trying to cut our royalties."

"They fucking what?"

Their voices slowly faded and after a moment of silence, my phone vibrated.

It's okay to come out. I'm out the back with John.

I tapped out a reply to Grace before I left the confines of her wardrobe.

I have to get back to work. You. Me. Wednesday night. I don't care where the fuck it happens, but it's happening.

It wasn't until I was back in the car and heading towards the office that I realised the issue of my backseat hadn't reached a satisfactory conclusion. Tomorrow night, I vowed. I would yell at her some more tomorrow night.

Chapter Sixteen
CASEY

Frank strode into my office just after lunch on the Wednesday. His pace was rapid and his brows drawn, telling me he meant all business. He shoved a report under my face without any preamble and barked, "We got that lead on the Janie Berg case."

Shoving all thoughts of getting my hands on Grace later that night aside, I read the page in front of me, my pulse racing in anticipation of closing this case quickly.

It held an address, the photo of a house, and a map where the house was clearly marked on the street. Frank had detailed all entry and exit points, including windows, along with the information of each neighbouring residence. I glanced up, meeting Frank's fierce eyes.

Janie Berg was a six-year-old little girl, kidnapped from school on Monday. It wasn't until the bell rang signalling the end of lunch that it came to light she hadn't returned from the school playground. Teachers were supposed to be monitoring the playground where the kindergarten kids played, but reports indicated a five minute window during a teacher changeover when the area hadn't been supervised.

Five goddamn minutes. That was all it took to bring someone's entire world to a grinding halt.

The only witnesses were the other six-year-olds in the playground. As eager as they were to help with descriptions, the information hadn't been worth the paper it was written on. All we managed to get was the kidnapper was male.

I snatched the report holding Frank's meticulous information and stood. "Sure you still want that retirement, Frank?"

Frank didn't answer the question, and I didn't expect him to. The man never did anything without investigating every angle first, all but getting a NASA report before taking action.

Moving around the desk, I started for our equipment room at the back of the office. Tim glanced up from his desk as we strode out. "He's going to have to call you back," I heard him say as we continued down the back hallway. Punching in the security code, I opened the insulated door, Frank following behind.

"Where's Travis?" I barked, grabbing two bulletproof vests from the shelving.

"Already on his way in. Said he'd be—"

"Here," Travis said quickly. Pushing past Frank, he grabbed two handguns from their box while I picked up a box of ammunition from the shelf on my right. Travis handed one of them to me.

"Talk, Frank," I ordered as I loaded the gun in my hand. The Janie Berg case was mine, but Frank needed to update Travis on the situation so he wasn't walking in blind.

"The information was called in by a neighbour two doors down. Said she noticed movement inside the residence indicated. Last night she heard a kid screaming," he continued as I passed the box of ammunition to Travis. Travis began loading his gun while Frank spoke. "When she got a good look, she rang the police, gave them a description that matched Janie. They rang us. We checked on the lead and it came through. The little girl is in that house."

"Tell him what the police don't know," I grunted at Frank.

Frank's eyes went flat and hard. "The kid's dad was a former member of the outlaw biker gang The Sentinels."

"Was?" Travis questioned.

"Dead in a drive-by three years ago. No arrest was made."

"Shit. Is this random then, or is the MC involved somehow?"

My expression was grim as I tucked the gun in the back of my pants. "We don't know. Sherry, the kid's mum, says it has nothing to do with the MC but something's not sitting right with me," I finished as we left the equipment room, Travis pulling the heavy door shut behind us.

"Tim, hold all calls," I barked as the three of us filed past. "Frank, I want you to get in touch with Detective Kerr. Give him an update on what we know." I glanced at the page again. The house was in Blackheath. Frank had listed the estimated travel time as one hour and thirty-six minutes. "Get hold of Blackheath Police. Let them know what's going on. Give them ours and Kerr's contact info and also our ETA."

I paused as we entered the car park. Travis and Frank stopped with me.

"We have to take your car," I told Travis. "Mines full of boxes."

His brows flew up. "Boxes?"

I shook my head, not having found the time to haul them over to document destruction yet. "Something to do with Jared nesting." Travis opened his mouth to speak. I held up a hand. "Don't even ask." I turned to Frank. "Give Blackheath Police our vehicle info, too."

"What about Sherry?" Frank asked as we loaded the back of Travis's Subaru.

I swiped a hand across my face. "Shit. Ring her. Tell her we have a lead and to remain on standby. If little Janie is there and alive, we want to have Sherry brought in ASAP. If she's not, we don't want her there to see anything. See if we can get a chopper pulled in."

Frank nodded as Travis and I both slid our vests on. "Roger that," he said, and headed back inside the office.

Fifteen minutes later we were on the M4 and heading towards Sydney's Blue Mountains, Travis moving swiftly between lunchtime traffic.

When Frank rang, I picked up the phone. "Yeah?"

"Blackheath Police on standby. They'll be parking an unmarked patrol two houses down from the target residence. Detective Kerr has a team on its way. The mother has been notified. It's a negative on the chopper at this stage."

"Thanks, Frank." I hung up the phone and gave Travis the update.

After shifting gears and changing lanes, he glanced at me. "The unmarked is going to go with our lead?"

"They will if they know what's good for them. I don't want them interfering in something we've had specialised training to deal with."

Exhaling heavily, I leaned back in my seat and closed my eyes, feeling a cold sweat break out across my brow.

"You okay?"

"Yeah," I muttered, opening my eyes and focusing on the passing scenery. "Just … brings it all back. Every damn time." Travis glanced across at me again, concern furrowing his brow. "Stop fucking looking at me like that. I'm fine," I lied, because I wasn't. I was exhausted. I had the sudden urge to wrap my arms around Grace, bury my face in her neck, and just breathe her in. Five and a half weeks. That was all I had left of her. Taking a deep breath, I emptied my mind and forced a smile for Travis. "This is why we do this job, right?"

"Casey—"

My phone rang then, cutting him off. Thankful for the interruption, I answered without checking the screen. "Yeah?" I barked.

"Casey," Morgan replied. "I've been trying to get a hold of you. You're a busy man."

"Sorry about that. Look, now's not a good time. We're—"

"Listen. I've got some information for you." I sat up in my seat, suddenly alert and unable to breathe. "Let's do dinner. Tonight. It's been too long since I had my hands on you. We need to remedy that."

I wanted to repeatedly smash my phone against the dashboard of Travis's car. Tonight was my night with Grace. It was all I'd thought about since Monday morning.

"Casey?"

"That sounds like a plan, but I'm heading out to an undisclosed location and I don't think I'll be back until late tonight."

"That's perfect. I'm working late. Come over when you're done, doesn't matter how late. I'll cook."

"Sure," I forced myself to say while I scrambled internally. What the fuck else was I supposed to do? She had information I'd been trying to get my hands on for ten damn years. I couldn't just throw that out the window.

"You don't step out on women?"

"No. I don't."

Shit. Just … shit.

I closed my eyes, rubbing a hand across my brow. I'd do dinner, let Morgan know that whatever this was, it was over, and then hope like fucking hell she was still willing to give me the information anyway. "Thanks. I'll let you know a time when I have more of an idea."

"You remember my address?"

"I do," I replied.

"Great. See you soon, Casey."

"Later," I murmured and hung up.

Travis checked his mirrors before returning his gaze to the road. "Who was that?"

"Morgan." Knowing I may as well get it over with, I added, "She has information."

His brows flew up as he glanced at me quickly. "She does? Well, fuck. Maybe I overreacted about you and her," he admitted. "I thought you were chasing a dead end. What information does she have?"

"Don't know yet. She wants to do dinner tonight."

After a minute he replied, "Well that's good, right?"

I sighed deeply and stared unseeing out the window. "Yeah, it's good."

Picking up on my flat mood, he frowned. "You do like her, don't you?"

"She seems okay," I hedged as I sent a brief text message to Grace, disappointment leaving a bitter taste in my mouth.

I can't make it tonight. Sorry.

A year ago I would have been pumped at finally getting a lead, but now I just felt empty. If this lead turned into a dead end, then I needed to find a way to let go of the past. I couldn't keep going the way I was because the guilt was killing me.

Grace's reply came back ten minutes later.

Okay.

That was it. Nothing else. Just … okay. She didn't even question why. God, she was so fucking beautiful and perfect and I was an asshole. I would see Morgan tonight, have dinner, get the information, and end it there. Whatever happened, I couldn't keep leading Morgan on, and hurting Grace was out of the question.

I tapped out another message while Travis drove silently beside me.

Reschedule for Thursday night?

She replied instantly.

No can do, Batman. Friday is also out. We have a show.

"Are we doing security for Jamieson this weekend?" I asked.

"I think so," Travis replied. "Friday night. Nothing Saturday and Sunday. Jared and Coby are taking care of it. Why?"

"Just checking," I murmured.

I sent a message to Coby.

Take your Friday night security shift?

After reading his reply of "Fuck yeah. Owe you one," I sent another message to Grace.

I'm doing your Friday night security. Come home with me.

I waited another twenty minutes for her response.

How would I explain that?

The sneaking around had to stop. After Friday night, I was telling Henry, consequences be damned. Grace and I were both adults. She could make her own decisions and he needed to trust that she was safe with me.

I sent a quick reply.

Make something up. I don't care. I need to see you.

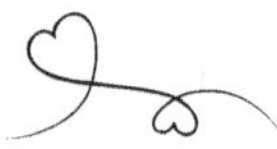

Travis was just turning onto the street Frank had marked out on the map for us when he rang again.

"You have to pull out."

"What? Why?"

"The elderly couple who own the house? Their nephew is a member of The Sentinels. It looks like the place is used as a safe house. You were right, Casey. Janie's abduction wasn't as random as we thought."

"Janie's mother said she no longer had ties to the MC."

Frank gave a weighty sigh. "I guess she lied."

There could only be one reason why. She was involved with another biker and they were taking care of it. Bikers did not involve police in their business. No exceptions. They handled it within the "family." I racked my brain trying to think. The kid's father was a Sentinel, which means even if Sherry no longer had ties to the MC, Janie was theirs. The only reason why Janie would be inside the house of Sentinel was because Sherry had done something to piss them off. But what? Date a rival gang member?

I cursed crudely. "This is part of some goddamn biker war, isn't it?"

The police were going to shut us down the minute we opened our mouths and said "biker war." Those situations instantly became a no-fly zone for outside consulting firms like ours. Not only because their relationship with the police was volatile, but because no insurance company in the world would take us on for that.

"Goddammit!" I yelled and kicked the dash, not hiding my frustration at being blocked. Two biker gangs were using her as a pawn, and we were right there—the third party who wanted her out of the situation and safe. And our hands were tied.

"I know," he said, his voice resigned. "Wait up." When I heard him talking on another phone, I muffled the speaker and updated Travis before Frank came back on. "Kerr's team is thirty minutes out. Your orders are to vacate the area immediately."

"There's a little girl inside that house, Frank. I don't give a fuck about orders! We're not going anywhere."

I looked at Travis. He met my eyes and gave a single nod. After ending the call, Travis drove past the unmarked patrol car and pulled up alongside the kerb another fifteen metres down the road.

Picking up Frank's report, I searched for the contact information for the neighbouring house on the left. "Bingo," I muttered when I saw their home phone number listed down.

I started dialling.

After six rings I got a message service saying "You've reached the Abbott residence. Sorry, we can't take your call right now. If you'd like to leave your name and—"

I hung up.

"Neighbours aren't home," I told Travis. "I'm going through their backyard. Scope out what I can see over their fence. If I don't get anything, I'll climb over for a closer look." I paused. "You cool with that?"

If a child's life was in immediate danger, we had all agreed we would go against any higher authority, regardless of the damage to our firm's reputation, to make that child safe. However, we hadn't been caught up in a situation involving rival motorcycle gangs until now. Falling under their radar could potentially be the worst thing our firm could ever do.

Travis swiped a hand across his face, staring out the window while he processed the situation. After a moment, he glanced sideways and nodded. "I'm cool with that."

After checking the safety on the handgun, I leaned forward, tucking it into the back of my pants.

"Just scope it out and come back, okay?"

I agreed quickly and after setting my phone to vibrate only, slipped it in my pocket.

I glanced at Travis before opening the car door. "Ring Frank. Tell him to update Jared and Coby on the situation, just in case shit hits the fan."

After a quick nod, I left Travis to his phone call and strolled casually across the road to the neighbouring house. It was a single-story brick home, similar to every other house in the street. Closed blinds covered the two front windows so I couldn't catch a glimpse inside. Not wanting to give myself away by scanning the street, I kept my gaze focused on the front door as I walked up the paved pathway. I knocked softly on the metal frame of the screen. After thirty seconds of silence, I tested the handle. Locked. Putting my hands in my pockets, I strolled around the far side of the house. The back gate wasn't latched properly and I slipped through, relieved to see a thriving green hedge lining the timber fence. It provided good cover from the target house.

Crouching low, I ran alongside the length of the hedge until I found a decent vantage point. Pulling out my phone, I dialled Travis.

"Speak," he answered.

My eyes scanned the neighbouring lawn. "The backyard is clear." I shifted my gaze to the house. "All blinds are closed, no gaps. Place looks locked up tight."

"What do you want to do?"

"What's the ETA of Kerr's team?"

"Eight minutes," he told me.

"I want inside that house, Trav. It's so fucking quiet. I'm not hearing a thing. If she's in there on her own, this could be our opportunity to get her out quickly and quietly."

There was silence on the other end and I knew Travis was thinking hard. "And if she's not on her own, then we're escalating a kidnapping into a potentially dangerous hostage situation."

"And if it was your child in there?"

"I would scale the fence. I wouldn't even hesitate."

My voice was grim. "Then I'm going over."

Keeping Travis on the line, I pocketed the phone and grabbed the top of the timber fence. After levering myself up and over, I hit the ground hard and ran for the back of the house. Heading straight for the back bedroom window, I crouched beneath it.

Fumbling quickly for my phone, I put it to my ear. "I'm over," I panted. "What do you—"

"Pull the fuck out, Casey!" Travis ordered, his voice low and urgent and I realised why when I heard the rumbling sound getting closer. "At least six biker members just turned down the street and are heading right for you."

I cursed vehemently. "Sentinels?"

There was a pause and when his voice came back on the line it was filled with dread. "Worse." Then he named the most violent and savage outlaw biker gang in Australia. "The Black Vipers."

But it was too late to do anything. The back door of the target house banged open hard, the sound barely audible over the thunderous growl of approaching motorcycles. A man flew outside, vaulting over the three back steps. He was running as soon as his feet hit the ground. For a guy who was built like a brick shithouse, he moved fast. I dropped my phone and ran at the guy. Leaping at him, I took him down in a tackle. The wind was knocked out of me when I landed hard beneath him.

"Where's the girl?" I gasped.

"Fuck you," he snarled, pushing off me as he scrambled to his feet. His fist slammed into the side of my head before I could get up properly. My neck snapped back. Jesus. It was like getting hit by a Mack Truck. Disoriented, I still managed to turn and sweep my leg out when he took off for the back fence. He stumbled and went down, landing on his stomach. The sound of gunfire barely registered in my already ringing ears when I straddled his back. Pulling out my handgun, I engaged the slide and pressed it quickly to the back of his head.

"Move and die," I panted furiously, still winded from the tackle.

It was then that I heard the sound of a little girl screaming. My initial reaction was relief she was still alive until the sound of gunfire cut through the air. The screaming stopped instantly. So did my heart.

Before I could turn around, something flashed in my peripheral vision. I felt something crash into the back of my head and the world went black.

When I came around, Travis's face came into focus. He was hovering above me, his fingers running over the swelling lump on the back of my head. The tender spot throbbed into a sharp spike of pain. I rolled over and puked in the grass.

"Do that again and I'll punch you," I rasped, wiping at my face.

Travis remained abnormally silent as he sat back on his heels. He wiped bloody fingers on his jeans with eyes that were raw and bleak. A small crack began forming inside me, growing wider until my whole body felt ready to shatter.

"She's dead, isn't she?" I whispered.

He shook his head. "She got caught in crossfire. It doesn't look good for her."

"No," I moaned. Rolling onto my back, I put a hand over my eyes. The long, drawn-out wail of a siren hit my ears. "Where is she?"

"Detective Kerr has Janie out the front. That's the ambulance arriving for her now."

I tried sitting up and the world tilted. "I need to see her."

Travis pushed me back down. "The medics have her now. Let them do their job."

Emotions were running high when we met with Blackheath Police and

Detective Kerr and gave our verbal reports. No one yet knew the full story but from we could gather, I was pretty spot on. Sherry was dating a member of the Black Vipers. The Sentinels didn't take too kindly to that considering it was Viper that shot her old man. The brother of the dead guy, Janie's Uncle, was the one that kidnapped Janie. The police managed to arrest him along with two bikers from the Vipers, and they were all taken in for questioning. The rest had scattered like cockroaches. After being checked over by the medic, our firm was cleared of any wrongdoing, but we were put on notice. If we went against a direct police order one more time, we were done.

The drive back to the office that night was silent.

"You gonna be okay?" Travis asked, keeping the engine idling when he pulled up beside my car.

I nodded, unable to speak past the lump in my throat. After grabbing my car keys from the centre console, I opened the door and slid out. Sticking my head back in, I muttered, "I'll see you tomorrow."

Our firm had a rule about dealing with on-the-job trauma: you followed routine and returned to work the next day; you surrounded yourself with those who knew what you were feeling; and you spoke up if you weren't coping. It was the only way that worked for us.

"Tomorrow. Ring if you get any news on Janie's condition."

I gave him a brief salute in response because I didn't want to think about the slim odds of her survival.

It was eleven p.m. when I got inside my own car and started the engine. With eyes that burned from exhaustion, I got out my phone and sent a message to Morgan.

On my way.

Chapter Seventeen
GRACE

I'd spent the past hour tossing and turning in bed, picking up my phone to message Casey and then changing my mind. After seeing John off at the airport earlier, I'd been thinking of nothing else but seeing Casey later that night. The disappointment when he messaged to cancel was enough to see me reaching for the ice cream. What cured sexual frustration—Chunky Monkey or Peanut Butter Fudge? Turns out neither because Henry had eaten both, leaving the empty cartons in the freezer.

I tossed them in the bin, miserable enough to not bother complaining. Who was I kidding anyway? Ice cream was no replacement for Casey and the way he made me feel. Desire for him was a knot inside me, coiling tighter and tighter as each day passed until I was ready to explode. I hadn't even seen him fully naked yet which was surely some sort of crime. What I had glimpsed was enough to know the man was virile and beautiful. His shoulders were rounded and muscular, his abs tightly defined, and his thigh muscles powerful and strong.

I bit back a moan just thinking about him.

Mac speared me with a look of sympathy.

"What? It's hot, okay?" I waved my hand at the broken air-conditioner. We were all suffering. The night was steamy and oppressive. A storm was supposed to hit earlier and sweep the humidity away, but it obviously had better things to do. I grabbed a hair tie from the dining table as I walked past. My hair was wrapped around my sweaty skin like damp tentacles. I peeled it off me and tied it in a knot on the top of my head.

"Give me that," Henry growled at Mac. He reached for the frozen bag of peas she had plastered over half her face.

"Get lost, Henry." She slapped his hands away. "I'm not wrestling with you over iced vegetables. It's too damn hot."

"It's too damn hot to do anything," I complained as I flopped in the chair beside the three-seater couch they were splayed over.

"Or wear clothes apparently," Mac replied with a pointed look at Jake. He was sprawled across the other couch in nothing but a pair of boxer-briefs. Granted, we were all wearing next to nothing, but this was Jake and he was built like a tattooed Thor. No wonder Mac had cried dibs on the frozen peas because all that rippling muscle was making me sweat on a whole other level.

"It's even too hot to jack off," Cooper piped up from the floor where he lay watching television.

"It's never too hot for sex," Frog countered from the couch opposite me. Rather than watch television like everyone else, he was busy sticking a skewer down the cast on his arm. I felt sorry for him. Having a plastered arm in this heat must suck donkey's balls.

"True that," Cooper agreed. I looked his way. He watched me, his lips curled suggestively. "Maybe Grace and I could test that theory."

"I'd be willing to test that theory on the first person who fixes the air conditioner," I joked.

"Me too," Mac added.

Jake's eyes fell on Mac as he stood and if I said I averted my gaze from all that sexy, rippling muscle, it would be a big, fat lie. I glanced across at Mac to see if she was similarly affected. She was studiously watching the television. I didn't believe it for a second. Not because Cooper had flicked the channel to an old episode of Murder She Wrote, but because from the time it took for Jake to walk across her field of vision and out the front door, she didn't blink once.

I heard the neighbouring front door of the duplex slam where Jake, Frog, and Cooper lived. Five minutes later, he returned wearing a tiny pair of football shorts. Was that his definition of getting dressed? Because they were smaller than his boxer-briefs. The guy rarely wore a shirt when he was playing the drums. Granted it was sweaty work, and that sheen of perspiration on his pecs reeled in the female groupies, but he hardly wore a shirt when he wasn't playing either. I assumed it was how he was most comfortable, but maybe he was doing it to get a reaction out of Mac. With her being unusually quiet, I'd give him points for it working.

Cooper dragged his eyes away from the television as Jake returned. He strode back through the middle of us, carrying a large metal toolbox.

"What're you doing?"

Jake dumped the toolbox on the timber floor with a clank, answering

Cooper all the while looking at Mac. "Fixing the damn air conditioner, idiot, what does it look like I'm doing?"

Henry, Frog, and Cooper all shared a smirk as Jake crouched and began rifling through a bunch of metal gizmos.

"Nothing like the incentive of sex for a guy to get his tool out," Cooper quipped, and all three of them laughed.

Jake looked directly at me and winked. With a metal doovalacky in his hand, he stood and said, "Of course. Grace said she'd be willing to test the theory. There's nothing sexier than a willing female."

Everyone faltered, including me. Was this his tactic—making Mac jealous? That was like poking a tiger with a really big stick, and I wanted no part of it. I hope he wasn't firmly attached to his balls.

"I think that I … uh … might go to bed." I started inching off the couch as I spoke. "To sleep," I added hastily as I stood. "Good luck with the … er…" I ran my eyes over Jake and exhaled a sharp puff of air as I tried to think "…air conditioner. The air conditioner. Night all."

A chorus of goodnights were called out as I made my way up the stairs. Mitsy followed on my heels. Surrounded by other people, the dog came off loyal. I could almost believe I was the only important person in his life. It all changed the minute we were alone. Reaching my room, he peeled off towards his bed, and I to mine. He growled when I walked past him, breaching his personal space to set my phone on the bedside table.

Stripping down to a tiny pair of rainbow striped cotton and lace panties, I slid under the sheets and promptly closed my eyes. After a minute, memories of Casey—the way he kissed me, his tongue and hands on my body—had my heart racing and the sheets sticking to my body. I kicked them off with an irritable huff. Another minute later and I'd peeled the panties down my legs and tossed those too. Now completely naked, I was spread across the bed like a starfish and praying for a cool breeze.

I closed my eyes again, and this time I must have drifted off because Mitsy growling woke me.

"Shut up, dog," I mumbled into my pillow.

His growling got louder.

"Gonna kill you," I slurred tiredly. "In the morning though. After sleep. You're gonna get it."

Mitsy's growling reached offensive levels.

"What, dammit?" I sat up, scooting out of bed half asleep. When I stumbled over to Mitsy's area by the open window, I realised it wasn't even him growling, it was Casey's car parked out the front by the kerb. My brow furrowed. He'd cancelled tonight, hadn't he? Was he here for me or some other reason? Maybe someone had been hurt. Fear knotted my belly. I grabbed for my panties and tank top, hopping about as I slid them on hastily.

My heart hammered with apprehension as I made my way quickly down the stairs. It turned to confusion when I noticed no one was around. The duplex was dark and still. With a quick glance behind me, I slipped out the front door, letting it softly click shut behind me. Casey was sitting in his car, staring straight ahead as I walked down the drive. Opening the car door, I slid inside and shut it. He didn't acknowledge my presence, or even look at me at all. He simply shifted gears, and with a quick glance in his rearview mirror, pulled out onto the road.

I clicked my seat belt into place. "Casey?"

With a hard swallow, he shook his head, keeping his eyes on the road as we drove. Despite his controlled composure, his face was pale and tension surrounded him like an aura.

"Casey, you're scaring me."

"I'm sorry." Our eyes met for a brief moment, the connection intense. Raw pain flickered in his eyes before it was quickly banked. "That's the last thing I want to do."

His palm slid over my bare thigh, riding upwards as he continued to drive. The touch sent arousal spiking through me, but not enough to override the concern.

"Where are we going?"

He shook his head as if he had no clue. After a moment, he replied, "I want to drive, but I don't want to be alone. I want to be with you."

My eyes fixed on his profile as he drove. The knuckles of his right hand were white on the steering wheel and his jaw tight. Something wasn't right. In fact, something was very wrong. I slid my hand over his, my pulse racing when he flipped his palm over and grabbed hold.

"Casey?"

He glanced over at me.

"I want to be with you too."

His answer was a squeeze of my hand before letting go.

We sat in silence as he drove. I stared at the dashboard, having no idea what to do or say or how to fix what was wrong.

"Are you okay?" I asked.

"Sure." A smile came to his lips. It was forced because it never reached his eyes. "Just a bad day at work, you know?"

"No, I don't know. Maybe you should tell me."

The roads were eerily quiet when he pulled to a stop at a red light. "I don't want to talk right now." His hand fell on my thigh again, the calloused palm scraping my skin as it slipped upwards. Reaching between my thighs, he dragged my panties to the side and slipped his fingers inside, gently massaging my clit and dragging a moan from my throat. He leaned over, putting his mouth on my ear, his breathing coming harder and heavier.

"I want to fuck you, Grace. Not just tonight, but every night," he professed, his fingers working me expertly. The red light turned green, but with no cars around, Casey ignored it. "Hard enough for it to hurt, so that when you leave, me fucking you is the only thing you can think about."

I closed my eyes, my head falling back against the headrest. I wanted him to fuck me that hard. I wanted to feel him inside me even when he wasn't there, but not like this. Not when he was using sex to mask a hurt so painful and deep I could feel the ache of it surrounding me until I felt suffocated.

"No," I gasped.

He froze at the single word, his hand stilling instantly.

"There's something wrong, Casey. I can feel it."

His hand slipped out of my panties and I mourned the loss. "I don't want to talk about it," he snapped.

Tension bled into the car as he put it in gear and accelerated swiftly. My eyes burned. When we were good, it was wild and intense and consuming, but we always spiralled into such a hot mess. I wasn't sure if Casey and I would ever find a happy medium.

Drawing a deep breath, I forced calm. "Maybe you should take me home."

"No."

My brows flew up. "No?"

"No." He shook his head, his tone cold and harsh. "This was your deal, and now you want to turn it into some kind of relationship? That's not what this is. This is about you and me and sex. So maybe you should spread your legs so we can both get what we want."

I flinched, his words a slap in the face. Clenching my jaw, I ground out, "Take me home."

Casey pulled the car over, jerking the wheel so hard I lurched forward, the seat belt cutting into my chest. I winced as we pulled to a sudden stop. He wrenched on the handbrake and turned the car off. Twisting in his seat, he faced me, furious.

"If I've had a bad day, I'm not inclined to share it with you, or share anything else for that matter. I just want to have it fucked out of my system. Don't you get that? I want to lose myself in fucking you until I can't feel anything else." He grabbed the bulge in his jeans, raking his eyes over me brazenly before returning to my face. "Don't tell me this isn't what you want."

I sucked in a breath. "You asshole," I hissed and scrambled for the door handle, my heart pounding with hurt and anger and so much else I almost couldn't breathe from it.

"Where do you think you're going?" Casey grabbed at my arm before I could get the door open. "You can't go out there with barely anything on."

"I don't care!" I shouted, trying to shrug him off as tears started falling down my face.

"Grace!"

"God. Just leave me alone!" I slapped at his hands as we grappled in the car. "Anywhere is preferable to being in here with you!"

Casey stiffened at my words, both of us breathing harshly in the sudden quiet. He drew back in his seat, effectively distancing himself from me.

"Fuck," he roared and slammed his fist against the steering wheel. "Fuck!"

I sat there unmoving, trying to control my breathing. A thin sheen of sweat from the heat coated my body as I wiped at the tears on my face.

"Sorry," he rasped. Taking the wheel with both hands, he pressed his forehead against it, closing his eyes. "I'm sorry. I'm not…" he started and then paused, seeming unable to go any further. He shook his head in frustration before facing me. There was something fractured in his eyes, something that wavered between desperation and despair. It made my blood run cold. "A little girl got shot today. It doesn't look good for her," he admitted, his voice hoarse and tired. "And I'm fucking losing it because it shouldn't have happened. If I'd found her sooner, then maybe she wouldn't be in the hospital right now fighting for her life. I … God …" He breathed shakily. "I shouldn't have come over. I started falling apart and my first instinct was to come to you and I'm sorry."

His first instinct was to come to me? What was I supposed to do with that? It made me want to cry because being that person for him was only temporary. He needed so much more than what I could give. I took his hand and gave it a squeeze. "This is about more than that little girl, isn't it?"

"I can't talk about it right now." He swallowed, rubbing a trembling hand across his eyes. "I just can't. I'm sorry."

Casey let go of my hand and got out of the car before I could respond. The heat of the night swirled inside as he shut the door behind him. I watched as he walked around the front of the car. For a brief second, the glare of the headlights illuminated his pants and rolled up sleeves of his dark shirt. He looked tired and rumpled and so completely defeated my heart gave a lurch.

"Dammit," I muttered when he leaned up against the hood. Glancing around, I spied his jacket on the backseat. I grabbed it and slipped it on, the sleeves falling past my hands. Pushing them up my forearms, I reached over and pulled the keys from the ignition and slipped them in the jacket pocket. When I opened the car door, the sound of crashing waves was loud and the smell of salty ocean thick in the air. We'd pulled off somewhere along the headland of one of Sydney's beaches. A cliff top coastal walk ran somewhere along here, from Bondi to Coogee. I knew because I'd been meaning to do the two-hour walk since arriving and hadn't yet had the chance.

I walked around to the front of the car. Rather than looking out to the dark waves crashing below, Casey's head was bent, his arms folded.

He was right, in a way. This was about sex and the wild attraction we had for each other. Expecting a relationship for the short period of time I was here was unfair. What was also unfair was expecting him to talk about what was in his head if I couldn't do the same.

I stood in front of him and he looked up. "Grace," he whispered. Unfolding his arms, he reached out and tucked a loose strand of hair behind my ear.

My chest brushed against his when I stepped in between his spread legs. Wrapping my arms around him, I hugged him, not letting go as I spoke. "It's okay to lose it, Casey. Maybe you think I don't see you, but I do. You're always the first to smile, and to laugh and tease, but underneath it all, you're scared of letting everyone down so you hide what hurts the most so you can be the person they all need you to be. You put everyone above yourself, but whatever it is that hurts will never heal while you keep doing that." I exhaled shakily before continuing. "I know, because I used to do the same thing."

Feeling his body tremble, I squeezed tighter. His arms came around me, wrapping tight enough to squeeze the air from my lungs. A sob tore from his chest, and then another, until his face was buried in my neck. I held on, my eyes burning at seeing such a big, strong man hanging on by his fingernails.

"Whatever you're doing now is not enough," I whispered thickly when he drew back. "You have to let go of what hurts."

"What hurts you, Grace?" His beautiful blue eyes watched me intently, waiting.

I released the breath I'd been holding and gave him a faint smile. "Country music mostly, and algebra. Falling down stairs is up there too. That never ends well." Casey chuckled softly just like I'd hoped he would. The sound lifted my heart. "What hurts you, Casey?"

He rubbed his hands up and down my arms, the touch soothing me. "Getting kicked in the crotch," he replied and I laughed. "The Hawks beating Freo in the AFL final. The thought of you leaving." His eyes locked on mine. "When I'm with you, touching you, breathing you in, I forget who I have to be and I'm just me. When you leave, you'll take that with you."

I leaned in and pressed a long, lingering kiss to his cheek. He shuddered, his grip on me tightening. Turning his face, he brushed his lips against mine. I relished the brief contact before taking a step back, the small rocks jabbing into my bare feet. The sharp stab of pain was a welcome distraction from the ache in my heart.

"Casey." I looked away. "This … thing between us. I never expected it. Whatever it is, the intention was never for it to hurt. Maybe we should stop before it gets worse."

Casey shook his head, opening his mouth to speak but his phone rang. Frowning, he dug in his pocket and pulled it out. His body tensed when he checked the caller ID. It rang and rang, the mechanical tune cutting through the crashing sound of waves.

I looked from the phone to him. He was staring at the screen with drawn brows. It was clear there was an internal battle raging inside him. "Casey?"

As though reaching a decision, he tucked the ringing phone back in his pocket and grabbed hold of my hands. "Then let it hurt," he snarled as he dragged me close. "Let it. We're not stopping, Slim. You're mine. Every night for the next five weeks. Just you and me. Fuck everything else."

Chapter Eighteen
CASEY

"I can't. We can't," Grace amended as she tried tugging her hands free. I refused to let go. Instead, I spun her around and walked her backwards without taking my eyes from hers. "We should stop this now."

When she collided with the hood, I lifted her up. She gasped when I sat her down on it. The sound was sweet and had my cock throbbing and filling in my pants. Resting her feet on the front bumper, she hiked up her knees, and I took a moment to enjoy the display. "There's no such thing as can't."

Grace arched a brow, her pupils dilating when she glanced down at the growing bulge in my pants. "Are you trying to dazzle me with logic?"

"It's either that or I dazzle you with my cock." Spreading her legs, I pushed my way between them, groaning when she wrapped them around my hips and rubbed up against me. "Which would you prefer?"

"Jesus, Casey," she breathed. "You want to just go for it right here on your car?"

"Fuck," I growled, so turned on at the very thought I felt dizzy. I'd fantasised about doing her in an endless number of places. Starting with the hood of my car would suit me just fine. "Yeah. I do."

Grace scanned the darkness around us. The road was quiet in early hour, and though we could hear the odd passing car, shrubs along the roadside hid us from their view. Houses were dark and quiet. People were asleep. Satisfied no one was around, or likely to be, she took the tie out of her hair and leaned back on her elbows, staring up at me as she licked her lips.

"So do it," she challenged, her hair falling down in a fiery tangle against the gleaming grey hood.

"You think I won't?" Leaning over her, I planted both hands on either side of her and ran my tongue along her bottom lip, nibbling it between my teeth.

"I'm gonna fuck you so good," I crooned in her ear, "you won't ever want to leave." I took hold of her hips and dragged her against my erection, rubbing it between her legs. The layers of clothing had to go.

"Oh my God," she muttered. "We're going to get arrested for public indecency, I know it."

"If we do, I'm telling them you forced me."

She laughed and I swallowed the sound as I kissed her, sweeping my tongue inside her mouth. Her hands came around me, holding on as I tilted my head, deepening the kiss.

Grace was breathless when I broke away, moving my mouth to her neck, licking and sucking her overheated skin.

"Casey," she moaned.

I pushed her back against the car, drugged with lust. Nothing short of the world ending would stop me from having her now. I grabbed the hem of her top and shoved it up until it bunched beneath her armpits. Her tits were a small handful yet utterly perfect, her nipples a dark rose. I ducked my head and took one in my mouth, biting it gently with my teeth. She gasped and the sound went straight to my cock.

A loud crack of thunder cut through the sound of our heavy breathing. Grace jerked at the signal of an imminent storm and tipped her head to the sky. "It's going to rain. I can smell it in the air."

"I don't care," I told her, having no intention of stopping what we'd just started. Latching onto her nipple, I sucked it deep in my mouth. With one hand pinning her down, I used the other to undo my belt buckle and slide the zipper down on my pants.

I shifted to her other nipple, biting it before laving the sting with my tongue. I sucked the rigid peak until she cried out my name. It still wasn't enough. Letting go, I straightened up and pushed my boxer-briefs below my straining erection. My cock sprang free, swollen and aching. Grace dropped her gaze, watching as I grabbed it in my hand and tugged, needing desperate relief.

"Suck me," I demanded, wanting her mouth.

She sat up on the hood and shifted closer, her knees up around her ears as she leaned in and pressed a kiss to the head. I shuddered, fisting my hand in her hair as she did it again.

A cold raindrop splattered across my arm when Grace opened her mouth and took the head of my cock in her mouth. My head fell back and I closed my eyes, groaning her name when her hot tongue swirled around the tip, teasing me.

Another raindrop hit, fat and heavy, when she sucked the length of me deep inside, swallowing me in her hot, wet mouth. Her beautiful stormy eyes met mine and pleasure hit in waves. God, I was going to come watching my cock slide in and out those pretty lips of hers.

Heavy rain started falling while her tongue stroked over my cock. I ignored the cold drops when an orgasm came screaming up inside me. Grabbing the base of my erection, I pressed hard, staving it off as I pulled out of her mouth.

"We should get out of the rain!" she shouted as the heavy drops turned into a shower. She went to slide off the hood of my car and I put one hand in the middle of her chest, halting her.

"No." I pushed her down. She fell back on her elbows, her wet hair beginning to plaster itself to her skin. While she was busy catching her breath, I grabbed her panties and yanked them down her endlessly long legs. Grace watched, her mouth open, as I tossed them away. They sailed over her shoulder, hitting the wet windscreen with a loud slap. Taking hold of her knees with a firm grip, I spread her legs.

With her body sprawled across the hood of my car, Grace looked wild, soaked to the skin, and crazy beautiful. I knew then I was falling in love with her. It wasn't a good feeling. My heart thundered in my ears and my chest felt tight, like I might hyperventilate at any moment. I shouldn't want this. There would be no easy way out.

"Casey," she gasped, goose bumps skittering along her skin as her stormy blue eyes found mine.

Since when have you ever taken the easy road, Casey?

"I'm not waiting for you any longer!" I shouted over the downpour. She shivered when I dug my fingers hard into her hips and yanked her towards me. "I need to be inside you, Grace." I rubbed my bare cock between her legs, nailing her wet, swollen clit with each thrust. Her head fell back on a moan and she grabbed my hips, holding on. "Right now."

Blinking away the drops of water pooling on my eyelashes, I reached for my wallet in the back pocket of my pants. "Dammit," I growled when my hand came up empty.

"What?"

"Condom," I bit out. "Dammit!" I found Grace's eyes, wanting to cry like a baby. "I don't have one."

I don't think I'd ever been caught in a situation where I'd ever not had one. I wanted to punch myself in the face. Of all the times, not having one now was just fucking cruel. Like some sick joke. I should just—

"Do we need one?" she yelled back, blinking rapidly as the rain pelted her in the face. "I know I'm clean."

I swallowed hard at the thought of fucking her bare, of coming inside her. Then I let the image go. "Yes, Grace, we do. I've never gone bare before, and holy shit, right now I want to more than I've ever wanted anything, but trusting me with your body like that is a decision that should be made carefully, not in the heat of the moment."

"I trust you!"

I shook my head, then remembered that the glove compartment in my car had condoms the last time I'd rummaged around in there. "Don't move!"

After finding one quickly, I slammed the door and was already ripping it open with my teeth as I came around the hood of the car. After rolling it down my cock, I shifted between her legs.

She took hold of my swollen erection with both hands. I watched, my breath heavy, as she guided me inside her body. My hips surged forward when she let go. With my head buried in her neck, I slammed home. Not even pausing to catch my breath, I began a hard and fast thrust.

"Feels so good," she moaned when I rolled my hips. We were getting pummelled by rain and cars were driving past not even ten yards away. I didn't care. I was caught up in the intensity, in the vice she squeezed my cock in. I turned my head to kiss her, forcing her mouth to open for my tongue. Grace took it and gave it back, making me groan.

Then she tore her mouth from mine, taking a deep gasping breath. "Make it hard, Casey," she said, her eyes inflamed. "So that when I leave, you fucking me is the only thing I can think about."

My fingers dug into her ass at the sexy words thrown back in my face. "You want it hard?"

I pulled out with agonising patience, until only the head of my cock remained in her body. Shifting my gaze downwards, I pushed back in slowly, gritting my teeth from the drawn-out pleasure as I watched myself disappear back inside her.

"Casey, please." Grace moaned and fell back against the car, her back arching as she tried to pull me deeper inside.

I wanted to freeze the moment so I could enjoy it a little longer—the abandonment, the desperation on her face, the chill from the rain contrasting with the heat of her body, the wild surge of hunger for her and no one else. No. Not hunger, I realised, but craving. I wanted to build a wall around us, brick by brick, until no one else could get inside and Grace couldn't leave.

Pulling back out again slowly, I shoved in hard, my hands pinning her body in place so she could take the force. She cried out, her legs wrapping around my hips. That was when the last thread of control snapped. I began fucking her with abandon. There was no finesse, just need.

The outside world faded as I focused on making Grace feel good. "Come," I bit out breathlessly, knowing I couldn't hold on for much longer. "God, please," I begged, my hips burning as I slammed her hard.

Reaching between us, I pegged her clit with my thumb, massaging the swollen nub expertly.

"Casey," she gasped as I kept pounding my cock inside her. "So damn good."

Her breathing was deep and ragged now, her grip on my bare hips tight. I knew she was close. Pulling my thumb away, she watched as I sucked it into my mouth, using my tongue to sweep the taste of her over my lips. It was so hot it almost ripped an orgasm from me then and there.

Grace cried out my name, her eyes rolling back in her head as she came. Her body contracted violently around my cock, forcing a groan from my chest. I braced my thighs further apart, unable to slow down to ease her through the aftershocks. "I'm gonna—"

"Yesssss," she moaned slowly.

She reached down and grabbed my balls with one hand, tugging hard. I thrust once, twice, and squeezed my eyes shut, coming with a shout.

Ducking my head, I kissed her as I rode out the pleasure, my hips slowing to short, sharp thrusts. The weight of my heavy body pinned her to the car.

She grinned against my lips, panting hard as the rain pelted us. "We need to do this again soon."

After accelerating out onto the main road, I glanced across at Grace. With the little clothing she had now wet, she was wrapped in the beach towel I kept in the back of my car. It was tucked loosely around her slender body. If I reached over and gave it a small flick, I was sure it would just fall away. Returning my eyes to the road, I shifted gears and settled my hand on her bare leg.

The heavy rain had died off minutes ago, settling into a light, steady patter that the windscreen wipers cleared away intermittently. We were on our way back to my loft. I wasn't sure what plan Grace had in mind, but mine was to finally get her in my bed and fuck her all over again.

I would have to return her to the duplex before anyone woke up and noticed she'd left. I didn't like the idea of taking her home in the middle of the night—I wanted to wake with her in my bed—but I liked the idea of Henry waking up to find her gone even less.

"Why are you angry?"

"I'm not angry," I replied.

"You're frowning," she answered, shivering from the cool change the storm had brought with it. I took my hand from her leg to turn up the heat before returning it.

"Because I don't want this whole thing with your brother to come to blows."

"What? Why would it come to that? Henry's not violent." Grace looked confused, her furrowed brow now mimicking mine. "You're not going to punch him, are you?"

"I'm not going to punch your brother, Slim," I replied calmly, but Henry was going to punch me, of that there was no doubt. He'd made it a point to ask me to keep my distance and I'd gone against his wishes. All over the hood of my car. Which could now quite possibly be dented and scratched. "But I am going to tell him about us."

"No you're not," she declared, raking her eyes over my near-naked form. I was wearing only my boxer-briefs. The rest of my wet clothing had been tossed in the boot of the car along with hers.

My cock stirred in interest at her attention, and I took my hand off her leg to rub it absentmindedly. "No, I'm not going to tell him right now."

Her brow smoothed with relief before furrowing again. "When?"

"Tomorrow night," I told her, deciding that would be a good a time as any.

Grace pursed her lips, smug. "Jamieson has their contracted show at the Florence Bar tomorrow night. Henry won't be home."

"I know," I replied, taking a right turn onto Ocean Street when the light changed to green. "I'm doing your security."

"No you're not. Jared and Coby are."

"Jared and Coby were," I corrected her. "Now Jared and I are, remember? I texted you about it earlier today."

After a moment of silence, she blurted out, "I'll tell him."

"No." I shook my head at the idea. "I'll handle it."

The closer we got to the city, the busier the roads became, filling up with mad taxi drivers taking their tired, drunken fares home after a Thursday night out. I shifted gears and took the next left on o New South Head Road before glancing quickly at Grace. Seeing the hem of her towel falling precariously close to her nipples, I reached over to tug it up, mindful of peeping passengers.

"Why do you get to handle it?" Grace folded her arms, thwarting my efforts. The towel inched lower. "Because you have a penis?"

"Yes," I conceded, glancing across at the towel with frustration. "Henry is going to be pissed off. You get that, right? I'd prefer him to be pissed off at me rather than you."

Comprehension dawned in her eyes. "Because you think he's going to punch you!" She waved her hands around as she spoke and the towel gave up its fight, falling into her lap.

My cock stood to immediate attention, saluting the sudden display of nudity. I groaned. "Jesus, Slim." With one hand, I grabbed the towel and yanked it up under her chin while I tried to watch the road. "You're going to cause a car accident. And he won't punch me," I lied. I'd tell him just before he went on stage. At least then he would be holding his guitar. It would give him less opportunity to get violent.

"You're right. He won't punch you."

I smiled at Grace reassuringly, pleased that she'd realised I could handle the matter. Henry would get over his fury when I made him understand that I had no intentions of hurting his sister.

"Because you won't be there when I tell him," she added as I navigated the car into the underground car park of my building. The area was well lit. It hadn't always been, but when the elderly couple living in the space below were mugged soon after Jared and Travis had moved in, we'd made some changes to make the area safer.

"That's very noble of you to sacrifice yourself, Slim, but—"

"Oh, it's no trouble—"

"—I said I could handle it. I know how to take a punch or two."

Grace went suddenly quiet as I parked in my assigned space and turned off the ignition. Pocketing the keys, I got out and went around to the passenger door. After opening it, I ducked my head to check on her when she didn't move.

"Grace?"

I crouched down until I was looking up at her bowed head. Her eyes looked suspiciously wet.

Reaching over her lap, I unclipped the seat belt and pulled her towards me. She came easily, wrapping her arms around me. I nuzzled the side of her throat, inhaling the sweet, feminine scent of her skin.

"Baby, what's wrong?"

Grace pulled back, her eyes searching my face. "That day at the beach when you told me your story. It wasn't just your mum, was it? He hit you, too."

My heart raced and my mouth went dry, hating to dredge up old memories.

"He did," I replied, using my thumb to wipe a tear that spilled down her cheek at my admission. "I would act out deliberately, because if his rage was focused on me—"

"Then he would hit you instead of your mum or Kelly," she finished for me, her voice thick with hurt.

I nodded, unable to form words.

Grace drew a deep, shaky breath. "That's why you want to talk to Henry instead of me. You want him to take his anger out on you instead of me."

I stood up, dragging Grace with me. "I won't let him hurt you, Slim," I told her as I shut the car door and locked it.

"But it's okay for him to hurt you?"

Taking her hand in mine, I led her up to the loft. "I told you. I can take it." I punched the security code in and opened the door, motioning her inside. The minute she stepped through the doorway, I spun her around, using my bulk to push her up against the wall and kiss her, making us both forget the entire conversation.

Forcing her mouth open, my tongue swept inside. She grabbed my shoulders, her fingers digging in as she kissed me back, whimpering and rubbing her tongue against mine until I shook from wanting her.

She broke the kiss with a gasp. "We haven't finished our conversation."

"We'll finish it later," I lied and started kissing her again. Damn, she tasted good. I reached for the towel to rip it away.

The sound of a throat being cleared echoed through the dark, quiet loft. We both froze for a minute before I reached over and flicked on the light switch. The living and dining area lit up, highlighting Coby standing in the kitchen. His hair was mussed and like me, he was wearing only a pair of boxer-briefs.

"Well," he drawled with a crooked grin, setting his glass of water on the kitchen bench. "This is awkward."

It wasn't the first time either of us had caught the other with a woman, but this was Grace, and she was barely dressed. I pushed her behind me, but not before Coby caught sight of her distinctive deep red hair and the colourful tattoo that wound over her shoulder and down her arm.

He blanched, his brown eyes growing wide with shock. "Grace?"

Grace peeked over my shoulder, giving him a brief wave and a once over with her eyes. "Hi, Coby."

I glared at her.

She lifted her shoulders in a shrug.

"Shower," I muttered and herded her towards the bathroom. "Excuse us," I threw at Coby as we passed by.

He was still standing in place, stunned, when I shut the door behind us. Letting go of Grace, I reached inside the shower stall and flicked on the taps. I held my hand under the spray while I waited for the water to heat. When steam started rising, I turned around to find Grace with her head stuck in the bathroom cabinet.

"Need something?"

"No." She shook her head. "That's a big-ass box of condoms, Casey." She took the box out, peering inside. "Half empty. You're a busy boy, aren't you?"

I didn't hesitate. "They're Coby's."

Grace laughed. "I don't care about who came before me, Casey." Putting the box back, she shut the cabinet door and faced me.

"Really?" I took a step towards her. "Because I'm crazy jealous of every man who ever came before me." With a quick movement, I flicked the edge of the towel. It dropped to the floor and my mouth went dry as I looked at her. "Of every man who got to see this." I ran my palm down the smooth skin of her belly and over her hip. "And feel this." She closed her eyes at my touch. "Every inch of your body is mine now, Slim. No one else gets to touch you."

"Yours," Grace moaned when my hand slipped between her legs, my fingers gliding over hot, slick skin before finding their way inside her body. She rested her forehead against my shoulder, her breath fanning out across my skin in ragged pants. "Until I leave."

That's what you think, but I'm never going to let you leave.

"Casey?" she breathed. I looked up, unable to hide the possessive gleam I knew was clear in my eyes. "You promised."

My jaw clenched at the reminder and I nodded stiffly. Withdrawing my hand regretfully, I took a step back. "In the shower, Grace. I need to go have a word with Coby."

She grabbed my arm when I turned to leave.

"He won't say anything to Henry, will he? I mean, it's one thing for him to know we're seeing each other, but hearing it from someone else would be so much worse."

"He won't," I assured her.

Leaving Grace to her shower, I headed to my room and plucked out a pair of sweatpants from the dresser. I tugged them on, knowing they were loose enough to cover the erection that wouldn't go down. Picking out my old football jersey with "Daniels" and the number 85 on the back, I took it into the bathroom for Grace to put on when she was finished. Leaving it on the vanity along with a clean towel, I left to face Coby. He was still standing in the kitchen, arms folded while he waited.

"What the fuck, Casey," he growled the second I appeared. "Does Henry know? What am I saying," he muttered, pinching the bridge of his nose with his thumb and forefinger. "Of course he doesn't know or you'd be dead right now."

I leaned my hip against the kitchen bench, waiting for Coby to get a hold of himself.

"Christ." He started pacing. "When I found out about Jared and Evie, it was all I could do not to weigh his body down with cement bricks and drop him out in the middle of the ocean."

I shook my head, remembering that particular day clearly. Coby had gone so far as to hire a deep-sea fishing charter for the day. We'd all gone out under the guise of Coby telling us we were guaranteed to catch a marlin—the holy grail of offshore sport fishing.

With the captain occupied at the wheel and his two-man crew getting equipment from below, Coby had whipped out a gun and ordered Jared to his knees. Everyone froze in place, thinking he'd gone mad. Being the closest, I'd tackled Coby to the floor of the boat. In my effort to control his sudden psychotic break, I cracked my head on the side of the built-in metal fish box, splitting open the skin. Blood oozed down my face in a fountain, spilling out over the deck.

When Mitch got close enough to wrestle the gun away from Coby, he slipped in the blood and would've gone overboard if Jared hadn't grabbed his legs and pulled him back in. With Jared now in arms' reach, Coby slammed the butt of the gun in his face. Jared stumbled back, letting go of his hold on Mitch. Coby used the opportunity to deliver a hard kick to Jared's groin, along with the verbal threat that he would die a slow, torturous death if he went near Evie again.

When the crew returned to the deck, they found it covered in blood, Mitch pointing Coby's gun at Coby, me getting woozily to my feet, Jared finally on his knees, ready to puke as he cupped his groin, and Travis leaning against the side of the boat, casually drinking a beer. We were kicked off the boat and the word was spread. There were few fishing charters that would take us out now, thanks to Coby.

Coby paused his pacing to glare at me. "What are your intentions?"

"What are my…" I looked at him, incredulous. "Why? Are you planning another 'fishing charter?'" I air-quoted.

"No, but if Henry comes to you and tells you he's booked one, don't go," Coby said in all seriousness as he resumed pacing. "I still can't believe those assholes kicked us off their boat," he added, obviously still pissed and holding a grudge over the whole fiasco. "It's not like the gun was loaded or anything."

"You know I heard of a charter up the coast that might take us on," I told him as I yawned and stretched, feeling the physical and emotional drain of the day catching up to me.

Coby's eyes lit up. Despite his original intention being only to scare the living shit out of Jared, he was still hell-bent on catching that marlin he was promised.

"Casey?"

We both turned. Grace stood in the entryway to the kitchen. She looked unbelievably sexy with her skin flushed and damp from her shower. She was wearing the jersey I'd left out for her, but instead of it reaching her knees like I thought, it barely hit mid-thigh because her legs were so damn long. Glancing sideways, I saw Coby was busy noticing that particular fact.

Irritated, I pointed towards my room. "My bedroom's that way, Slim. I'll be there in a minute."

Her eyes narrowed at my rude dismissal.

"Can I get you a drink, Grace?" Coby asked.

She gifted him with a smile and I heard his sudden intake of air. I knew the effect it had on him because it did the same to me.

"No," I told him sharply. "She doesn't want one."

"I think Grace can speak for herself," he replied, returning Grace's smile with one of his own.

"A water would be nice, thanks."

Before Coby could react, I had the fridge door open and a bottle of water in my hand. I held it out to her. She took it, and I knew she must have seen the exhaustion on my face because her eyes softened.

"Thanks, Casey." Stepping close, she cupped my cheek and brushed her lips against mine. "Don't be long," she whispered and disappeared inside my bedroom.

Suddenly I had no idea why I was in the kitchen with Coby. I started to follow when a hand slammed into my chest, halting me. I met Coby's eyes and saw the question in them, knowing instantly what he was asking.

"I'm going to tell him," I said, referring to Henry.

"Good." He gave me a single nod and removed his hand. "She's wearing your jersey."

I raised a brow, wondering why the conversation had suddenly spiralled into talk of fashion. Had we somehow grown vaginas when I wasn't looking?

"You don't let anyone wear your jersey," he expanded. "Ever."

I shrugged the comment off and turned my gaze towards the now closed bedroom door, envisioning Grace spread out on the bed waiting for me. "She looks good in it."

"I noticed."

My eyes narrowed on my roommate. "Stop noticing."

Coby grinned. "You're being an irrational twat. You know that, right?"

"Yes," I agreed, knowing he was right and finding it hard to give a shit. I opened the fridge door. "What's your point?"

He shrugged and in an abrupt change of subject, said, "Frank filled Jared and me in on what happened today."

Janie Berg's face swam in my head when I reached for another bottle of water. I slammed the fridge door shut, the contents rattling noisily behind me as I turned and cracked the lid on the bottle.

I had no response for Coby—no words to justify the number of ways in which I'd failed that sweet little girl.

Coby didn't say anything more. He didn't need to. It was spelled out in his eyes and the weight of his voice. He took hold of my shoulder and squeezed, then walked silently back to his room.

After a quick shower, I walked naked to my room and shut the door behind me. Grace was spread out in the middle of my bed liked I'd imagined, but she wasn't waiting for me. Her body was tangled in the sheets and her head was tipped back on the pillow. A smile spread slowly across my face as I looked down at her. She was sound asleep and snoring like a sailor.

I switched off the lamp on the bedside table and climbed in beside her.

I should leave her alone, I told myself as I unravelled her body from the linen and situated myself between her thighs. She mumbled something in her sleep and slapped at my hands when my fingers trailed lightly up her thighs. Undeterred, I didn't stop until my jersey bunched around her hips, revealing her lack of underwear. Her mutterings turned into soft sighs of pleasure when my hand slipped between her legs and began teasing her.

Pressing my weight gently onto her body, I licked a path up her neck before sucking on the pulse point underneath her jawline.

"You make me ache for you, Grace," I muttered softly against her skin. "Just you and no one else. How do you do that?"

She swatted at me when my tongue tickled her ear, mumbling a very unladylike curse. I laughed silently and set about seeing how close I could bring her to the edge without waking her up.

I soon discovered Grace was a heavy sleeper. Her eyelids barely cracked open when I slid my cock inside her, yet her legs wrapped instinctively around me, taking me deeper. I pressed my forehead against hers and she tilted her head finding my lips in a long, lazy kiss that didn't end until I felt her orgasm. Thrusting harder and faster, I let go and came, burying my head in the crook of Grace's neck until my heart rate slowed down and I was breathing easier.

"Grace?" I whispered.

Nothing.

"Grace?"

My eyes widened with amazement. She was fast asleep again, leaving me to wonder if she ever actual woke. I chuckled as I shifted my weight off her body, envying her ability to switch off so quickly. Rolling over on my back, I saw my phone light up, reminding me I had voicemail from the call I'd rejected earlier. Getting out of bed, I picked it up and left the room, shutting the door silently behind me.

Swiping the screen, I opened the voice message and put the phone to my ear.

"Casey? It's Morgan," I heard as I walked into the living room. "I can't help but notice you're not here. I hope everything is okay. I was waiting to tell you when you got here, but well … it's about that information we talked about. It turns out the coroner on the case is an old friend of my Uncle's." Her words sent my pulse rate skyrocketing. "I have the report, Casey. The coroner's report." My knees buckled beneath me and I sank onto the couch. "We should …"

The rest of her message drowned out over the blood roaring like thunder in my ears. She had the report. The one I'd been trying to get my hands on for ten damn years. My hands shook as I pressed the button to end the voice message.

Sitting back on the couch, I swiped a hand over my face, wondering what the hell I was going to do now.

Chapter Nineteen
GRACE

I woke late in the duplex the next morning after Casey deposited me home at four a.m. The first thing I did was check my appearance in the mirror on the back of the wardrobe door. It was just as I suspected—last night with Casey was written all over my face. Dark smudges had taken up residence beneath my eyes, there was stubble rash on my neck, my hair looked like rats had made a nest in it, and there was a ridiculous grin on my face.

After locating the concealer in my makeup case, I leaned close to the mirror and dabbed it on my face, doing my best to hide the evidence. Deciding to deal with my hair later, I tied it in a knot on the top of my head and left my room.

In an effort to remain nonchalant, I kept my expression cool and my head high as I jogged casually down the stairs.

"Henry's not here."

Mac's words caught me by surprise and I skidded on the bottom step. When I couldn't regain my balance, my legs gave out beneath me and I landed in a heap on the floor, gasping for breath. So much for being cool.

"Oh my God, are you okay?" Evie cried out, rushing over. She grabbed at my arms, trying to lift me.

I swatted her hands away, embarrassed to see Mac, Frog, Cooper, and Jake witness my undignified entrance from their seats at the dining table. A flush climbed my cheeks hearing their laughter. Gaining my feet awkwardly, I turned the attention on Evie.

"You shouldn't be trying to lift me or you'll bring on labour," I reprimanded, knowing full well that was an impossibility. She was only four months along after all.

"You too?" She threw her hands up in disappointment and stomped back to her seat. Picking up her fork, she pointed it at us in a sweeping gesture as she sat down. "You're all driving me daft. I can't do anything—even sleep! I woke in the middle of the night to find Jared staring right at me. It was creepy. I almost had a heart attack."

Mac narrowed calculating eyes on Evie. "We need to start thinking about scaling back Jamieson's commitments. We should cancel that tour."

"No!" she shouted, standing back up. "I'm perfectly fine. By God, I'll have this baby on stage if I have to."

"You're not having the baby on stage," Jake ordered. Standing up from the table, he pushed Evie back down until he had her restrained in her seat. "I won't allow it."

Evie huffed and tossed her fork on the table. "I'm not having the baby on stage."

Cooper looked up from his plate. "But you just said—"

"I think you're right," Frog said to Mac. He glanced meaningfully at Evie's full plate of food. "She's not even eating."

"Because no one is giving me a chance to eat!" she shouted, her eyes getting teary. I limped unobtrusively towards the kitchen, feeling guilty for having thrown her under the bus. In my defence I had no idea it would escalate so quickly.

Jake glared at Mac. "Now you've made her cry."

"I've made her ..." Mac looked at Jake, incredulous. "You can't be serious. You ate all the Doritos during band practice yesterday. Evie fell apart when she found out. I had to hug her while she sobbed for a full ten minutes!"

"Someone call the press," he barked with a voice full of sarcasm. "Mac had to be nice."

Mac's eye started twitching.

"I did not fall apart!" Evie shouted as I got an orange from the fridge. I put it on the chopping board and got a paring knife from the drawer. As I started peeling the piece of fruit, I realised that everyone was eerily quiet all of a sudden. I glanced up and froze. They were all staring at me. Evie's face was smug.

"Uh ... what?"

"I said," Evie enunciated in a loud voice, "how long have you and Casey had a thing for?"

I turned an accusing glare on Mac. "You told them we had a thing?"

"Ah ha!" Evie squealed at the same time Mac said dryly, "No, but you just did."

"Sonofabitch!" Cooper shouted. "They don't even give you a fighting chance." He stood up, bringing his half-empty plate to the kitchen. "I quit, Mac," he said to her on his way past. "I work for Jamieson and Valentine Consulting now. If you have an issue, you can take it up with them." He dumped his plate beside the sink before looking at me with a wounded expression. "Casey? Really? What does he have that I don't?"

"A big gun?" Evie offered before I could speak.

Mac raised her brows at Evie with apparent interest. "Is that so?"

She shrugged and shook her head. "I was making an assumption. I haven't seen it." Both of them turned their gaze my way.

"Why would I have seen his … Oh." I shut my mouth, realising that Mac and Evie were talking in euphemisms. "Casey is very … impressive," I admitted, thinking back to last night and the way he had me spread out over the hood of his car. The man had me in such a haze of lust the Pope could've passed by with a wave from his bulletproof glass contraption and I wouldn't have noticed.

I looked up from the massacre I'd made of my orange. Mac and Evie were nodding at me as though my answer was just as they'd suspected.

"Of course he is," Cooper muttered under his breath from beside me. He stole a piece of orange from the chopping board and popped it in his mouth.

"But it's not just that," I added. "It's the way that he …"

"Looks at you?" Evie finished for me when I trailed off.

"Yes," I breathed.

It was how I imagined it felt getting too close to the sun. I wasn't used to being looked at that way; I was used to being looked at like a tool of trade. My body was hired to sell products or as an accessory for publicised events. It wasn't exactly a hardship. I got to travel extensively and was paid ridiculous amounts of money for it, but after years of having my appearance scrutinised and criticised for all manner of imperfections I'd become detached.

"How did you know?" I asked Evie.

Cooper leaned over me, grabbing for another piece of orange. Using the knife, I scraped the fruit his way. He popped more in his already full mouth and winked at me in thanks.

Evie picked up her abandoned fork off the table and began stabbing at her food. "It's the same way Jared looks at me," she said, and shoved an enormous pile of bacon in her mouth.

I shook my head at the comparison. The love in Jared's eyes when he looked at Evie was bright enough to hurt your eyes. Casey looked at me like a man in lust, not love, and it would be foolish to confuse the two.

"You're his wife," I reminded her, as if she'd somehow forgotten that important fact. "He's supposed to look at you that way."

Cooper plucked another piece of orange from the board. "Does Henry know?" he asked as he chewed.

"Of course he doesn't know," Mac told him as Frog stood from the table and brought his own plate to the kitchen. "Otherwise, Casey would be dead, wouldn't he?"

"And none of you are going to tell him either," I added, pointing at them all with the paring knife. Satisfied my warning was heard, I returned to the fridge and retrieved another orange.

"Henry won't kill him," Evie said and smiled reassuringly as I started peeling the skin away. "He's not violent like that. I would know. He's my best friend."

"He will," Frog contradicted with a nod. Putting his plate down next to the sink, he leaned against the kitchen bench, his expression grave. "Henry could be the Dalai freaking Lama and he'd still go all Kill Bill on Casey's ass. When it comes to some dude's little sister, it's like flicking a switch. They just blow like some ticking time bomb." I flinched when he made the sound of an explosion, spreading his hands wide to emphasise his point. Turning to Jake, he said, "Remember the fishing charter incident with Coby and Jared?"

Evie put down her fork and frowned at Frog. "What fishing charter incident?"

I caught Jake shaking his head at Frog in a quick motion as I brought my bowl to the dining table. When I sat down, his eyes landed on my orange with a frown. I looked down at the bowl, wondering if an insect had landed on it without my knowledge.

"What?" I asked, seeing it pest free.

His response was to pick up his own plate, lean over the table and scrape half the contents over the top of my orange.

"Thanks," I muttered, staring down at the greasy pile of bacon now covering my piece of fruit.

"No problem," he replied. Sitting back down, he went back to reading the magazine spread out in front of him.

"What fishing charter incident?" Evie repeated, her voice gaining volume.

"Once upon a time …" Frog began, as though recounting a fairy tale. We all paused to listen. "… Five men went to sea with the daring ambition to hook and capture a marlin, the elusive fish of the sea. But never in their wildest dreams could they have imagined the depths of treacherous intent brewing in one of their own." Frog narrowed his eyes and lowered his voice to a raspy hush. "You see, the fishing expedition was a ruse. The real plan was for five of them to head out to sea, and only four to return."

"He didn't!" Evie shouted, her face flush with anger. She'd obviously reached the conclusion of the story before it had barely begun.

By the time Frog finished the alarming tale, her face looked red enough to catch fire. It made me realise how imperative it was for me to talk to Henry before Casey got anywhere near him. Evie abandoned her plate in favour of her phone, stabbing at the screen furiously as she dialled.

"Does Henry own a gun?" Cooper asked Mac.

"No." She shook her head emphatically. I felt a measure of relief until she followed it with, "But he knows where I keep mine."

Jake glared at Mac. "You told me you didn't have it anymore."

"Yeah, well, I lied," she told him with a smirk.

"That's not all you lied about, is it?" There was enough anger underneath Jake's voice that I wasn't fooled by the soft tone. I stopped mid-chew and glanced at Mac. Her face had paled considerably, suggesting she wasn't fooled either.

"Excuse me," she muttered as she stood from the table. "Some of us have work to do."

My phone beeped from the kitchen as Mac walked away. Cooper picked it up and brought it over. Putting down my bacon-flavoured piece of orange, I swiped the screen, thanking him as I read the message.

Don't forget you promised to let me handle Henry.

"Damn the man," I mumbled under my breath. Casey's ears must have been burning.

"Damn who?" Henry called out as he walked through the front door with sweat dripping down his face. He was wearing running shorts and holding two dog leashes in his hand. On the end of one was Mitsy and on the end of the other was Evie's little dachshund, Peter.

"Goddamn bat ears," I muttered as he leaned over and unclipped the leashes from their halters. Both dogs were panting and snapping at each other, not caring that Henry was caught in the middle. My heart swelled at his thoughtfulness in caring for my rabid pet. There was no street cred in jogging outdoors with a psychotic white ball of fluff and a sausage dog.

"I heard that too," he said, using his forearm to wipe the sweat away from his brow.

I fired a quick message back to Casey as Henry made his way into the kitchen and Mitsy to my side. You made me promise under duress. That means it doesn't count.

Keeping half an eye on Jake to make sure he wasn't watching, I waved a piece of bacon to Mitsy under the table. His teeth bit into my skin as he snatched it from my fingers. I hid the wince.

"I saw that," Jake told me, his eyes never straying from the magazine in front of him.

"Of course you did." I exhaled in a long, exaggerated sigh and he rolled his eyes.

Henry was getting a bottle of water from the fridge when Casey's reply came through.

Duress? Is that what they're calling sex these days?

Yes, I responded.

I bit back a smile at his next message.

Fine. We should have duress tonight, and lots of it.

Three times hadn't worn him out? I knew he'd barely slept all night. He was worried about the little girl.

Any word on Janie?

His response was immediate. She made it through the night. Doctors say she's gonna pull through.

I sighed with relief. Good news.

The best.

"Grace, can I talk to you for a minute?" Henry asked as I hit send. Everyone froze at the serious tone and I thought furiously for a quick second. I might have promised Casey I'd let him tell Henry—even though the promise was made under duress and shouldn't count—but there wasn't much Casey could do if Henry found out all on his own, could he?

"Privately?" he added to the silent room.

"Of course," I murmured, feeling a sense of impending doom wash over me.

It was one thing to boast I was going to tell my brother, but actually doing it was something I hadn't fully considered. I wouldn't have been so anxious if everyone had kept their opinions to themselves, but there appeared to be an overwhelming consensus that Henry was going to bathe himself in Casey's blood. I didn't like to doubt my brother's capabilities. Henry was certainly tall and muscular and capable of handling himself, but Casey was, well … Casey.

Henry turned and started for the stairs. I abandoned my breakfast and followed him, feeling everyone's eyes watch our retreat. Mitsy brought up the rear of the procession, making sure his growl of contempt encompassed the room as he trotted up the stairs behind us.

After following Henry into my room, he spun around and faced me. I noticed with some surprise that the expected anger wasn't there. Maybe Henry hadn't found out like I thought.

"Grace," he began, folding his arms.

"Let me speak first," I blurted out.

Henry shrugged. "Okay."

I began to pace, trying to think of how I could tell Henry about Casey without actually breaking my promise. Flat out telling him was off the table but at the least I could be proactive about the situation. Perhaps I could somehow bamboozle him.

I stopped pacing and looked at my brother. "Sometimes things just happen whether you want them to or not."

"Uh … okay," he agreed.

"So you agree?"

"Sure. I guess." He shrugged again, his blue eyes clouding with confusion over my sudden line of questioning.

I resumed pacing. "So if something happened that you didn't want to happen, you would be suitably calm and non-violent and not punch anyone in the face, because you understood that those things just happened, right?"

I paused and looked at him again, waiting for an answer.

Henry narrowed his eyes on my face. "What happened, Grace?"

I folded my arms and narrowed my eyes in return. "Answer the question."

"Why do I feel like I'm being led into a verbal trap?"

"Don't be ridiculous," I lied as I tried to form an appropriate response. I walked over to the bed and sat on it, tucking one leg underneath me. "I just want to clarify you aren't the type of person to go around punching people who do things you don't like. Take Jake for instance."

"Jake?" he echoed.

"Yes, Jake. This morning he dumped bacon all over my orange. That would constitute him doing something I didn't want him to do, right?" I tried not to wince at the ridiculous example. It was hardly the same thing, but I was thinking on the fly and had to roll with it. "I have to watch my weight or risk losing work, Henry," I continued before he could reply. "That means I can't go around eating bacon whenever I please, no matter how much I want to."

Henry's brows rose slowly as I spoke until they reached his hairline. "What's your point, Grace?"

"My point is that I didn't punch him."

Silence reigned for a moment as Henry stared. Was he waiting for me to say something else? I calmly folded my hands in my lap. "What is it you wish to talk about, Henry?"

"I have no idea now," he muttered.

"Well, okay then." I stood up from the bed and he gripped my shoulder, pushing me back down before I got anywhere.

"I think you should stay," he said.

I looked about the room, wondering why he would want me to stay. Did he see through the concealer to the dark smudges under my eyes? Granted, a nap would be nice, but we had a show tonight. "There's no time to sleep today. We have a set list to prepare," I reminded him.

"I meant stay here. In Sydney. Permanently." He let go of my shoulder and stepped back. "That's what I wanted to talk to you about."

"Wow, Henry, that's …" Unexpected? Nice? A really bad idea? This break from my everyday life had shown me just how lonely I really was. I loved that I couldn't get a moment's peace living here. I loved the constant bickering. I loved that Mac bossed me around. I loved how Frog and Cooper entertained me with their stories until I couldn't breathe from laughing. I loved the way Jake tried to take care of me while pretending not to. I loved having my big brother back in my life, but not enough to get him, or any of them for that matter, caught up in my problems. "That's really nice, but … I can't."

Hurt and disappointment clouded Henry's eyes. "Why not?" he asked, coming to sit beside me on the bed. "You can do your job better here than in Melbourne, can't you? I mean, you're signed with an international agency, but I read the other day that the majority of fashion designers are based here. It would make sense for you to move."

"Where did you read that?"

Henry's tanned skin flushed slightly. "In one of Mac's fashion magazines," he admitted.

My brows flew up. "You're reading Vogue now?"

He grabbed hold of my hand and got to his feet, pulling me with him. After leading me into his room, he flung open his wardrobe and took a bulky folder from the shelves. He held it out expectantly.

"What's this?"

"It's my sister's life," he said simply.

Curious, I took the folder and opened the first page. Staring back at me was a fourteen-year old Grace from the cover of a magazine. Not just any cover, but my first, I realised as I sank to the edge of his bed. It was with Dolly, a magazine targeted to young teenage girls. My hair was mousy brown back then and my freckled nose more prominent. I was wearing a white lace top, lilac jeans, and dangly earrings so alarmingly huge they could've anchored a small boat. I ran my eye over the cover's captions—"The Brave Girl's Guide to Life" sat in bold font above "Be his best kiss EVER!" To the left read "What is your skin trying to tell you?" and beneath that "Mind tricks to get the guy EVERY girl wants!"

I looked up at him, my eyes wide with surprise. This was why my brother was reading Mac's fashion magazines. "I can't believe you kept all these." Returning my attention to the folder, I flipped the page over, followed by another, and another, until I'd silently made my way through the entire book full of clippings from my career. It was staggering to see the transformation from mousy brown tomboy to the unconventional redhead I was today. My look had an edge and I played it up by getting the wild, colourful tattoo on my arm and shoulder. My agent was pissed about that and admittedly I hadn't been booked for bridal wear since, but it had scored me the coveted contract with the Hendrix label. Their latest campaign was the last picture in Henry's folder.

I'd been photographed by John on the back of a moving Harley Davidson, clutching hold of a real life hard-core biker named Bingo as I grinned at the camera. Bingo was immense and sported a beard so impressive he could've braided it. At the end of the three-day shoot, Bingo and his biker friends, who were photographed riding with us, hosted a bonfire on our behalf. Hendrix must have paid them a whopping sum for their time because I sat there with my water, watching as they guzzled back full bottles of rum before tossing the remaining contents in the fire. They hollered like excited cavemen discovering fire as the flames blew up wildly. The whole affair escalated quickly when sparks flew out and caught hold of Bingo's beard. Reacting on instinct, I tossed my drink in his face, drenching his impressive beard and leather vest. He stared at me, open-mouthed, and before I could apologise, John tackled me into his car. After slamming the door behind me, he flung his equipment on the backseat with reckless abandon and the wheels spun as we skidded away. Unfortunately, John's driving skills left much to be desired. We took out three bikes in our haste to leave. I could only pray I never encountered Bingo ever again or I'd be a dead woman walking.

The muscle in Henry's jaw ticked as I recounted the story. "No more biker photo shoots," he ordered.

"Getting that contract was a big deal. A really big deal. Do you know how much I was paid?"

"How much?"

He blanched when I told him the sum. "What?"

I told him again.

He shook his head. "I don't care if it pays ten dollars or ten million. No sum is worth your life, Gracie Bean."

While his words were heartwarming, they were also ridiculous. "I'm sure Bingo wouldn't have hurt me," I lied. Saving his beloved facial hair from a fiery death didn't negate taking out a biker's ride in a hail of spinning wheels and gravel.

Henry shook his head. "Bikers are wild and unpredictable. Add an unlimited supply of rum to the mix and you've got trouble. If …"

I tuned his lecture out and focused on smoothing the pages in the folder before closing it neatly. Knowing Henry had followed my career made me realise I hadn't been as alone as I'd thought. He really did care. Maybe I should have reached out to him more than I did. I placed the folder on my lap and looked at him.

"Thank you," I said, my soft words interrupting his rant.

Henry paused. "What for?"

I gave him back the folder. "For being more of a brother than I realised you were."

He put the folder down and pulled me off the bed and into his arms, squeezing me hard. "Thank you, Grace. For dropping everything to help us out. I'm sorry I said you chose your career over your family." Taking hold of my shoulders, he pushed me back until he was looking me in the face. "I was angry over losing you. I missed you."

I pressed my lips together. "I missed you too."

Henry let go of my shoulders and picked up the folder. "Does that mean you'll stay?" he asked, placing it back on the shelf in his wardrobe.

"I'll think about it," I hedged.

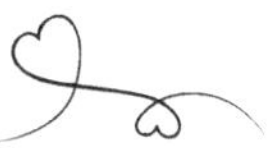

We spent the rest of the day tinkering with equipment and going over last minute song changes. The afternoon passed by and before I knew it, we were arriving at the Florence Bar for our Friday evening show.

The streets were bursting with people waiting to get inside. We bypassed them all, driving through the gates that led to the back entrance. Casey and Jared were there waiting for us. My pulse thumped at the sight of him. He was wearing their standard security uniform of black pants and snug black tee shirts. Bold white lettering on the back declared him Jamieson Security. His face was all hard angles and flat eyes, as though he'd put his "security face" on.

Despite the venue providing their own manpower, Casey and Jared took charge. Jared sprang forward and opened the car door, leading us swiftly towards Casey.

I watched for a reaction after making an effort with my appearance—choosing to wear the high-waisted black leather hotpants Mac had salivated over in my suitcase. They were decorated with three front buckles and silver studs around the sides. Into the pants, I tucked a white tee shirt with rolled up sleeves and my black boots. John called it my "greaser" look, but there was nothing greasy about it. It was supposed to be cool and rock chick sexy and get Casey's attention.

It didn't.

Casey's eyes passed over me like I was yesterday's news. I deflated when he turned, giving me his back as he led us directly to the dressing room. A five-man crew had come before us and set up our equipment on stage, so once we were all inside, he left with Mac and Quinn to do the stage check, leaving Jared with us.

"Long gone are the days of doing it ourselves. We're too big for that now," Frog boasted as he stretched out on the dusky red couch. It was vintage, with clawed feet and button leather. The whole room was styled similarly; gilded mirrors decorated the walls and black shagpile rugs covered the floorboards. The bar was one of Sydney's most upscale music venues and it showed.

Cooper leaned over from behind the couch and punched Frog in the gut.

"Oomph." Frog clutched his stomach and rolled inwards. "What was that for?"

"In one of those magazine articles, the interviewer asked how you were coping with your 'sudden fame,'" Cooper air-quoted, "and you said you had plenty of friends to keep you grounded."

"Yeah?" Frogs brows flew up. "So what?"

Cooper grinned. "That was me keeping you grounded."

After what felt like an eternity of bickering, the dressing room door opened to reveal Casey. Knowing he wanted to talk to Henry before the show kicked my nerves into gear. His eyes swept the room, passing right over Henry before locking on mine. "Grace." I blinked in surprise. "Mac needs you for a minute."

"That was subtle," Cooper muttered under his breath from beside me when I got up to leave.

Casey closed the door behind us. Without saying a word, he turned down the well-lit hallway. Curious, I followed him. He led me out towards the stage where Mac stood expectantly. I smothered the disappointment. We were both working after all. It wasn't like we could go for it in some random closet.

"Grace, your bass amp sounds patchy. I don't know what happened because it sounded fine before we left," she told me. Her eyes narrowed on the crew as if they'd had something to do with it. They all began to look busy when I stepped up on the stage. I picked up the plugged-in guitar and fingered the strings quickly, wincing at the distorted sound. "Someone's on the way with a spare," she shouted, her loud voice competing with the noise of the bass, "but you're going to need to check the tuning before the rest of the band comes on stage. Are you cool with that or do you want Frog to do it?"

"I'm cool with that." I plucked at the strings a bit more and then rested the guitar against the amp. "Just let me know when you need me."

She gave me a thumbs-up. When I turned to leave, Casey called out, "Wait up, Grace." I paused. "I go first," he ordered.

I go first? After a night of hot sex, that was all I got? Obviously, because he was already walking away.

With a shrug, I followed behind as he headed back to the dressing room. Hurt at being ignored, I remained silent and kept my eyes focused on the lettering of his shirt. They strayed regardless, trailing across his broad, muscular shoulders and down to the firm, round ass that flexed enticingly as he walked. I almost moaned at the memory of how that ass felt beneath my hands when he thrust himself inside me last night.

"Wha—" I was so caught up in staring at his backside that when he grabbed my hand and veered us off course I stumbled. Suddenly we were going left when we were supposed to go right. "Casey?"

"Shhh," I was told.

Heavy bass began vibrating off the walls. The Florence Bar had opened the doors to the public. That meant whatever Casey had planned, we had no time for it.

We turned another corner when he spun around and pushed my back against the wall. The beat pounded into me from one side, his body rubbing me from the other.

"I thought you were ignoring me."

"This is me ignoring you?" He thrust his hips, letting me feel the hard heat of his erection against my belly. "I'm trying to do my job and I have to do it with you looking like this? Thanks for that."

A slow smile overtook my face. "My pleasure."

"Well, now you've got my attention," Casey said with a smirk, "what are you going to do with it?"

That was a challenge I wasn't backing down from. I grabbed his shirt in my fist and dragged him closer. "I'm going to kiss you," I told him.

He slipped a warm palm around the back of my neck and brought his lips to mine, hovering with tantalising invitation but not quite touching. "Beg me."

I pushed up against his erection, rocking my hips. "Is that how you want to play it? Because I think that maybe you should be begging me."

Casey grinned and slid his other hand beneath my shirt. He spread his fingers wide and trailed them upwards until my breast filled his palm. "Did I hurt your feelings earlier, Slim?"

Casey thumbed my nipple over the lace of my bra. It peaked from his touch and shot hot, pulsing sparks between my legs.

"Yes," I hissed.

The fire in his eyes softened at my admission. I dragged in a breath at the tender affection. "Damn you, Grace," he breathed against my lips. "Beg me to kiss you."

"No." I rocked into him again. He responded by pinching my nipple until I rode the edge somewhere between pleasure and pain. I gave in.

"Please, Casey," I begged.

It was all I could manage to say but it must've been enough because suddenly his mouth was on mine. I wrapped my arms around his neck, holding on for the ride. He shoved me against the wall, grinding his hips, his hot, hungry tongue rubbing against mine until I gasped for breath.

He broke off, panting as his gaze dropped to my hotpants. He ran his hands over the pointed metal studs. "I'd spank you for wearing these if they weren't so sharp. They're so fucking sexy."

Leaning up, I took his earlobe in my mouth and sucked on it. "I wore them for you."

He groaned as I nibbled and licked along his ear. "Don't ever wear them again when I'm working. I've been rock hard from the moment you stepped out of the goddamn car." He rubbed his cock between my thighs to emphasise his point. "I would've given us away if I'd looked at you for a second longer."

"Everyone knows about us anyway."

"They do?"

"Well, everyone except Henry. I don't think we've been as stealthy as we thought."

"I'm good with everyone knowing. I'll talk to Henry tonight and then it's no more hiding for us."

His lips were back on mine before I could tell him that we would be telling Henry tonight.

"Casey?"

We broke apart at the voice, Casey muttering a curse under his breath as he spun around. Over his shoulder, I glimpsed a woman watching us with arms folded and brows arched. He took a step backwards, pressing me against the wall behind him. I peeked over him at the woman watching us with a calculated expression.

"Morgan," he replied. "What are you doing here?"

"We seem to keep missing each other. When I spoke to Mitch this afternoon, he said you were working here tonight. So here I am."

Casey turned back around. "Grace. Go back to the dressing room. I'll be there in a minute, okay?"

My eyes went back to the woman. Hazel eyes speared me with enough venom for me to recognise the look. It was the same look Selena used to give me when Dalton and I were together.

Was she an ex-girlfriend? I gave her an assessing gaze. Her red dress was three seasons ago. It would have looked nice if she wasn't wearing it a size too small. My gaze fell to the red stilettos on her feet. They were nice shoes, I'd give her that, but they were too much for the dress. She should have gone with pale pointed slingbacks in nude. Dismissing her fashion blunder, I returned my gaze to Casey's pleading eyes.

Knowing I was staking my claim and unable to stop myself, I put my palms on Casey's chest. With Morgan watching, I took his bottom lip between my teeth and bit gently before kissing it better.

When I was done, I said softly, "Okay."

"Thank you," he mouthed.

A quick glance at Morgan confirmed her triumphant expression at seeing me walk away. I blanked my features carefully, not allowing her to see the sudden burst of fury. Instead, I winked, tamping down on the satisfaction when the gesture threw her.

"Nice shoes," I murmured as I passed by her to reach the dressing room. "Enjoy your minute."

Chapter Twenty
CASEY

"So," Morgan spoke, dragging my attention from the door Grace just disappeared behind. She took a step towards me and I was surprised she could move her dress was that tight. It strangled her tits until they popped out the top, as though gasping for air. She folded her arms, thrusting them to greater heights. "That was Grace."

My eyes narrowed at the sly calculation on her face. "What do you know about Grace?"

Morgan laughed before answering me. "I'm a detective, Casey. Did you forget that little fact?"

"You've been stalking me?" My entire body tensed. I realised then that I had no clue who this woman really was.

"Stalking?" Morgan cocked her head. "That's a weighty accusation. Have I left notes on your car? Harassed you with phone calls? Turned up at your place of work?" She took another step forward and ran her finger down my chest until it hooked in my belt buckle. "Tell me, Casey … Do you feel threatened in any way?"

I unlatched her fingers from my belt. The flare of annoyance in her eyes told me she didn't like that. "We had a good time once, Morgan. I think we should leave it at that."

"I don't."

"You don't?" I folded my arms, my glare turning feral. "What do you want,

Morgan?"

"I want you to forget about Grace," she snapped, "but I think the bigger question is what do you want, Casey? Oh wait!" She snapped her fingers and grinned. "You want that report I have at home, lying between the sheets of my bed, right where you should be." She bit her lip and I knew she was remembering the first night we fucked. When I'd handed her a drink at the bar, I leaned in and spoke in her ear telling her that lip she was biting down on looked tasty and would she mind if I took a bite too. Half an hour later she was in my bed. Now I was left wondering why I'd ever thought fucking her was a good idea. Nothing was worth this big bunch of crazy disguised in a red dress.

"What do you think, Casey? Shall we do a trade?"

"What do I think?" I think if she'd asked me a few weeks ago I wouldn't have hesitated. I would've slammed her against the wall, yanked up her dress, and shoved my cock inside her—giving her just what she was asking for. Transaction complete. See you the fuck later.

But that was before Grace.

"I think, Morgan, that you shouldn't be back here." Taking hold of her shoulders, I spun her around and led her out past the stage to the main room. The area was already at capacity—all seats were taken and the bar was crowded three feet deep with loud partygoers waiting on Jamieson to take the stage. A DJ sat in the booth, pumping "Do I wanna know" by the Arctic Monkeys while bodies ground together on the dance floor.

"I also think," I yelled over the noise, leaning in close so Morgan could hear, "that there's plenty of available cock in this room." I looked pointedly at her tits. "If that's what you're looking for, then you should have no trouble finding one."

She pressed close and rubbed those tits against my body. "I don't want any of the available cock in this room. I want yours."

"Mine's not available anymore." I took a step back and almost knocked someone to the ground. Twisting sideways, I steadied the girl behind me with a quick apology.

"Then I guess you don't want that report after all."

"Are you serious? You really want my cock that bad? Would it get you off knowing the whole time I was fucking you, it wasn't you I was thinking about but some goddamn piece of paper?"

"I like your cock. No one fucks the way you do, Casey—hard and rough, just the way I like it." Morgan went to place a hand on my chest, an eager smile playing about her pretty, painted lips.

I snatched her wrist before she could touch me. She hissed, biting her lip and I knew she was getting off on the roughness of my actions. I shoved her hand away. "Give me the damn report, Morgan."

Her eyes narrowed. "You've told me what you think. You want to know what I think?"

I didn't, but I knew I was going to hear it anyway.

Morgan scanned the room before she leaned in, placing that damn hand on my chest before I could stop her again. "I think you're nothing but a whore," she breathed in my ear. I froze. "I've been watching you long before Mitch introduced us. Drinking yourself into a stupor almost every weekend. Taking home a different woman every single time. None of them really want you—they just want to fuck a hot, muscled body with a pretty face. They get up the next morning and go back to their lives—careers, husbands, boyfriends, loving families—and they forget you exist. None of them want to keep you because you have broken, used-up whore written all over your face. Grace is no different. She'll go back to her life and forget you too."

I fought to keep my face blank. I didn't want Morgan to see how the words hit home. None more so than Grace going back to her life as though I never existed. "You're wrong, Morgan." I shook my head. "Grace isn't leaving."

She isn't going back to her life, because her life is with me. She just doesn't know it yet.

"Oh, but I'm not. You see, her return flight is already arranged. She booked the ticket yesterday morning."

Yesterday morning?

After being in my bed all night, her naked body stretched over mine like a lazy cat and her head resting over the steady thump of my heart, my first instinct had been to damn the consequences and keep her there. Hers had been to book a flight home?

Fuck you, Grace.

"Don't you see?" Morgan placed a hand on my crotch and rubbed. Leaning in, she licked a path up my neck until she reached my ear. "Grace doesn't want you either. But I do."

Lips curled with distaste, I grabbed a fistful of hair and yanked her head back, detaching her mouth from my body. Morgan laughed, her gaze directed over my shoulder.

I turned, following her gaze, and cursed.

Grace was there on the stage and she was watching us. Her lips were pressed together, trying to hide the hurt, but I could see it in her eyes anyway.

Jake stood beside her, veins bulging from the hands fisted by his sides. Dismissing me with a look of contempt, Jake took hold of Grace. Cupping her face with his palms, he pressed his forehead against hers. It forced her eyes to shift from mine to his. Then he said something I had no hope in hell of hearing.

I shoved Morgan away—hard. "Don't touch me again."

She stumbled and a man nearby threw me a filthy look as he helped steady her. When she gained her balance, she looked at me, her lips pressed flat in a sneer. "The apple doesn't fall far from the tree, does it?"

"What's that supposed to mean?"

"That you're just like your loser father."

"What do you know about my father?"

She raised her brows, triumphant. "It's all in the report."

With the band getting ready to play, the DJ's music died off so I didn't need to shout my next words. "I don't know what your game is, Morgan, but you need to stop. You want the truth? Yeah, I used you, and believe me, I'm feeling real fucking sorry about that now, but you need to stop watching me and stop watching Grace. Not only is it against the law, it's creepy."

"Feeling real fucking sorry?" she echoed with an angry flare in her eyes. "Believe me, you'll be sorry."

"Is that a threat?"

"You can take it any way you want to."

I jabbed my finger towards the entrance of the bar, furious. "Leave. Right now. I'll get the damn report some other way."

Morgan shrugged and spun around. Satisfied to see her disappear in the direction of the exit, I dragged in a deep breath of air that didn't calm me one bit.

There was more than one pair of pissed off eyes to greet me when I reached the side of the stage. I ignored them. The only pair I cared about right then were the ones that refused to look at me.

"You didn't just piss in one bowl of Cocoa Pops this morning, did you? You pissed in everyone's," Jared said from beside me.

I folded my arms and grunted, no doubt in my mind I was public enemy number one tonight. "Seems so."

"You want to talk about it?"

"No."

My eyes scanned the crowd as Jake kicked in with the drums, the loud, steady thump getting everyone's attention. Relieved that I couldn't see Morgan amongst them, I turned my eyes back to Grace. It was hard to look away, even when she was pissed at me. Her outfit was pure sex, and the way she plucked those guitar strings so confidently, her hair falling in her eyes, made her downright sinful. I dragged my eyes away and focused more on doing my job.

"You and Grace, huh?"

I raised my brows at Jared questioningly.

He shrugged and grinned. "I'm not blind. Does Henry know?"

"What do you think?"

His grin widened. "I'm gonna say no."

"Let me guess," I said, my tone sarcastic, "because I'm not dead?"

Jared chuckled. "Not yet anyway."

A heated argument off to the side of the crowd drew our attention. A quick check showed one of the Florence Bar's security guys already heading their way. Satisfied the matter was being handled, I turned back to Jared. "You think it's funny, do you?"

Amusement flashed in his eyes. "Yeah, I do."

"I took five stitches to the head for you, asshole," I growled in reference to the fishing charter incident.

"And so you should, because you're one of my best friends, asshole. And when the time comes, which will probably be sooner rather than later with the way you were just eye-fucking Grace, I'll have your back."

My response was another grunt and we fell into companionable silence until the last note by Evie rang out into the captivated crowd. Wolf whistles, wild shouts, and heavy stomping followed the band off the stage. We rushed them to the dressing room, Jared leading the way and me bringing up the rear. Jake and Cooper closed ranks around Grace when we reached the dressing room, not letting me close.

"Grace." My voice was firm as it rang out over everyone, including Henry. Her eyes cut to mine, wide with surprise that I would call her out in front of her brother. "A word, please?" I nodded at the door, indicating I wanted that word outside the dressing room.

Jake stood up, his body tense. "You don't get shit, Daniels."

The room fell silent and I folded my arms, keeping my cool. "That's not for you to decide, Romero."

Henry sat his guitar down and looked between the both of us. "What the hell is going on?" He stood up next to Jake, brows drawn with tension.

Grace pushed her way between the middle of the wall they created in front of her.

"Grace," Jake muttered and went to push her back.

"No." Grace swatted his hands away and gave me her attention. "I stood out on that stage and told myself that it shouldn't hurt, that I shouldn't be pissed, and I sure as fuck shouldn't care…" she took a step forward until she was in my space "…because I have no right to feel that way. I'm leaving and you have your own life to do whatever you want with. But you know what? It hurts anyway. Not just because I thought better of you, but because I'm tired of being a chump. Being here in Sydney was a chance to put all that crap behind me, but now I'm getting it from you." Her voice got louder as she spoke until she was shouting at me, her eyes welling with tears. "Damn you for making me feel that way all over again! It fucking hurts!"

"Grace," I whispered, my voice gruff as I wiped away a tear that spilled down her cheek. "I'm sorry."

Grace slapped at my hand. "You want a word?" she growled.

Grabbing my shoulders with both hands, Grace yanked me towards her and crushed her mouth on mine in the most wild and aggressive kiss of my life. I felt it all—anger, betrayal, and underlying arousal. I gave it back just as hard, bruising her lips, my cock filling rapidly in my pants. She made me forget there was anyone else in the room. I was ready to find the nearest wall to shove her against when she pulled away. Then without warning, she slammed her knee in my groin.

"Arrghh fuck!" I bit out, stars exploding behind my eyes. I sucked in a breath, trying to fight past the pain and not puke.

"There's your word, asshole!" Grace shouted.

I staggered when she dug her hand inside the pocket of my pants. She yanked it back out, bringing with it the sound of jangling keys.

"Whatever we had is done," she bit out, brushing swiftly past me as I hunched over against the wall.

"You're dead," was Henry's ominous warning before he cocked back a fist. I waited for the hit, prepared to take it, when Jared stepped in front of me. Henry's eyes widened for a split second, but it was too late to stop the momentum.

There was a grunt of pain and a muttered curse when Jared took the fist meant for me. It wasn't that hard. Henry had managed to slow it down, but Jared still swayed a little. "Don't just stand there like a stunned twat," he barked with a hand held to his jaw. "Go after her."

"Shit." I threw an apologetic look his way and ran for the door.

"Don't think I won't be digging your grave while your gone, Casey!" Henry shouted after me.

I rounded the car park out the back in time to see Grace sitting in the driver's seat of my car. She was frantically thumbing through the keys to find the right one.

"Grace!" I yelled, running towards her.

She glanced my way quickly before her eyes returned to the task. Holding up the right key in her hand, she slotted it in the ignition and turned it, chanting, "Come on, come on," as the engine kicked over effortlessly.

The loud, throaty purr echoed through the dark night like hot sex. Taking no time to admire the erotic sound, I ran for the passenger door just as she thrust my baby into gear.

"Back off, Casey!" she shouted when I opened it. "I'm taking your Marjorie for a wild ride and you're not invited!"

"Get out of the car, Grace!"

"Fuck. You." Her jaw locked and her foot hovered over the accelerator ominously.

My eyes narrowed. "Don't you dare!"

She planted her foot down. Hard. I had just enough time to slide inside the car before she careened Marjorie out of the car park like she was unleashing a wild animal. I slammed the door shut before it was ripped off.

"Grace," I panted, still catching my breath. "Pull over."

"Were you sleeping with that woman with the horrible shoes at the same time as me?"

"Horrible shoes?" I echoed.

"They don't match her outfit," Grace muttered. After a beat of silence, she slammed a fist against the steering wheel. "Answer me!"

"No, Grace. I wasn't sleeping with her at the same time I was with you. Or anyone else," I added before she could ask that too. "Now pull over," I ordered as she fishtailed my baby around a left turn.

She glanced sideways as we dashed through an orange light, her expression both pissed and sceptical and I knew she didn't believe me. "I saw her in the bar, Casey. She was attached to you like a barnacle."

"Believe me, I know," I muttered under my breath.

"You had your hand all fisted in her horrible hair!"

"Her horrible hair?"

"Yes, horrible. It needs a protein treatment. It's all dried out from God knows how many bad dye jobs she's killed it with."

"I don't give a shit about Morgan's hair, Slim."

"Well it's obvious she doesn't give a proper shit about it either, isn't it?"

"Jesus fucking …" I trailed off, shaking my head. Grace careened through another orange light. "At least slow down if you're not going to pull over."

"Is she an ex-girlfriend, Casey? God. You know what? Why do I even care? You and I are only temporary so it's not supposed to hurt like this."

"No. She's not. I slept with her once before I met you. And it hurts because this is more than temporary."

"What?" Grace took her eyes off the road to scowl at me. "No it's not."

"Grace," I growled warningly, jerking my chin at the road. The car lurched when she gave her attention back to the road. "Just pull over. I'll drive us back to the loft and we can talk about this properly."

"No. Let's just clear the air now."

Fine. If hearing the shitty details was what it took to make her pull over then I'd give them to her. "I slept with Morgan. I thought she might be able to help me with information on a case. Turns out she can, but she won't give it to me."

"What, unless you sleep with her again?" Grace took her eyes off the road again to shoot me a look of disbelief. "Is that how you operate over there? You fuck people for information?"

"Grace!" I barked. "Watch the road." Her focus returned to the random street we were driving down. "And no, that's not how we operate. This case … it's important."

"I see," she muttered, her tone telling me didn't see at all. But why would she? It wasn't like I'd been an open book. "What case?"

I didn't answer. I didn't want to open that book. At least not right now. It was hardly the time or the place.

"Casey?" She frowned across at me as we flew through the green light at an intersection. "What case?"

My eyes widened, horror punching through me when I saw the headlights bearing down on us. The car was heading right for Grace and it wasn't deviating. "Grace! Look out!"

She screamed and I grabbed for the wheel. But the warning came too late, and the car wasn't just coming at us too damn fast, it wasn't slowing down. At all.

The sound of impact was no less than what I imagined it would sound like for a plane to hit the ground after hurtling from the sky. It was a roar of grinding, crunching metal and smashing glass, followed by eerie silence. Then everything went black.

I woke fuzzy and lightheaded to Grace sobbing my name over and over. The sound of sirens screamed in my ears and my eyes blinked open, my vision distorted.

"Grace," I rasped, my head falling back against the seat when I tried to lift it.

"Oh God, oh God, oh God," she chanted.

I don't know how long I was out for because a fire crew already surrounded the car. My door was ripped open quickly. "You okay in there?"

"Yeah, I think so."

"What's your name?"

"Casey," I panted, sweat breaking over my brow when bolts of pain shot through me. Gritting my teeth, I tried turning my head to see Grace and cried out.

"Don't try moving," I was told.

"Grace," I mumbled, my vision fuzzy and grey around the edges.

"Grace. That your girl's name?"

I blinked, trying to focus on the guy talking to me. "Yeah."

"Hold tight, Casey, we're gonna get you and Grace out in a minute. Just waiting on the paramedics. In the meantime, I don't want you moving. We need to get a neck brace on you as a precautionary measure, okay?"

"Okay."

The fireman stood up and spoke to someone standing behind him. "What's the ETA on the ambulance?"

The answer came quick. "Two minutes."

"We're gonna need two," I heard him say. "We'll get him out first. They'll need to get a line in on the girl. She's trapped in there. Gonna need the jaws to get her out. Get someone on it now."

"No!" I cried out, my voice cracking at hearing she was trapped. "Grace?"

Nothing.

Panic clawed at me. Bracing against the pain, I turned my head. Grace slumped against the headrest. Blood spattered her face and neck and all down her right side. Shards of jagged glass littered her clothes and hair. Her side of the car was crumpled inwards, showing just how much of the impact she'd sustained. She looked so broken.

"Grace!" I cried hoarsely, fighting back tears. "Answer me!"

The fireman spun back around, crouching low at the open door. He fixed his eyes on mine. Finally able to focus, I could see they were dark brown and firm. Straightforward eyes you could trust. "What's your name?" I asked him.

"Lieutenant Saunders, but you can call me Liam."

"I'm not leaving her here, Liam," I rasped. "You get her out first."

"We're working on getting her out right now, but I can't let you stay with her."

"I'm not leaving her here."

Liam shook his head. "I'm sorry. Is there anyone I can get in touch with for you?"

"Travis." He was my next of kin, had been for almost as long as I'd known him. "My phone is in my back pocket."

"I don't want to move you. How about you just give me his number?"

He tapped it in his phone as I recited the number. "Be right back," he told me and stood, taking a few steps away from the car. While he murmured in quiet conversation on the phone, I felt movement on my right.

"Casey?" Grace moaned.

"Grace, baby, you're gonna be okay."

The screaming of sirens getting closer filled the cool, dark night air. At the same time, four firemen surrounded Grace's car door. The sound of the hydraulic pump thumped and whirred, competing with the sirens as two of them began cutting the metal of my car. Two more stood behind, ready to provide assistance.

God.

They were cutting Grace from my car.

My stomach rolled.

"I'm sorry," she whispered, and I almost didn't hear her over the grinding crunch of metal. She moved her arm, inching her hand across the seat.

"Don't be sorry. It's not your fault." I took it in mine. The fit felt perfect but her hand was so cold. I gave it a light squeeze, letting her know I was there and wasn't leaving. "That car came out of nowhere."

Then I realised something that made me frown. Liam had only mentioned two ambulances—one for me and one for Grace. What about whoever was in the other car? "Liam."

The man crouched again, meeting my eyes. "Travis is already on his way to the hospital. He's going to meet you there."

"Thanks." Sharp bolts of pain stabbed from somewhere inside me. It was a pain unlike anything I'd felt before. I gasped, shifting.

"You okay?"

"I'm fine," I told him, shaking off the dizzy sensation. "The other car?"

He shook his head, his eyes grim. "Fled the scene."

I cursed. It could've been an accidental hit and run, but I remember the car not slowing down. That didn't spell accident to me. Someone hit us deliberately.

"Casey," Grace whispered. "Your car."

"I don't care about the car, baby. I don't. I care about you. Just you."

"I'm sorry. I had no right to get so angry. I just saw her touching you and—

” Grace shifted and cried out.

“Grace—”

“—and I saw red.”

“Don’t.” I shouldn’t have strung Morgan along. That was on me. I just couldn’t give up on my family and finding answers. Letting go was hard. Just the thought made my eyes sting. I wasn’t ready. “That case was important to me because it was my family,” I said, blackness closing in again. I fought to stay awake. To explain. “My brother, Kelly. My mum. Dad … They’re all gone.”

“Gone?” she whispered.

“Dead, Grace.” I closed my eyes and swallowed, my head tipping back against the seat. “They’re all dead.”

“Casey.” I felt her trying to squeeze my hand, the sound of a sob breaking from her chest. “How?”

“Shot.” One single word to explain the loss of my entire world. “My father was a violent man. I promised my little brother and my mum a new life away from him. I promised and I failed. They needed me,” I whispered, bile rising in my throat, “and I was too late.”

“Failed? Casey, no,” she replied, “I don’t believe it.”

Her faith was misplaced, but now wasn’t the time to set her straight. “Let’s just focus on getting you out of the car,” I said when her head lolled forward.

Then she coughed, and I didn’t like how it sounded. “Hurts so much.”

I ground my teeth, frustrated at being unable to move. “They’re getting you out right now, baby, okay? Just focus on my voice. I’m right here with you okay. I won’t leave you.”

“I’m scared,” she whispered. “I don’t want to die. I don’t. I’ve only just starting living, Casey.”

My eyes burned, but my voice was fierce. “You’re not gonna die, Grace. I won’t let you,” I told her, because that was what happened when you found the woman perfect for you. You refused to let them go. “I promise.”

A male paramedic filled the doorway of my car and crouched, running an assessing gaze over my body.

“Casey?” she called out, her voice thready and weak.

“Yeah?”

It sounded like she was trying to laugh. It came out more like a strangled cough instead, but the sound was sweet, because she might’ve been scared, but she was strong, she was dealing, and I was fucking proud of her. “I believe you.”

“Good,” I replied and blinked, seeing two of the medics when he reached in and unclipped my seat belt. “I’m not leaving,” I told him. My voice came out slurred and suddenly keeping my eyes open became too damn hard.

Grace’s hand slipped from mine.

“Grace?”

I fought to remain conscious, my heart pounding so hard in my chest it hurt.

"Don't leave me, Slim, please," I begged hoarsely.

The paramedic reached across in front of me and grabbed her wrist, feeling for a pulse. "Fuck," he muttered. He pulled back out of the car and spun around. "You need to hurry up with that door and get her out!" he yelled at Liam. "You." He pointed to another fireman. "With me. I want you to …"

I tried hard to hold on, so damn hard, but the blackness won and my eyes closed.

Chapter Twenty-One
CASEY

I came to inside the ambulance. The rocking motion told me we were already en route to the hospital. My eyes opened. A male paramedic who looked a lot like Travis hovered above me—same build and blond hair, except tattooed sleeves covered both arms. My shirt had been cut down the middle and his dark brown eyes were focused on my chest where he was checking my vitals. The guy was well-trained, performing the task efficiently, his hands and body remaining steady as the vehicle swayed through night time traffic.

I closed my eyes, my breathing erratic when I remembered the grinding, screaming crunch of impact. It was no less horrific than the feel of Grace's hand slipping from mine.

"Grace," was all I could choke out. The raspy sound was barely audible. I yanked the oxygen mask down, letting it rest around my neck. The paramedic met my eyes with drawn brows. "Grace," I whispered again, willing him to understand.

"Grace?"

"My wife," I lied, knowing it would get me answers otherwise reserved for family members. "In … the car."

He shook his head. "I don't know. I'm sorry. They were cutting her out when we left."

I turned my head and breathed, fighting the urge to puke.

"You gonna be sick?"

A loud groan echoed through the ambulance and I realised it was me. I drew another deep, rasping breath.

Pull it together, Casey.

"No." I swallowed and turned my head back. "I'm fine."

"Good." He reached over and lifted the oxygen mask back over my face. My breathing eased instantly. "Keep this on."

I yanked it back down with a glare. "I said I wasn't … leaving her," I gasped out. "Take me back."

"No can do."

"Take. Me. Back." Grabbing hold of either side of the stretcher, I struggled to sit up, hissing when my vision greyed, sharp pain stabbing at me from every direction.

The paramedic put a gloved hand on my chest to stop me from moving. "No." My eyes cut to his, blinking to gain focus. His expression was that of a man quickly losing patience. "I can do one of two things. I can find out your wife's status when we arrive, or I can strap you to this stretcher and sedate you. I'm really hoping you'll pick option two because it's been a long damn day and they don't pay me anywhere near enough to deal with people like you." He fixed me with a firm glare. "What's it gonna be?"

Knowing he had the upper hand, I exhaled through the pain and lay back down.

"Not quite the answer I was hoping for," the paramedic muttered wryly, indicating he was all for sedation, "but you can't win everything, right?"

I glanced at the guy's nametag. Luke Fox. "What do you know about winning?"

"Everything," Luke answered while he worked. "I don't like to lose. That means I'm damn good at my job."

If Luke was so damn good, he should've been the one attending to Grace rather than to me, and I told him so. He shook his head and assured me the paramedic with Grace was the best there was. "Better than me," he added, then muttered under his breath, "not that I'd ever tell him that."

"How do you know?"

"Because the guy's my brother and he's even more of a stubborn asshole than I am." Luke placed both hands on me and began palpating my abdomen. "Let me know if anywhere hurts," I was instructed.

I sucked in a sharp breath and glared. "It all hurts."

Luke's brows drew together. "Do I know you? You look familiar."

"Is that a pickup line? Because I don't do dudes."

He grinned. "Well you're safe with me. I don't do them either."

"Good to know," I muttered.

"Your next of kin's listed as Travis Valentine. That's not Mac's big brother, is it?"

"Yeah it is. You know Mac?"

Luke shook his head while his hands manipulated my torso, his grin widening. "I'm an old friend of Mac's from high school."

"Old friend, huh?"

"Yeah. We know each other. Though not as well as I'd like."

"And you plan on rectifying that?" I asked, thinking Jake would be mighty interested in Luke's answer.

Luke shrugged. "I don't know. I kinda like my balls attached, you know?" I could only agree. It would take a helluva man to take on Mac and her brothers and come out the other side with all body parts intact. Luke shifted his hands and ran them slowly down my right leg, asking, "You on any medications?"

"No."

Done, he did the same to my left leg. "Allergies?"

"No."

He began checking my blood pressure. "When did you last eat?"

"Lunch," I muttered. "Midday."

When he was done with the examination, he wrote a quick note down on the chart to his left, speaking as he scribbled. "You're responsive and your speech is fine, but you have a concussion, minor lacerations, and your vital signs are unstable, meaning your pulse is fast, your breathing rapid, and your blood pressure too low." He put the chart back and looked at me. "You're lucky it's not worse."

"Lucky, huh?" I let that one go and when the ambulance slowed to a crawl, said, "You can just let me out here."

His brows rose. "Or I can just do that sedation thing."

"Is that how The Dummies' Guide to Being a Paramedic teaches you to treat a concussion?"

"You're a funny guy. I don't like funny guys." The ambulance picked up speed again. "I should just open the back doors and roll you out into oncoming traffic. Finish the job someone started earlier."

"Your bedside manner sucks."

"Thanks," he replied.

The ambulance came to a stop moments later. Luke ripped off his latex gloves and tossed them in a container to his right as the back doors swung open. Leaping out, he and another paramedic wheeled the stretcher into the path of an oncoming nurse. Luke ran through my vitals quickly while she assessed me, pausing on my chest as she listened to him speak.

I sat up on the stretcher. The effort dragged a groan from my chest. Both Luke and the nurse pushed me back down.

"Stop," I ordered, shoving their hands away.

I sat back up again, ripped off the oxygen mask from where it rested around my neck, and tossed it on the stretcher.

"Casey!"

Everyone turned in the direction of the shout. Travis was jogging towards me, Quinn close behind. They'd been at his parents for dinner tonight with Sam, which was closer to the hospital than their place. It explained how they arrived here at the same time I did.

"I'm fine," I said quickly.

He nodded his response but scanned over me regardless before returning to my face. Noticing the man beside me, he lifted his chin, saying, "Luke. Been a long time. Almost didn't recognise you. I'd say it's good to see you but …"

"Yeah, mate. I get that a lot."

They shook hands briefly, Travis asking, "You were on scene?"

"Yeah."

"Good. Wanna stop in after your shift? Might have a few questions."

Luke nodded. "Sure."

Travis turned back to me, his brows drawn. "They wouldn't tell me who the girl was in the car with you."

"Grace."

He blanched, the golden hue of his skin paling rapidly. "What was Grace—"

I interrupted him. "Long story."

Quinn took my hand, wrapping it in both of hers. The gesture was meant to be soothing, but it wasn't working. I was too wound up, too fixed on Grace. "Is she okay?"

"She took most of the impact," I told them because that was all I knew. "The other car fled the scene."

Travis cursed sharp and loud while Quinn covered her mouth, visibly upset. He grabbed Quinn by the back of her neck and pulled her close, wrapping her in his arms.

"Travis." His eyes cut to mine. "I don't have a good feeling about this."

He was silent for a moment, absorbing the words. "Where is she?"

"I don't know. I don't even know if they're bringing her here. Last I remember they were cutting her from the car."

"I'll find out," he told me.

"We'll find out," I corrected. I ripped the IV from my arm carelessly. Blood began seeping from the wound I created. I pressed down on the torn skin with my hand and got to my feet, fighting back dizziness and protests from the surrounding medical staff.

"Stubborn sonofabitch," Luke grunted. He grabbed my forearm and slapped a bandage strip on my inside elbow. Done, he fixed his eyes on mine. "Grace is en route."

"Here?"

"Here," Luke confirmed.

"She okay?"

"She's breathing."

I closed my eyes for a brief moment and felt myself sway. I quickly opened them.

"We need to get you inside. Get back on the stretcher," Luke ordered.

"Not until Grace arrives," I replied and turned to Travis. "We need to ring Henry."

"I'll do it." Travis yanked his phone from his back pocket, dialled and held it to his ear. "He's gonna lose it," he said as he waited for Henry to answer.

I held out my hand, knowing the call needed to come from me. "Give me the phone."

He handed it over wordlessly. I put the phone to my ear, my eyes on Travis as I listened to it ring. It wasn't just Henry that would lose it. They all would. Not just because Grace was Henry's sister, but because Grace had become family. One of their own. And when one of them hurt, they all hurt.

"Travis!" Henry shouted in my ear. The steady thump of music in the background and rowdy laughter told me they were still at the bar.

"It's Casey," I corrected.

"Casey?" he shouted. There was a pause, and then, "Where the hell are you and Grace? What's going on?"

"I'm at the Prince Alfred. Grace has been in an accident."

"Fuck!" Henry spoke to someone as the music in the background began to fade. He was already on the move. Then he came back on the phone. "Is she okay? What happened?"

"My car was T-boned at an intersection. They're bringing her in now by ambulance."

"I don't understand. Weren't you with her?"

Luke's radio crackled and within seconds, he and his partner were folding the stretcher back in the van, getting ready to head back out. "I was. We were both in the car. They brought me in first."

"You sonofabitch!" he exploded. "You left her there? How could you do that? I told you she'd get caught up in all your bullshit and end up getting hurt." I swallowed the lump in my throat and turned for the hospital's emergency entrance. The bright lights and sudden movement made my head spin. "Were you drunk driving?"

"Henry, you know me better than that," I replied, not bothering to correct his assumption about me being behind the wheel. Emotions were running hot. Explaining anything right now would be pointless.

"Yeah? Well it turns out I don't know you like I thought I did."

"I'm sorry," I replied. When the world tilted, I stumbled to my knees. Travis was at my side in an instant, his hand on my bicep to help me up. "I'm fine," I bit out and shrugged him off. "Henry, I—"

"Save it," he growled. "We'll be there soon."

Henry hung up.

Travis knelt in front of me. I handed him back the phone.

"Travis," I began. I wanted to explain how much Grace meant to me, but I didn't know how without sounding like some girly Hallmark card. "This is so fucked up. I didn't mean for this to happen, but Grace is … She's…"

Travis shook his head. "You don't need to explain, Casey." He took hold of my shoulders and looked at me. The effect of both actions steadied me. "You think I haven't seen the way you look at her? Or the way she looks at you? Jesus, Casey. It doesn't matter if you've known her ten years or ten minutes. There's something there and it makes my heart fucking sing to see it." The sound of approaching sirens cut through the night and my control wavered. It was Grace. It had to be.

Please be okay or I'll fucking lose it.

My lungs began to burn. Travis shifted his grip and grabbed my head in both hands. He dragged my face to his until our foreheads pressed together. "Stay strong, okay? Whatever happens, I'm in this with you. Always."

I nodded wordlessly.

"Good." He let go. "Now get up," he growled.

My body responded to the command.

The next few minutes were a blur. The ambulance bringing Grace arrived. I held my breath when the back doors flew open, the paramedic barely waiting for the vehicle to come to a full stop. He already had the stretcher half out when his partner jumped out to assist him. I ran over at the same time a trauma team rushed out from the emergency exit. The paramedic, a bigger, older version of Luke, started shouting stats. The noise was fuzzy static as I focused solely on Grace. Her smooth skin, usually flushed with laughter or anger, was pale and streaked with blood.

I went to take her hand, but before I could, Henry was there. And Jake. And Cooper. And everyone else.

I let myself get pushed back as Grace was rushed towards the hospital entrance. The doors whooshed open and they disappeared inside.

Travis glared. "What are you doing? Get in there."

"I can't," I muttered.

I bent over, resting my palms on my knees, fighting for air.

"Casey? Are you okay?"

"I don't know. I can't breathe," I panted.

Travis started shouting but this time when the world tilted, I let go, letting it rise up to meet my face.

I woke in a hospital bed. Bright, streaming light told me night had given way to morning and loud, angry voices announced an argument in progress. Powerful drugs must have been pulsing through my system because I couldn't feel a thing. I tensed a leg muscle. Nothing. A bicep. All good. I drew a deep breath and sharp stabbing knives attacked me like a posse of ninjas.

"You need to take lead on this!" Travis thundered across my bed.

I opened my eyes. He was standing on my left, Jared beside him, Tim wedged between the both of them. Coby stood on the other side next to a tense looking Mitch, the apparent target of Travis's thunder. My brows drew together as I studied the guy standing at the end of the bed. His arms were folded, his eyes pinging back and forth as he followed the argument. He was somehow familiar. Luke, I suddenly remembered. The paramedic.

"Lead? I work homicide, dipshit," Mitch growled back at Travis. "Clearly Casey is not dead!" His arm swept over my prone form, introducing my breathing body to support his case.

"It's attempted homicide. Close enough," Jared countered. "That means we need you in on this."

"We don't know that yet," Mitch replied, his expression tired and irritated. The look came from years of cleaning up the mess of his little brothers. "You're acting like a bunch of melodramatic egomaniacs."

"You weren't there, Mitch," Coby informed him. "So you don't know what you're talking about."

"You weren't there either!" Mitch pointed out, frustration making his voice loud and his brows pinch tight.

"That's why Fox is here," Travis said. "He was there. He can tell us what he knows."

Everyone turned to Luke at the end of the bed. The guy was still in uniform and looked like he hadn't slept. He shook his head at them all. "I don't think whoever hit Casey's car wants him dead."

Jared narrowed his eyes on Luke. "Yeah? What the fuck would you know?"

"Enough!" I roared, wondering if they'd all suddenly lost their minds. Six pairs of eyes swept my way. "Would someone please tell me if Grace is okay?"

"She's fine," Travis said quickly. "She's in surgery but she's going to be okay."

"Surgery?"

"Her arm," he replied. "She has a wrist fracture but the impact broke the bone in her forearm clean through the skin."

My stomach rolled. "Jesus."

"We don't know much else yet but as soon as we do …"

Tim pushed through both Travis and Jared and grabbed my hand in his. He began petting me like a zoo animal. "How do you feel?"

"Like a guy who got hit by a car," I muttered, the aches in my body pulsing now that I was fully conscious. I pushed myself up and bit back a groan. Tim went immediately for the electronic device beside the bed. A whirring noise filled the room and everyone watched patiently, waiting for my bed to raise me to a sitting position. Except it didn't. The end of my bed began lowering instead. It caused a pull on my stomach muscles that made me want to puke.

"Tim, what the hell?"

"Shit. Sorry." The whirring noise ground to a halt before starting up again, and my legs returned to a horizontal position. He pressed another button and the front end of my bed began dipping down until my eyes encountered the wall behind me.

"Oh, for the love of … Tim!"

"Give it here," Travis barked and snatched the device. Tim yanked it back, clutching it to his chest like it was the last pair of Prada shoes on sale. I knew he loved Prada shoes because he bought me a pair every year for my birthday and they were always, conveniently, three sizes too small, and, naturally, unreturnable. "I got this, okay?"

A whirring noise once again filled the room. The back of my bed rose until my eyes once again encountered ceiling. There was a loud clunk and the bed kept rising until I could finally see everyone's face from a less prone position. Lips twitched as my bed continued to whir onwards and upwards. What felt like half an hour later, I reached a seated position. Tim clipped the device back on the side of the bed with a loud click. Travis reached over and flicked it sideways out of Tim's reach.

"Talk," I barked.

Everyone turned to Luke. I was anxious to hear his take on the accident. Lack of skid marks on the road would confirm what I already knew, but I wanted it confirmed nonetheless. He picked up my chart and scanned it. "Splenorrhexis. Grade I. Emergency splenorrhaphy not required. Fractured costal left upper quadrant. Contusion across left clavicle—"

"In English," Coby clarified.

Luke rolled his eyes and muttered something under his breath before he began again. "Your spleen was torn from impact. It was only minor so they gave you a blood transfusion and they're letting it heal on its own. Fractured ribs. Bruising along the collarbone—"

"Not me, dammit," I interrupted. "The accident. Tell us what you know."

"I know I wanted to cry like a baby when I saw your car." Luke's nostrils flared. "Whoever wrecked that beautiful piece of machinery doesn't deserve to live." Nods of agreement filled the room and sympathetic looks darted my way. "There were no skid marks on the road. The car that ploughed into the driver's side of Casey's car didn't slow down, suggesting it was deliberate." Travis arched a brow at Mitch over that piece of information. "But they didn't want Casey dead," Luke continued. Mitch arched a brow back at Travis. There was a pause. "They wanted his wife dead."

"His wife?" Tim said faintly and turned accusing eyes my way. Everyone started talking at once.

"I wasn't driving the car. Grace was."

Silence fell for a minute.

Travis was the first to speak. "Grace was driving your car?"

"There was an altercation at the bar," Jared began, and proceeded to fill them in on the events of the night. I gave a few brief facts to complete the missing pieces, which included the whole sorry mess with Morgan, and everyone stood silent for a moment, absorbing the new information.

Travis rubbed at his jaw and I knew he was trying hard not to say I told you so. I was grateful for that small mercy. After carefully weighing his words, he spoke. "I think Morgan sounds like a deranged bitch."

Jared nodded his head in agreement. "I agree. Besides, no one's cock is that good. Unless it can perform magic tricks. You got a magic dick, Casey?"

I willed myself to stay calm. "I do," I replied, my tone thick with sarcasm. "Every time I get a woman in bed I like to perform a little trick I call now you see it, now you don't."

Jared snorted.

"Now if we're finished discussing my cock and the amazing things it can do, can we get back to the matter at hand?"

Coby eyed me speculatively. "You think Morgan had something to do with this?"

"It's possible," I conceded. But if I distanced myself from Grace to keep her safe and it wasn't Morgan but someone else, then Grace would be left wide open for them to make another move. A more permanent move.

"Are you all forgetting something?" Mitch interjected with a fold of his arms. "Morgan is a newly appointed detective with the Sydney City Police."

Travis shrugged. "So what? You think all the coppers who make the rank of detective are squeaky clean?"

"We need to talk to Morgan and we need to talk to Grace," I informed the room.

"I agree," Travis said and pulled out his phone. "I'll ring Frank, get him to make a start on the background checks."

"Seth, Travis. Seth," Tim reminded him. Frank had finished up his last day of work yesterday. As of today, Seth McKinnon—Frank's replacement, former agent with the AFP, Travis's father-in-law and recipient of the mean right hook Travis possessed—was now on the clock.

Lips twitched when Travis tucked his phone back in his pocket at the reminder. He turned to his brother beside him. "Jared, you ring Seth, tell him to do the background checks."

Jared shook his head, green eyes amused. "You're gonna have to speak to him sooner or later, Travis. He works with us now."

"Well let's make it later," he snapped.

The door to my hospital room flew open. Mac strode through first, followed by Evie, who was followed by Quinn, the latter two both holding strawberry shakes in their hands. Luke, who'd been mostly quiet throughout our exchange, sucked in a sharp breath. Mac glanced his way and stumbled slightly, her eyes widening.

Evie veered off, dumping the remains of her shake in the corner bin. Quinn went to the side of Travis, who wrapped one arm around her and yanked her close. He used the other to snatch her shake. Recovering quickly, Mac kept going until she stood between Coby and Mitch. "You wankers finished with your little pow wow? Because Grace is just coming out of surgery, and now that we know she's going to be fine…" Mac looked at me when she said that, her eyes softening slightly and hardening again real quick. "…we have a bitch to take out, so let's get on it."

"A bitch?" Jared echoed the question for all of us.

"Morgan."

Coby's eyes shot to his hairline. "How do you know about Morgan?"

She gave him a look that said bitch, please. "The things I know would chill your blood."

"Mac," I said quietly, my tone warning her to explain.

She huffed. "Remember in the bar when you and Morgan were having your 'conversation,'" she air-quoted. "You stepped back and stumbled into someone behind you. Well that someone happened to be me."

"Of course it was you," I mumbled as I swung my legs over the side of the bed, determined to be there when Grace woke up. The effort forced a sweat to break out across my brow.

"Where's Henry?" I sucked in a deep breath at the stabbing pain in my ribs.

"He's out in the waiting room and Nate is on his way," Quinn told me.

"Who's Nate?" I asked.

Quinn cocked her head, her lips pressed together in a look of heart-felt sympathy. "Grace's dad."

I closed my eyes and cursed.

Fucking awesome.

Chapter Twenty-Two
GRACE

I breathed in a lungful of sterile antiseptic air and knew where I was before my eyes opened. It was the smell of my past. Not the kind that brought good memories, but the shitty ones. The ones where my mother was so tired and sick it hurt just to look at her. Those memories usually left me cold, but I didn't feel it this time. Instead, it felt like my body was plugged into a heater. Warmth radiated its heavenly blanket all down my left side. I wanted to cocoon myself in it and not move.

I turned my head and the smell of antiseptic changed to one of musk and man. I opened my eyes. Casey was lying on his side next to me in a hospital bed, his head resting on the corner of my pillow. His eyes were closed and his long lashes rested softly on his cheeks. My heart beat a little harder. Not only could I feel it, I could hear it. The monitor beside my bed echoed the sound through the room as I stared.

Brilliant red and purple bruises lined the left side of his face, across his brow, and down to his jawline. Dark smudges circled his eyes.

"Back off, Casey! I'm taking your Marjorie for a wild ride and you're not invited!"

Oh no.

I pressed my lips together. What had I done?

"Grace! Look out!"

I hadn't seen the car until it was too late. Had I gone through a red light? All

I could remember was the blinding glare of headlights; the ear-splitting crunch of metal; and the sharp metallic taste of blood on my tongue. The memory made my stomach roll and my lungs scream for air.

I drew a deep, shuddering breath and let it out slowly. As though Casey sensed me watching him, his eyes opened, blinking twice before focusing on my face.

There was silence for a moment as we stared at each other wordlessly. Then I lifted my hand and cupped his face, feeling the soft, scratch of his beard beneath my palm. I liked it. I liked this. Us. Together. No matter if we were on some romantic gondola ride along the Venice canals or here in a hospital bed. Waking up with Casey beside me felt right.

Huh.

Was I falling in love?

If I was, then I was well and truly screwed but I couldn't seem to care.

"Hey," he whispered roughly.

"Hey," I whispered back.

"How are you feeling?"

"Like an idiot." I went to shift slightly and realised my right arm was bound tight to my chest. Had I broken it? Two bass guitarists with broken arms? Mac was going to be pissed. I drew my hand from his face, and he took it in his, threading our fingers together.

"Are you okay?" I asked, taking in the graze on his left brow.

"I'm fine, just a few scrapes is all," he replied as I stared at all his bruises. The impact must have been tremendous to cause those. His car had been rammed clear across the intersection.

Oh God.

His car.

His car.

I closed my eyes and braced for Casey's anger. I'd destroyed his pride and joy. His baby. Just a bit of scratched leather on the backseat and he'd been ready to put me in the ground, but this was so much worse. "Are you here to finish me off?"

"Finish you off?" he echoed.

"I broke your car. No, wait. I stole your car and then I broke it. I don't know what comes after being dead, but whatever it is, that's where your car is. And I sent it there," I breathed, utterly horrified.

"Open your eyes, Grace."

I cleared my throat. "No. I'm good."

"Open."

"Uh uh." I squeezed them tighter. "I can't."

"Open."

"No."

"Yes."

"No."

"Grace. Open your eyes."

His hand loosened on mine and I panicked. Was he going to pry them open himself?

"Wait!" There was only one way I could fix this. I squeezed his hand so he wouldn't let go. My grip was feeble but he halted anyway, perhaps out of pity. "I'll open my eyes."

I peeked them open, directing my focus to his neck. It was a nice neck—strong and tanned, his pulse visible in the thick veins. My gaze wandered downwards. There were bruises all along his collarbone too, right where his seat belt would have been. The bruises blurred and I realised it was because my eyes were brimming with tears.

"Grace." My name on Casey's lips was deep and low and rough. He tucked a finger under my chin, tilting my head until I couldn't look anywhere else but in his eyes.

"I was thinking …" My voice sounded raspy so I cleared my throat. "Maybe we should start again."

"You want another do-over?" A slow, sexy smile overtook his face until his dimples popped. When the beep of my heart monitor increased in time with the flutters in my stomach, his look changed to one of amusement.

"Yes. I think that would be best."

"Okay." Casey shrugged and then winced, as though the slight movement hurt. "You start."

I paused, unprepared. Casey always started our do-overs. "You sure you don't want to start?"

"I'm sure."

I paused for a moment, buying time as I tried to think about what I wanted to say. Casey watched me, waiting. It made me nervous. "Okay then. I'll start, shall I?"

His response was a grin.

I went back to staring at his neck. "My name's Grace Paterson," I began. "I currently play guitar in a band, I have the major hots for the guy who does our security." I stole a peek at Casey and saw his eyes flash heat. I had to draw a breath before I could continue, "and apparently in my spare time I like to trash cars. Expensive, restored types of the uh, muscled variety. With motherfucker tyres," I finished. "And I'm really, really sorry."

Casey's brows rose. "Motherfucker tyres?"

"Tyres so big they could mow down King Kong without losing traction."

His body shook with silent laughter.

"It's funny I trashed your car?"

"No, it's not funny at all, but you don't need to apologise for it. You didn't trash my car, Slim. Someone else did that."

"They wouldn't have if I hadn't stolen it," I pointed out.

Casey shrugged and the response surprised me. Where was the anger? The deep burning rage? The threats on my life? Perhaps he was in shock and it hadn't sunk in yet. I went with that for now because his casual response didn't make sense.

"Your turn," I told him.

"Okay. My name's Casey Daniels," he began in his deep, rumbling voice. He reached up, trailing a finger slowly down my nose and along my brows as he spoke, his eyes following the path of his finger. The touch was sweet and whisper soft. "I do security for a girl in a band who makes me burn hotter than the sun. I'm also an asshole who makes mistakes that hurt the people I care about and for that I'm sorry." He paused, his eyes sombre as his thumb trailed a path along my bottom lip. "And in my spare time I like restoring trashed cars … with motherfucker tyres," he emphasised with a twitch of amusement.

I held my breath when Casey leaned in and brushed his lips softly on mine. The touch was light, but it held just as much impact as the wild and passionate ones we shared earlier that night.

Casey drew back, running his eyes over my face. "Are you in any pain?" His question was like a catalyst because everywhere suddenly began throbbing like a bass drum. He took a second to press the button on the side of my bed before taking my hand back in his threading our fingers together. "You took most of the impact, Grace. God, you're lucky to be breathing right now. That car hit us so damn hard."

I shivered because I'd never been in a car crash before. It was the oddest sensation. Almost like it was happening to someone else. "How bad off am I?"

He grimaced. "Lacerations cover pretty much the entire right side of your body. Busted ribs, bruised shoulder, concussion, and a hairline fracture in your right wrist. You broke your arm too, Grace. It was bad enough they had to do surgery to put it back together."

I winced. "That sounds bad."

"Because it is bad."

"There's no way I'll be playing a guitar again anytime soon." Being in the band was like having another family, except you experienced something amazing together that the outside world would never understand. I swallowed the disappointment at losing it. "I loved being up there on stage, being part of something special."

"Hey." Casey gave my hand a squeeze. "You don't have to leave the band. They can find a place for you."

My heart leaped at the possibility before reality intruded with a rude slap, reminding me that sometimes life just wasn't that easy. For a second my eyes stung with tears. I looked down at our joined hands so Casey wouldn't see. "You know, I think they really would, but I can't."

"There's no such thing as can't. I'm sure I already told you that."

"You did." I peeked up at him from beneath my lashes, a smile forming on my lips. "Right before you defiled me all over the hood of your car."

Casey's lips twitched in response. "That was fun. You should let me defile you again some time."

"Well now that playing guitar is out, my schedule is wide open." I wasn't sure how well two injured people would go having sex, but there was no way I wasn't going to try.

"I'll miss watching you play," Casey replied softly, looking into my eyes.

Casey always stood on the right of the stage wherever we played. I figured it was the side he was most comfortable on. I always found myself gravitating towards him, shooting quick glances his way. His focus would always return to me, his eyes full of heat and something that looked a little like pride. "I'll miss you watching me play," I replied equally as softly.

Mac always stood off to the right side as well, iPad in hand, taking charge while still keeping one eye on the stage watching us. Come to think of it, her eyes always had that streak of pride too. Then I realised something. "I'm going to have to tell Mac I can't play. She's going to have a stroke."

"She already did." Casey's lips twitched again. "You were too busy snoring and missed it."

"I don't snore." I drew my face back from his, making sure he could see my frown. "Why would you say such a thing?"

A light rap came at my hospital door, saving Casey from an explanation. It opened and in walked a doctor wearing green scrubs. A surgical mask hung casually around her neck and her tousled black hair was pulled into a knot at her nape. It didn't detract from the incredible colour—a black so deep it reflected blue in the light as she clicked the door shut and walked to the end of my bed.

"Miss Paterson. You're awake."

"Grace, please," I told her.

"And it appears Mr Daniels is too." Dancing eyes of sea green turned Casey's way as she went straight for my chart. Casey started to get up. "You can stay for a few minutes if you like. I was going to come visit you next anyway."

"Thanks," he replied and lay back down with a heavy breath.

"I'm Doctor Rowan James, Grace. I took care of you when they brought you in." She flicked through my chart, scribbled something, set it back down and walked to the side of my bed. Flicking on a penlight, she asked how I was feeling while she checked my eyes.

"Sore," I mumbled, hissing at the glare of the light. I blinked a couple of times and refocused.

"That's to be expected." She tucked her penlight in her coat pocket and lifted the stethoscope from around her neck. She ran through the list of my injuries while she checked me over, adding that someone would set my arm in a couple of days when the swelling went down.

"You're lucky your injuries weren't life-threatening. With the kind of impact you sustained, the medics rushed you in with suspected internal trauma. The CT scans came back clear. We've put a soft cast on your arm for now. When the swelling goes down we'll put a hard cast on for you but otherwise, you're going to be fine. Grace …" She paused, casting an assessing gaze between both Casey and myself. "We noticed your recently healed scar in our exam. I think it's best if I contact your GP to inform them of your injuries. They'll need to take this into consideration—"

She broke off when the door opened again. Henry came through, followed by—

"Dad," I said loudly, my body tensing with shock when he stepped inside my room.

My father was usually a handsome man—tanned, shoulders broad and imposing, his eyes the same bright blue my brother inherited. Today he looked like he'd gone through the wringer. His clothes were rumpled, face pale and drawn, his lips tight with fear. My actions put that fear on his face and the knowledge made my insides twist with guilt.

"Hell," I heard Casey mumble under his breath.

With a painful hiss, he turned his body and sat up. Planting his feet on the floor, he stood slowly and faced my family. I liked that he didn't leave or let go of my hand. Instead, he gave it a squeeze and sent a reassuring smile my way. I got lost in it, somehow forgetting for a second my father was there. Casey had that ability to make me forget everything. I returned his smile.

Henry cleared his throat pointedly.

"Dad," I said, ignoring Henry because I knew he'd have nothing good to say, "this is Casey Daniels." Dad was busy looking between the both of us and our linked hands. I guess that meant I didn't need to explain the nature of our relationship. The tightening of Dad's jaw told me he got it loud and clear. "Casey, this is Nate, my dad."

"Son," Dad replied, holding out his hand.

I hadn't mentioned Casey to my father so his response had me sighing with relief. Perhaps it was only in deference to our injuries and the inquisition would come later. Either way, I was taking it.

Casey cleared his throat. "Sorry to meet you under these circumstances, sir." He let go of my hand and took hold of Dad's, giving it a firm shake. Dad would appreciate that. He was a strong, no-nonsense man and it showed. His brown hair was lightly peppered with grey and closely cropped, and his tall frame displayed his usual weekend attire of jeans and a polo shirt. The clothes were a little worn because it was Dad's belief that shopping was akin to purgatory. I'd tried sneaking trendier items into his wardrobe a time or two but I'd yet to see him wear any of it.

"Call me Nate," Dad barked before letting go. Then he dismissed Casey, his face paling further as he took me in.

"Oh, love," he murmured, and I knew what he saw because his face was sad.

Mum and I looked so much alike—right down to the exact same shade of eye colour—so seeing me laid out in a hospital bed just brought it all back for him. Tears threatened. I hated seeing him so defeated and alone. Hated it.

Doctor James stepped away from bed, allowing room for Dad to step in. Telling me she'd be back later, she returned my chart to the end of the bed and gave us privacy.

Dad leaned over and pressed a kiss on my forehead. When he pulled back I saw his jaw tremble.

"I'm fine, Dad," I assured him.

"She's not fine," Henry interjected from beside Dad. Folding his arms, he glared across my hospital bed at Casey.

"I don't look that bad," I insisted, despite having no clue what I looked like.

There was no purpose to Henry making a big deal over it. It would just upset Dad further. Not to mention I didn't like the way he glared at Casey as though it was his fault this happened.

"You do," Henry contradicted. "You're a mess. Both your eyes are bruised along with your cheekbone and jaw. You've got stitches in your head and dried blood all over you!"

I believed him. Not only because the tone of his voice rose with each word, but because he looked just as upset as Dad did. I also winced because Casey had lay next to me in bed and seen all that up close. "Well." I brushed a hand over my forehead and encountered a bandage. "If I'm that hideous, maybe you should leave so you don't have to keep looking at me."

"Look at you? I'm lucky I can look at you because you almost died."

Casey straightened his shoulders under the laser beams Henry shot his way. The move would've hurt with the pain he was in, but his face was like stone, giving nothing away. "None of this would've happened if you'd stayed away from Casey like I told you. He almost got you killed, Grace."

"Enough," Casey said. His voice was quiet but there was underlying steel behind the words. "I was going to talk to you, Henry, and I'm sorry I didn't do it sooner. I fucked up—"

"Damn straight you fucked up," my brother interrupted. "I told you to stay away from Grace. Instead, you did the exact opposite and went behind my back."

"Henry," Dad said in his scary warning tone that always stopped me in my tracks no matter what.

Henry wasn't deterred. "You didn't even listen to what I said, let alone consider it, did you, Grace?"

"Because you can't tell me what to do, Henry. Casey was all for telling you. Keeping it quiet was my decision. You and I went through a long, rocky patch. Knowing how you felt, I was scared to make it worse just when it was starting to get better."

"And going behind my back wasn't making it worse anyway?" he pointed out.

"Henry," Casey began, beginning to sound pissed off.

I interrupted, not wanting him caught up in our fight. I took his hand and squeezed in silent apology. "You're right, Henry, and I'm sorry, but it's not up to you to decide whether Casey is good or bad for me; it's my decision. And while I respect your advice, I need you respect the choices I make."

"Like the choice you made to leave?" he asked, his tone still bitter when I thought we'd started to move past it.

"Enough," Dad roared at Henry, his voice a whiplash that reverberated off the walls. "I won't have the two of you fighting. Henry, you need to let it go. Grudges are ugly. I raised my son better than that."

Henry went to open his mouth but dad didn't let him speak. Instead his gaze shifted to Casey. He had his determined face on. His brows were drawn, jaw set, and he wanted answers. "My little Gracie was in your car at the time of the accident?"

Casey nodded. "Yes, sir, she was."

"I see." Dad folded his arms, giving his intimidating glare. I was impressed when Casey didn't appear intimidated. Dad's glare could part the Red Sea and was the only look that worked on me when I was in trouble. "And this other car, they rammed the side she was sitting in?"

Casey nodded again. "Yes, sir, they did. A hit and run," he added.

Dad sucked in a deep breath, his nostrils flaring as he absorbed this piece of news. "And were they caught?"

My gaze shifted from Dad to Casey. I hadn't known the other driver fled the scene. Who would do something like that?

"No, sir," Casey answered with that steel back in his voice. "Not yet."

"This car of yours, it have side airbags?"

"Yes, sir, it did."

"I see," he murmured, his nostrils flaring even wider. "I want to speak to the police. See what they're doing to find the sonofabitch who would ram a car and then leave my daughter for dead." I winced at dad's dramatic turn of phrase. "I want to see the car too," he added.

Dad knew a thing or two about cars. He'd been employed as a mechanic at Dave's Family Auto from his teens, working his way up to the Office Manager position he was in now. That's how he met my mum. She brought her car in with a broken thermostat and I guess he knew just the right way to fix it.

He still worked there because he didn't like change. Dad was all about the status quo, and while they paid him for his loyalty, it didn't pay enough to live a life of luxury. He still lived in the same house we grew up in. The only updates to the furniture were the wide-screen television on the wall and surround sound. Dad told me Henry bought it for him—sneaking in one day to have it installed while Dad was at work. It was the weekend of the Bathurst 1000 (Dad's favourite weekend), where the V8 Supercars took to Mount Panorama Circuit in a festival of exhaust fumes, rumbling engines, and blazing testosterone. Dad had insisted the installation would stay only for the weekend, but the weekend came and went and the television stayed.

It was obvious he was a proud man, so when I covered mum's medical bills, paid out the home loan and all our schooling, as well as contributing to food on the table, it almost broke him.

He promised me it would only be a loan. He saved every year, and at the end of that year, he would deposit those savings in my account as repayment, and every year, I would transfer the money into an investments account I had under his name. It was building nicely, and when he was ready to retire, I'd hand it over and tell him to do that trip around Australia Mum told me he'd been itching to do all his life.

"I can arrange a meeting with the police for you," Casey told him. Then he picked up his phone from where it sat on my hospital side table and said, "I also have a photo here of the car that one of my guys took for me if you want to have a look."

Dad's brows rose in question. "One of your guys?" He held his arm out over the top of my bed, indicating for Casey to hand him the photo. "What do you do, son?"

Casey tapped at the screen, calling it up before giving it to him. Casey gave dad a brief rundown while Dad stared at the photo, his jaw ticking ominously.

"That's a damn shame about your car. It was a real beauty." His eyes narrowed on the photo. "You say they hit Grace's side of the car?"

Casey nodded. "Yes, sir."

"I see," Dad replied for the millionth time, each time sounding more growly and tense than the next. He handed the phone back to Casey.

"Seems Casey's car had enough side airbags to inflate the Titanic," he told Henry. "Did you know that?"

Henry folded his arms, his expression mutinous. "No."

"A beautiful car like the one in that photo, they don't come standard with side airbags like that. Casey would've had those installed special." Dad glanced at Casey. "Right, Daniels?"

Casey nodded and Dad continued. "After looking at that photo, it's pretty obvious our Gracie could've died without them. You know what else, son? It was a hit and run. You know what that means?" He didn't allow Henry time to answer. His voice gathered speed and momentum and we both knew to keep shut when that happened. "It means some goddamn sonofabitch hit my little girl and then fled the scene like a coward. Also," he whipped out and Henry flinched, "the impact was on the driver's side. Do you know what that means?" Dad didn't wait to see if Henry knew what that meant because he was on a roll and stopping for no one. "It means Grace was the driver, not Casey here. So out of all that, what makes you figure this man here…" he jerked his chin in Casey's direction "…almost got our Gracie killed?"

"Jesus," Henry muttered when he could finally get a word in. He looked at Casey, his eyes full of apology.

Trust my dad to get to the heart of the matter in the most roundabout way possible. It warmed my heart that he wasn't letting Henry be a right prick to Casey. It wasn't deserved and being an outsider to the situation, it was easier for Dad to see that.

Dad sucked in a breath, indicating he hadn't yet finished. "You a criminal?" he barked at Casey.

Oh no.

Casey was getting the inquisition now? I wanted to pull the sheet up and over my head and block it all out. "Dad!" I wailed.

They both ignored me, and Casey answered him with a, "no, sir."

"Nate."

"No, Nate," Casey repeated. "I'm not."

"You married?" my dad continued.

"No."

"Divorced?"

"No."

"Dad!" I interjected. "Do you really—"

"Kids?" he boomed over the top of me.

I squeezed Casey's hand to get his attention. His eyes cut to mine briefly and I mouthed, "I'm sorry."

He winked at me and my heart squeezed. He turned back to my dad and answered, "No kids, Nate."

"Do you own a chainsaw and a goalie mask and run by the alias of Jason?"

I smothered the snort of laughter. Dad might have checked out for a while after Mum died (and who could blame him because my mum and dad were the definition of crazy, stupid love) but when he'd checked back in, he did it with guns blazing. By that time I was embedded in my career, because like my dad I was content with the status quo and focused on trying to be the type of person he would be proud of: polite, calm and well-mannered.

"No, I don't," Casey replied, his eyes hiding a glint of amusement that I'm sure only I recognised. "Should I, sir?"

"Nate," my dad barked again.

"Nate," Casey dutifully repeated.

Dad shrugged. "Might come in handy for Halloween if you're into that shit."

His next comment made me cringe because I knew he was revisiting the time Dalton and I took him to dinner in the city. It was winter so Dalton had his blond highlights for the summer fashion shoots and a dusting of bronzer on his face. Dad only picked up on the bronzer because there was a smear on Dalton's collar. Dad thought it was from me and remarked on it. Dalton replied that it was winter and he wanted a bit of colour on his face. Spending all of his life working with grease and metal, Dad couldn't relate and it showed.

"Do you get highlights or wear makeup?"

Ugh.

Dad!

So what if he was divorced, had kids, got highlights, or ate only white food. It shouldn't matter. Either Dad was just being a big old meanie, or he was trying to make a point somewhere in there.

Casey scratched at his short, scruffy beard, hiding a grin. "No, sir."

Dad, it seemed, finally got to the point. He turned to Henry with disbelief written all over his face. "This is the type of man you tell your sister to stay away from? Did you not meet Dalton? That man was about as useful as a Hyundai Excel," he said, spitting out the words with distaste. Dad hated cheap import cars so that insult was huge. "When Grace rang and told me she'd given him the boot, the whole workshop erupted in cheers. We closed a whole half hour early that Friday and everyone stayed back for a beer to celebrate. Even Warren," Dad said to me pointedly, "who you know always goes straight home because he's whipped by that wife of his."

"Dad, you're being dramatic," I told him, embarrassed to hear about the celebration and all warm on the inside at the same time. "The workshop always stays back for a beer on Friday afternoons."

"Yeah, yeah," he waved me off. "But that Friday we lashed out on the good stuff."

"Good stuff, schmood stuff," I muttered.

Dad dragged the chair from the corner towards the side of my bed. The sound of it scraping along the linoleum floor was loud. He picked up the newspaper that someone must have left in the room. Then he sat down, put on his reading glasses, and snapped it open. He glared at Henry over the top of the pages. "I don't know what your issue is, young man, but you need to leave your sister alone."

"Dad," I said in warning.

Dad ignored me, focusing on the page in front of him. "I understand your protective instincts, but your sister's worked hard. Grace is entitled to live a little so you need to give her space to do just that. She's been there for you more than you know, so—"

"Dad!"

"There for me?" Henry shouted. It was clear he'd had enough of Dad shoving the wonders of Casey down his throat. It was also clear he wasn't ready to let go of that grudge just yet. "She hasn't been there for any of us! Not since mum died."

"Screw you, Henry," I snapped, because I damn well had.

"Not there for you?" Dad crumpled the paper in his lap, and I knew he was ready to swallow his pride and tell Henry the truth. I really didn't want him to because I didn't want to see my brother hurt over it.

"Daddy," I whispered. He glanced at me and I gave a brief shake of my head. "Don't."

"You think after everything you did, I'd sit back and let you take that kind of hit from your brother?"

"Everything she did?"

Dad sighed heavily. He put the paper back on the table and tucked his reading glasses into the pocket of his shirt. "Grace paid out our mortgage and all your mother's medical bills because the debt was about to put us on the streets." Henry blanched. "She helped pay for the food you ate, the clothes you wore, and the university education you and your sisters got. That was so you could keep your weekends free playing guitar with your band and going to parties rather than working to earn your education and the apartment you rented with your friends."

Henry stared at me, tears building in his eyes.

"You think your sister wanted to be a model? You think she wanted to leave a family still in grief to trip around the world, get pinned and poked, and miss out on being a teenager? All those years of sneaking into clubs underage, getting detention for wagging school, being taught how to drive, and hanging out with friends on the weekends. You got all that. Grace got none of it. You think her life was so great? She had no friends because it turns out teenage girls are a pack of jealous bitches who can't stand seeing another girl prettier than them do well for themselves. She gave up regular school for tutoring. She didn't go to movies, or parties, or cut loose at all, because she was working. If you think—"

"Enough!" Henry shouted at Dad without taking his eyes from mine. Dad shut up, glancing at me with guilt. I don't think he'd meant to lay it all out so harshly.

"Is it true?" my brother whispered. "You did all that for us? Paid for everything all those years when it was all I could do to get Dad that damned television?"

"Henry," I said softly. I didn't know what to say. I never wanted him to feel what he felt right now.

"Is it true?" he shouted, his knuckles white.

"Yes."

"Fuck!" Henry's chest heaved up and down.

"Son." Dad went to grip his shoulder in a supportive gesture but Henry's hand flew up, halting him. "Screw all of you for this," he hissed. He spun on his heel and took off out the door.

There was a pause and then my father piped up with, "Well that went as well as expected."

"Dad! Go after him."

Dad shook his head. "He needs time to cool off, Grace."

"I'll go," Casey said.

"No!" Henry obviously had a lot of anger to work through. I didn't want him working through it on Casey. "You need to go lie down, Batman. Not fight our family battles."

"I'll be fine." He bent over my bed, not without a wince, and in full view of Dad, kissed me. It wasn't a polite peck like you'd give your nanna either. There was a quick sweep of tongue too—enough for me to forget myself and grab his hair with my good arm, holding him there for a second longer. Then he was gone.

My dad arched a brow at me. "Batman?"

"Yeah," I replied on a soft, drawn-out sigh.

"I like him."

Chapter Twenty-Three
CASEY

"Henry!" I called out after shutting Grace's hospital room door behind me. I checked left and right, but the man must have been quicker than I realised because I didn't see him. What I did see was my nurse bearing down on me and she was breathing fire. I'd already nicknamed her Houlihan from M.A.S.H because the woman had a take no prisoners attitude with a glare to match. She would've been better placed inside a war zone.

"Back in bed, Mr Daniels," she instructed in her gravel voice.

"In a minute," I told her. "I just have to—"

"How about I give you a minute to get your butt back in bed?" Her drawn on eyebrows pinched together, creating one long squiggly line. I tried not to stare and forced my gaze down to her eyes. "This is a hospital, not command central like you and your posse seem to think it is."

My brows flew up. "Posse?"

"You heard me."

Travis appeared behind her and I widened my eyes in silent communication to help a guy out.

Using his middle finger, Travis rubbed at his brow in silent reply to let me know I was on my own. My eyes narrowed and Houlihan glanced over her shoulder to see what I was looking at. Travis quickly snapped his arm back down by his side.

"Visiting hours are over," she barked.

"Yes, ma'am." He disappeared quickly, no doubt waiting until Houlihan returned to her station.

Because it was easier not to argue, I let the nurse hustle me towards my room. Deposited back in my bed, pain meds delivered, and chart checked, I was ordered to rest, and then she was gone.

I lifted the blankets and was half out of bed when Travis materialised.

"Pussy," I muttered at him, wincing and holding my ribs as I slid the rest of the way out and to my feet.

"Bitch."

"As delightful as this conversation is, I need to find Henry." I started for the door, opening it cautiously as I asked, "Did you see him?"

"I passed him in the hall on the way to your room," he replied as I stuck my head out and peeked left. No Houlihan. "What was up with him anyway? I said hey and he shot past as though I wasn't even there."

I looked right, not even knowing where to start with that question. "Don't ask," I muttered.

Travis stuck his head out beside me. There she was. Houdini Houlihan. Her back was to me and she had Jared barrelled up by the wall. He looked nervous. Travis snorted beside me when he caught sight of his trapped brother.

"Jared's a pussy too," I muttered with a smirk sent his way. Jared's caged glance caught us and relief swept his features.

"Quick," I muttered and shoved Travis back inside and shut the door, sacrificing Jared for the greater good. "Fucking Houlihan." I turned around, facing my friend. "What are you two doing here anyway?"

Travis folded his arms, eyes flattening in an unhappy gesture. "Jared and I spent the past couple of hours at the Florence Bar, reviewing the security footage."

"And?"

He exhaled audibly. "Morgan didn't leave like you thought. We placed her inside on two separate occasions after the time of your accident."

"Hell." It would have been easier if it was Morgan who'd hit us. At least then we knew who we were dealing with. Now we were left with the possibility that someone was after Grace and no idea who it was. "Are you sure it was her?"

He nodded, grim. "Even if her features weren't clear on screen, you couldn't miss that red dress she wore."

I tipped my eyes to the ceiling for a minute, resigned to the possibility that Grace was hiding something important from all of us. Something big enough for people to want her dead.

"I haven't heard from the police," I said, looking back at Travis. They'd taken my statement not long after I woke, barrelling me up before I could go climb into bed with Grace. "Have you?"

"Jared spoke to Mitch. He says they got black paint samples off the side of Marjorie. Forensics can try piecing back the make and model of the car but that won't be a quick and easy answer."

The door opened and Jared slipped inside. He was on his phone, muffling the mouthpiece to mutter, "Thanks, assholes," in our direction before returning to his conversation.

We waited for him to finish. "Good news," he said after hanging up the phone and tucking it into his back pocket. He looked from Travis to me. "A witness identified the car. Bad news. The police found it abandoned and burned out near a reserve on the south end of Penrith."

That confirmed the crash was deliberate and not the work of complete amateurs.

"Maybe it was young kids," Jared offered. "Stole a car, lost control, and panicked at getting caught."

"Or maybe someone wanted Grace dead," Travis said bluntly. "Then incinerated the car to cover their tracks because they're already known to police." He looked to me. "What's your gut say, Daniels?"

I swiped a hand over my face, scratching idly at the light growth of beard on my face. "My gut's saying this has something to do with Morgan." *Believe me, you'll be sorry,* her acid voice echoed in my head. "There's too much coincidence for it to be otherwise, but you placed her at the bar."

Travis shrugged. "She could've got someone else to do it."

"That seems a bit overkill, don't you think?"

"Then who is it who wants Grace dead?" Travis asked.

"This is not happening again." I jabbed my finger at both Jared and Travis in turn, my eyes flashing angrily. Between Evie being shot and Quinn kidnapped, we'd all had it. Enough was enough. "As soon as Grace gets the all clear to leave the hospital, I'm taking her somewhere safe and I'm not letting her out of my sight until this situation is contained."

Travis looked at me as though I'd just told him I planned on picking up Mount Everest and moving it several metres to the north. "How do you plan on managing that?"

"How do I plan on managing that?" I folded my arms. Jared and Travis might have married two stubborn women, but they kept making the mistake of telling them what to do. They'd have better luck telling a cat to sit and roll over. "By putting her in the car and driving, that's how. Straight to the beach cottage in Terrigal." Our firm owned the central coast property, acquiring it under an assumed name. It made the cottage a haven to retreat to when one of us needed to lie low for any reason. I couldn't think of a better place to keep Grace safe right now than there. "Mac can pack Grace a suitcase for me. When she's released from hospital, I'll let her assume I'm taking her home to the duplex and just keep driving. She's hardly going to leap from a moving vehicle, is she?"

"She could," Jared interjected. "I've learnt never to assume anything when it comes to women."

The door opened and Mac slipped inside. She looked unusually severe. Her blond hair was pulled back in a tight knot and she was wearing a long-sleeved, fitted black shirt and tight black jeans tucked into combat boots. "Christ, you were right, Casey." Mac rolled her neck as though she'd just gone a round with Muhammad Ali. "Houlihan is hardcore."

She held an A4 yellow envelope in her hand. Seeing all three of us standing in my room, she tucked it quickly behind her back.

My eyes narrowed at the furtive gesture. "What's that?"

"What … this?" She brought the envelope back into view, looking at it as though she'd never seen it before.

"Yes. That," I replied.

"I'm not sure. I found it on the floor outside your room just now, " Mac replied with widened eyes. My body tensed. Mac's widened eyes was her tell that something had just gone down, and whatever that something was, she a) had no plans on sharing it, and b) it was likely to cause a stroke.

"Jared, was that envelope on the floor outside when you walked in five minutes ago?" I asked without taking my eyes from Mac.

Mac looked everywhere but at the three of us and began tapping the envelope against her thigh impatiently.

"No," Jared growled.

Tension crackled in the room.

"Well, fun chat," she said casually, "but I've got shit to do."

Jared barred the door, green eyes narrowing on his sister.

"Out of my way," she barked.

Travis snatched the envelope from her hands and passed it to me. A quick glance over her shoulder and Mac's eyes widened further. She turned back to Jared. "Move, asshead."

Jared folded his arms in reply.

Taking the envelope, I flipped open the lip and took a peek. There were several harmless looking white sheets of paper inside, but it was the print on the top of the first sheet made my hands shake.

"Mac." My voice cracked on the word. She spun around, facing me, and her eyes softened. I cleared my throat. "How did you …"

Travis peeked over my shoulder when I trailed off, peering into the envelope. He jerked visibly.

"What is it?" Jared asked from his position by the door.

"It's my parents' autopsy report," I told him and his body stiffened.

All eyes fell on Mac and the crackling tension reached new heights as we took in her uncharacteristic outfit with a whole new perspective.

"What. The. Fuck?" Travis growled.

"Damn," she muttered, knowing we were on to her. "I should've posted it anonymously."

My voice was a whiplash. "You broke into Morgan's house and stole the report?"

Mac shrugged, the gesture nonchalant and frustrating. It only served to piss me off even more. She risked her damn life and was trying to make it sound like a cakewalk. "I only did what you guys were going to do anyway."

"After we finished her background check and knew what we were dealing with!" I roared, completely losing it. "You do not put your life in danger! Not for me, not for your brothers, not for anyone, and least of all…" I flung the envelope fisted in my hand across the room and Mac flinched "…for this!"

"And what if Morgan destroyed it while you were all dithering around with background checks?" she shouted back, sounding far more frustrated than she had a right to be. This wasn't her fight.

"Then it would've been too damn bad!" I yelled back, going nose to nose. Her nostrils flared and I forced myself to soften my tone. "What you did was stupid and dangerous and not worth risking your life!"

"I happen to think you're worth it, Casey."

Then her eyes filled with tears and I sagged like a whipped puppy. These girls were going to kill us all. I might as well just accept it. I shook my head and met her eyes. "Thank you." A slow, happy grin overtook her pretty face. "But …" I added and her eyes narrowed. "If you ever do something like this again—"

"We'll tell Mum," Jared finished for me.

Mac gasped with horror and spun to face her brother. "You wouldn't dare!" she shrieked. She looked to her other brother. "Travis, that's—"

"Shut up," Travis whipped out, his green eyes shooting sparks. "There are no words for how pissed I am at you right now."

Travis stalked to the door and Jared shifted. He launched it open without thought or care to where Houlihan was lurking. Grabbing Mac's bicep, he dragged her out the door behind him. "Hey!" she yelled.

"We're going to have a conversation, Mackenzie 'Lone Wolf' Valentine, and by conversation I mean I'm going to talk and you are going to keep your piehole shut and listen!"

When they disappeared, I shook my head at Jared. "Your sister needs a leash."

His eyes were flat and unhappy. "Mum and Dad already tried that. It backfired. Big time." He glanced at his watch. "I need to get to the office. I want to see what Seth has managed to pull together for us on Morgan."

"Is Tim there?"

It was Saturday and Tim rarely worked weekends, but I'd asked him to clear my schedule. It would probably involve some heavy duty grumbling because it meant dumping all my current cases on Travis, Jared, and Coby. They would have to deal. I was due time off.

"He was just turning up when I left so he's probably still there."

"Do me a favour? Tell him I'm going to be out of town for at least a week once Grace gets out of hospital. Then get him to contact the property agents for the cottage, have someone come in on Thursday and give it a clean and stock the fridge and pantry."

"Good idea," Jared replied and then smirked. "But you can tell Tim yourself. He mentioned plans to visit you sometime this morning. Said he wanted to bring you coffee and a brownie."

"Awesome," I muttered, hoping he took pity on me just this once and got my coffee somewhere else.

When Jared left, I picked up the envelope off the floor. With everything going on I knew I wasn't in the right headspace to deal with whatever was inside it. Reading it would have to wait. Opening the cupboard beside my bed, I pulled out the bag Travis dropped off for me. After tucking it inside, I zipped it back up, put the bag away, and went in search of Henry again.

First I did a quick detour by Grace's room. She was fast asleep, her head tilted back on the pillow, mouth open and emitting a light snore. Nate sat by her bed, reading glasses on while he perused The Sydney Morning Herald.

I stepped up to the side of her bed, watching her breathe noisily. Grace had put her family before herself. It was admirable and I was proud of her, hearing how she'd stepped up for her family during such a shitty time, but that needed to stop now. Her family was strong enough to stand on their own feet, and from the sounds of her father, they had been for some time. She needed to learn how to put herself first for a change. That would start now.

Nate looked at me over the top of his newspaper. "How's my Henry? Cooled off yet?"

"I hope so but I'm not sure. I got waylaid," I explained. "I just wanted to check in on Grace again before I went looking for him."

Nate's eyes, blue like Henry's, lit with amusement. "As you can see here…" he jerked his chin towards his snoring daughter "…my little girl is resting just fine and I have no plans to be anywhere else today. If you're looking for Henry, try the cafeteria or the vending machine at the end of the hall. The boy never stops eating."

"Will do." I ran the backs of my fingers gently down Grace's cheek, reassured when it felt warm to the touch. When I looked up, Nate was watching the gesture. I drew my hand back. "Can I get you anything while I'm gone?"

"Coffee," he boomed and went back to the article he was reading, adding, "Black, no sugar."

"Oh, and Casey?" he called out when I was halfway out the door. I turned back, meeting his eyes. "My Gracie needs a man who looks after himself. You're useless to her if you don't give yourself time to heal too, yeah? So after you're done talking sense into my bullheaded son, go lie down."

"Yes, sir."

"Nate," he barked.

My lips twitched. I gave him a short nod and left.

Grace's dad was right. I found Henry in the cafeteria. He was sitting alone at a table with a packet of chips, but by no means had his presence gone unnoticed. I watched two girls, maybe around twenty, approach him. One of them said something and Henry grinned. After replying, he stood up and the girls took turns getting their photo with him. More giggly chatter followed before they left, one of them slipping a piece of paper into his pocket. They moved a distance away, nearer to me, and paused to look at the photos on their screens, both arguing over whose picture was better.

Henry looked up when I reached his table. He sighed and waved for me to sit down, saying, "Nothing like a couple of pretty fans to make you feel less like a fucking loser, right?"

"Looking out for your little sister makes you a loser now?"

"I'm sorry, Casey." He looked at me, his eyes sad and defeated. "You were a friend and telling you to stay away from Grace was pretty much saying you weren't good enough. I guess after everything that happened with Evie and then Quinn, I got scared."

My brows flew up, surprised. "You think I am good enough?"

Henry shrugged. "Yeah, I do."

"I'm not. But for Grace I want to be. Do you get that? I've never cared about being good enough for anyone until I met your sister. I'm sorry for going behind your back, and I had every intention of speaking to you about it, but I'm not here to give you excuses. I'm here to tell you that no one is in safer hands than she is." I locked eyes on his, letting him see the seriousness of my words. "No one."

Henry swallowed, and after a pause, nodded.

I breathed a heavy sigh of relief because that just went down a whole helluva lot easier than I thought it would. "This whole thing with Grace and stepping up for your dad when he needed help, that's something you need to talk to your sister about, but she did it because she loves you and she wanted you to have your dream. You would've done the same thing for her. So rather than get pissed off and make Grace upset, let it go. In her eyes, you've already paid her back because you didn't stuff around. You worked your ass off to get where you are now and you're doing something you love, just like Emma and Ava are. And because of that, she gets to sit back and be happy with the choice she made to put her family before herself. Let her have that happiness, Henry, because without it, you'll make everything she did mean nothing."

Henry, eyes trained on the table as I spoke, nodded again. Then he looked at me. "I know you're right." His voice was hoarse and he cleared his throat. "I'm not pissed at her. I'm pissed at myself. For not knowing. For giving her hell for leaving us when the whole time leaving us was the last thing she wanted to do. We lost our mother, and we had each other to lean on, but Grace left and she had no one, and I was an asshole because I hated her for leaving. I hated her because I thought we didn't matter enough, when all along, we mattered too much. And the whole time I was a prick to her about it, she didn't say a word." His eyes filled and he let out a shaky breath. "I don't know how to fix this."

"You can't fix the past," I told him because I knew that firsthand.

"No, I can't." He shook his head. "But I can be there for her now, right?"

"You can." I stood up to leave. After stealing a chip from the packet on the table, I slapped him on the back. "We cool now?"

Henry's voice hardened. "Not quite."

I paused, the chip halfway to my mouth. "Oh?"

"Is someone trying to hurt Grace?"

I pressed my lips together. I didn't want to scare him but after the whole speech I just gave, I needed to be honest. "Possibly."

Henry closed his eyes at the word, muttering a low, "Fuck. Who would do something like this?"

"Henry." He opened his eyes. "We're looking into it. Right now I think it's best if I take Grace away for a while. Our firm has a house up the coast. She'll be safe there with me. It'll give her time to heal while we work out what's going on."

He stood up. We were the same height so he was looking at me directly. "On one condition."

"Okay. What?"

"You keep me in the loop. If I find out you've been keeping any more shit from me, I won't care if you're my sister's boyfriend or the fucking Pope. I'll punch you out."

I wouldn't have expected anything less. Popping the chip in my mouth, I crunched it hard between my teeth and held out my hand. Henry took it, shaking firmly. "Agreed."

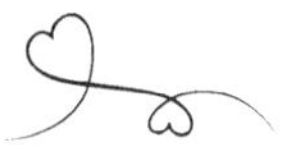

I spent the next few days in hospital because it was a good excuse to keep watch on Grace. Her room was situated opposite a small bench of seats. Beside that sat the vending machine Henry liked to frequent, Evie too, judging by the number of chocolate bars stashed in her bag. When I wasn't with Grace, either Travis or Coby sat on the bank of seats, keeping watch on her door and fielding conversation from Henry and Evie when they visited the vending machine to replenish their stash. The rest of my time was spent in clandestine meetings, dodging Houlihan, popping painkillers, and getting to know Grace's dad.

When I asked, Grace was adamant the crash was an accident. She couldn't come up with a single name of anyone who might have it in for her. I made her ring John so he could weigh in on the conversation via speakerphone. He told me the modelling industry was a bitchy, jealous world but it wasn't full of people trying to kill off the competition. Regardless, we kept Seth busy looking into all her current and past jobs.

By the time Friday morning rolled around, we had yet to find answers. I got up and showered early. Today we were both getting out of here. I wanted to be ready so I could help Grace.

After pulling on a pair of board shorts, Houlihan materialised. With military style precision, she began re-strapping my ribs and barking post-care instructions.

"The car's all fuelled up," Coby told me as he strode into my room. I was borrowing his car for the trip—the same tricked out Toyota Hilux that Evie had, only in black. Seeing Houlihan, he started backing away.

"You know you're a big girl, right?" I called out.

"Yeah, so?" he called out over his shoulder.

"I'll tell Evie about the fishing charter incident if you don't get back here with those car keys."

Coby changed direction, coming back in the room. "You're such a bitch, Daniels," I was told as he dug his hand in his pocket. "Besides, she already knows."

"Yeah?" I chuckled. "How'd that work out for you?"

"My ears are still fucking ringing," he muttered.

"Language!" Houlihan snapped.

Coby set his jaw and tossed the keys on the bed while I fought not to laugh. I'd been copping it all week. It was refreshing to have it directed on someone else for a change.

"Thanks," I told him and pocketed the keys, causing Houlihan to grumble. "You pick up Grace's suitcase from the duplex?"

"Yep."

"You're blocking my light," Houlihan growled at Coby.

He scowled and shifted back a step, folding his arms. Houlihan returned to her task. When done, she scooped up the empty bandage packets off the bed, tossed them in the bin in the corner, and left the room, over her shoulder, saying, "Goodbye, Mr Daniels. I see you in this hospital again, I'll have your balls for breakfast."

My balls shrank back up inside my body at the thought of Houlihan anywhere near them.

"Jesus," Coby muttered, cupping his own protectively while I tugged a tee shirt over my head and yanked it down. "Does the father-in-law know you're whisking his little girl away for a week of sex?"

I tucked my wallet in my back pocket and picked up the duffel bag off the bed, sparing Coby a glance. "Father-in-law?"

He smirked as he snatched the duffel bag from my hand. "You know his only son is into playing his guitar and partying, right? And then you come along and bond with him all week over fishing and cars. And then rather than ask him, you go all take charge and tell him you're taking Grace away until you're satisfied she's safe. The man was impressed. But then we've all heard about Dalton." Coby shrugged. "Any guy following that douchebag would look like the Second Coming to Nate. In his eyes, you and Grace are already hitched. Welcome to the Paterson family, mate," he said with a grin.

I looked at him sideways as we left the room, not hiding the smirk. "Of course the man's impressed. No one can handle this much awesome and remain unscathed. If you're lucky," I told him as we walked side by side down the hall towards Grace's room, "I might let a little of it rub off on you."

Coby snorted. "You're so full of it, Daniels."

I shook my head in mock sympathy. "Jealousy is an ugly look, man."

"You would know," he retorted.

"Any news on Beck?" I asked him, switching topic midstride. I wanted to find out what he knew before we hit Grace's room. Beck, our part-time surveillance guy, was tasked with watching Morgan. Seth had put together her background check but it came up clean. Too clean. Morgan was no angel, yet according to the report, she was set for sainthood. With someone of her background who now worked in the cybercrime division, she held the power to abuse the position if that was the way the wind blowed.

"Still nothing," he muttered, pissed, because I wasn't the only one who wanted this shit done with. "Goes to work, occasionally the laundromat, shops, comes home. She had two friends over last night. Both female. He's working on identifying them."

We rounded the corner to Grace's room. "When he does, put someone on following them too."

Grace was perched on the edge of her bed wearing a tiny pair of ratty denim shorts. The length of beautiful toned leg on display sent a surge of blood to my cock. Seeing the bandages covering her right side quickly took care of that.

The shirt she wore was white and floaty, with big red lips painted on it. It hung off her left shoulder, baring more skin than I could handle seeing right now. It made me itch to get her underneath me.

Soon, I promised myself. I just had to get past the initial outrage when she realised I was stealing her away. Then we could get down to the serious business of sex.

The cast on her right forearm had been set two days ago. Her wrist was now strapped to her chest with a sling, protecting her bruised shoulder. The bandage looked too tight, indenting the skin around her neck and leaving no doubt it was Houlihan's handiwork.

Henry knelt tying the laces on her runners, and her father stood behind her, looking uncomfortable as he tugged a brush through her hair.

"Ouch, Dad!" she squealed, her head snapping back as the brush caught on a knot. "I've just come out the other side of a concussion. Are you trying to give me another one?"

"Quiet!" he boomed, looking tense and red in the face. "And stop moving around or I'll cut your hair off and solve both our problems."

"You threatened that every time you brushed my hair when I was little."

My lips twitched as Coby and I stood in the doorway taking in the scene.

"So?" Nate retorted as Henry finished with her shoes and stood up.

"So you haven't done it yet," she pointed out. "You're nothing but a big bunch of hot air."

Grace's head snapped back again, and I'm pretty sure it was deliberate that time. Coby chuckled from beside me. Her eyes flew our way at the sound, her face breaking into a smile when I stepped into the room.

"Oh thank God," she announced.

I walked over, pressed a kiss on her lips, and picked up her bag. "Ready to go?"

"Damn straight I'm ready to go." Nate went for one more drag of the brush and she batted him away with her free hand, snatching the brush and giving it to me. I opened the zip partway on her bag, stuffed it inside, and closed the zip.

Nate took the bag from my hand. "I'll walk you both down to the car," he muttered gruffly. The man was flying home to Melbourne later that day. There wasn't much else he could do but return to work, though he was leaving with the promise that I'd keep both him and Henry in the loop.

As we left the room en masse, Henry gave me a fist bump, knowing it was all up to me to squirrel Grace out of the city without her leaping from the car in a fit. "Good luck."

Grace furrowed her brow. "Good luck with what?"

"Er …" Henry scratched the back of his head. "I don't know." Grace's frown deepened and I shook my head. Henry was a shitty liar. "Stuff," he mumbled.

"What stuff?"

Nate started moving a little quicker, no doubt trying to avoid the questioning his son had inadvertently set off.

"Where's the fire, Dad?" Grace called out as he raced ahead of us.

"Don't be impolite by dawdling, love." He frowned back at her sternly. "Coby's got his car in temporary parking to pick you up, you know. Do you have any idea how much hospital parking costs these days? Why they may as well ask a man to hand over his left nut."

Grace snorted, rolling her eyes at Coby who, along with me, was busy fighting back laughter. "Sorry I'm injured and can't Olympic sprint to your car, Coby. I'll be sure to pay the parking fee so you won't have to sacrifice your left nut for us."

Coby cleared his throat. "That's mighty polite of you, Grace, but I think I've got enough cash to cover it."

I took hold of Grace's hand and she leaned in close to my ear as we walked. "My family's not usually this odd," she whispered furiously. "I think it must be a full moon."

I looked down at her, grinning. "It's only a quarter moon, Slim."

"No, you're wrong," I was told, her voice ringing with authority. "It's a full moon."

My grin widened and I squeezed her hand. "You're adorable, even when you're wrong."

"Adorable? You should check out all my bruises. Then you'll change your mind."

"I've seen your bruises," I replied. My nostrils flared with anger because they were a reminder that someone had done this deliberately. I cracked my knuckles. "Every time I look at them I want to hit someone," I muttered under my breath.

Grace looked from my knuckles to my face, not missing the anger or the words. "Maybe you shouldn't look at me then."

Everyone had walked on ahead while we were talking so I halted her with my hand, using the opportunity to nudge her gently back against the hospital hallway. "Stop looking at you?" I pressed my forehead to hers, staring into her eyes. "Why don't you ask me to take you time travelling while you're at it, or ask me for the cure for cancer?"

Grace sucked in a breath, paling rapidly.

"What?" I paused. Oh shit. Then I winced. I was trying to point out that what she was asking was impossible, but I couldn't have been more of an idiot if I tried. "Dammit, Grace. Baby, I'm sorry. That was insensitive of me. I—"

Grace cut me off, saying, "No, it's fine," but she was a shitty liar, just like her brother. "Really," she added when my brows rose suspiciously. "We should catch up to Dad before he gives himself a hernia from moving too fast."

She pushed away from the wall, but I held fast to her hand. "Grace, I …"

"You what?"

Christ. She had no idea how much I cared about her, did she? She was strong enough that I couldn't walk all over her, teasing when I was in a pout, hot when I wanted a hard fuck, and sweet when I needed her in my arms.

I wanted to tell her exactly that but my balls must've done a disappearing act because what came out instead was a lame apology.

It was pathetic.

"Casey." Grace reached up cupping my cheek. Her thumb brushed over the short scruffy beard on my face. She seemed to like it. She was always touching it like she was doing now. I liked her doing that so much I hadn't yet bothered to shave. "You're amazing. So much so, that the fact you can't cure cancer surprises me, because you give off this…" she shook her head, as though searching for the right word "…aura of intense capability that makes me believe you can do anything."

I turned my head and pressed a kiss to her palm. Then I winked. "That's because I can. I'm Batman, remember?"

Grace rolled her eyes, but I could see the amusement. "Like I could forget."

She slid her hand from my face and I watched her walk away, her laughter trailing down the hall, and I knew I didn't just care for her. My heart was lost, and even if she didn't want it, I wouldn't take it back.

Chapter Twenty-Four
GRACE

I glanced sideways at Casey from the passenger seat of Coby's Hilux. His brow furrowed in concentration as he drove so I wiped my left palm furtively on the denim of my shorts. Being back in a car made me break out in a sweat. A cold, clammy sweat. I hadn't given it a thought until we pulled out of the hospital, but once we did, out came the meltdown. Not Casey though. His actions were so calm and unruffled you would think he was in a major car accident every other week. I could see him at the dinner table. "Can you pass the salt? Oh, and by the way, I was in a fiery crash today. Just in case you see it on the news. Tomorrow I plan on diving off the Harbour Bridge into a mob of great white sharks, but I'll be fine, because I'm Casey."

The man was as cool as the Arctic.

Setting my jaw, I beat back the imminent panic attack before it went nuclear. I hadn't come this far in my life to fall apart at the thought of being inside a speeding metal box.

I could do this.

If Casey could be ice cold, then by God, I would be cooler than that.

"What's colder than ice?"

"Dry ice," Casey answered, glancing across at me. "Why?"

I am dry ice.

It didn't have a very good ring to it. I shook my head. "What else?"

"Liquid nitrogen."

I am liquid nitrogen.

That made me sound like a lame villain out of a Spiderman movie. "Anything else?"

"A polar bear's nutsack?" Casey chuckled at his own joke, which made him just as lame as the idea of me being liquid nitrogen.

He grinned across at me and I rolled my eyes. "You just lost some of your cool factor."

His grin widened. "You think I'm cool?"

"Not anymore," I mumbled, brows pinched as I stared dazedly out the window. My visions of flurries and Polar Ice Caps were interrupted by the view of a six-lane dual highway and forest. My eyes swung to Casey. "Where are we going?"

He indicated right and changed lanes, shifting into fifth gear as he overtook a little Suzuki Swift. Wherever we were going, he planned on getting us there in a speedy fashion. "For a drive," I was told.

"Oh?" I prompted for a further explanation. After a lengthy wait where one didn't appear forthcoming, I gave up and asked, "A drive where?"

"North."

"Where north?"

Casey hesitated, looking like he was going to say something and didn't.

My eyes narrowed because he was acting shifty. "What's going on?"

"Nothing, Slim."

He may as well have said he was driving us to Kakadu for a spot of fishing because I didn't believe it for a second. "Then why won't you tell me where we're going?"

"I'll tell you when we get there."

Casey accelerated a little harder and the car picked up speed. I tried not to notice the scenery blurring out my window and grabbed for my new phone from the centre console. Coby had taken my old one and put the new one in easy reach before he left with Dad and Henry. He called it a 'temporary burner phone.' I called it overkill. The idea that someone could be tracking me or listening to my phone conversations was outrageous. I was Grace Paterson, not the President of the United States.

I scrolled the contact list, grateful to see he'd at least transferred all my numbers in. Even Casey was still listed under Batman. After finding Mac's number, I dialled.

Casey glanced at me. "What are you doing?"

"Ringing Mac. She won't lie."

"I'm not a liar."

"You're a deflector," I retorted. I put the phone to my ear and trained my gaze out the window. "It's practically the same thing."

"Grace," Mac barked by way of answering the phone.

I then realised my mistake by focusing on the outdoors. The blurring scenery forced the tight rein on my panic to snap like a rubber band. Suddenly, I couldn't breathe and began to gasp and wheeze.

Mac's tone of voice changed from annoyed to alert. "Grace?"

"Breathe, Slim," Casey ordered from beside me.

"No, I won't breathe!" Having a panic attack in front of Casey was embarrassing. I didn't want him seeing me fall apart. It wasn't going to be pretty. "In fact, I'm holding my breath until you pull this car over. Then you can tell me what's going on!"

"Uh oh," I heard Mac say.

Casey backed off of the accelerator, slowing the car a little. "That better?"

"No." My efforts at being liquid nitrogen weren't working. I was getting worse. Every breath I took forced my lungs to squeeze painfully. The realisation I was somehow suffocating freaked me out. Screw being cooler than ice. This wasn't irrational fear of being in a car, this was a goddamn heart attack. "I can't be in this car," I gasped. "Let me out."

"I can't pull over on the freeway. It's not safe." Casey glanced across at me again, real concern on his face. "Grace, are you okay?"

"No," I wheezed, my body starting to shake harder than Shakira live in concert. "Pull over. I need to get out!"

"Look at me," he ordered. "Don't look anywhere else. Just at me."

I looked at him, my chest pounding so hard it hurt.

"Grace, you're having a panic attack, okay? You need to fight it by focusing on me, okay?" I shook my head. Who cared about focusing? I couldn't breathe. He placed his palm on my bare leg, connecting us. Warmth seeped into my skin from his touch. He began to rub, soothing me. "Focus on breathing with me. Slow and deep."

I tried doing what he said because I didn't have any other choice. It took a full minute for my breathing to even out, slow and deep like his. The burning in my chest began to ease slowly. With that came the return of rationality followed by a nice big helping of mortification. "Thank you," I murmured, my cheeks flushing pink.

"Grace?" Mac's voice floated up from somewhere on the seat and I realised I'd dropped the phone mid-conversation. "You there?"

I went to reach for it but Casey stilled my arm. "Grace … It's okay to be scared."

"You're not," I pointed out.

He shrugged. "I've rolled my car once before, been rear-ended, spun out on a sheet of ice and hit a tree, and shoved into guardrail by an out-of-control truck."

"So what you're saying is once I have a few more accidents under my belt, I won't be scared anymore?"

Casey glared. "You're not having anymore accidents. That was your first and your last."

That was a ridiculous statement. Casey couldn't predict the future. If he did it would include something far worse than a car crash. Not that someone ploughing into the side of Casey's car was an accident. "It wasn't an accident though, right? Someone wants me dead."

After a beat, he said, "That's why I'm not taking you back to the duplex." He glanced across at me. "I'm taking you up the coast. Our firm has a cottage by the beach. I think it's a good idea for us to stay where you can rest safely for a few days."

I did my best to turn and look at him properly, but whatever painkillers I was given were wearing off fast and it hurt to move.

"Whatever you're going to say, save it. I'm not taking you back," he informed me, his tone rigid. "You need time to heal and have hot sex on the beach, and I'm going to make sure you get both. You're not going to complain about it either. You're going to like it. Or else," he added.

Casey looked tense and wary, his jaw ticking. I knew he expected me to spaz out at any moment. It was possible I might. Time away to clear my head? An entire week of sunshine, sand between my toes, and hot sex with Casey? Sign me the fuck up.

"Grace!" Mac yelled and I jumped, amazed she'd had the patience to hang on the line for this long. I picked up the phone and this time Casey didn't stop me. He'd obviously said what he needed to say and sat back waiting for the fallout.

"I'm going on a road trip," I said to Mac, dazed.

"Congratulations. Are you okay?"

"You don't get it. I can't even remember the last time I got in a car and left everything behind to lie on a beach." Granted, it would be awkward—I was bruised and bandaged, but even that couldn't dampen my rising spirits. "This has to be done right. I need you to pack a bag of beach essentials."

"I already did. I put it in Coby's car this morning."

My eyes flew to Casey. An untraceable phone, my bags already packed and in the car, a cottage by the beach? This wasn't some spur of the moment getaway. Casey had this planned long before we left the hospital. Wedging the phone between my shoulder and ear, I opened the glove box in front of me. A slate grey handgun sat inside, silent and deadly. He obviously wasn't taking any chances with my life. My breath hitched and tears climbed my throat.

Casey glanced over. I knew he could see the gratitude written all over my face because he went all hard and fierce. "Whatever it takes to keep you safe, Grace, okay?"

"Okay," I agreed quietly.

"You all good now?" Mac boomed in my ear.

I closed the compartment and took the phone back in hand. "I don't know. Is there anything else I need?"

"Booze and snacks."

"Yes!" I turned back to Casey. "We need to hit the shops." I was going to eat, all week, and it was going to be awesome.

Casey shook his head, unamused. "We're not going shopping."

My lips pursed. "Yes. We are. What else?" I asked Mac.

"Nothing else. I've packed some books and movies in your bag, but honestly, if you need those for entertainment then there's something seriously wrong with you."

"Wait," I breathed. "What about Mitsy?"

"Yeah," Mac agreed quickly. "It's not a road trip without a dog."

"No," Casey snapped.

"We have to turn back," I told him.

"Hell, to the fucking no," he snapped again.

"We're on our way back," I said into the phone. "Can you pack some things for Mitsy?"

Casey dug in his heels. "I'm not turning around."

An hour later we were back on the highway. The back window was down and Mitsy's fluffy white head stuck out the side, tongue working furiously as he lapped at the wind.

I passed him a Dorito from the packet on my lap, slipping it around the left-hand side of the passenger seat. He crunched it furiously before returning to the window. I grinned. While I would never associate the word jubilant with Mitsy, he appeared to be having a good time.

Casey's jaw ticked each time his gaze returned to the rearview mirror to check on my dog. The chips kept Mitsy occupied so he hadn't taken to chewing the upholstery. Yet.

My burner phone buzzed. I put down the chip packet and picked it up, reading a message from Coby.

Just received news from Evie that Mitsy is currently en route to the cottage via the backseat of my car. He better be in his dog carrier or heads will roll.

I typed a reply. Of course he is. Relax, dude.

After hitting send, I put the phone back in the centre console. Then I picked up the chip packet and passed Mitsy another Dorito. Casey shook his head. "If Mitsy chews the backseat of Coby's car, we're dead," I announced.

His brows flew to his hairline, incredulous as he looked at me quickly. "We're dead?"

I shrugged. "You know how when you're driving and the police pull you over because your passenger isn't wearing a seat belt? And they fine you because you're the driver and responsible for all occupants of the vehicle? It's kinda like that." While Casey looked a little dazed I added, "And if he asks, Mitsy was in a dog carrier the whole trip."

"Firstly," Casey began, nostrils flaring dangerously, "if I ever hear about you being in a car without wearing a seat belt, you will be dead and I'll be the one doing the killing. Secondly … I agree. If Coby asks, Mitsy didn't leave the dog carrier, but," and that but was loud and firm and rang in my ears, "if he chews any part of this car, he's going home in a pine box."

I gasped.

"That's me being humane, Grace," I was told. "I'll make sure it's done quickly. Coby wouldn't be so nice. He doesn't like dogs. I do."

I ignored his threats and ate a chip. Casey glanced at me, lids lowering when I licked the flavouring off my fingers. That proved harder to ignore. I reached for another chip. "You know why I refused to give Mitsy back to Dalton?"

"Why?"

I shifted, trying to get comfortable and failing miserably. "Because Dalton abandoned him and Mitsy got shafted because no one wanted him. I feel bad about that because initially, neither did I. So of course he's going to be angry at the world. Mitsy had a rough start to life and deserves to get his happily ever after." I watched Mitsy from my side passenger mirror as I spoke. His head was still out the window, licking the wind with enthusiasm. "He just needs someone to love him. That's all."

"Playing eye-spy with you sucks," I muttered to Casey after our fifth game. Which I lost. After losing the last four before that.

He grinned. "Don't be a sore loser, Slim."

"A sore loser?" I huffed. "Using words like automotive navigation system and engine malfunction light is not in the spirit of the game."

"You said I couldn't name anything outside the car," he pointed out.

"I know, but I'm not an aeronautical space engineer. Simple words like steering wheel and dashboard would suffice."

"You want to play again?"

My nostrils quivered. "No."

Ten minutes later we pulled into a paved driveway.

Casey got out of the car, but I sat for a moment and stared. When he'd said beach cottage I assumed some kind of rendered beach house within walking distance to the water, but this was right opposite the beach, and it wasn't some modern monstrosity; it was quaint and pretty and well kept. The outside was white weatherboard with a sweet timber porch and a brightly coloured hammock. The front lawn was thick and lush, and the gardens were a riot of bright shrubs and colourful flowers.

This wasn't a house, this was a home. A place you could see kids running around the front, bikes overturned, a pile of shoes by the front door, and a hanger by the porch railing that held things like skipping ropes, and a leash for the dog.

Tears blurred my vision when longing hit me hard.

This.

Just … this.

This was what I wanted. A home. A family. Maybe a veggie garden and a cat too. One with long hair that looked like a wild lion.

I opened the car door before Casey reached my side. He took my hand, helping me out. "This place is beautiful."

"It's not fancy," he warned me. Moving to the back of the car, he started getting our bags out.

"I don't need fancy," I called out, opening the back door. Mitsy leaped out and immediately cocked his leg on the big tyre. I waited patiently for him to finish.

"Yeah?" Casey walked over and dumped one of the bags on the porch. Holding the other, he dug in his pocket for his keys. I followed him over, Mitsy trotting behind as Casey plucked them out. "What do you need?" he asked when I stepped up onto the porch.

I hooked a finger in his board shorts and tugged him closer. "Just you."

He grinned and brushed his lips against mine. "Just me, huh?"

"Mmm hmm." I rubbed a hand over the bulge in his shorts, my pulse accelerating when he started getting hard. Casey dropped the bag in his grip. Then he cupped my face in his hands and kissed me, sweeping his tongue inside my mouth. Need exploded as I kissed him back. My hips cradled his and he rocked his erection against me.

The pulsing between my legs reached critical levels and I broke off, anxious to get inside. "Give me the keys."

He held them up and I snatched them from his hands with a smirk. Turning, I unlocked the front door, over my shoulder saying, "Last one inside has to spend the entire next day naked, waiting on the other hand and foot."

Mitsy raced under my feet to get inside, tripping me. I spun, trying to catch my balance and Casey grabbed my hips before I toppled over.

"Arrghhh!" I cried out, fire trailing up my bruised body where he caught me.

He cursed and picked me up in the doorway, cradling me against his chest. I could hear the rapid thumping of his heart so I knew the effort cost him. Casey was always so capable he made me forget he was injured. "You okay?"

"I'm fine." I jerked my chin at the floor. "You can put me down."

"In a second." Casey turned around and started walking backwards inside the house. It would effectively make him first inside and me the loser. "Let me just carry you inside."

"No." I reached out and grabbed hold of the doorframe before he could move. It forced him to shift sideways or risk dropping me on my ass. "This is my stop, right here."

Thwarted. There was no way Casey could peel my fingers from the doorframe without having to let go of me first. I was impressed he could still hold me as tightly as he was without breaking a sweat.

"It seems we're at an impasse," he said.

My brows rose coolly. So help me God I wanted a naked Casey all day waiting on me hand and foot. He was not going to win this. "So it would seem."

"What's your plan, Slim? Because my arms are getting tired."

"They are?"

His lips twitched. "No. I could stand here all day."

"Fine. I don't have a plan," I declared, "but I've never had a naked man wait on me hand and foot before." I let my lids lower lazily, focusing on his mouth and letting my voice go all husky. If my one working hand didn't have a death grip on the doorframe, I'd have trailed it down my body suggestively. "The things I could do to you …"

"Yeah?" Casey's lips brushed mine again, slow and teasing. "What things?"

"What things?"

"Mmm hmm," he answered against my mouth. "I want you to list them out. One by one."

Did he think I wouldn't?

Newsflash, buddy, I thought, my eyes narrowing. You are going down in a ball of flames.

"First, I'll make you watch while I slide my hand down my belly and inside my panties." My cheeks heated because I'd never touched myself in front of a man in my life. If Casey asked me to though, I would. He had that effect. I lifted my chin, soldiering on. "But I'd keep them on so you couldn't see what I was doing." Casey's breathing got heavier. Buoyed that my plan was working, I kept going. "Then I'd—"

I was cut off by the sound of a man clearing his throat from inside the cottage. My eyes flew towards the sound and my flush almost set me on fire. A man—black suit, white shirt, red tie—was leaning up against the kitchen bench, juggling a set of keys. He looked like a property agent. Slick, handsome, and amused.

My hand fell away from the doorframe and Casey walked me in, setting me carefully on my feet. I didn't care that it made me first inside the cottage because I wanted to die. I glanced quickly at Casey. He hadn't been breathing heavy like I thought at all. He'd been laughing. His lips pressed together when he caught my glare.

"Hello," I managed politely to the man. Then I started for what I prayed really hard was the bedroom and not the pantry. "It's been a long drive so I'm just going to go to the bedroom now and die. Please excuse me." Mitsy followed, pausing to growl at the man as we passed by. "Mitsy," I snapped. "Come."

"Grace." My wrist was snagged before I could make my escape. I was turned to face the man so I pasted a smile on my face. "You're dead," I hissed quietly at Casey through gritted teeth. "I'm going to smother you in your sleep with a pillow. And I'm going to laugh while I do it."

His lips twitched as he made the introductions. "This is Wesley Brennan of Brennan Marks Realty. Wes, this is Grace."

There was an awkward hand shaking movement where he held out his right hand and I had to shake it with my left. He quickly changed hands and took mine in his. "I'm sorry about before," I told him. "We weren't— I mean, I wasn't … I didn't know anyone was going to be here."

I felt Casey shaking beside me and I wanted to elbow him. Not one of those lame elbows in the side either, but the kind where it packs a punch and when they double over from the pain, you crack your elbow in their face, thus breaking their nose. They did it all the time in those Jackie Chan movies. It didn't look that hard.

"I arranged for Wes to meet us here when we arrived," Casey explained. "He's heading out of town tomorrow so I wanted to catch up before he left."

I offered Wes another smile before I hissed quietly at Casey through gritted teeth. "Perhaps you could've told me this earlier."

"I could've," he murmured.

"Sorry for the interruption, Grace," Wes offered, fighting back a grin. "I was checking some of the fencing along the back line so I came through the side entry, which is why the front door was still locked."

Deciding to get over it, I offered Wes a drink. God knows I needed one.

He accepted so I left them to talk while I made a beeline for the kitchen. It looked out over the backyard. A large window sat above the sink, offering a beautiful view of more flowering shrubbery and a deep, blue pool. The kitchen and living area boasted a lot of white, but the gleaming timber floors added warmth—as did the accents of colour dotting the interior. The kitchen splashback was a bright tangerine and the beige modular couch was decorated with a navy throw and large, coloured cushions. The overall space wasn't huge, but high ceilings with exposed beams added an airy feel.

Deciding I'd be happy living here on a permanent basis, I opened the fridge door. Cool air blasted outwards and I let it cool my residual embarrassment while I perused the contents.

Spying a bottle chilled Sauvignon Blanc in the side door, I plucked it out. After finding some glasses from a nearby cupboard, I poured a hefty amount in each. Casey and Wes walked over and I pushed a glass across the kitchen bench in each direction, only catching on to their conversation after I'd returned the bottle to the fridge.

I slammed the door and spun around. "Wait a minute. You're putting the cottage on the market? This cottage?"

Casey shrugged. "Yeah, why?"

"I'll buy it," I blurted out.

Casey took my elbow gently. I was hustled away from Wes and towards the corner of the kitchen. Wes politely wandered into the living room with his wine, pretending to peruse the books on the shelves to give us privacy.

"Grace."

"What?"

"This property is right opposite the beach."

"And you're pointing out the obvious because ..."

"Because it's a million dollar property."

Did he think I was destitute? That I didn't have financial investments up the wazoo? Because I did. And this place? This would be an investment in my future. I may not get the kids with the overturned bikes and the husband in the backyard manning the barbecue, but I had Mitsy and my future cat.

"That's nice," I replied. "It will free up some capital for you."

I opened the fridge door again and began pulling out contents at random—olives, cheese, prosciutto, crusty bread—and put it all on the kitchen bench.

"Is that why you want to buy it?" he asked as I searched the cupboards for a platter. Casey walked to the high cupboard by the range hood and took one out. He handed it over and then leaned up against the bench, folding his arms. "We don't need the capital, Grace. We're offloading the property because it's a sellers market right now. House prices are hitting their peak. Now's the time to realise a good profit."

I paused what I was doing and picked up my wine, raising my brows at Casey while I took a sip. My insides quivered with delight at the crisp, cool taste.

"I just think that maybe you're making a rash decision," he added.

"Look," he said when I didn't reply. He began manoeuvring me out of the kitchen. "Why don't you go sit down and rest while I finish this and we can talk about it later. You have all week here. Take the time to look around first and see what you think."

I took another sip of wine, contemplating Casey over the rim of my glass. I was still buying it, but what he said made sense. There was no need to rush it. "Okay."

He paused, his expression suspicious. "Okay?"

"Yeah. Okay. You're right. I'll take the time to look around first."

Casey scratched at his beard, looking a bit thrown by my easy agreement. I grinned and walked away with my wine towards the living area and Wes.

"Oh, and Grace?" Casey called out. I paused to look at him. "You shouldn't be drinking alcohol. You're on heavy duty painkillers. The combination will—"

I cut him off. "Don't push it, Casey."

Wes half stood when I made my way over, hesitant about whether I needed assistance sitting down or not. I waved him off and sat, but I couldn't restrain the hiss when it hurt.

"Are you okay? Casey told me about the accident?"

"I'm a bit bruised, but I'm okay. I'm more upset about Casey's car to be honest. I don't think it stood a chance from the moment I arrived in Sydney."

Wes's brows rose in question.

"It's a long story," I replied and nodded at his glass. "Top up?"

He shrugged. "Sure. I don't have anywhere I need to be tonight."

I started to shift off the couch.

"I can get it," Wes said hastily.

"I'll get it," Casey called out. He walked over with the platter. Leaving it on the coffee table, he left and came back with the bottle of wine.

"I'm not imposing, am I?" Wes asked when Casey topped up his glass and took a seat beside me, his own wine glass in hand. I couldn't help but notice the double standards.

"Not at all," I told Wes and fixed a smile on my face. "Tell me about the area. I haven't been to Terrigal before but from what I saw on the drive in, it's really beautiful."

His face warmed with pride as he began spouting off some of the spots I needed to see while I was here. Casey put his hand on my leg, letting it rest there while Wes spoke. I finished my wine all too soon and Wes topped it up for me without thinking.

Casey didn't look happy but he didn't say anything. I went back to my chat with Wes, asking him about the local shopping and walking trails as I sipped at my second wine.

Chapter Twenty-Five
CASEY

"Oh my God," Grace moaned from somewhere beneath her pillow. I sat a coffee on the bedside table next to her, my first duty of the day after losing the challenge. Then I climbed back in bed. "How much did I drink last night?"

I chuckled, lifting the corner of the pillow to look at her. Her eyes were puffy and her hair everywhere. "Two glasses."

"Two? Just two?"

I opened my mouth, ready to tell her she shouldn't have combined her alcohol and painkillers.

"Don't you say I told you so," she mumbled, yanking the pillow from my hand and hiding back underneath it.

My lips twitched. "Okay."

I propped up my pillows and sat against the headboard of the bed, checking emails on my phone with one hand and sipping my coffee with the other. Grace was muttering from beneath her own pillow beside me when suddenly it flew off the bed. "You're naked," she breathed, her eyes running down the length of me and back up again.

"I am," I confirmed, going back to my phone.

"No. You don't understand. You're not wearing anything. At all."

I peered at her over the rim of my coffee cup as I took a sip. Her interest made my cock twitch in response. "That's usually what naked means. Wearing no clothes."

"I've never seen you fully naked before."

"And?"

"And you should never wear clothes again," she declared.

I laughed as I set my phone back on the bedside table, giving up on the emails for now. "With this?" I grabbed my cock suggestively. It was semi-hard already and all she'd done was look at it. "Could be dangerous," I joked. "I might poke someone's eye out."

"Oh my God," she groaned with a laugh and a roll of her eyes.

A pillow came flying my way, knocking my hand that held the coffee and just clipping my face. Hot liquid splashed carelessly over the pale blue sheets.

"Oops," Grace muttered. "Sorry."

I brushed it away with my hand, setting my coffee next to my phone before Grace did any more damage. "It's okay. That can be my first order of business today. Washing the sheets."

"No. I want a shower. You can help me with that first."

Help Grace with getting naked and wet? I grinned. "Yes, ma'am. But with your injuries, it might be easier if you had a bath instead."

"Yes, ma'am?" Grace repeated. She turned on her side and rested her head on her left hand. "I like that. You can do that all day too. Call me ma'am."

"Yes, ma'am." I rolled out of bed, the manoeuvre not hurting so much after taking a low dose of painkillers earlier this morning. I pointed to the ones I left next to her side of the bed. "Take those first. I'll make you something to eat so you can have them with food."

"Food?" Grace plopped onto her back with a loud, heavy sigh. "I don't think I can ever eat again. I ate so much crap yesterday my tummy still hurts. I'm not used to, well … eating." Then she groaned, holding a hand over her eyes. "I made an ass of myself in front of Wes last night, didn't I? I vaguely remember you apologising for me every five minutes."

"You were guarding the food platter like a pit bull," I told her as I walked through the double doors of the bedroom. Being a small, two-bedroom cottage, they opened directly into the kitchen so I could still see Grace as I pulled the toaster from the cupboard. I rested it on the counter, catching her eyes doing a lazy descent over my body. I angled myself so she got a better view and winked. "How's that?"

"Perfect," she said with a sigh. "Don't move."

I had to move to get the bread. Grace let out another mortified groan as I popped two slices in the toaster. "I'm so embarrassed. I pretty much ate that entire platter myself, didn't I? I'm such a pig."

"Don't be embarrassed. I don't think Wes cared. I had to stick him in a cab because he was just as shitfaced as you were."

"Probably because I didn't let him eat," she mumbled.

"Probably," I called out, chuckling as I opened the fridge. I stuck my head in, looking for the butter when a warm hand landed on my back.

"Mmm, nice," I said, straightening when the hand trailed down my back to my bare ass. Grace ran her palm over it, squeezing. I glanced down at my cock, watching it fill from the simple touch.

Her hand slid around my hip, taking it in her hand. Her grip was hard and I thrust into it. "Fuck the toast," I managed to get out when she squeezed and began to stroke. "I'm gonna eat you for breakfast."

"Uh uh," Grace tutted and pressed up against my back. "Today I'm in charge."

I slammed the fridge door shut and braced my palms on it, fucking into her hand. I shuddered, knowing I'd come like a freight train if she didn't stop soon. My dick was on a hair trigger after a forced week of abstinence.

"Yeah?"

"Yeah."

"That's what you think."

Her hand fell away when I turned around. Grace was still wearing her shirt from yesterday, but the shorts were gone and her panties were nothing but a scrap of black lace.

"Hey!" was all she managed before I sucked her bottom lip into my mouth. I used her distraction to my advantage. She squeaked into my mouth when my hand slipped inside her panties. I slid a finger through the slick heat and inside her. She broke off, gasping.

So hot and tight.

I wanted inside bad but I wouldn't last that long. I pulled out and sat her up on the kitchen counter.

"You said you'd stick your hand in your panties and touch yourself," I reminded her. Then I dragged her panties down and off and spread her wide. "But I wanna see you do it."

"Casey," she breathed, hesitating.

"Do it, Grace."

She reached down and began rubbing her clit. It dragged a soft moan from her throat.

"Fuck," I bit out. I had to grab my cock at the base before I came all over her. "That's so hot."

Her cheeks flushed and I knew she was embarrassed. I didn't care. She was so sexy I was tempted to grab my phone and take a picture. Stuff my mental spank bank. I could use that photo to jack off to for life. I palmed my phone off the kitchen counter and held it up. "Can I?"

"No way!" Grace pulled her hand away.

"Don't stop," I told her. I put the phone down and slipped a finger back inside. She tilted her hips at my invasion, taking my finger deeper with a groan. I added another one. "Keep touching yourself, Grace."

Her finger found the swollen button and began rubbing again. My cock pulsed and I fisted it, jacking myself at the same time. "Okay," she panted.

"Okay?"

"You can take a photo."

Fuck. I almost came right then and there. "Really?"

"Two conditions."

"Anything," I told her truthfully. "Tell me."

"The photo gets deleted before we leave the cottage and I get to take one of you."

"Done," I said quickly.

She giggled. It ended on a gasp when I twisted my fingers, finding her G-spot. "Oh God. I can't believe I'm agreeing to this."

"You can't back out now," I said with a grin. I pulled back and tugged at the hem of her shirt. "This has to go first." I helped her take it off, carefully slipping it from her injured shoulder. I tossed the shirt aside and ducked my head, sucking a nipple in my mouth. "You're gonna kill me, Casey," she gasped.

I let her nipple go with a pop and grinned. "Not if I go first."

I palmed my phone again before Grace changed her mind. After finding the camera, I held it up in front of her.

"I don't want my face in it!" she cried, holding out her hand to ward me off.

"You can be the one to delete the photo if you don't trust me to do it," I told her because I wanted her face. The look on it when she was all worked up and flushed was just as hot as the rest of her.

Grace bit her lip. "Okay. I'll delete it."

She didn't trust me to do it. I was okay with that. What I was asking was pretty huge. I knew if I had a daughter, I'd rip the head off any guy who got near her with a camera. Then I'd jam it up his ass.

Forgetting the whole photo thing for minute, I dropped between her legs and sucked her clit in my mouth. I wanted that look back on her face. Her head fell back and she moaned, rocking her hips forward. I shifted lower. "Touch yourself, Grace," I said before pushing my tongue inside her.

She did just that. I withdrew my mouth and licked my lips as I picked up the phone. Taking a step back, I focused the camera and took the shot. "So fucking hot."

"Just the one," she told me.

"Just the one," I confirmed, setting the phone aside. And it was a good one. Grace let out a little gasp. "You close?"

"So close," she managed to get out.

I dropped back down, spearing her with my tongue, competing with her finger as we both worked to get her off. "Come on, baby," I urged, palming my cock when it demanded attention. "Make it a good one."

Grace cried out and came, her body tensing on the counter. I laved at her gently with my tongue, soothing her through the aftershocks. When she was done, I straightened and wrapped her in my arms. She giggled weakly into my neck. "Your turn."

"Yes please," I replied.

She took my hand and guided it back to my cock. Soon she was taking a photo of me jacking off. Unable to hold back after that, I came hard all over her belly, my cock pulsing until I wondered if it was ever going to stop.

"Jesus, fuck," I breathed, pressing my forehead against hers. I gave her a quick messy kiss. "I think that was the hottest thing I've ever done."

"Me too," Grace replied and a grin broke out across her face. "Today's going to be fun."

I groaned. "Today's going to kill us."

After breakfast, my next duty was to run Grace a bath. She sat in the steaming water with her cast resting off the edge. I climbed in behind her, realising I'd overfilled the tub when water sloshed onto the floor.

"Oops," Grace muttered.

"It's just water. I'll throw a few towels down."

I uncapped the shampoo bottle and began lathering her hair. The sweet smell of strawberries rose from the steaming water as I worked it through.

"Mmm," she moaned. "I could get used to this."

"Yeah?" I massaged her scalp, liking the sweet whimpers she made. "Because I could do this for you every day if you wanted me to."

Grace stilled. "Every day this week?"

I calmly picked up the plastic jug by the tub and filled it with water. "Tilt your head back."

"Casey?" she prompted, tilting her head back.

I poured the water, carefully rinsing out the shampoo, and said, "No, Grace." I filled the jug and ran the water through her hair again. "Not just this week."

She didn't respond, so after I finished rinsing, I uncapped the lid on the conditioner and began combing it through her hair with my fingers. "Look," I began. "I know we haven't talked about this but—"

Grace cut me off. "No buts, Casey. We had a deal and you promised."

I lowered my hands, rinsing them in the water. Screw the deal. I wanted Grace to stay. I nudged her backwards, settling her against my chest, and I slid my hands down her belly. "And this," I said in her ear, my voice dropping to a husky whisper as I reached between her legs. "I could do this every day too." Grace moaned as I massaged her clit.

"Casey." She put a hand over mine, stilling me. "Stop. Please." Her voice cracked and I withdrew my hand, hurt as all fuck and not knowing how to hide it.

"Is the thought of something more permanent that awful? I'm just someone to fuck until you return to your real life?"

Because that played into exactly what Morgan said when she called me a whore. I didn't want to be that guy to Grace. That douche from her past that she got over with a stiff drink because she knew he didn't deserve her. I wanted to be the guy that did. The guy she'd never get over.

"Don't, Casey. You know it's more than that." She pushed off me to get out of the bath. I snaked my arm around her waist, pinning her back to my chest. We were far from done with this conversation.

"Of course it's more than that," I snapped. "You think I went against what Henry said just for sex? I had no intention for this to last only eight weeks."

"So when we agreed to this deal, you lied." She turned her head, looking at me.

My chest thumped with anger. "No, I didn't fuckin' lie," I bit out. "If you want me to walk away, I'll walk away. I'm just saying that I agreed to the deal hoping you'd change your mind."

"You did?"

"Yeah," I muttered, pissed. I hadn't wanted to play my hand so soon. I wanted time to warm her up to the idea before I went shooting my mouth off.

"Casey … I'm not going to change my mind. Even if I did, whatever this is, neither of us is ready for it."

"I'm not ready? Are you speaking for me now too?"

"You dated Morgan because she had information on a case. Your family's case. A case I know nothing about because you're not willing to share."

"Grace—"

She held up a hand cutting me off. "I'm not saying you have to share anything, Casey. Not if that's what you don't want to do. I'm just pointing out that if you were ready for something more, you'd be more open about your life, same as I would."

"Same as you would?" I cocked my head, locking eyes with hers. "What are you hiding from me, Grace?"

"How has this conversation gone from me saying we're not ready, to me hiding stuff?" Grace turned back around and went to push up and out of the tub again. "I thought this week away was about both of us having time to recuperate, not argue. I'm getting out, and then I'm getting dressed," she said calmly, "and then you can drive me back to Sydney."

My arm locked tighter around her waist, not letting her move, and she sucked in a breath. "Casey that hurts."

"I'm sorry." I immediately loosened my arm but didn't let her go. Grace was definitely hiding something but pushing her on it wasn't going to work. Maybe Henry knew something I didn't. After resolving to ring her brother tomorrow, I rubbed her belly, soothing her until she relaxed back against my chest again. "You want to know about my family? About Kelly?"

"Casey—"

"I want to tell you, okay?"

After a moment, she nodded against my chest, so I took a deep breath and forced the words from mouth. "Kelly was my little brother. Younger than me by four years, so I was always looking out for him, you know? I had to. My dad was a mean drunk. He wasn't too bad otherwise. We just had to watch out for him when he'd been drinking."

Grace's tone sounded stiff. "Did he drink a lot?"

"Every day," I told her. "But weekends were reserved for getting shitfaced."

"Why?"

"Why did he drink?"

"Yeah."

I ran my fingers through her hair as I spoke. It made the words easier to get out somehow. "I don't know. It's not really something that he sat down and talked to me about. Maybe he wasn't happy with his life. Maybe a wife and kids wasn't what he signed up for and he drank to forget about us. It's something I'll never know. We just knew to stay out of his way when the whiskey bottle was out, but most times it wasn't that easy. We got beat pretty regular."

Grace turned, water sloshing in the tub and anger blazing in her eyes. It surprised me. Not looking at her when I spoke meant I had no cues to what she was thinking.

"I want to kill him," she hissed, seeming to forget that my father was already dead.

"Grace."

"I want to—"

"Grace!"

She stopped suddenly. I could see her brain ticking over as she stared at me. "This is why you don't have any good stories, isn't it?"

"Pretty much," I admitted. "I have good ones now though, yeah?"

"That doesn't absolve all the bad ones, Casey."

I turned her back around and took my time rinsing the conditioner from her hair.

"See, that's what you think." I hesitated for a moment and then thought, fuck it. "But sitting here with you makes the bad ones easier to bear."

"Casey …" Grace tried to turn but I wouldn't let her. "What about Kelly and your mum?"

The pain hit sharp and swift then. Because I'd failed them. It was that simple. "I tried to bear the brunt of it, but I couldn't always be there. Kelly was a good kid, Grace. The complete opposite of our dad. So sweet and kind. I tried to keep him that way. I really did. And most of the time we were okay, but …"

Grace tried turning again and this time I let her. She straddled my lap, taking care to keep her cast dry. Then she looked at me. "But what?"

"But when it wasn't okay, it was bad." All my childhood fears came rushing back and I didn't hide it. I wanted Grace to see it because I wanted her to see me, not some guy she fucked to pass the time. "It was really, really bad."

Grace gripped my forearm and squeezed. "You're scaring me."

"I'm sorry."

"Don't." Her eyes searched my face. "How bad?"

"You want another shitty story? Because I've got a few of those."

"Just one. Give me one, Casey. I need to know how bad."

I shrugged as if it were okay, but speaking this shit out loud was hard. "There was one afternoon when I got caught up late after school. I told Kelly to go on ahead because I didn't think dad would be home. It was a Friday. He liked to celebrate the start of the weekend at the pub," I explained. "But it turns out he didn't go that day. And what I came home to scared the shit out of me."

I tilted my head back against the lip of the bath and closed my eyes, seeing it all in my head as though it happened yesterday. "I came home through the side door from force of habit. It was easier to fly under Dad's radar by sneaking inside that way rather than walking in through the front door. It opened to the kitchen and Kelly was standing there in the centre of it. Blood poured down the side of his face from a split brow, and … Jesus," I muttered, swallowing hard, "he had a knife. My sweet little brother who was only twelve had a knife pulled on our dad." I opened my eyes, looking at Grace. "He'd just had enough, you know? I grabbed for it, worried he was going to hurt himself. That was a mistake. He hadn't realised I was there and the move freaked him out. He cut my arm, slicing it wide open from here…" I twisted my right forearm and pointed to the scar that began at my inner elbow "…to here," I said, trailing my finger down the long, thin line where it finished near my wrist.

Grace paled. "Kelly did that?"

"He didn't mean it," I told her, defending my brother. "He wasn't thinking straight. It wasn't until after the knife sliced through that he realised who it was, but by then it was too late."

"What do you mean it was too late?" Even though it happened over fourteen years ago and I was right here and okay, Grace's eyes were round with fear. "Casey?"

"Dad grabbed the knife during the commotion and he came at Kelly. He came at his own son with a knife," I bit out.

"What did you do?"

"I stood in front of my little brother," I said simply, "and I took the hit. Just like I always did."

Grace stared at me, her jaw quivering and tears filling her eyes. Suddenly she stood up, water sloshing everywhere. "I have to get out. I don't feel well." She tripped getting out and I grabbed for her. "Oh God, I can't breathe," she choked out, sobbing.

I stepped out of the bath and took her shoulders in my hands. "Look at me, Grace."

"Show me." She pulled from my grip, trying to push me away. "Show me what he did!" she shouted, her breathing heavy and erratic.

"Grace! Stop. Just breathe."

"I can't." Her legs gave out and I sank to the mat right along with her, holding her shaking body in my arms. I rocked her slowly, hating that my past was hurting her now too. It was hurting both of us, and that was the one thing I didn't want to do but I didn't know how else to let her in.

"Show me," she whispered, her voice hoarse. She turned her head into my neck, pressing a kiss right where I could feel my pulse thumping.

"I can't show you, Grace. I covered the scar with a tattoo because I couldn't stand looking at it anymore."

"This one?" Grace pulled back slightly and pointed to the tattoo of an ancient sword that covered the left side of my torso. A dragon curled around the blade, his head resting above the handle.

"That one," I confirmed.

She covered it with her hand, letting her fingers trail over it, feeling the long, raised scar hidden beneath. Peering closer, Grace read the script I had inked into the sword's handle. "Glory is not in never falling, but in rising every time we fall." She looked up at me, horror clear in her eyes. "This almost killed you, didn't it? He almost killed you."

I nodded.

"Can you …" She paused, her breath shaky as I wiped tears from her face. "Can you kiss me, Casey? I know it sounds stupid because you're right here, but I need to feel that you're okay."

"I can do that."

I took her face in my hands and kissed her. She opened her mouth and I took everything she was willing to give. Using it. Letting it soothe the ache in my heart.

When I pulled back, I kept her face cupped in my hands. She watched me carefully, hesitating before she asked the question. "How did they die?"

I shook my head, letting my hands fall away. Getting to my feet, I reached for a thick, fluffy towel and helped her stand. "Not today." I wrapped it around her first before meeting her eyes. "Just … not today, okay?"

When she was dry, I put her back in bed. My stomach growled, letting me know it was nearing lunchtime, but I couldn't think about food. Instead, I lay beside her, spooning her. She put a hand over the arm I tucked around her, but even then I couldn't find sleep.

The rest of the week followed much the same. We slept, watched movies, walked along the beach, and traded more stories. We laughed and teased each other, and we fucked—sometimes slow and sometimes hard, and sometimes it was explosive and other times calm, but every single time, it was fucking perfect. We got time just to be together.

We went to the local GP for our post hospital check-up, and once while Grace was sleeping and I was horny, I got to jack off to her photo and it was awesome. I wasn't looking forward to having that deleted from my phone.

Between all that, I messaged Nate daily and I also rang Henry, fishing for information, but he had nothing. Whatever Grace was hiding, she wasn't just keeping it from me, she was keeping it from all of us, and that worried me.

On our last night at the cottage, I carried a snoring Grace from the couch to the bed after she fell asleep watching a movie. When she was settled, I removed the yellow envelope from the bedside table where I'd placed it after we'd arrived.

Moving to the kitchen, I grabbed a glass, a bottle of scotch, and along with the envelope, carried it out to the small table on the front porch. The sound of waves crashing on the shore was loud and the air cool on my bare chest as I poured a glass. I took a sip, contemplating the envelope.

If there were no answers inside it, then I knew I had to let go. This was it for me. I had to move on from my past, and I wanted to move on with Grace.

I set my glass on the table and pulled the sheets from the envelope. I skimmed them quickly at first.

"Male skull showing bullet exit wound on parietal bone …" and on my mother's report, "Despite extensive injuries, cause of death was a single gunshot wound to the chest."

Then I sat back and read the entire report in full. The coroner had declared the death of my parents a murder-suicide. There was nothing to indicate otherwise. Turning the page, I flinched, not expecting to see crime scene photos.

Jesus.

My eyes stung and my stomach rolled. I shook my head, trying to clear the images before they stuck.

"Casey?"

"Go back to bed, Grace," I told her without turning.

She came up behind me. I tried to hide the photos but she saw them anyway because I felt her flinch too.

She didn't say anything. She simply took them from my hands, set them on the table, and crawled into my lap. Then she wrapped both arms around me and held on.

I buried my head in her neck, swallowing a sob. My family was gone, and nothing could've prepared me for seeing it right there in a bunch of old, gritty photos. "Grace," I whispered, my voice hoarse as I clutched her to me. "It's my fault."

"No."

"It is. I left them. I left Mum and Kelly there alone."

"You couldn't be there all the time, Casey."

I drew back, angry because she didn't get it. "I left them!" I shouted right in her face and she just sat there calmly and let me.

"Okay. So you left. I get that. That's what your mum would've wanted you to do, right? Where did you go?"

"My whole life I wanted to be a policeman so I could arrest assholes like my dad. I moved to Goulburn to study at CSU. That's where I met Travis. He was studying the same policing major. I bunked with him. It was supposed to be temporary because I promised Mum and Kelly I'd come back for them. It was only supposed to be six months. The plan was to get settled, find them accommodation, a job for Mum and schooling for Kelly, and I'd fucking come back for them. But jobs and places to live were limited and six months dragged to seven, and then eight…" I hung my head, feeling sick "…and then I got called into my Associate Professors office, and that's when I found out I was too late. Mum and Dad were both dead and Kelly missing. They never recovered his body. My whole family was gone, Grace, just like that. My life ended right there, in her office."

"It didn't end there because you're here." Grace cupped my face in her hands, her eyes fierce. "You're right here and you're still fighting for them. And you're not giving up. We're going to find Kelly. And I'm going to help you."

I gave a humourless laugh. "No offence, Grace, but I've been looking for ten years. You think you can help…" I waved my hand at all the papers "…then go right ahead, but Kelly's gone, baby. He's gone. There's no way he wouldn't find his way to me if he were still alive. Not after ten years. No way."

Grace started reading the autopsy report as I spoke, going straight to cause of death. "Murder-suicide?"

I shook my head. "I don't believe it. I can't. Someone else did it and then they took my baby brother somewhere and killed him too." My eyes burned. "Someone killed my family, my brother. He was out there scared and alone, and I let it happen. I promised I'd come back, and I didn't."

Grace grabbed my shoulders, the pages in her hand crumpling because she hadn't let them go. "Look at me, Casey."

I met her eyes, broken and defeated.

"This tattoo here…" she placed a hand over the sword without taking her eyes from mine "…tell me what it's about."

"It's about rising stronger from falling."

"Fuck that," she growled. "Tell me what it means to you."

I rubbed at my face. "Grace, I—"

"Okay. I'll tell you what it means then, shall I? It means that life cut you down, but you didn't fail, because you didn't just lie there and give up. You got to your feet, stronger and fiercer than before, and you did Not. Give. Up." Her fingernails dug into my shoulders as she glared at me. "So don't do it now."

I thought back to when it happened. I had given up. I was ready to walk into that ocean and end it all. But Travis hadn't let me. I hadn't risen when I fell, he'd fucking picked me up, just like Grace was trying to do now.

And I loved her for it.

I fucking loved her.

My heart hammered at the realisation.

"Okay then," I said with a calm I didn't feel. I reached behind Grace, plucked the papers off the table, and handed her half. She looked at me warily as she took them from my hands. "Help me find my little brother."

Grace shifted off my lap and disappeared inside the cottage. She returned with her reading glasses and sat on the seat beside me. After smoothing out the pages, she stole my scotch, tipped her head back as she took a hefty gulp, poured another, and then focused on the partial report in front of her.

After five minutes of me studying the autopsy report again, Grace interrupted with, "This is the case report?"

I glanced at the pages she had spread out in front of her. "Uh huh."

Her brow furrowed. "I think I'm missing the second page."

I rifled through what I had, found the page and handed it over. After another five minutes, she waved the page underneath my face. "Casey, what's this?"

I looked at it.

"It's the on scene report," I replied. It was the only report I'd managed to recover at the time of the shooting.

"And this." She pointed to the bottom of the page. "This is a list of attending officers, right?"

"Right," I confirmed.

"Look here." Her finger moved to the very bottom of the page. I leaned in, focusing on the section of names. "It looks like a name has been cut off the bottom. You never noticed that before?"

I looked closer. Grace was right. Just the tiniest smidge of ink on the bottom of the page made it look like a name had been cut from the bottom of the list. "No I didn't. But this is just another copy of the case report that Morgan had in the envelope. I have the same one in a file at the office, but I never saw this on mine."

My pulse started racing and my hands shook. "Wait here," I ordered and went back inside. Grabbing my phone I came back out and sat down. I called up my own case report I'd stored in the files on my phone and zoomed in on the bottom of the page. Nothing.

Grace shrugged. "Maybe it was just the photocopier leaving marks or something."

I held up a finger, indicating for her to shut up so I could focus.

She shut up.

I closed the report on my phone, called up my contacts and dialled Travis.

It was well after midnight but this couldn't wait.

"Yeah," he answered after two rings, his voice sleepy.

"I don't have the background report on Morgan here. I need you to check on something."

"Give me a sec," he replied without hesitation or question. He murmured something quietly and Quinn's sleepy voice responded before I heard the sound of a door closing. "What do you need?" he asked.

"I need you to tell me how old Morgan is."

"Okay." I heard the sound of a computer coming to life and the whine of a dog. "Go back to bed, Rufus," Travis muttered. The whine came again.

"Fuck. Hang on," he said in the phone. "Damn dog's gotta take a piss."

Grace sat quietly while I waited for Travis. Curled in the chair beside me, she sipped at the glass of scotch and watched the ocean. I stole the drink from her hand. After tipping a decent mouthful down my throat, I handed it back.

The muffled noise of Travis picking the phone back up came through and after a pause, he said, "Morgan's thirty-three."

"So that would've made her twenty-three at the time my family was shot."

"You think she did it?" Travis sounded doubtful.

"No, but I think she was one of the attending officers and for some reason, she didn't want a record of that fact."

"But her name wasn't listed on the report. Are you sure about this because it sounds like a fuck of a long stretch?"

"It is a stretch but a name has been cut off the bottom of the report and my gut is telling me it's hers. It explains why she got her hands on all this information so quickly and easily. I don't care how good she is with computers. No one's that good."

"It turns out the coroner on the case is an old friend of my uncle's."

I grabbed for the autopsy report and checked the name of the coroner listed. "Graham Bennett. He's the listed coroner. Get Seth to run a check on him in the morning and then we'll go pay him a visit."

"Done."

"Oh and Travis?"

"Yeah?"

"Thanks."

He hung up.

I put the phone down on the table and looked at Grace.

"We're going home tomorrow?"

I nodded.

"There's only one problem with that."

"Oh?"

Her lips curved slowly. "You promised me sex on the beach. So far we've had sex in the bath, in bed, in the kitchen, and on this very chair." Was I developing a fetish for sex in public? Grace had unzipped my jeans last night and straddled me, lowering herself on my cock right here on the front porch. We were still fully clothed but anyone could've walked past. "But not on the beach."

I stood up and held out my hand. Grace looked at it. "Well? What are you waiting for?" I jerked my chin at the beach across the road. "Let's go."

She shifted her gaze from me, to the beach, and back again, her eyes excited. "Should we get a towel?" she asked, taking my hand as she stood.

"No towel." I led her across the road. My cock should've been worn out but it rallied determinedly, punching against my jeans as we walked down the small, sandy incline. "It's not a proper experience if you don't get sand in all the wrong places."

It wasn't until an hour later that everything went to shit. I'd ducked quickly into the surf to rinse off the sand. Grace waited by the shore, not wanting to get her cast wet. I was just getting out when sirens sounded in the distance. My eyes cut quickly to Grace, relieved she was still in sight, when suddenly she wasn't.

She was running.

"Grace!" I shouted.

She disappeared over the incline, not looking back.

"Grace!" I screamed.

Shoving on my jeans, I took off after her. Running hard, my legs powered through the soft sand. The sound of sirens got louder and louder. And my chest pounded harder and harder.

I hit the top of the incline and my heart stopped.

Smoke poured from the back bedroom of the cottage and fire trucks flew down the street, red lights flashing and sirens screaming.

But Grace didn't stop running and I couldn't breathe, fear strangling me as she flew straight towards the front porch.

"Grace! No!" I yelled hoarsely, still running.

"Mitsy's in there!" she screamed and disappeared through the front door. I tore after her, never running so hard in my life, my heart lodged in my throat for entire seconds that felt like long, agonising minutes.

"Not again," I begged, not knowing how I'd survive losing one more person I loved. "Please not again."

A fire truck halted in front of me and I weaved around it when suddenly I was grabbed from behind. Two firemen held me back. One of them shouted, "You can't go in there!"

"Let me go!" I yelled, my voice cracking as I fought to get free. "Grace is in there!"

A fireman, all suited up, disappeared inside the cottage door as neighbours filtered out on the lawn and flames started licking up the side of the house, black smoke filling the sky. "Let us do our job."

"You don't get it," I yelled, pulling free of their grip. "Keeping her safe is my job."

Turning, I ran for the front door just as the back half of the house exploded, hurtling me backwards. The air in my lungs emptied as I landed hard on the ground. I rolled over, coughing as I dragged myself to my feet.

"Grace!" I cried, my ears ringing from the blast. "No."

Chapter Twenty-Six
GRACE

"Casey!"

He spun around, coughing, his chest covered with dirt and ash and his eyes wild. "Grace!"

Casey grabbed for me, and I dropped the wriggling Mitsy from my arms when he wrapped his around me, burying me into his chest, one hand fisting my hair. "Oh my God."

He held on, squeezing me. My ribs screamed and I couldn't breathe, but I didn't care. I was freaked. Someone had been trying to kill us. I hadn't truly believed it—maybe I hadn't wanted to—but hell, someone had just blown up the ass end of the cottage right where we would've been sleeping.

"Casey," I said again, having no idea what else to say.

He pushed me back, grabbing my face in his hands, his chest heaving up and down like he couldn't breathe. "That was so stupid! Why did you do that? Jesus. When that back room exploded I thought you were dead!"

"I'm sorry!" I cried. "I didn't think," I told him, because I hadn't. It was like my mind had completely detached, leaving my body driving the car. I just ran inside, grabbed Mitsy, and tailed it out the side entrance because it was closer than coming back through the front door. "I just reacted."

He kissed me—fierce and quick. "Next time, you think! You fucking think, okay?"

"Next time?"

"There'll be a next time, Grace," he warned, his voice flat and grim. "It would be a mistake to think otherwise."

I turned to look at the cottage. Firemen surrounded the back, flames dying under the deluge of water. If I'd been just a few seconds later, I would've died.

I really was stupid.

I'd just proved it.

By running into a burning building.

My brother was going to shit a brick if he got wind of what I just did. I looked at Casey. "We don't have to tell Henry, right?"

Casey's eyes went flat and hard. "What did you just say?" he snapped, anger evident in his tone.

"Casey, I—"

He let go of me, hands fisting at his sides as he took a step back. "You think I'm pissed because I have to explain to your brother you almost died in a damn house fire?"

"No, of course not—"

"I just watched the woman I love run into a goddamn burning building!" he roared at me, pointing at the smouldering cottage without taking his eyes from mine.

I froze.

"What?" I whispered.

"I love you, dammit!" Casey yelled, his voice cracking. "And I almost lost you. I almost …" He trailed off, sucking in a lungful of air.

Oh no.

My breath caught in my throat and my stomach pitched.

I'd pegged Casey as the guy who didn't do commitment. Who didn't fall in love. This whole thing was meant to be about living and loving life, and wild sex with a hot, irresistible man who both made me laugh and set me on fire. A moment in time to pretend everything was normal before I went home to face the music.

I hadn't cared about my own heart. I knew before I'd even made the pact that leaving Casey would break it. And I could deal with that.

But I couldn't deal with breaking his heart too.

That wasn't meant to happen.

That wasn't part of the deal.

Casey searched my face as I stared wordlessly, and I knew he was reading my thoughts. Seeing my hesitation, he turned away, hiding the hurt I already saw on his face.

"Casey."

He shook his head and pulled his phone from the back pocket of his jeans. "I need to make some calls."

My heart slammed against my ribs as I felt him draw away, not just physically, but emotionally, and I should've let him. I should've just let him make the calls and wait for him to realise that it wasn't love, it was just wild, crazy adrenaline that would fade by tomorrow.

But I couldn't.

Because I loved him too.

And seeing the hurt in his eyes and the slump of his shoulders made my heart ache.

"You, uh …" I drew a shaky breath and tried again, my eyes burning. "You remember when we first met?" Casey stilled, and after a moment, turned and looked at me. "I thought you were an asshole. Hot, but an asshole nonetheless."

"I know, Grace. You called me an asshole."

"You called me a bitch first."

He held up his phone, indicating he had better things to do than argue about it. I couldn't blame him. I started this off all wrong, but I didn't know how else to say what I needed to say.

"What's your point?" he asked.

I knew what my point was, but getting to it wasn't quite as simple as saying three little words, so I forged on. "When Mitsy chewed your backseat on the ride to the duplex, I told myself it was payback, plain and simple, for you assaulting me in the airport bathroom—"

"That wasn't assault!"

"You say potato, I say po-tah-to," I muttered, remembering him shoving me against the tiles, his thigh wedged between my legs, his fierce glare. If his actions hadn't been so outrageous, it would've been kind of hot.

"But I realised it wasn't payback," I continued. "It was me pissing you off to make keeping my distance easy because I knew you were trouble. I mean, look at you." I waved my hand over the length of him, wearing nothing but a pair of jeans, his firm, tanned chest on display. "Even covered in dirt and bits of grass, you're still the sexiest man I've ever seen. Every man I've ever been with I've kept at a distance, but doing the same with you proved impossible. Right from the start you were there in my face, pissing me off, making me crazy, and making me feel. And somehow I kept coming back for more. And then you took me surfing that day and I knew there was more to you than I'd ever realised. So much more. There was a fierce loyalty for your friends, pain from losing your family, and this wildness underneath it all that with the slightest provocation, you would unleash, leaving me completely captivated."

"Grace," he breathed, his eyes going dark.

He took a step towards me and I held up a hand. "I'm not finished." My gaze shifted to the waves crashing on the shore as I tried to find the right words. "People come and go, Casey. Some crash into your life and leave in the blink of an eye, others stay with you for years, but it doesn't matter how long you have them for," I said, looking back at him, hoping he understood what I was trying to say, "because the way they make you feel stays with you with forever, and you've made me feel so much." Tears climbed my throat and I had to swallow them down so I could keep going. "You've made me laugh and made me cry, pissed me off, completely infuriated me and made me want you all at the same time. But underneath it all, you made me ache, and you made me love you so hard." I took hold of his hand and pulled him close until his chest hit mine. The breeze had picked up, fanning my hair across my face. He reached up, brushing it away as firemen shouted and people moved around us. "That's what makes you beautiful to me, Casey."

A smile grew slowly on his face, and he rubbed his nose gently against mine. "That has to be the longest 'I love you' in the history of the world."

I grinned in reply as people threw varied looks of disbelief our way for smiling in the middle of a war zone. "But definitely the best, right?"

He shook his head, his body quaking with laughter as he kissed me. "You're the only woman who's ever said that to me, Grace. I never knew how good hearing it would make me feel."

Casey made his calls. It wasn't safe for us to stay out the night for obvious reasons, so after we finished speaking with the police, he arranged for Coby to drive up. He would take over dealing with the cottage and subsequent repairs and we would head home.

I was dozing in Casey's arms in the chair on the front porch, my head tucked into his chest, when Coby pulled in the drive at five a.m. He drove up in Evie's Hilux. The plan was for us to drive it back and leave his car here with him.

I heard him step onto the porch, but opening my eyes to greet him was a feat of strength that was beyond me right then.

"Is she okay?" I heard Coby ask quietly.

"Solid," Casey replied. The deep rumble of his voice as he spoke was soothing and I burrowed deeper.

"You right to drive back now? I can watch her if you want to have a quick nap."

Casey's arms tightened around me, and I sighed softly as he stood up bringing me with him. "No, but thanks. I want to get her to the loft. She'll be safe there."

"What about Morgan?"

"What about her?"

"She knows where you live."

"I can't believe she would do this, Coby. She had her alibi for the night of the accident. We saw it on the security tapes. And she might be a bitch…" total bitch, I agreed silently "…but she's a detective. Bombing a house? That's taking it a bit far, don't you think?"

"No. Women do crazy shit."

I was pissed at Coby's comment, but not pissed enough to wake up and join the conversation, so I let it slide. I couldn't possibly refute his statement and make it sound believable anyway. We did do crazy shit. I, for one, could add stealing a car, crashing it, and running into a burning building to my crazy shit repertoire.

My eyes opened lazily when Casey started walking. He was carrying me towards the car just as the sun appeared over the horizon, casting soft pinks and orange into the sky. It was beautiful and I didn't want to leave. Being here with Casey had been one of the best weeks of my life, despite it ending in a semi-blaze of glory.

Coby opened the passenger door and went to pick up Mitsy while Casey set me down in the seat.

He bent over the top of me, his eyes focused on doing my seat belt, not noticing I was awake and watching him intently. I could feel the warmth of his breath on my arm as he clicked the belt in place. He pulled back and glanced at me.

Seeing my eyes open, he smiled slow and sexy, and with a husky whisper, said, "Hey."

"Hey," I whispered back, my eyes dropping to his mouth, remembering how he'd pushed me back on the soft sand last night, shoved up the skirt of my cotton dress, yanked down my panties, spread my legs, and put that mouth on me in the most toe curling way imaginable. It seemed to be one of his favourite things to do. I wasn't complaining.

"Stop looking at me like that," he muttered, his lids lowering as he placed a palm on my thigh and began swirling his thumb on the bare skin.

"Like what?" I bit back a moan, wanting his hand to shift higher and not wanting it to because Coby was somewhere nearby putting stuff in the back of the Hilux.

"Like you want me to eat you." Casey's hand started moving higher and my pulse accelerated. "Because damn, I want to, and knowing you want me to just makes me hotter, and I can't be hot right now. I need my head in the game so I can get you home safe. Visions of burying my tongue between your legs won't help me do that."

I stopped breathing.

He grinned. "Breathe, baby."

"I don't think I can right now," I muttered. "Maybe later." When I'd fallen asleep again and unconsciousness took over.

Maybe not even then.

We left soon after and I don't remember the drive home because I slept the whole way. When I woke, we were parked in the driveway of the duplex. Casey stood by the car next to Henry. He was talking and Henry's eyes were hard as he stood there listening, his arms folded. I quickly closed my eyes again, playing possum so when the brick shitting began over my exploits, I didn't have to deal with it.

Five minutes later the car door opened.

"Grace. I know you're awake."

I focused on keeping my face serene and my eyelids still, but the more I tried, the harder it was. Damn, playing possum was a skill I had never fully mastered.

"Grace," Henry repeated. "I know you're awake because you're not snoring."

I cracked an eyelid open. "I don't snore!"

My phone buzzed, saving me, and I sprang for it.

"Hello."

"Grace, love."

Fantastic.

I'd watched a show on TV the other night. One of those current affair type programs with the scare tactics. You know the kind that led you to believe flesh-eating bugs were invading the country and if you didn't watch the show, you wouldn't know how to combat them and subsequently face being eaten alive. It was one of those types, and after much eye rolling on Casey's part, he caved and we watched the show. This one was on sinkholes, where the earth's surface just falls away below you in a startling tidy kind of circle.

I needed to find one of those because according to the show's host, they were opening up all over the earth's surface when you least expected it, sucking you into the never-never.

That was where I needed to be right now.

"Dad," I muttered.

Suddenly Casey stood right there in front of me, and he said something pretty damn amazing. "Give me the phone, Grace."

If I didn't already love the man, I would've after that. I flung the phone at him like it was a hot potato.

"A burning building, Grace? Really?"

And it was back to Henry while Casey put out the fire that was my dad.

His voice rose alarmingly as he spoke. "When I told you to stay safe, you interpreted that as run towards danger without passing go and collecting two hundred dollars?"

"You're being dramatic."

Henry's jaw went tight, indicating I'd chosen the wrong response.

I tried again. "I'm sorry."

His jaw kept ticking.

Casey eyed us from a small distance away, one arm holding my phone to his ear, the other tucked across his chest. His brows rose at me in silent question and I felt a rush of love. I had to bite down on the goofy smile that threatened for fear Henry would think me amused. I shook my head at Casey, silently telling him I had it covered. He nodded and half turned, focusing again on whatever he was saying to my dad.

"What good is sorry if you're dead, Grace?"

"Henry."

"What?" he snapped.

"It was stupid and it won't happen again."

His eyes narrowed cynically. "I don't believe you."

"So what now? Should I write it in blood? Will that make it more believable?"

"Maybe," he muttered, backing up as I slid from the passenger seat to the ground. My body protested the movement after sitting down for so long and I winced. Henry reached for me, steadying me when I faltered.

I looked up at my big brother, time seeming to stand still for the longest moment. "I love you, Henry Bear."

"Ah hell." He blinked back tears and rather than letting me go, he wrapped his arms around me. I burrowed in, fighting sadness that I'd missed this for so many years. "I love you, too, Gracie Bean."

An hour later, Casey had me situated at his loft. That involved him rolling my suitcase into his room, running me a bath, helping me wash my hair again, and dragging me naked to his bed, because apparently I needed to rest. I only complied because he was joining me.

Casey lifted the sheets and I slid in gratefully. He slid in behind, spooning me, all warm skin and hard body, his breathing soft and even against the nape of my neck. He pulled the sheets up over both of us, cocooning us in delicious warmth.

"Casey?" I murmured.

"Mmm?" He pressed a kiss where the base of my neck met my shoulder, making me shiver.

"What's our plan?"

"Our plan?"

"Yes. Our plan. I'm still helping you find your brother," I reminded him, and knowing they had someone named Seth from their office tracking down the coroner, I added, "And I'm coming with you when you talk to this Graham whatshisname."

I braced for an argument but he surprised me by agreeing. "I don't want you leaving my side right now."

"I heard you talking to Coby. I know you don't think Morgan instigated the accident and the fire, but I think she's involved somehow and it's something to do with your brother."

His arm tightened, his hand cupping my breast as he cuddled me close. "I think you're right," he admitted, "but I can't seem to fit any of the puzzle pieces together."

"So stop trying. Put it out of your head until we talk to Graham, and then maybe they'll start falling into place."

His thumb flickered over my nipple and my blood heated as it hardened. "And how do you propose I do that?"

I pushed back, wriggling my ass against him, finding him half hard already. He exhaled harshly. "Grace." He wedged a knee between the backs of my legs, parting my thighs. I sighed in anticipation. "I told myself I'd let you sleep," he murmured in my ear. His fingers found their way between my legs.

I moaned softly. "So be quick then."

His tongue snaked out, trailing a path along the back of my neck as he rocked his hips, rubbing his erection against my back, his fingers never ceasing their rhythm. "A quickie with you, Slim? That's like drinking champagne when you're already drunk. A waste of something that should be savoured."

"Savour me after, Casey, please. I need you inside me."

He drew his hand away, over my hip and down my leg. I felt him reach for a condom and moments later he lifted my thigh and filled my body with his. I gasped, my head falling back against him.

"Ah, fuck, Grace," he groaned, pressing his forehead against my shoulder.

He thrust into me, once, hard, then he stilled.

"Casey," I moaned, shifting, wanting more.

"Grace?"

"Mmm?"

"I almost lost you last night." He thrust again, once, harder, his body trembling and his heart pounding. It was like he'd been keeping himself in check since the fire and now he was crashing hard. "I'm not sure I can be gentle."

I stretched my arm behind me, my fingers running through his hair. "I don't want you to be gentle."

"Please be sure," he whispered hoarsely, grinding his hips, making me moan.

"I'm sure."

With that, Casey pulled out and before I could protest, I was rolled onto my back with him kneeling between my thighs. His big hands gripped my hips and yanked upwards, taking the pressure off my injured body. Then, with his eyes locked on mine, he slammed back inside me with a hoarse shout.

He didn't pause. His strokes increased and I clutched the bedsheet in desperation, holding on, breathing erratically, taking his fear and anger and hearing it transform into groans of pleasure.

"Grace," he panted, his eyes fluttering closed. "I can't … Fuck," he bit out.

Casey pulled out suddenly. He ripped the condom off, jacked himself hard and came with a hoarse cry. I felt the warmth of it hit my belly and I was left wanting more.

"Why did you do that?"

"Because…" he shifted down, still breathing hard "…I want to do this."

He looped one of my legs over his shoulder, slid two fingers inside me and buried his mouth between my thighs. My eyes closed and as my body came alive, my heart ached.

How was I going to say goodbye?

Chapter Twenty-Seven
CASEY

My phone woke me from a late afternoon nap three days later. Grace and I had started out the day by going to her hospital check-up where she complained they took at least a litre of blood from her arm. After that, I took her shopping to replace what she'd lost in the fire.

Shopping and I had never seen eye to eye, yet somehow I was always the one roped into going—first with Evie when she had trouble, then with Quinn, and now with Grace. Only with Grace it was a thousand times better because not only did I get to help her try the clothes on, I got take them off her. I also got to watch her flush with embarrassment when we got caught doing more than just changing outfits in the dressing room.

My eyes opened when the phone kept ringing, revealing Grace in my bed. The fact that she hadn't ventured from my side while I slept left me satisfied. She sat, curled up, her colourful tattoo bright against the crisp, white sheets that bunched around her body. Her hair was a tangled mess down her bare back, black-framed reading glasses adorned her face, and her brow furrowed as she read through the case files in front of her.

I grinned, ignoring my phone when it started ringing again. My eyes drank her in and my cock hardened at a rate that made me dizzy. "You're so sexy, Slim."

She tilted her head at me, making a face at my comment before nodding at my phone. It was on the bedside table on her side. "You going to get that?"

"Who is it?"

With a quick glance at the screen she said, "Travis."

I yawned, scratching the back of my head as I tried to wake up. "You can answer it."

She shrugged, put the pages down in front of her and reached for it. The sheet slipped, baring a whole bunch of naked torso and the swell of her breast. My hand slid up her ribs, cupping it in my hand before I even realised I was doing it.

Putting the phone to her ear, she answered, "Hey, Travis."

I pinched her nipple between my thumb and forefinger, barely feeling it harden before she giggled and twisted away. I growled playfully.

"He's right here," she said. "You want to talk to him?"

I ripped the sheet away, exposing her nakedness. Papers fluttered carelessly to the floor by the bed. I ignored them as I focused on Grace before me. "Tell him I'm busy."

Moving to the end of the bed, I grabbed her by the ankles and yanked her down. "Oh," she cried and into the phone said, "He's, uh, in the middle of something. Can I take a message?" Another pause while I splayed my hands wide on her calves and slid them upwards, massaging her thighs. She shivered at the touch and my lips curled. "You want to talk to me?"

Grace tossed her reading glasses on the bedside table, and I shifted closer, trying to listen. I could hear Travis's deep voice, but I couldn't make out what he was saying. I looked at her questioningly and she shook her head at me.

Then she looked at me, her lips parting in surprise. "He is?" A moment later her eyes filled. "Oh, I don't—"

She didn't get to finish because I snatched the phone and put it to my ear, my hard-on dying a quick death. "Travis," I growled, my tone lethal. Vaulting off the bed, I stalked naked from the room. "What the fuck?"

"Casey," he said in my ear. "Thought you were busy?"

"I was until you started upsetting my girl. You want to tell me what the hell you were saying to her or you want me to just come over there and punch you?"

"I've got a better idea. I'm out the front. Why don't you buzz me up?"

I veered from my direction towards the kitchen and started for the front door. With a quick flick, I switched on the security screen. Travis was standing there, phone to his ear, waving at the camera with a smirk. My eyes narrowed as I hit the buzzer, unlocking the building door and then the front door of the loft. "Come up at your own risk, asshole."

"Aww, I love you too."

With the phone still to my ear as he made his way up, I asked him what he said to Grace.

"You remember what you said to Quinn that night before Evie's big birthday bash? I pretty much said that same thing to her."

"Quinn told you what I said?" I frowned, closing my eyes briefly as I thought back.

"I know what Travis was like before you, and I know what he's like since you, and I like the latter. He smiles like he means it, even after a long, shitty day like he's dealing with today." I'd tapped a finger to my temple and said, "Up here, there's you at the back of all that, making his day not so shit because at the end of it, he gets you. You leave, he loses that and we lose him, and I don't like that."

"Not sure why that would've upset her, Daniels," he said in my ear as I exhaled heavily. "I just wanted her to know it makes us happy to see you happy. I don't want to see you lose that." The door to the loft opened and Travis stepped through. He arched a brow, drawing the phone from his ear. "And maybe you could've put some pants on so I wasn't blinded when I walked through the front door."

I rolled my eyes. Hanging up the phone, I tossed it on the kitchen bench, not caring about my nakedness in front of my best friend. We'd not only shared a room during our uni days, we'd shared girls too. "What about all those three-ways we use to have," I threw over my shoulder as I started for the bedroom. "Are you saying my cock blinded you then too?"

Travis grinned. "You think I was looking at your cock when you fucked some girl while she sucked me off?"

"I can hear you both, you know!" Grace shouted from the bedroom as I approached the open door. I winced.

Travis chuckled. The sound faded when I walked into the bedroom to find Grace sliding black lace panties up her thighs. Her brows rose. "Three-ways, huh?"

Pausing to watch, I cocked my head. "Mmm why? You want one?"

Her answer was a huff as she turned her back and began rummaging through her bag. Out came a black lace bra. I spun her around, snatching the bra. Tossing it on the floor, I pulled her close. Her tits crushed against my chest and I groaned, liking it. "Because you can't have one. You're mine and I don't share well with others."

Grace arched a brow. "Not according to what I just heard."

"That was before." My palms slid down her back until her ass was in my hands. "You don't care about what's in my past, do you, Slim?"

"As long as you don't care about what's in mine," she retorted.

Suddenly I cared. "Oh?"

She licked her lips, and my gaze dropped to her mouth, just catching the determined glint in her eyes before she kissed me. I changed the angle, sucking her bottom lip into my mouth and biting down.

"Ouch," she muttered, tearing her mouth free.

"I mean it, Slim," I warned, leaning in to kiss her mouth better. "The thought of you being with another guy makes me want to rip someone's head off."

"You finished?" Grace pushed me back, reaching again for her bra, snapping it on with short, sharp movements that told me I'd pissed her off.

"Grace."

"What?" she muttered, grabbing for a pair of jeans that looked damn near a hundred years old yet cost me ten times as much.

"Grace," I repeated, wanting her attention.

"What?" she snapped, yanking them up her legs. They fit like a second skin, hugging her ass and showing off her long, slender calves. I wanted to go back and buy her another dozen pairs.

"Would you look at me?"

Grace faced me, folding her arms.

"I've never been in love before." Her breath hitched and I knew how she felt. Just saying the words had my heart slamming against my ribs. "I don't know what the hell I'm doing and I'm sure that's obvious. I was only trying to tell you how I felt. That I want you to be mine, and mine alone. That I love you."

The sound of rattling bottles indicated Travis opening the fridge. "Can you guys wrap up your love fest?" he called out. "We've got somewhere to be." A bottle was uncapped. The lid made a clatter in the sink where he flung it while I stood waiting for Grace to say something. "Like catching up with Graham Bennett for instance," Travis added.

I froze and my insides clenched with both anticipation and building tension. "We got an address?" I called out after a moment.

We'd spent the past three days searching, but the guy was in the wind. It didn't make any sense. The guy was a coroner, not with the damn mob. It only made him more circumspect in my eyes.

"Yep," he called back.

I reached immediately for a pair of boxer-briefs, my mind narrowing it's focus to one thing only—finding out what he knew. Sliding them on along with a pair of jeans, I went for my bedside table and pulled out my handgun. After making sure it was loaded, I checked the safety.

"Casey."

Tucking the gun into the back of my jeans, I turned. Grace stood there, still half-dressed, her face pale.

"You think you'll need that?"

"Maybe," I muttered, hoping the hell I didn't, but I wasn't leaving anything to chance, least of all Grace's safety. "Get dressed," I told her, reaching for a shirt from my dresser. I tugged it over my head and yanked it down.

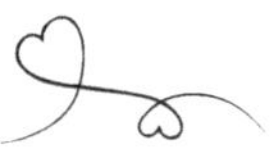

A half hour later we pulled up outside a small house—pale brick, one storey, two-car garage. It gave nothing away except maybe the guy was lazy because the lawn was overgrown and untidy. As we got out of Travis's black

Subaru, I grabbed for the coroner's report and looked at Grace.

"Stay behind me, okay?"

She gave me a brief nod.

As we walked up the small path and two sets of stairs onto the small square porch, Grace stayed behind me like I asked, making me breathe a little easier.

Travis took my side when I rapped hard on the door.

When no one answered and no sound came from inside, I glanced at Travis before knocking again.

"Yeah, yeah! Hold on," someone yelled from inside.

The door opened after another moment. The guy standing there looked too young to be Graham Bennett. I was imagining some old dude in his retirement years, but this guy was maybe late-thirties and a little unkempt with his overly long dark hair, sweatpants, and threadbare tee shirt.

My brows rose dubiously. "Graham Bennett?"

His hazel coloured eyes turned wary and guarded. "Who's asking?"

"My name's Casey…" I nodded my head at Travis "…and this is Travis." Grace cleared her throat behind me. "And this is Grace. We're consultants with the Sydney City Police."

The guy took a step back, carefully eyeing each one of us as he wiped his hand against his torso in a nervous gesture. My body tensed and my pulse accelerated a little, making my fingers twitchy for my gun and that was downright stupid. I needed to calm down.

Sensing my tension, Grace stepped a little closer behind me.

"Why are you here?" the guy asked.

I held up the pages in my left hand and he squinted at them. "To ask you some questions about an old case. According to this report, you were the coroner who conducted the autopsies on the victims. It was around ten years ago, so—"

I was cut off. "Oh shit," he muttered, his eyes going wide on the report he stared at before flying back to my face. Suddenly the door slammed hard and fast.

"What the hell?" Travis arched a brow as we glanced at each other.

I rapped hard again on the timber frame of the door.

"Open the door, Graham!" I shouted. "We just want to talk."

Nothing.

Using my fist this time, I pounded the door. It rattled beneath the force. "Open the goddamn door or I'll shoot it open!"

The sound of another door slamming from the back of the house hit us and Travis met my eyes. "Motherfucker's running," he said with disbelief.

"Stay with Grace," I ordered and took off running around the side. Met with a gated timber fence, I rammed it hard, putting the full force of my shoulder into it. Ignoring the shooting pain from the impact, I shoved through when it slammed open.

I scanned the yard quickly. It backed onto a reserve and was only partially fenced. It was almost as though someone got halfway through erecting it and gave up. Tyre tracks on the turf suggested it was used as a back entrance so comings and goings couldn't be seen from the street. Graham was headed directly for the unfenced section. It probably meant he had a car parked out there somewhere.

Sprinting hard, I caught him easy and tackled him to the ground.

"Ooomphf." We landed with a bone jarring thump. My ribs—not fully healed from the accident—took the full brunt. I gritted my teeth, pushing past the pain while Graham scrambled away. His fingers dug into the damp soil beneath him for leverage as he launched off the ground.

I caught him and he spun around, trying to tug away from the hold I had on his shirt. He lost his balance and crashed down again and I straddled him. He flailed and I grabbed his arms, pinning him to the ground.

"Fuck," he panted.

"You want to tell me what that was about?" I growled.

He shook his head, trying for casual and falling far short of the mark. "Nothing. Seriously. Thought you were someone else."

"Bullshit!" I jerked him up and slammed him back into the ground, his head cracking backwards. "Why did you run?"

Graham pressed his lips together.

"Talk!" I yelled.

He locked his jaw so I grabbed his shirt in my hand and slammed my fist in his face. His head snapped sideways. Despite the sharp hiss of breath, he remained impassive, unwilling to speak.

Adrenaline and desperation built inside me and I cocked back my fist, ready to throw another punch. "Talk, damn you!"

His dark eyes narrowed. "I'm not telling you shit."

My control snapped. Years of nothing and when I finally get the chance for answers, this jackass decides to shut his mouth?

Fuck. That.

Letting go, I reached for my gun, pulling it from the back of jeans. Cocking it with a quick, deliberate movement, I held it out straight in both arms and pressed it against Graham's head.

He froze, fear making his eyes wide. "Tell me what I want to know or I swear to God I will blow a motherfucking hole in your head," I growled, my chest heaving and eyes blazing with anger.

"Casey!" I heard Grace cry.

Movement from the corner of my eye told me Travis had both arms around Grace, locking her down. I kept my focus on the man frozen beneath me.

"Talk!" I jammed the gun in harder and he winced, sweat breaking out across his brow.

"I ain't rattin' on a brother," he gasped. "So if you're gonna shoot, get it the fuck over with."

"A brother?" A chill slithered down my spine. Graham was talking about bikers, meaning he was in a motorcycle club. Which MC was it?

Holding the gun steady to his head with one hand, I used the other to grab the neckline of his shirt and rip it away. It revealed a tattoo on his chest of a grim reaper with red eyes standing in front of Hell's Gates. The tattoo made him as a member of the second most dangerous outlaw biker gang in Australia.

The Sentinels.

Jesus Christ. Whatever this guy was into, he was in it up to his eyeballs.

"I have no beef with the Sentinels," I snapped. "I just want to know about the case I'm investigating."

"The Daniels case," he muttered.

"Yes, the fucking Daniels case."

The guy shook his head again. "That case is Sentinels business, not yours." He glowered at me, the muscles tightening around his eyes. "So get that gun the fuck outta my face. If you shoot me you'll have every fuckin' Sentinel in Sydney after you."

"What the hell are you talking about? The case is family business, my family business, and that makes it mine." I jammed the gun harder into his head, showing him his threats didn't mean dick. "Mine!" I roared.

"Oh shit." Graham paled. "You're Casey Daniels, aren't you?"

I stared hard into his eyes, his question making my gut roll unhappily. "You know me?"

"Maybe."

"Jesus," I muttered, my heart beating faster as another piece of the puzzle fell into place. "The Sentinels were involved in my parents' murder?"

"It was murder-suicide."

Graham's eyes shifted to the left and down as he spoke. The guy was a shitty liar.

"They had you cover it up by calling it a murder-suicide. The coroner's report, your report, is a fake."

He didn't deny it but his silence was answer enough.

"Why?"

His lips pressed together.

Goddamn sonofabitch.

Shifting the gun, I fired a single shot at the fence post behind Graham. He jumped at the loud crack before I rammed the gun back in his face.

"Answer me or I'll put a bullet in your fucking head!" I roared.

"I don't know shit!" he yelled, the lie so obvious I wanted to throw him against the fence until he gave it up.

"Casey!" Grace cried out again.

"Quiet, Grace," Travis ordered. "Let him do this."

"He's going to shoot him!" she replied, horror edging her voice.

"And if he doesn't, I will."

Graham's panicked gaze shifted from Travis and Grace back to me. "I don't! I do what I'm told and don't ask questions."

My eyes bore into him, hard and unyielding. "Who told you to cover it up?"

Graham swallowed. Not wanting to give him time to think on his answer, I cracked the butt of the gun in his face, splitting his lip. He cried out. His mouth filled with blood as I pressed the weapon back to his forehead.

He spat a mouthful of it out, refusing to answer. I tried another tactic. "Do you know a detective on the force by the name of Morgan Rhodes?"

His eyes shifted to the left and down. "No."

My lips peeled back in a sneer. Graham just made her as a member of the Sentinels without even realising. It made sense for the MC to have members on the inside with the law. She was someone they would never suspect. The biker tattoo would have to be on her somewhere. Hell, I fucked the woman. I should've seen it. I know there was something on her left ass cheek but no matter how hard I strained my memory, I couldn't see it because I never really looked at it. I was drunk, and the next day I was busy getting rid of her.

I pulled the gun off him. Putting the safety on, I tucked it back in my jeans and pushed up off the ground.

"You fuckin' done now?" Graham growled, suddenly finding his balls now my gun was tucked away.

I got to my feet and shrugged, my eyes full of contempt. "Don't leave town, asshole."

Turning, I headed towards Grace and Travis. My eyes hit Travis first. "You know Morgan's address?"

He gave me a nod.

"Good. Let's go."

I grabbed Grace's hand as we headed back to the Subaru. It was cold and clammy. Now wasn't the time to wrap her in my arms so I settled for squeezing her hand and opened the car door for her. "You okay?"

She went to slide in the car without answering. I slid my hand around the nape of her neck before she could get in. I pulled her close, pressing my forehead to hers. "Grace. You with me? I need you to be okay. You said you wanted to help me find my brother. If you can't do this—"

"I'm with you," she said quickly.

Not wanting to linger, I helped her in the car. Before I shut the door, I leaned down, meeting her eyes. "Good."

Chapter Twenty-Eight
GRACE

After arriving at Morgan's house, she opened the door and my reaction was immediate.

I bristled.

I could see why Casey had been with her. She was really quite beautiful, but that was on the surface. Underneath it all she was like a snake in the grass, and also a member of the Sentinels, an outlaw biker gang that fought on the side of evil. The biker name actually rang a bell. Casey didn't look pleased when I mentioned that particular fact, but they were apparently notorious. Maybe I'd seen them on the news or something. Either way, I put it out of my head because Sentinel, detective, or trash collector, whoever the hell Morgan was, someone needed to take her down. Considering God was not currently available for a good smiting, I was happy to nominate myself in his stead.

Leaning casually against the doorframe, she gave Casey a deliberate once over and turned, doing the same to Travis. "So nice to see you both again." Then her eyes hit mine, flashing a smile that wasn't the least bit genuine. Maybe Casey's earlier violence was rubbing off on me because I wanted to tackle her to the ground. I knew I could do it. I had an older brother. I knew how to initiate an effective smackdown. "And what a pleasure to see you brought Grace with you."

I smiled in return, but it was more like a baring of teeth because anger was burning the lining of my stomach clean away. "The pleasure's all mine,

Morgan."

Casey must have heard the threat in my tone because he shifted right, blocking me from launching myself at her.

"Can we come in?" he asked with what I knew was forced politeness. I took satisfaction in knowing he'd never spoken to me with that chilliness. Even when he'd found out about the destruction of Marjorie's backseat, his tone had still been all spark and fire.

Her eyebrows rose but she widened the door in invitation. "By all means."

Morgan stepped back as we filed inside the house. I gave her my own once over as I walked through a tiled entryway that led towards the living area. She wore jeans like me, but hers were dark wash and bootleg and somehow, somewhere, the nineteen-eighties screamed for them back. Wasn't she a detective? Didn't that mean the woman should be able to detect what decade they belonged to?

I arched a brow her way as I followed Casey and Travis into the living area. "Nice jeans," I murmured, my smile genuine when I saw her tug at the waistband.

"Thanks," she replied. She cocked her head at me in mock sympathy. "Though they're probably a little dark for your colouring, sweetie. You're so … pale."

Bitch, I growled internally.

What she did by withholding those reports was not cool. I bet she had no intention of Casey ever seeing them either. She just used them to string him along. My eyes narrowed on her face and I could literally feel my claws extending.

So not cool.

I pasted a smile on my face as she shut the door behind us. "Well. I guess it's lucky that dark jeans like yours aren't the height of fashion right now then, isn't it?"

Her eyes narrowed and I wanted to laugh.

"Morgan," Casey barked, interrupting our verbal sparring right when I was getting warmed up for round two.

Her gaze shifted his way. "I'm not sure why you're all here, but make it quick." She made a point of looking at her watch. "I have somewhere to be."

"Works for me." Widening his stance, Casey folded his arms, his expression intimidating. "Let's cut the bullshit, then. I know you were there. I know you were the first cop on scene at my parents' murder. We're here so you can tell us what happened. That's all we want, okay? Then we'll leave you alone."

I watched her reaction closely. Her brows rose, her expression cold and derisive, but I still caught the flicker of surprise before she banked it. That screamed guilt in my eyes. Yeah, she was there. "What led you to that far-fetched conclusion?"

Damn. She wasn't stupid. That didn't bode well for us. She was waiting for

Casey to incriminate himself by acknowledging he had the stolen reports from her house. Even if she was in this up to her eyeballs, admitting to breaking and entering a detective's house—a detective with an unblemished record—would not work in his favour.

"Well, Casey?" She arched a brow. "Aren't you going to explain why you think I'm somehow caught up in this when all I did was bust my ass to find those reports for you? The ones that seem to have suddenly vanished into thin air?"

Yeah, she was good, but Casey? He was better.

I waited for him to take her down, but he was quiet—Travis was too—and I wasn't sure why. Maybe this was why men resorted to violence so quickly. Verbal sparring with women took a certain skill. Men weren't masters of using catty comments to throw off their opponent.

When he didn't respond, Morgan took his silence as some kind of admittance of guilt because her face flushed with triumph.

"What reports?" I quickly threw out there. I wanted to fold my arms, mimicking Casey's intimidating stance, but it was too difficult with the damn cast on my arm. I settled for a sneer instead.

Casey frowned across at me, his expression silently telling me to shut the hell up. I shrugged. Someone had to say something. Where was the badass Casey of earlier? Pulling a gun seemed like a language she might better understand.

"What reports?" Morgan pressed her lips together like she was fighting a smile. "Really, Grace?"

She walked casually to the coffee table where a laptop sat, the screen closed. Leaning over, she flipped the lid, typed in the password when prompted, and the screen flickered to life.

After sliding a small USB into the side of the laptop and a few taps on the keyboard, a black and white video began to play. With our eyes glued to the screen, she took a step back. "You might want to be careful about what you come around here accusing me of. I don't take kindly to being backed into a corner."

When I realised I was looking at Mac on the computer, rage made my fingers curl into fists. She was dressed all in black, hands gloved up as she systematically searched a bedroom—opening drawers, rifling through books and papers on a small corner desk, and peering under the bed. Eventually she lifted the mattress and came out holding an A4 sized envelope. Lifting the flap, she took a quick peek and with what looked like a grin of satisfaction, disappeared from the room, envelope in hand.

With a quick tap, Morgan shut the video down. "Your parents died in a murder-suicide, Casey. Stop trying to make into something it's not and let it go."

There was no time to think through my actions. Casey and Travis had remained impressively impassive throughout the clip, but I wasn't some kind of trained badass like they were. I simply reacted. Shoving Casey to the side, I yanked the USB from the laptop. With the evidence now safely in my possession, I spun around and slapped Morgan. Despite having to use my left hand, the fury behind it made the impact brutal.

Unfortunately, my smiting didn't come complete with Morgan exploding into the ether, but I did experience some satisfaction in seeing her head snap back. It far outweighed the sting it caused my palm.

"You bitch," I hissed for good measure.

She came back at me, her cheek red from my imprint and her hand raised and ready.

I lifted my chin and braced for impact, silently telling her to bring it, but Travis intervened. Coming from behind, he locked his arms around her, leaving her completely immobile in a matter of moments.

"I'll have you arrested along with Mac," she spat at me, struggling in Travis's tight hold as she lost her cool. "Assault on a police officer. Cops don't take kindly to that."

Shit.

I'd made it worse, hadn't I?

No wonder Casey and Travis had stood there with their mouths shut. They knew how to speak badass. My language was more territorial kitten. I should've stayed in the car with Travis like Casey ordered me to, but leaving him alone to deal with Morgan? Yeah, no. The itch to scratch her eyes out had been strong. I'd jumped from the car and was halfway to the door before he could even catch me.

Casey shoved me behind him before I could do any more damage. I glared at her from over his shoulder.

"Assault?" he said, his tone calm and almost amused. Yep. Definite badass. "I didn't see any assault here." His gaze turned to Travis, his brows raised coolly. "What about you, Travis? Did you see anything?"

Letting go of Morgan, he stepped back and she huffed, yanking herself from his presence. "Nope." He shrugged and it felt good having the both of them take my back. Despite the tense situation, my heart still managed to produce a warm fuzzy. "I didn't see shit."

That was when Casey made his move, and I had to link my hands together to restrain a juvenile fist pump in the air.

"Have you heard of Chief Inspector Valentine? Mac's father?" he asked Morgan, referring to Steve. I'd met him several times when he visited the duplex with his wife, Jenna. I had no idea he'd been such a high-ranking member with the Sydney Police. He was a huge guy, handsome and fit, and fanatical about World News. He'd bailed me up in a conversation about the separatist rebels ambushing Ukrainian soldiers, throwing current peace talks into crisis. Rather than appear ignorant of the situation (which I was), I offered him a drink when he came up for air.

"He may be retired," Casey continued, "but he's a close personal friend of Deputy Commissioner Alan Rossiter. The same Deputy Commissioner that owes Chief Valentine for saving his life. You try to have either Mac or Grace arrested and not only will the charges get thrown out, I'll inform Rossiter that you're a member of the Sentinels." Morgan flinched when Casey threw that out there. After a pause to allow that particular piece of information to sink in, he continued. "I'm giving you two days. If you don't tell me by then what you know, you can kiss your career goodbye. The force won't accept a member of the Sentinels within their ranks. Every single case you worked on during your entire career will come under investigation." Casey jabbed a finger in her face, some of his fury leaking through. "I'll fucking ruin you."

Casey stood there with confidence as he spoke, his glare intense and unwavering. His demeanour wasn't just inspiring, it was hot. He had her. We all knew it. Even Morgan, because underneath the eyes that flashed fire was a layer of panic she couldn't hide.

"Prove it," she hissed.

"I don't need to." He shrugged casually. "Maybe you thought I was too drunk to notice, or too stupid to eventually put two and two together, but the proof is right there in the ink on your skin. How long have you been covering up the Sentinels' crimes for, Morgan? Your entire career? Come on," he tutted with a chilly smile that gave me goose bumps. "We know Graham Bennett isn't an old friend of your Uncle's. He's a member of the Sentinels, and somehow you—a twenty-three-year-old officer fresh out of the academy—managed to get him to falsify an autopsy report. You know what that tells me?" Morgan didn't answer, her expression mutinous. "It tells me you're in deep, Morgan. You know what else? I don't care how deep you're in it. If I don't hear from you in two days, I'll take apart every single Sentinel member one by one, including you, and damn the consequences. Someone murdered my family and for that, they're going down."

"Two days!" Travis exploded when we were back at the car. Casey opened the car door and I slid onto the backseat, knowing exactly how Travis felt. We were so close to getting answers I could taste it.

Checking my phone quickly after leaving it in the car, I saw two missed calls from John that set my stomach churning. I knew why he was ringing. It was time to go home to Melbourne and face the music.

I wasn't ready.

God, just two more days, I pleaded silently. Let me be here for Casey just a little bit longer.

Unaware of my sudden, inner turmoil, Casey huffed with frustration as he slammed the car door behind me. Hopping into the front passenger seat of Travis's car, he slammed his own door for good measure. "What did you want me to do, beat it out of her?"

"A valid option," I pointed out as I buckled my seat belt, forcing the missed calls from my mind.

Casey turned in his seat as Travis pulled onto the street, accelerating quickly. He raised his brows at me. "Since when did you get so bloodthirsty?"

"Since I met you," I retorted.

"Jesus," he muttered, turning back around. To the both of us, he said, "We've backed Morgan into a corner. Let her cool off and we'll get it out of her, okay? I've waited this long. Two more days is not going to hurt."

Of course it would hurt. I was already hurting for him so I couldn't even imagine how bad it was for him.

It was going on dusk when we hit traffic on the return trip to the loft. Travis must've had his phone hooked up by Bluetooth to his car because the sound of it ringing came blasting through the speakers.

"Yeah?" he answered as he pulled up at a set of red lights.

"Where are you, asshead?" Mac barked and the sound was amplified by a thousand, her voice booming at us in surround sound.

"Fuck," Casey muttered.

"Working," Travis replied.

There was a pause where Mac appeared to be waiting for her brother to elaborate. He didn't. The light turned green and he accelerated, his car growling powerfully as we shot off the line like it was a drag race. The car beside us rallied valiantly but faded fast and we left everyone behind. It was impressive and even though I was still shaky getting behind the wheel of a car, it didn't lessen the urge to take this one for a test drive. Somehow I knew Travis wouldn't be cool with that. Wreck one car, one, and it ruined you for life.

"Working where?" she eventually asked.

"Working at none of your damn business. What do you want?"

"Don't be such a wanker, Travis," her voice boomed, and I felt like ducking for cover. "You've been acting like a little bitch ever since I stole that report."

Travis white-knuckled the steering wheel. "Your little escapade could possibly get you arrested. Did you know Morgan has video surveillance of you ransacking her room?"

There was a pause. "No shit?" Then a bit more cautiously, "How do you know that?"

"How the fuck do you think I know that?" Travis growled.

"That bitch!" she fumed, and I nodded my agreement even though Mac couldn't see it. "You're not going to tell Dad, are you?"

She sounded worried so I figured Steve would probably lock her in prison himself if he heard about what she did. It wasn't easy being a girl and being badass. People tended not to like it. Not that Mac cared about whether anyone liked it or not. She was a law unto herself. "I will if you don't stop going all Dirty Harry on everyone. It's got to stop."

"Yes, of course," she replied quickly.

Travis slammed a fist on the steering wheel, obviously not believing a word of it. "I mean it."

"So what happened?" she asked, deflecting. "Did you go pay her a little visit? Did she hand over the video?"

"Yes, and no. It was on a USB, but Morgan isn't stupid. She'd have more than one copy floating around. Grace took it before she delivered Morgan her own little message." Travis glanced at me in the rearview mirror and I caught a flash of amusement.

"She did?"

"I did," I called out from the backseat.

"Yes!" Mac hissed gleefully and the sound echoed through the car. "Did you make her bleed, Grace? Why wasn't I invited to the smackdown?"

"For the exact same reason you just called it a smackdown. This is not the WWE," Casey replied, weighing into the conversation. "As if it isn't hard enough doing our jobs without worrying about you girls in lockup for breaking and entering, and assault and battery."

"She threatened to arrest Grace too? Bitch!" she growled again. The reminder of Morgan's threat made me hot with anger all over again, so I pressed the button for the window. It came down quickly, emitting subzero air into the car. I quickly put it back up before icicles formed on my eyelashes. "Did you throw Dad's name about like confetti?"

"Casey did," Travis confirmed.

"Good. Let her know we have people in high places. Make her sweat. I think we should—"

"Mac! Dammit. There is no we. You're not involving yourself in this any further. Are we clear?"

"Christ, Trav!" she yelled and my ears smarted. "Let it go! Yes, I broke in, and yes, I stole the report. And you know what? I'd do it again and if I got arrested, then so be it. I happen to think it was worth doing jail time for. I'd even—"

"Mac," Casey interrupted, but she was on a roll.

"—get a cool prison nickname like Lil' Em Vicious, and—"

"Mac!"

She paused.

"Thank you," he told her.

Another pause, then, "Anything for a guy as hot as you, Casey. Sorry, Grace," she threw my way. "It's just a fact."

Casey laughed but Travis looked ready to pop a vein.

"You're forgiven," I told her. "I would've been right there with you if I hadn't been strapped to a hospital bed."

"Great. Then we'd have both of you working the chain gang," Travis muttered dryly. "We need to keep you two separated."

"Speaking of separation, it's Mum and Dad's thirtieth anniversary tonight."

"Nice segue, Mac." Travis told her, shifting across two lanes and into the right turning lane that led us onto Casey's street. I had to hold on at the quick, zippy manoeuvre.

"I thought so. So back to my original question. Where are you, asshead? Everyone's arrived at the back function room of the Florence Bar for the surprise party and the three of you are still a no show. Mum and Dad will be here soon."

"Shit," he muttered.

"You forgot!" Mac accused in high-pitched surround sound and I flinched. "How could you do that? Your wife organised the whole thing! Did you even give Casey and Grace the invitation?"

Travis widened his eyes at me in the rearview mirror, a silent plea to lie.

I cleared my throat, relieved to see the loft up ahead. I'd long mastered the art of rapid dressing. A quick shower to wash off the evil that was Morgan and I could do my makeup in the car. "We're on our way, Mac," I told her.

"Sure you are," she grouched, not believing a word of it.

"With everything going on, I'm not sure taking Grace out right now is a good idea," Casey interjected.

"Rubbish," Mac told him. "You have to be there, Casey. Mum and Dad are like your surrogate parents. Besides, the entire Badass Brigade will be at the party, not including the bar's own security. What could go wrong?"

Casey groaned, rubbing a hand across a face that was weary. I wasn't sure Mac should have added the "what could go wrong" part to the end of her speech. Throwing something like that out there always preceded something bad happening.

"Fine," he told her after a long hesitation. "But we won't stay long."

"Good. Maybe I should duck back quickly and grab Polly," I heard her mutter.

"No!" Travis shouted as he pulled into the loft's underground car park.

"Who's Polly?" I asked.

"My gun," she replied. "Polly Pistol."

My brows flew up, not just at the part about Mac owning a gun, but because she'd named it. "Nice."

"I know, right? Anyway, I have to go, assheads. Your drinks are on me tonight, Grace."

She hung up before I could reply.

Chapter Twenty-Nine
CASEY

Quinn sent a message to let me know the party was black-tie, so with Grace in the bath, I pulled my tux from the wardrobe and began to dress. I was frowning into the mirror, tying the bow, when the loft intercom buzzed. I gave up, letting the tie hang around my neck while I went to answer it.

I flicked on the security vision, revealing a guy standing there with a huge box. He was dressed casually—jeans, hoodie, and cap—but he was shuffling from foot to foot. My eyes narrowed suspiciously. He was either up to something, impatient, or busting to take a piss.

I hit the intercom button. "Yeah?"

The guy cleared his throat. "I have a package for Grace Paterson. She here?"

Mitsy's head perked up at the unfamiliar tone flooding the loft, letting out a little woof from his dog bed in the corner of the living room. I raised my brows at the little bastard. "Tough guy, huh?"

He woofed again, adding a bit of growl to the end of it as though saying, "Tougher than you, asshole."

Shaking my head because I was having a conversation with a dog, I hit the intercom button again. "Who's it from?"

I watched the guy check the tag then lean close to the intercom speaker on the outside wall. "Says it's from Mackenzie Valentine?"

"Give me a minute," I replied. Palming my phone off the kitchen bench, I called up Mac's number and dialled.

She answered after two rings. "Casey."

"Mac. Did you order something for Grace? There's a guy here with a package. Says it from—"

"I knew you weren't on your way," she snapped. "That package was supposed to arrive two hours ago."

"What is it?" I asked and returned to the security monitor to eye the big, glossy looking box.

"It's a dress for tonight. I figured Grace wouldn't have had time to shop. There should be matching shoes in there too, okay?"

I hit the buzzer, saying, "Come on up," to the delivery guy. I watched him disappear through the downstairs door. Into the phone, I said, "Thanks, Mac."

"You wait 'til you see her in the dress. You can thank me then." She chuckled and hung up.

I shook my head, a grin on my face as I opened the door. Mitsy began barking, the sound both savage and ear-splitting, which was quite a feat considering his small size. His claws ticked rapidly on the timber flooring as he raced to my side, his teeth bared in tiny, razor-sharp points.

"Holy shit," the delivery guy exclaimed, taking an abrupt step back. "What the hell is that?"

"It's a dog, dude," I replied dryly. Grabbing Mitsy off the floor, I tucked him under my left arm like a football. He was a quivering, snapping bundle of fur, his eyes fixed on the guy while he put the box at his feet and handed over an electronic pad for me to sign. I quickly scrawled my signature, took possession of the box in my other hand, and shut the door with my foot.

"Good boy, Mitsy," I praised, deciding his ferocity deserved a treat. Returning him to the floor and the box to the kitchen bench, I opened the pantry cupboard. The shelves were bare. Spying a lone packet of Doritos leftover from Grace's holiday binge, I opened it and tossed a handful into his doggy bowl before taking one for myself.

Mitsy crunched loudly just as Grace stepped out of the bathroom wrapped in a towel. Her eyes narrowed with suspicion. "What are you feeding him?"

I swallowed the chip in my mouth and shifted in front of the packet, blocking it from view. "A doggy treat."

"No you're not. You're feeding him Doritos."

"Why did you ask if you already knew?"

"Because I wanted you to know I knew exactly what you were doing."

My brows flew up, confused. "By asking me what I was feeding him?"

Grace huffed. "You're just trying to make Mitsy love you more than me, luring him to the dark side with your bribes."

"What, I'm the 'dark side' now?" I air-quoted. And didn't she know the words Mitsy and love in the same sentence was ridiculous? The dog was about as loveable as a cactus.

With a roll of her eyes, Grace started for the bedroom. Grabbing the box,

I followed behind. Her skin was damp and flushed and a cloud of the rich, honey-scented body wash she favoured trailed behind her.

I checked my watch and my lips curled with anticipation.

We had time.

"What's this?" Grace asked, pausing to stare at the box when I dumped it on the bed. Noting the swirly black writing, she read out, "Collette Dinnigan." She turned, her face flushing with sudden pleasure. "You bought me a dress?"

The way she looked at me made me wish I had. I was fully dressed, my jacket on and the tie still dangling around my neck, but she was looking at me like I was naked.

With a quick flick of my hand, her towel unravelled and pooled at her feet. She sucked in a breath when I sank to the edge of the bed pulling her towards me. It brought her belly to eye level. I gripped her ass in my hands and leaned in, licking along the taut skin with the tip of my tongue

"Oh," she breathed, her fingers in my hair. She tugged a little, getting my attention. "Do we have time?"

"Are you kidding?" I answered, my palms running down the backs of her thighs. The world could have been imploding for all I cared. "Don't you know how sexy you are? All that fire under your skin gets me hot." I told her between licks of her skin. "I was so damn proud of you today. You didn't flinch once. You were strong and fierce and just watching you made my cock hard. So when you ask me if we have time, the answer is always yes." Her nails scratched through my hair, giving me goose bumps. I looked up at her, my heart thumping. "You're fast becoming my world, Grace, and that world is a place I never want to leave."

"Casey," Grace breathed and crawled naked onto my lap. My hands gripped her ass when she straddled me. I wanted to fuck her just like this. Leaning back on my elbows, I could thrust upwards and watch my cock disappear inside her. God, that would be hot. I reached for my fly and slid it down, freeing my erection. "There's something I have to tell you."

I could barely think for her words to register. Her tits were in my face and my dick was hard enough to pound nails. I reached between us and massaged her clit. "Uh huh."

I reached across and snagged a condom off the bedside table.

"Casey, I'm serious."

I rolled the condom down quickly and looked up, my eyes dazed with lust. "What?"

"We need to talk."

"Later."

Grace shifted upwards and I took advantage, my cock sliding home. Her head fell back as I drew back and rammed upwards. She moaned, squeezing me. "It's important," she managed to get out.

The worry in her voice snagged my attention, but my brain struggled to reengage. "Whatever's going on in that pretty head of yours, as long as we have each other, it'll work out, okay?"

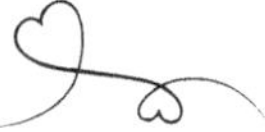

We were late.

I walked into the party of over a hundred people holding Grace's hand. Surrounding chatter died off and those closest to us blinked and stared. I couldn't blame them. Before we left, Grace pinned her hair at the nape of her neck in a messy knot, put something on her skin that made it shimmer under the lights, and slid into a short, gold dress with thin straps. It was covered in gems that reflected the light and came down in a V on her chest. My hand literally shook when I'd slid the back zipper closed, my fingers deliberately brushing the bare skin of her back.

I glanced at Grace, my eyes crinkling in a grin. "I'm so sexy in this tux everyone can't take their eyes off me. Hope that doesn't bother you."

Her glossy, pink lips curved in an answering grin. "As long as it doesn't bother you they're only staring because your cock is still hanging out of your pants."

"What the …" I glanced down.

Grace threw back her head, her laugh loud and throaty. Squeezing her hand, I tugged her towards the bar. "Come on, chuckles. Let's get you a glass of champagne before you do some damage with those terrible jokes of yours."

Turning to face the crowd after placing an order for champagne and whiskey with the bartender, Vince, I caught Mac heading our way. The red strapless number that clung to her body was no doubt giving her brothers a collective heart attack. As far as they were concerned Mac was still a virgin. A quick scan of the room showed two pairs of eyes tracking her. One set belonged to her eldest brother, Mitch, and they were busy telling the room to back the fuck off. The other belonged to Jake, and what his were busy saying had me chuckling.

I grinned at Mac when she reached us.

She paused to stare.

My brow furrowed. "You okay?"

She cleared her throat. "Fine."

Jake's gaze shifted from Mac to me and he scowled. I leaned into Mac's side experimentally, keeping watch on him from the corner of my eye. Placing a hand on the small of her back, I asked her if she needed a drink. His hands fisted and he started our way.

"Thanks, Casey," Mac replied.

Laughing silently, I removed my hand and asked Vince for another champagne.

"Casey," Jake muttered as I handed Grace and Mac their drinks.

"Jake," I replied with a nod and picked up my whiskey, taking a sip while the girls talked.

"First Evie, then Grace, and now Mac. You working your way through all the women one by one?"

His reference to Evie happened to be a kiss that was a long time ago. It was a weak moment at a time when we both needed it, but I knew it wasn't Evie or Grace he was caring about right now. "You mean all the women," I asked and arched a brow, "or just Mac?"

"I mean just Mac," he snapped.

"Mate." I slapped him on the back, shaking my head in sympathy. "Mitch, Travis, Jared, and Steve? A guy would need balls bigger than Mount Everest to take those four on. I wouldn't want to be you for all the tea in China. Good luck," I added and tossed back the contents of my whiskey.

On that note, I left my glass on the bar and guided Grace towards the centre of the room where Steve and Jenna held court. After offering our congratulations, I got caught chatting with Steve about China's brute coerciveness in disputing Asian waters and the potential risk of war with Vietnam.

He frowned at me, rubbing his jaw as he immersed himself in the subject. "The question is, how far is China willing to go?"

"They'll go as far as they can before the U.S. intervenes," I answered. "And the U.S. won't do anything until Obama identifies there's a national risk."

"Jesus, Dad." Travis shoved another whiskey in my hand as he joined our circle. "Relax. It's a party."

Steve ignored Travis and focused on Grace. "What do you think, Grace?"

"What do I think?" She puffed out her cheeks. "I think you need another drink." He laughed, and then paused when she added, "I also think China's assertiveness is driving U.S. allies, including Australia, closer together and now is the time to hedge our position. We need to work for the best outcome and prepare for the worst. It's a jungle out there. Sir," she added.

"That's interesting, Grace," he muttered, taking hold of her elbow as he leaned closer to talk. "Australia is in deep economic engagement with China. Now is the time to strengthen—"

"Dad," Travis interrupted.

"—relations with our allies, and the key to hedging—"

"Dad! Jesus."

Steve paused, looking at his son. "What?"

"Let the hostages go," he ordered, jerking his chin our way. Grace sagged with obvious relief as I led her away from the conversation.

I laughed. "Congratulations, Slim. Keeping up with Steve and his world news obsession makes me sweat."

"Same," she muttered as she finished off the last of her champagne. "That's why I googled."

My lips twitched. "You googled?"

"Mmm hmm. In the car on the way here. Current world news headlines."

"I'm impressed," I told her, taking the empty glass from her hand and placing it on the nearby table.

"Stick around, fledging grasshopper…" she winked "…and I'll show you the rest of my moves."

An hour later I was ready to leave. We'd made a decent appearance. It had been a hell of a day, starting off with the physiotherapist for Grace, and ending with the showdown at Morgan's house. I needed Grace. I needed a bed. I needed Grace in a bed. Knowing exactly where she stood in the crowd, talking with Cooper, Frog, and Henry, I met her eyes and indicated one last drink before we left.

She nodded and I headed towards the bar.

"Hang on," Vince told me. "The whiskey's run dry. I just need to run to the back room."

"Don't go to any trouble, mate," I told him, knowing he was busy. "I'll just head to the main bar."

I left via an exit I knew led inside the main section of the venue. Opening the door, I stepped into bone-thumping music and a crush of bodies. Winding my way through the writhing masses by the dance floor, I made it past the line of booths along the wall and put in a drink order at the bar.

"Are you following me now?" came a voice from beside me.

My body tensed and I glanced sideways. "What the fuck are you doing here, Morgan?"

She leaned casually against the bar, as though enjoying herself. A beer sat in her right hand and a smirk lined her lips. There were not enough mistakes in the world that could match up to the one I made by fucking her. Now the memory of her sucking my cock made me want a shower.

She arched a brow. "It's a public bar."

And it conveniently happened to be here? "Go drink somewhere else." My eyes narrowed on her face. "Unless you're ready to talk?"

Her attention shifted to the exit door of the function room. I turned around, following her gaze. "So that's Chief Inspector Valentine," she murmured, watching Steve walk through the door and head our way.

He slapped me on the back when he reached my side. "Order me a whiskey, son. We've already drunk the bar dry back in there." I signalled for another whiskey as Steve's eyes fell on Morgan beside me. "And who's this young lady?"

Morgan held out her hand and I gritted my teeth. "Steve this is Morgan." Steve shook it. "Morgan, this is Chief Inspector Valentine."

"Retired," Steve added. "Well, supposedly."

"Supposedly?" she questioned as another whiskey joined mine on the bar.

I handed it to Steve, eager to usher him away from Morgan.

"They won't leave a man alone to enjoy his retirement in peace," he explained after taking a quick sip of his drink.

"We better get back to the party," I interrupted.

Steve gave her a nod. "Nice to meet you, Morgan."

We both turned to leave and she called out, "Wait!"

We paused and Morgan handed me the whiskey I left on the bar in my haste to leave. Looking at Steve, she said, "I hear it's your thirtieth wedding anniversary."

"It is," he confirmed.

"Congratulations on a such a wonderful milestone." She raised her drink. Then she looked at me over the rim of her glass with a glint in her eye. "Cheers."

My eyes narrowed and she shrugged.

"Thanks, Morgan," Steve replied, holding up his glass in response. I tipped back my head and tossed the entire contents down my throat and left my glass on the bar. I felt her eyes follow me as we left, but I refused to acknowledge it.

Back inside, Steve peeled away to join Jenna while I headed towards our table, intent on collecting Grace's bag so we could leave.

Her phone sat by her little evening bag. Four missed calls showed on the screen from her best friend, John, and as I picked it up, he rang again. My eyes searched out Grace. She hadn't moved from where she stood talking with Cooper, Frog, and Henry. The four of them were caught in a huddle, laughing. Thinking John's call might be an emergency, I picked up the phone, hit answer, and put it to my ear.

"Grace!" John barked instantly. "Dammit. I've been trying to ring you all day." I opened my mouth to tell him it wasn't Grace but he kept on talking, his pissed tone putting me offside. My jaw ticked as I listened. "What the hell are you doing? You need to stop playing Russian roulette with your life and get home already."

Russian roulette with her life? I paused. What the fuck was he talking about?

"Grace? Stop ignoring me. This is serious. You can't put off coming home any longer. You shouldn't have even gone in the first place."

Waves of tension rolled through me. "It's not Grace."

"Oh. Shit," John muttered.

"Tell me what's going on, John." My grip on the phone tightened. "Right now."

"Is Grace there?"

I looked to where Grace stood with the guys, sipping the last quarter of her drink. "She's nearby. We're at a party."

There was a long pause before he spoke again. "I'm not sure Grace will forgive me for speaking behind her back, but this is bigger than our friendship."

John's cryptic conversation was making me lose patience. "Talk," I barked, needing to know what the hell was going on.

"Grace …" He let out a shaky breath. "Hell … Okay. Grace had a lump removed from her breast exactly nine days before she left for Sydney. Did she tell you?"

"I asked her about it," I told him, remembering the sudden worry after seeing the fresh scar for the first time. "She said it was a benign lump. I didn't have any reason to doubt her. She—"

"She lied."

"What …" I swallowed, my heart suddenly thumping so hard I had to grab the back of the chair behind me to steady myself. "What did you just say?"

"She lied, Casey," he told me, then paused. "Grace has cancer."

Blood roared in my ears as the whole world faded away. "No," I told him, shaking my head. Not Grace. Not my Grace. "You're wrong. She would've told me."

"Casey … Shit. I'm sorry."

My eyes fell on her. Henry hugged her close while she laughed at something Cooper was saying.

My heart cracked wide open, memories flooded me instantly.

"What if I want to keep you?"

Grace closing her eyes, hiding them from me. "You can't. After eight weeks we both walk away, no questions asked."

Then at the cottage.

"People come and go, Casey. Some crash into your life and leave in the blink of eye, others stay with you for years, but it doesn't matter how long you have them for, because the way they make you feel stays you with forever."

I should've seen it.

Why didn't I see it?

John spoke my name but the sound was more like a buzz in my ears because suddenly it was hard to breathe.

The phone fell to my side. "Grace." My voice cracked on the word and I didn't realise I'd said it loud enough for everyone to hear until silence fell around me.

Grace looked my way, her brows drawing together. "Casey?"

I fought for air as she started towards me, a million emotions punching through me in turn: hurt, betrayal, and the most crippling one of all—fear. All of it roiled inside me, leaving me sick. I tried to leash it and failed.

"You lied to me!" I held up her phone so she could see it. She flinched, seeing John's name there on the screen. I turned and pitched it at the wall. Destroying phones was becoming a habit.

Travis started towards me, winding his way through the frozen bodies, all of them seemingly stunned at the violent outburst.

"That was John," I managed to say, just so she was clear.

"Did he …"

She faltered and trailed off, so I finished the question for her. "Tell me?"

Her head jerked in a nod.

"Yes!" I shouted, feeling raw. "Yes, he fucking told me!"

My raging pulse wasn't easing and I stepped back, feeling oddly anxious and dizzy. Bumping the table behind me, I spun around, shoving it angrily, and stumbled again. What was wrong with me?

"Casey?"

Christ. Fucking cancer. It was something I couldn't see, something I couldn't beat the shit out of, put away in prison, or shoot with a gun. It was something I couldn't protect her from. I could only hold her hand and watch it happen.

Feeling everyone's eyes on me, I shook my head, trying to clear it.

"Casey … I'm sorry," Grace whispered from somewhere behind me.

A sob broke in my chest.

Why?

Why now when I'd just found her?

Why, goddammit!

I clenched my jaw hard enough for my teeth to crack, willing myself to pull it together.

"I can't do this here," she told me, her voice trembling. I turned but she pushed her way through the crush of people until she was simply gone.

I blinked, trying to focus, to breathe, to fucking move.

If I wasn't so disoriented, I would've noticed Coby behind me righting the table I'd knocked over. That Jared was calming Henry down from taking a swing at me. That Travis was in my ear, talking to me. But I didn't see it, or hear any of it.

Without even realising how I'd gotten there, I was out the front of the bar, cold air whipping past my face as I searched for Grace. Catching a flash of gold, I headed for it. She was hailing a cab, standing near the long line of bodies that were waiting to get in the same bar I just left.

"Grace!" I shouted.

She spun around just as a cab pulled wildly to the kerb beside her.

"Holy shit," someone in line muttered. "That's Grace Paterson."

Ignoring the people behind me as I made my way towards her, I yelled, "Grace, you can't leave!"

I didn't just mean the bar either, or even the city. I meant me. She couldn't leave me. God, please, don't fucking do this.

Grace shook her head at me, tears filling her eyes while some fucktard in the line beside us held up his phone and snapped a photo.

"Are you fucking kidding me?" I growled.

"Hey!" the guy cried when I snatched the phone from his hand. I hit the trash icon on the screen deleting the photo. Then I threw it because I was becoming a pro at destroying other people's phones. "Take another photo and

I'll rip your head off. Got it?"

"Casey!" Grace grabbed my arm, pulling me away from him. I stumbled when the world tilted. "You're drunk," she muttered.

From three drinks? That couldn't be right but my head wouldn't clear enough to work out why. I forced my eyes to her face. "Why didn't you tell me?"

"Because this is my fight. Mine!" she shouted, pounding a fist against her chest. "It's not Henry's, or John's, or yours. It's mine, and I'm not going to allow what happened to my father and to my family happen to you. Don't you see how much you've already lost? Why would you think I'd put you through more of that?"

My vision began to fade. I was hanging on to consciousness by my fucking fingernails. "Don't you get it, Grace? It's too late," I slurred and shook my head. Blinking again, I managed to meet her eyes, my heart shattered. "I lose you and it's game over for me."

"Casey." Grace pressed her lips together, tears spilling down her face. "I can't do this. I'm sorry. I love you, but I can't do this."

I reached for her but in a split second she was inside the cab and it was driving her away from me. Stepping up to the kerb, I managed to hold up my arm, hailing the next cab passing by. Sliding inside, all I remember mumbling was, "Follow that cab in front of us," before I slipped into darkness.

Chapter Thirty
MITCH VALENTINE

My phone rang, the distinctive ringtone telling me it was work. I dragged my pounding head from beneath the pillow with a groan and felt around for it, not willing to risk opening my eyes.

When my fingers closed around it, I dragged it back underneath my pillow with me, answering with a grunt.

"Valentine," my boss, Inspector Keith Burns, barked.

I replied with another grunt, wondering why he was so alert at whatever the fuck time it was in the morning. Was it even morning? Who even cared right now? I barely remembered leaving the bar last night when Mum and Dad's anniversary party wound down and my boss had still been there, unsteady on his feet.

I startled at the soft murmur of a female voice beside me. My morning wood twitched happily, liking the sound, but my mind immediately questioned who the hell was in my bed. Was it even my bed?

I lifted the pillow. The familiarity of my own room stared back at me—white walls, navy sheets, and the framed print of Kate Beckinsale from Underworld, complete with fierce eyes and gun in hand, on my wall. The print had been a birthday gift from my sister-in-law Evie and was both sexy, powerful and kick fucking ass.

"I need you in the office, Detective," Burns ordered in my ear. "I know it's Sunday and your day off, but this is important, and when I say important, I mean real fucking important, so get your ass in here ASAP."

It had to be if my boss was in the office on his day off too. I ended the call with another grunt. Tossing the phone, I scratched my balls with a long, drawn-out yawn and rolled out of bed.

"Wha…" came a mumble from somewhere beneath the covers. Getting to my feet, I turned, completely naked with my wood still saluting the morning, and waited for the woman in my bed to reveal herself. She didn't disappoint. The sheets were shoved down sleepily, unearthing dusky olive skin, long tousled dark hair that reached the small of her back, and an extremely well toned ass. She paused for a moment before rolling over. The front was just as hot. My eyes travelled up her long legs, past a taut set of abs and halted to a jarring stop. A fresh, thick jagged scar marred her ribcage and on her torso sat a tattoo of a coiled, deadly snake, its red eyes waiting for the moment to strike. Beneath the snake in old English font read Black Viper MC.

I also knew her, and as of last night, that intimate knowledge may or may not have been re-acquainted. Events were still hazy.

"Gabriella."

Her eyes flew open, widening on my cock before slicing up to my face. She flinched, cursing in Spanish. "Mierda!"

Ripping the sheets away, she slid naked from the bed, grabbing for her clothes. I stalked around the bed, seizing her bicep roughly. "Where the fuck have you been?"

"Let me go, you cula!" she growled in that husky tone of hers that always got me hard. She yanked her arm free, her gold-coloured eyes shooting sparks. Her nose, covered with a smattering of freckles, scrunched adorably in contrast to her anger. "I must have been off my face on snow to sleep with you."

My stomach rolled in disgust. "You doing coke now?"

She paused to rake her eyes over me, the look both lazy and suggestive. My cock jerked, not seeming to care about the whole drug thing. At all. Then she shrugged. "I'm doing a lot of things now."

Including me? I scanned the floor, not seeing any evidence of torn, empty condom wrappers. "Did we have sex?"

Her panties were already on and her bra snapping in place when I asked my question. "If we did, then God save us all, because Hell must have frozen over."

I couldn't blame her fury. We'd left things in a bad place. Her sudden appearance last night at the party on the arm of a man I didn't know had hit me like a solid punch in the gut. Where had she been all these years? With the Black Vipers? How the fuck had it come to that?

I waved a hand in the direction of her torso where no matter what angle I stood, the eyes of the coiled snake glowered at me. "What's with the tattoo?" I growled. "We went through the academy together, then all of a sudden you disappear, and now you're running with the Vipers?"

"It's none of your business," she hissed, her voice muffled as she yanked a tight black dress over her head and twitched it quickly in place.

"You woke in my bed." I folded my arms as she yanked her hair from beneath the neckline of her dress. It resettled down the delicious curve of her back. "That makes it my business."

"Arrghhh!" She threw up her hands. "Eres una cara tan verga!"

The Spanish words rolled off her tongue beautifully, making me realise how much I'd missed it. How much I'd missed her. "What did you say?" I asked as she grabbed her shoes and sat on the edge of the bed.

"I said," she enunciated sarcastically as she jerked the pair of black stilettos on her feet, "that you are such a dickface."

With that she stood and grabbed her small bag. It began to ring and she rummaged her hand around inside it. Yanking out her phone, she answered with, "Hola!" as she stalked from the room.

Wrenching open a dresser drawer, I tugged on a pair of jeans and a snug long sleeve shirt in dark grey. Gabriella was gone when I entered the living room of my apartment. Knowing I had to get to work, I didn't chase her down. I might've had no idea what her number was or where she lived, but I was a detective and damn good at my job. I'd fucking find her because we were far from finished. I wanted to know how the beautiful, determined, career-driven girl I had adored spiralled into a woman who talked drugs and biker gangs.

Palming my phone, I dialled Tate, my partner with the Sydney Police. "You get the call?"

"Yep, already on my way in," he answered. "You know what it's about?"

"Nope," I replied, tucking my wallet into the back pocket of my jeans and hanging my detective badge around my neck. "You?"

"No idea."

Twenty minutes later I was at the Surry Hills LAC—Sydney City's local area command centre, sitting opposite my boss and to the left of Tate.

"What's going on, boss?" I asked.

"I need you both to make an arrest. A new case. Came up overnight. Probable homicide."

Tate and I shared a quick glance of what the fuck? Pulled in on a Sunday for something any cop on duty could have handled? The only thing I could think of was that either the victim or the perpetrator was a celebrity and Burns wanted only senior detectives in charge.

"Who are we arresting?" Tate asked, running a hand over his dark, buzzed hair in a tired, casual gesture.

Burns looked directly at me, his nostrils flaring when he answered. "Casey

Daniels."

I stiffened in my seat, the only physical indication of the shock punching through me. That had to be a mistake. The idea of arresting my friend on suspicion of murder was some kind of sick joke. But Burns didn't play sick jokes, and his eyes were flat, and deadly serious.

My jaw ticked, suddenly furious on Casey's behalf. "And the victim?"

Burns sat back in his seat and swiped a hand across the stubble on his jaw, the strain in his demeanour showing through. "Grace Paterson."

"Bullshit," I growled and Tate tensed at my side. Getting to my feet, I jabbed a finger across the desk at my boss and shouted, "Bull-fucking-shit!"

"Lock it down, Valentine," he ordered.

Hands on my hips, I paced for a moment. The ramifications of what this would do to so many people I loved weighed on me.

Probable homicide meant there was no body but there was enough evidence to indicate survival was extremely doubtful.

Grace.

I closed my eyes and pulled in a deep breath. Gaining control, my eyes opened directly on my boss. "Tell me what you've got."

Tate leaned forward in his seat, his jaw ticking.

"You two are not running this case." I opened my mouth to argue and he kept going, his voice gaining volume in order to deter an interruption. "You're too close, Mitch. I've pulled you both in as a professional courtesy to Jamieson and Valentine Consulting. I don't believe for a second Casey would do something like this, but the evidence is stacked so high against him that my hands are tied right now."

"With all due respect, sir," Tate bit out, "you need to share that evidence."

Burns nodded his agreement. "I will. Just as soon as—"

A rap came at the door to his office, interrupting him.

He glanced up. "Ahh, here she is."

I turned and froze.

"What the fuck?" I bit out.

"Cabron!" Gabriella growled at the same time.

It translated to 'bastard.' A term I'd heard pass her lips many times in the past when she was pissed at me.

Long gone was the sexy black dress of earlier. In its place was a tight pair of black jeans, black calf-high boots and a fitted long-sleeved black top. A police badge hung around her neck. My eyes locked on it, my head spinning. Had I woken up in a parallel universe this morning? "What in the goddamn hell are you doing here?"

"Mitchell Valentine," she hissed, using my full name in her rolling Spanish accent. She'd never shortened it to Mitch like everyone else and hearing it on her lips when she was naked and writhing beneath me had always got me hot. "You work here?"

Burns looked between the both of us. "You two know each other? Good," he said without waiting for a response. "Come in, Detective."

"Detective?" I echoed as Gabriella stepped into the office.

"That's correct. Detective Gabriella Valdez, you obviously know Detective Mitch Valentine…" he nodded at me, and then at Tate "…this is his partner, Detective Tate Miller." Burns shifted his gaze to Tate and myself. "Valdez joined our team yesterday, coming in from another department. She's going to head up the Paterson case."

"Nice to meet you, Miller," she said and Tate stood so he could shake the hand she held out. I simply glared as she withdrew her hand, my eyes telling her we would be having a chat later. A big one.

I turned to face my boss. "Can we get the pleasantries out of the way," I bit out, "and get to the evidence you mentioned?"

Burns took a minute to bring Gabriella up to speed before tapping the keyboard of his computer and then turning the screen to face us. "This is the security vision of where Grace was last sighted."

The four of us focused our attention on the black and white footage as it came to life. First it cut to Grace exiting a cab out the front of Sydney airport. My brows drew together. She was still wearing the same dress from the night before. I checked the time of the footage. It showed midnight—just twenty-five minutes after her argument with Casey at the party.

I drew a deep breath as she headed around the side of the building. Why was she heading that way?

"Watch here," Burns said.

The office was silent as a man came on screen, following behind Grace. The camera only caught the back of him. He was tall, with mussed dirty-blond hair, and wearing what looked like a tux, the bowtie hanging untied around his neck. My pulse quickened because if someone asked me if I knew this man, without a doubt I would've said it was Casey.

To Burns, I said, "That could be anyone."

"Agreed, but we also have eye-witness accounts from people inside the party and outside the bar that attest to a volatile argument between the pair. One man said Casey threatened him where he stood with friends out the front. His friends corroborated his account."

"So why are you making the call of probable homicide?" Tate asked.

Burns opened the folder in front of him, spreading out an array of crime scene photos. Tate leaned forward in his seat and Gabriella and I stepped up to the desk, shoulders brushing as we leaned in for a closer look. The photos showed enough blood spatter over the brick wall of the building for a fatal shot.

"Forensics?" Gabriella questioned, tapping at the blood spatter.

"Matched it to Grace," Burns answered.

She pointed to the photo of the shell casings. "Ballistics?"

"Semi-automatic forty calibre Glock," he replied, passing over a photo showing a similar gun.

My brows drew together, ignoring Gabriella's closeness and her husky voice. "That type of gun could belong to anyone," I said, "I have the same one."

My boss shook his head. "This was the actual gun found on scene. We've already matched the registration back to Casey. The only prints on it belong to him and the gun's been fired. Twice."

I glanced up, eyes widening in disbelief. "The gun was found on scene?"

Gabriella looked across at me. "You think it's a plant? Someone's setting your friend up?"

"It's possible," I muttered, thinking hard. Travis and Casey had apprised me of yesterday's events at last night's party. The fact that Morgan was linked to the Sentinels MC was a topic I needed to broach with my boss, but Casey and Travis had asked me to sit on the information for two days. I didn't like agreeing to the condition. The only reason I did was because Casey was like a brother. He deserved to find out the truth about what happened to his family.

Now sitting on the information was an impossibility because if I was right, and this was a set up, it could only point back to one person.

Morgan.

I opened my mouth, ready to share the information when my mind flashed back to the coiled snake on Gabriella's ribcage. Was she working with us … or against us? I shut it quickly.

"Valentine?" Burns watched me closely. "You got something to share?"

"I do."

"And?" he prompted.

"The information's highly sensitive, boss."

He sat back in his chair, his gaze speculative. "You can speak freely in front of Detective Valdez."

I turned my head, staring at Gabriella and letting her feel every inch of my distrust. "With all due respect, boss," I replied, not taking my eyes from hers. "I don't think I can."

"Arrghhh!" Gabriella shoved at my chest and I stumbled backwards, surprised at the force behind it. "Cula!" she spat, waving her hands around angrily. "You don't trust me? You stand here wasting time with your bitch talk when your friend is in trouble. Get over yourself!"

Her chest heaved angrily and my hands fisted, ready to go nose to nose in an all out argument when Burns interrupted. "A word, Mitch." I looked at him. "In private," he added with a pointed glance at both Tate and Gabriella.

Gabriella huffed and stalked out. Tate followed behind, throwing me a questioning glance before shutting the door behind the both of them. I turned to face my boss.

"Sit," he ordered.

I took a seat, elbows resting on my knees as I rubbed at my eyes.

What a goddamn clusterfuck.

"What I'm about to tell you is none of your damn business, but you're the best goddamn detective I have and I need you to pull your head out of your ass. I also need you to keep this quiet because trials are still pending and making this information public could put the case, and Valdez's life, in serious jeopardy." He paused before continuing. "Valdez's transfer was an unexpected one. She's been with the feds for years, working deep undercover."

Undercover? Damn you, Gabriella! Why did you have to go straight for the most dangerous division of law enforcement in Australia?

"Her last assignment with them ran for over eighteen months. Despite getting the guys they were after, it ended badly. Very badly. A lot of people died, including her partner. Valdez almost died too. She came out of it scarred and addicted to drugs."

My boss steepled his fingers, watching me carefully. I gave nothing away on the outside. But on the inside my heart began to break for the girl I used to know and for the woman she was now.

"She's worked hard to get where she is now," Burns told me. "Damn hard. She doesn't need to earn your trust because she already has mine. Got me?"

I let out a breath, realising I'd been holding it, and stared at my hands. "Her last undercover assignment …" I looked up. "She was with the Black Vipers, wasn't she?"

"I'm not going to ask how you know that because I'm starting to get a fair idea already. Now…" he nodded at the door "…send them back in."

I kept my face impassive as they filed back in and with short, sharp sentences, filled them in quickly on Casey's background, right up to yesterday's run in with Morgan, both Burns and Gabriella firing questions at me during the recount.

My boss was rubbing his temples by the time I finished. He growled out a curse after allowing the information to sink in. "Okay," he said eventually, sitting back in his seat. He looked to Gabriella first. "Valdez, I need you to get hold of Internal Affairs. Morgan needs to be investigated. I don't want anyone else on this but you and your immediate team. Furthermore, the information relating to Morgan and the Sentinels does not leave the team, got me?" He eyed each of us in turn, getting our agreement. "Not until I work out where the fuck we go from here."

"Valentine and Miller. Go pick up Daniels. Send a forensics team to follow behind you so they can sweep his loft. Valdez," he said, standing up from his desk as he shoved all the papers from his desk back in the folder and handed it to her. "Come with me. I'll introduce you to your team and we can find out where they're at with the search for Grace."

Leaving the office, Gabriella and Burns peeled right and Tate and I went left.

"Gabriella," I called out.

She paused, waiting as I walked back. I handed her my card with my contact information. "The minute you hear about Grace, could you let me know?"

She glared.

"Please?"

Her answer was to simply snatch the card from my fingers, jam it in her jeans pocket, and walk away.

We hit the downstairs carpark and I tossed Tate the keys to one of the squad cars. "You drive."

I slid in the passenger seat, clicked on the seat belt, and was dialling Travis's number before Tate even started the car.

"Yeah?" he answered, his voice croaky and feeble.

"Rufus! Peter!" I heard Quinn screech in the background at the dogs. "Outside! Now!"

"Fuck," my brother muttered. "This place is a fucking zoo. Jared and Evie crashed here last night, and then Mum, who was watching Sam this morning, brought him home an hour ago, along with Peter, because apparently it's not a family gathering without all the dogs," he added sarcastically, "and she's still here."

"Travis," I said quickly before he kept going. "We've got a problem. A big clusterfuck on top of a steaming pile of shit kind of problem."

"What?"

"Tate and I are on way to pick up Casey."

"And take him where?"

"Into custody."

There was a pause and then, "Fuck. What happened?" I could tell by his tone that he was already on the move.

I explained it all as quickly as possible, leaving out the part about Gabriella and the fact that I'd shared the information relating to Morgan and the Sentinels. I'd worry about that later.

"Meet me at the loft, okay? Casey's going to lose it. He's going to need you."

The throaty growl of his Subaru barrelled down the line. "Already on my way. See you there."

Travis pressed the intercom at the entrance to Casey's building after we arrived. There was no answer so Travis used his key. We all had keys to each other's place in the event of an emergency. This definitely qualified as one.

After unlocking the front door, Mitsy barrelled us up by the entryway, his shrill bark splitting my head clean in two. The three of us took a step back. Mitsy took a step forward.

"You take the dog," Travis told me as he began inching sideways into the room.

Grabbing Travis by the bicep, I shoved him in front of Mitsy. "You take the fucking dog."

Tate pulled his gun. "If neither of you take the damn dog, I will."

"Christ, I'll take—"

"Wait," Travis muttered, pausing to scan the loft. Furniture was overturned, a broken lamp sat in the corner and Casey was on his stomach on the couch, passed out and completely oblivious.

He began to stir when Mitsy kept up his aggravating tirade. Rolling over, he sat up with a wince, rubbing his face. I ran a critical eye over his clothing. He was sans jacket, but still wearing his shirt and pants from last night.

There was no blood spatter on his shirt, I noted with relief. If he shot Grace, there would be spatter. That was one tick in his favour.

"What are you three doing in here?" He paused and I could see his mind ticking over for a brief moment before his eyes flared with panic. "Grace," he muttered. Then he stood up and stumbled.

Travis rushed over and Mitsy ran for cover, hiding beneath the dining table at the far end of the huge space.

Casey shoved him away, his expression confused. "I need to find Grace."

Travis opened his mouth to speak and I shook my head, silently telling him to let me handle this. He shut it quickly.

"Casey, do you remember anything about last night?" I asked.

Ignoring me, he grabbed for his phone and began dialling. "I don't ..." He put the phone to his ear, shaking his head at me. "Nothing. Not after leaving the bar." Casey looked at Travis. "Is Grace at the duplex? We had a fight. She ... Oh God." He ran a hand over his face. Pulling the phone from his ear when it went unanswered, he tossed it on the coffee table. "I need to get over there."

This was not the Casey I knew. The Casey I knew had it together. If someone asked me to name the coolest guy I knew, I would instantly say Casey Daniels. The guy in front of me was shaking and incoherent like he was coming down from a major high. His clothes were a rumpled mess and his eyes bleary and red.

If he was being set up for this, being drugged would make sense. It would explain his actions at the party last night and the memory loss. Tate and I shared a quick glance and I mouthed, "Roofied?"

Roofies were the street name for Rohypnol—a drug easily slipped into someone's drink when they weren't looking. I'd come across its use more often than not in the homicides I investigated. It had no colour, no smell, and no taste—making it popular. After a half hour, the drug had you in its control, making you weak, confused, and by all appearances, drunk. Your speech would slur, you would black out, and when you woke, your memory was wiped.

Tate nodded his agreement.

"Casey, when was the last time you saw Grace?" I asked.

"Why?"

I cursed under my breath. There was no easy way to say this. My eyes flicked to Travis where he stood next to Casey. His jaw was clenched, his eyes bleak, but he was holding it together for his friend.

I looked back at Casey. "Grace is missing."

He froze. "What do you mean, missing?"

I held his eyes as I spoke, willing him not to lose it. "I mean she disappeared last night and hasn't been seen since." Casey's chest started rising and falling and I knew panic was setting in. Keep it together, I pleaded silently before speaking past the lump in my throat. "I'm sorry, Casey, but we have evidence that suggests her disappearance may be a probable homicide."

"What the fuck," he breathed, his eyes searching my face. Then he roared it, shoving me in the chest. "You fucking liar!" He swung at me, clipping me in the jaw before Travis locked him down.

Casey struggled, but he was in no state to break the hold. It didn't stop him trying. "She's not dead!" he shouted, his voice breaking. A sob forced its way from his chest. "You fucking cunt!" came his hoarse cry. "You goddamn …" Casey pulled free and Travis grabbed at him again, locking his arms around his friend and holding on.

"Casey, I'm sorry." Then I said the words that killed me the most. "We have to bring you in."

He froze against Travis, his eyes narrowing with fury. "You think I killed her? You think I killed Grace?" He started struggling again and I could see the strain starting to wear on my brother. His jaw was tight and there were tears in his eyes. He was about to lose it right alongside Casey. "She's not dead!" he yelled. "Damn you, Mitch! Fuck you. Fuck all of you. She's not …"

Casey trailed off, his head tipping to the ceiling and his chest heaving as Travis kept hold of him "Let me go, Trav," he said softly. Too softly.

"No," he grunted.

"I don't want to hurt you so let me go. Right now."

"Let me say one thing, Casey," I interrupted, taking a step towards the both of them, appreciating that Tate had kept quiet and let me handle the situation. "Then Travis will let you go, okay? One thing."

"Spit it out," he growled in reply.

"Grace is out there, and if she's still alive, then she's hurting and she needs you. She's counting on you to stay calm, to keep it together, and find her. So help us find her. Help us by letting us bring you in. The sooner we can do that, the sooner we can get you cleared, the sooner we can get her back and find out who's behind this."

"Fuck," Casey whispered, sagging against my brother.

I reached slowly for the cuffs dangling from the back pocket of my jeans and Travis tensed, his eyes going flat and hard. "Cuff him and I will beat you so fucking hard you won't move for a week."

I didn't cuff him. I went so far as to let him ride to the station with Travis on the promise it was kept quiet. If it came to light there was a trial and proper police procedure wasn't followed—no matter how small the procedure—it could backfire on all of us.

When Casey arrived his eyes were red rimmed and raw, but he held his chin high as he followed us in.

We arranged his drug test to screen for Rohypnol. Then we bagged his tux while he changed into a pair of jeans, tee shirt, and hoodie Travis brought with them from his loft.

Travis went to the waiting area and I led Casey to an interview room. It held nothing but a table, four chairs, and a security camera in the corner. I pulled out a seat and indicated for him to sit down.

He just sat down when Gabriella opened the door and strode in. I took the seat beside him and she barely spared me a glance before focusing on Casey. "Casey Zachariah Daniels?"

He nodded.

"I'm Detective Valdez," she told him, placing the folder on the table in front of her without sitting down. Gabriella chose to stand, casually putting her hands in her pockets as she watched Casey carefully. "I'm in charge of the Paterson case."

I sat forward, interested to see how she would handle the interview. She started by reading him his rights and offering a lawyer.

"No," he replied, staring her down. She didn't blink. "I don't want to waste time with a lawyer. Let's get this over with."

"Okay. Good. We'll start with going over the events of yesterday, from the moment you woke until the last thing you can remember."

Casey eyes flicked to mine and I read the silent question in them. "You can trust Detective Valdez."

Clearing his throat, he ran through his day, Gabriella peppering him with questions along the way until he got to last night's party.

"You and Grace argued," she recounted, flicking through pages from the folder on the table. She ran her eyes over the report in front of her then cocked her head at Casey speculatively. "You got violent. Tell me, do you always get violent when you're drunk?"

Casey slammed to his feet. "You bitch!"

"Hey!" My protective instincts kicked into gear and I planted a hand on Casey's chest, shoving him back in his chair. His glare shifted from Gabriella to me. I held his eyes. "Not helping. Just answer the question."

"Déjame manejar esto o salir!" Gabriella snapped at me. "Let me handle this or get out."

I held up my hands, re-taking my seat with an arched brow. "Seguir adelante," I replied with my small knowledge of Spanish, telling her to go ahead.

Nostrils flaring, she looked back at Casey, waiting.

"No. I don't," he replied, answering her question.

"So what were you arguing about that caused this … unusual reaction from you? She cheat on you? Steal? Lie? Threaten you?"

Casey drew a deep breath before facing Gabriella with expressionless eyes. I knew that look. Whatever was underneath it hurt like a sonofabitch. "That's none of your business," he told her.

Gabriella slapped her hands down hard on the table and jammed her face right in his. "Grace is now my business, comprende? You withholding information will only drag this process out!"

Casey's jaw ticked. "Grace has cancer," he bit out. "I only just found out."

I closed my eyes. How many hits could one man take before he just couldn't get up anymore? Did Henry know? Wasn't that how their mother died?

"And that made you … angry?" Gabriella continued, inflecting her tone with incredulity.

"Yes. She lied to me about it. I only found out last night after talking on the phone with John, her best friend," he explained.

"Even still, you don't think your reaction was excessive?" She flicked through another page of her report and read out a small section. "He threatened to 'rip my head off,'" she quoted, "says an eyewitness to your outside argument."

"Oh, for fuck's sake," Casey growled, jerking angrily in his chair. "He was taking a photo of us arguing on his phone."

I looked at Gabriella. "I would've threatened the guy too if I'd seen him do that."

Her gaze went from me back to Casey and she shrugged. "I probably would've bypassed the threat and just gone straight for the punch myself." I didn't doubt her despite the casual delivery of her comment. I'd seen Gabriella in action from our training days on the mat. She was able to take out even the biggest guy in our class without breaking a sweat. Flicking over another page, she drew a deep breath. "So let's go back to Morgan. You say she was at the bar?" She checked some of her scrawled notes, reading from them out loud as she spoke. "After having said to you that very same day, 'I don't take kindly to being backed into a corner,' which came just before you backed her into that very same corner by giving her a two day ultimatum?"

"That's correct," Casey confirmed.

A knock came at the door. Gabriella walked over and opened it to one of the junior detective's on her team. Casey stiffened beside me and we watched as he muttered something in her ear. Gabriella's face gave nothing away as he spoke and when he finished, she nodded once, shut the door, and returned to the table.

"We have security footage in custody of your interaction with Morgan at the bar. You'll need to excuse me so I can view it."

I began to stand.

"Siéntate!" she snapped at me. "Sit your ass down! This is not your case."

"You can't stop me from viewing the footage," I replied, incredulous.

Her nostrils flared. "I am in charge here. I can stop you from doing whatever the hell I damn please. Now you can wait here with Casey or I can have him placed in a holding cell. What's it to be?"

Goddammit. Gabriella wasn't giving an inch. It pissed me right the fuck off. I shoved the emotion aside. Now was not the time.

I sat down, my eyes hard as stone. "I'll wait."

Casey made an unhappy sound and she shifted her gaze, softening just the smallest fraction. "Look at me, Casey," she ordered. He met her eyes. "I'm going out there right now to brief my team. I'll have them all working every possible lead to find Grace and I'm going to do everything I can to get you cleared. I believe someone has spent considerable energy setting you up, but what I want to know is, why? What do they get out of it? Revenge? Hmm…" she shrugged "…maybe, but I'm not buying it. If this is the work of the Sentinels, then it's because you're sticking your nose in where it's not wanted, but then they would just kill you rather than Grace." Casey flinched at her casual mention of killing Grace. "Something is not adding up for me, and it's something to do with the death of your parents, isn't it?"

Gabriella tapped a finger against her lips. "Maybe releasing you might force them to play their hand. I need to talk to Burns," she muttered to herself and strode to the door.

"Wait here," we were told and she left the small room.

Chapter Thirty-One
GRACE

Ten hours earlier…

I slammed the cab door shut, my pulse racing as the cabbie zoomed off into the street. I forced my eyes to the front because if I turned around and saw Casey standing by the kerb, I'd lose it. I'd tell the driver to slam on the brakes and I'd leap out and start running back, just like in the movies.

Five seconds.

That was how long I lasted.

Twisting in my seat, I looked out the back window but there were too many people. I couldn't see him.

"It's too late, Grace. I lose you and it's game over for me."

"I'm sorry, Casey," I whispered, turning back around. I was supposed to find myself in Sydney, let myself really live, before returning home stronger, ready to face treatment. I wasn't supposed to find love and then destroy the man who found it right along with me.

"Where to, love?" the cabbie asked.

Oh God, really?

He might as well have asked me to unlock the magical, sparkling door to the Fairy Kingdom and take him to meet the Queen of Mystical Beings.

My head spun from the champagne and I closed my eyes. My first instinct was to head to the loft and I shot it down quickly. The look on Casey's face had broken my heart. How could I go back when it was me who put it there?

"Bitch," I mumbled to myself.

Where should I go?

I opened my eyes, suddenly realising there was only one person who would understand and tell me what to do.

Dad.

Tears filled my eyes. I needed my dad.

Resolving to catch the redeye flight to Melbourne, I directed the driver to Sydney airport and reached for my phone. I'd send Casey a message to tell him where I was. He might still be pissed at me for running off, but at least he wouldn't worry. I could fly back in the morning and we could talk then.

After digging in my purse, I remembered my phone was currently in pieces all over the function room of the Florence Bar. Another day, another pulverised phone.

"Shit," I muttered.

"You okay, love?" the cabbie questioned, glancing at me in his rearview mirror.

"Yes," I lied. "Why?"

Did I have something on my face? I brushed at my cheeks, finding them wet and realised I was crying. How odd that I didn't even know.

I wiped at my face with both hands, likely smearing makeup over my face. The press would have a field day if they caught me like this.

"Why?" he echoed. "Because we arrived at the airport five minutes ago and you've just been sitting there cursing to yourself."

I shook my head, ordering myself to pull it together.

"It's been a long day," I told him as I handed over the fare.

"You and me both."

As I stepped out of the cab, he asked, "You need me to wait?"

"I'm good, thanks. I'm catching a flight." His gaze dropped to my dazzling evening dress, his eyes dubious. "It's a bit of an emergency," I explained.

"Well, good luck, love," he declared and when I shut the door, he zoomed off into the night.

I turned, starting for the entry of the airport when a strange scuffling noise came from around the side of the building. Deciding to investigate in case someone was in trouble, I followed the noise. My heels made a distinct clacking sound, so I hopped about on one foot and then the other as I shucked them off. I held up one of the heels in my left hand as a makeshift weapon and rounded the corner.

There was no one there but I couldn't shake the itchy feeling that something was very, very wrong.

"Hello?" I called out, peering into the darkness.

Nothing.

"Hello?" I called again, my heart hammering in my chest. Inching forward, I raised my heel higher so whoever was out there would know I meant business.

When I heard nothing back, I realised that Casey's Batman tendencies had rubbed off all over me. I had no current aspirations to join the Badass Brigade and dispense vigilante justice across the streets of Sydney. Especially not if it meant cold, dark passageways that gave me the heebie jeebies. Eager to get inside the airport where it was warm and safe, I spun around and smacked into a big, hard chest. "Oomphf!"

A set of huge palms caught my shoulders before I could land hard on my ass. I glanced down. Attached to one of those huge palms was a gun. When my mind froze in panic, my body took over instinctively, connecting my knee with a groin. The impact made me stumble backwards. I teetered before righting myself and when I opened my mouth to scream, a gun jammed against my forehead and a male voice growled, "Don't even try it."

"Go fuck yourself," I declared.

Opening my mouth wide, I let out an ear-splitting scream.

He backhanded me across the face. My head snapped sideways and my stomach pitched. Damn, that hurt!

I blinked, dazed, as he took a step forward, the moonlight hitting his face. My eyes widened and my stomach pitched all over again. "Oh my God," I breathed, taking in the familiar features with a pounding heart.

"Grace, babe, you need to shut the fuck up, yeah?" He glanced behind me, his sharp blue eyes doing a quick scan. When he turned back to face me, it was just in time to catch me whacking him with the heel of my shoe.

"What the fuck?" He held up his forearm, deflecting my aim.

"You hit me!" I fumed, my blood pulsing with anger. I tried whacking him again. "You held a gun to my head!"

His response was to grab both shoes from my hands and toss them sideways. I watched them sail across the passageway, bounce off the wall, and fall to the ground. My eyes returned to his.

He used his gun to point at the ground by the wall. "Plant your ass there."

I folded my arms. "No."

"Yes."

"No."

"Fuckin' do it," he growled.

I lifted my chin. "No."

After calling me a stubborn bitch, he firmly grabbed my shoulders and I was shoved to the ground, my back hitting the brick wall behind me.

"Hey!" I started to get up and he held me there, his hands pinning me down. I strained to move until I thought my eyeballs would pop, but his arms packed too much strength and I was still recovering from my injuries.

Realising I wasn't going anywhere, I paused to catch my breath and glare up at him. "Ass."

He grinned and removed one of the arms that pinned me down to cup my face in his hand. The gesture felt almost tender. "You're beautiful when you're angry, Grace." His fingertip ran a line down the length of my nose, his eyes following the path. Leaning in, he planted a kiss on my lips. I froze in shock, his tongue licking a line along my bottom lip before I could jerk my head away.

"Don't touch me," I snapped.

He grinned, his face close to mine. "I like a bitch with fire inside her."

"Then you won't like me," I said quickly. "I'm cold. People call me the Ice Queen I'm that cold."

His eyes crinkled and his chuckle rumbled deep and soft through the passageway. "Classy and fuckin' sexy too." The butt of his gun trailed down the side of my cheek, cold and more than a bit terrifying. "Casey scored the trifecta with you, didn't he?"

I pressed my lips together because he couldn't be more wrong.

He cocked his head. "You don't think so?" A sound came from the end of the passageway and he turned swiftly, staring down into the dark. When nothing happened, he straightened and took a step back. "Move from that wall and I'll put a hole in you."

"So put a hole in me," I retorted and scrambled to my feet. Arms locked around me from behind before I could even run. "Dammit," I huffed, pausing my struggles to take a breath.

"Babe," he muttered in my ear, his warm breath setting off shivers. "Gotta stop with the running. People want you dead. I'm tryin' to fuckin' help you here."

I spun in his hold and he let me. "By putting a 'hole' in me?" I air-quoted.

"It's either that or ask you to trust me. You gonna do that, Grace? Trust me?"

I pursed my lips.

"That's what I thought. Now sit the fuck back on the ground and shut that sexy mouth of yours. I can still put a fuckin' hole in you without making you dead."

His eyes turned flat and hard when I tried to stare him down.

I glanced at the gun when the sound of it cocking reached my ears.

I sat.

"You have a lot to answer for," I told him. "You better start talking. Fast."

"Scratch that," he growled and crouched down, grabbing the small black duffel bag nearby. "You're not a trifecta. You might taste sweet as fuck, but you're a pain in the fuckin' ass." After unzipping the bag, he glanced over at me. "You got an off switch, babe?"

"Fuck you," I retorted. "And stop calling me babe. I'm not your babe."

His brow pinched with disapproval. "If you were, you'd know your place."

My heart hadn't stopped hammering and when a set of surgical gloves were pulled from the bag and snapped on, I was sure it would explode from my chest. He tucked the gun he'd been waving in my face into the back of his pants and pulled out another one.

"What are you doing?" I asked. Reaching back in, he came out with a small bag that looked like some kind of dark, liquid pouch. "And what's that?"

"It's blood, and shut the fuck up."

"Gross," I declared, scrunching my nose. That was a crap load of blood. Then my brow crinkled. "Whose blood?"

"Yours."

"Mine?" I squawked. "How did you get—"

"For fuck's sake," he growled, interrupting my outburst. Putting the pouch down, he jammed his hands back in the bag and came out with a roll of silver duct tape. Ripping a piece off, he slapped it across my mouth.

"Mmmmmm!" I screamed from behind the tape when I was yanked to my feet. He grabbed my hands and taped them behind my back. The agony from wrenching my tender shoulder and arm brought tears to my eyes. The asshole shoved me back down.

Picking up the pouch, he held it against the brick wall behind me and aimed his gun.

What the hell was he—

He fired two quick shots at the bag and I yelped from behind the tape, ducking my head. Blood sprayed out everywhere, the metallic smell of it filling the air. I jerked when it splattered my face and chest. Glancing down, I saw red flecks all over the dress that cost the equivalent of a small car. Mac would be pissed.

I glared at him but he was busy ripping off the gloves. They went in the bag while he tossed the gun away. It landed with clatter, skittering across the concreted ground.

I paused, staring at it. I knew that gun. I'd seen it in Casey's hands earlier today.

My eyes flew back to catch him taking off his black jacket and white shirt, both covered in blood. They also went in the bag. Then I was given a quick glimpse of a chest so wide it deserved its own postcode. Ridges of tattooed muscle filled my vision before a fitted black shirt went over his head. It was tugged down quickly.

My eyes returned to the gun.

Casey's gun.

Then to the blood spatter up the brick wall.

My blood.

He was setting Casey up for murder.

Not just any murder.

Mine.

My body tensed, tears of anger burning my eyes. Why would he do that?

He approached me again. Seeing the comprehension in my eyes, he crouched in front of me and used his thumb to wipe the blood from my forehead. "You know what I'm doing, don't you?" I met his eyes, breathing hard through my nose. "People want you dead. I'm making it look like you are. I'm saving your fuckin' life, babe."

By setting Casey up for murder?

When he saw the question in my eyes, he said, "Casey's messing in business that he shouldn't. Tried warning you, Grace. The car. Planting the bomb in that cottage. Knew you weren't in it, babe," he added when my eyes went wide. Then his lips curved. "You were busy fuckin' your man on the beach."

He saw us? I closed my eyes, hating that I flushed.

He grabbed my bicep and my eyes flew open. He yanked me to my feet. I faltered and he held on, steadying me, before putting his face in mine. "This is how it's gonna be. I'm gonna take off the tape covering those pretty lips of yours and you're gonna keep your mouth shut. You know why?"

He waited and I glared, my eyes saying, no, asshole, but I'm sure you're going to tell me. "Because if you scream or call out, I'm gonna shoot the first person who comes to your aid." He waited. "Give me a nod that you understand."

Silently fuming, I nodded.

"Good girl."

He ripped the tape off.

"Arrgghhh!" I cried, my face stinging.

I was spun around and he removed the tape from around my wrists. Then my shoes where handed to me. "Put 'em on."

I took my shoes, hopping about as I slid one on and almost toppled over. He grabbed my hand and put it on his shoulder, making me use his body to steady myself as I put on the other one.

He threaded our hands together and we walked out of the passageway, taking the opposite direction that I came in. He was making it look like we were simply a couple leaving the airport. I was pulled in close behind him, practically rubbing against his body as we walked and I realised he was hiding my bloodied dress.

We reached his car without incident. The fact that it was a hot car with motherfucker tyres just like Casey's didn't surprise me. After doing a quick scan of the car park, he opened the passenger door wide and growled, "Get in."

I lifted my chin. "Where are you taking me?"

"To Luna fuckin' Park," he declared sarcastically as he went to shove me in the car. "As if I'm gonna tell you, babe."

"No one's going to believe Casey killed me. No one," I hissed. "But mark my words, he's going to kill you for this."

He paused, staring down at me, the cocky glint in his eyes so familiar it made my heart pound. "You really think he'd kill his own brother, babe?"

"Kelly," I breathed, struck all over again at how much he looked like Casey. They could've been twins. "I honestly don't know what he's going to do. What I do know is that you're going to hurt a man who's already hurting enough."

Kelly's eyes flattened, but not fast enough for me to miss the pain flashing through them. "I don't give a fuck. He left me with that asshole. Compared to what I went through, he doesn't know the meaning of hurting," he sneered. "Now get in the fuckin' car."

"Is that why you're doing this?" I asked, my chest aching with grief for what these two boys had gone through. I put a hand on his arm. He glanced down at my hand before meeting my eyes. "Because he left you?"

"No, but that's all I'm givin' you, babe. The rest is between him and me."

Chapter Thirty-Two
CASEY

Present time...

She's not dead, I repeated to myself for the thousandth time. I would know it, right? I would feel it.

Gabriella returned to the interview room, interrupting my pacing. I spun around, searching her face as she strode towards the table. She gave nothing away as she slapped her folder down. My eyes fell on it and I had to clench my hands to fight reaching for it. Sitting back while someone else ran this investigation was bullshit.

"Goddammit, Gabriella," Mitch growled from beside me, echoing my sentiments. "You've been gone two hours!"

She jabbed a finger his way. "Don't start with me, Mitchell!" she snapped in that husky rolling Spanish of hers. Gabriella was not only intelligent, she appeared to have balls bigger than most guys I knew. Mitch must have a hell of time working with her. "I've had to drag forensics to the lab on a Sunday. Do you know how hard it is to do that when you've been working in this department for two days?"

"Two days?" I nailed Mitch with a savage glare, wanting to punch something, namely him. "You said we could trust her and you've known her two fucking days?"

"Suficiente!" Gabriella snapped again, sweeping a lock of hair from her face and tucking it behind her ear. "This is not a pissing contest over who knows who and for how long!" She turned her livid, gold-flecked eyes to mine and jabbed that finger in my direction. If she wasn't a girl I would've snapped it in half by now I was so pissed off. "I work for the good guys, comprende? But most importantly, I work for Grace."

"You work for Grace? I fucking live for Grace!" I shouted, unable to keep my raging emotions in check. Grace was mine to protect and I was stuck in this shithole interview room, unable to do a damn thing. "She's out there right now and she needs me. Not you, not Mitch, not your team, or the goddamn Tooth Fairy. Me! So hurry up and get me the hell out of here before I fucking lose it."

A rap came at the door before Gabriella could tell me I'd already lost it.

"Sit," Gabriella barked, pointing at the chair in front of me. I resisted the urge to kick it across the room and sat, hanging my head in my hands.

She murmured quietly with another detective at the door when I heard someone yelling. I glanced up and saw Henry pushing through the door, his eyes red and swollen and wild with fury.

"You can't come in here," was all Gabriella managed to get out as she grabbed for him and missed.

I stood abruptly as he came at me. My chair fell over, skittering backwards as I planted both feet apart, bracing.

His fist connected with my jaw and I managed to keep my feet, welcoming the sharp burst of pain. My lip split on impact. I felt the skin bust open, tangy, metallic blood flooding my mouth. This. Fists. Rage. Pain. In a world without Grace, where nothing made sense, this was what I knew, and it somehow grounded me with its familiarity.

"You motherfucker!" he shouted, swinging again. I lifted my chin, wanting it. I wanted that burst of pain. I wanted to feel my stomach roll and my head scream from the jarring impact. It was no less than I deserved, letting Grace out of my sight the way I did.

"You need to leave!" Gabriella grabbed for him again, but Mitch got there first. Twisting Henry's arms behind his back, he locked them in place. Henry bucked, his chest heaving as he tried to get at me.

"Let him go!" I ordered, my voice harsh to my own ears.

Mitch met my eyes from behind Henry, veins straining on his neck as Henry fought his tight hold.

I nodded once and Mitch let his arms fall away.

Suddenly free, Henry came at me again. Fisting my shirt in both hands, he slammed me up against the wall. My neck snapped back at the aggressive manoeuvre, air leaving my lungs in a rush.

I shook my head, dizzy.

Henry's back was to Mitch when Mitch came up behind him, ready to restrain him all over again. I held up a hand, holding him off.

"What did you do? Where is she?" Henry shouted in my face, so close his nose almost touched mine. Before I could answer, he jerked me forward and slammed me against the wall again. My teeth snapped together on impact.

Dazed, I had to force myself to look at him.

"Henry." I blinked away spots. "You know I wouldn't hurt her. You know me. Trust me on this. Please," I begged, locking eyes with his. "Grace is still alive. I know it. Mitch and Gabriella are working hard to clear me so I can get out there and find her, okay? I'll find her. I promise you. I fucking promise you."

Henry swallowed hard, the light slowly leaving his eyes as he sagged against me, his arms falling slack from their hold on my shirt. I knew then that he didn't believe I'd hurt Grace. He was scared, just like we all were, and taking it out on me was easy.

With a shake of his head, Henry found my eyes. "Grace has cancer," he said, his voice cracking and his knees suddenly buckling. I wrapped my arms around him as we sank to the floor.

I looked up at Mitch and nodded at the door. "Go," I mouthed.

Without a word, he turned. Putting a hand on the small of Gabriella's back, he pushed her out the door. The sounds of her protests were muffled when he closed it behind him.

My eyes burned as Henry cried, each sob from his chest making my own squeeze a little tighter. "I know, Henry," I whispered thickly, my heart so damn heavy that nothing could pick it up off the floor.

"She kept it from all of us," he told me, his voice hoarse as he pulled away. Wiping his eyes with the heel of his hands, he looked at me as we sat there together, huddled on the floor. "When did you find out?"

I tipped my head back against the wall, my eyes trained on the ceiling as I willed myself not to cry. "I found out last night. I picked up a phone call from John that was meant for Grace. He told me."

I shut my eyes, her face coming to life behind closed lids as she straddled my lap on the bed.

"We need to talk."

"Later."

"It's important."

"Whatever's going on in that pretty head of yours, as long as we have each other, it'll work out, okay?"

"I think she was going to tell me before the party but I put her off." I opened my eyes, shifting them in Henry's direction without moving my head. "What about you?"

"When I rang John this morning. He and Dad are already on the next flight. I've tried getting hold of the twins. Someone in the naval office is tracking them down for me. Dad's a mess," he admitted, "but I suspect Grace would know that, which is why she didn't tell us. Our family kind of imploded when we lost Mum. She's scared of it happening again." Henry's eyes filled and he drew a deep, shaky breath. "I don't want her to die, Casey. I can't lose my little sister. I can't."

"You won't lose her," I vowed. It was a promise I didn't know I could keep, but I made it anyway. I had to for my own sanity because the thought of losing Grace would send me mad.

Henry stared down at his knuckles. They were red and starting to swell. Glancing up, he said, "Sorry for hitting you."

I shook my head. "No you're not. You've been wanting to do that since you found out Grace and I were seeing each other."

There was a silent pause. "You're right. It felt good."

"Same."

His brows rose. "It felt good for me to hit you?"

Gabriella and Mitch returned, saving me from trying to form a response. I got to my feet and held out a palm to Henry. He took it and I pulled him up.

"Casey, you're free to go."

"What?" I faced Gabriella. "How?"

"Several things. First, we found your cab driver. He just left after giving his statement. He says you passed out after telling him to follow the cab that Grace was in. He lost her cab in traffic so he got your address from your wallet and returned you to your loft, helping you inside. We have your security footage of you returning home at the time he stated, which corroborates his story. Further, there's no record of you leaving before Travis and Mitch arrived this morning," she told me. "Forensics have you cleared of gun powder residue and blood on your clothes, and you've come back positive for Rohypnol. We've got experts analysing the footage of your interaction in the main bar," Gabriella told me with a quick glance at Henry. She obviously kept her words deliberately vague in deference to his presence. "While it's clear your drink was handled, what's unclear in the footage is the exact moment the drug was slipped in your drink."

Henry's mouth fell open. "Someone drugged you?"

"Someone's trying to set him up," Mitch informed him with drawn brows.

"Who?"

"That's not clear at this stage," he replied.

"Have you picked her up?" I asked.

Mitch and Gabriella shared a quick glance before she said, "Not yet. We're trying to locate her."

"Right," I muttered. Good. Because then I'd get to her first. "So I can leave?" I asked Gabriella.

"Sí." She splayed a pile of printed pages on the table. Clicking a pen, she held it out. "You need to sign your statement and official release papers first."

Taking the pen, I began scrawling wherever she pointed, not knowing what the hell I was signing and not caring. I needed to get out of there and get my hands on Morgan.

Minutes later I was walking out of the interview room.

Gabriella called my name. I halted at the doorway and half turned to look at her. "Officially, I need to warn you to keep out of the investigation."

"Warning noted," I replied with a nod, and duly ignored, I added silently, feeling her eyes on me as I walked out the door with Henry following behind. Gabriella knew full well I had no intention of heeding her official warning, yet she was letting me go anyway. I would owe her for that.

I faltered when I reached the waiting room and found it full. All eyes turned my way and relief hit me when I didn't see a single accusatory pair in the bunch. Tim broke from the herd as soon as he saw me walk out. He launched himself at me, wrapping his arms around my neck and his legs around my waist. I didn't break stride. I didn't have time. Not even when I felt the splash of his tears on my neck.

"Casey," he squeaked when my arms came around him and squeezed as I kept walking.

"You okay?" I muttered in Tim's ear as Travis fell into step beside me. Tim might piss me off most times, but he was like a little brother to me and I looked out for him.

"No," he managed. "I've never been so angry in all my life. I can't believe they would arrest you while Grace is out there, scared and alone and hurt." He pulled back to search my face. "Are you okay?"

"No. I'm not. I'm barely holding it together," I admitted.

"What can I do?" Tim asked.

"You can round up the entire team and get them in the office. Get Mitch to brief them. We need everyone to hit the ground running."

"Done," he declared.

"Thank you." I told him, grateful for the unwavering support. Loosening my grip, I unlatched him and set him on his feet. He returned to the huddle in the waiting room while Travis and I kept going. Mitch had been bailed up by the group and appeared to be explaining everything. I would owe him for that, too, because right now I didn't have the time, nor the inclination, to speak to anyone. My favours were racking up.

"Casey?" Tim called out when we reached the bank of elevators. "Where you are going?"

Half turning as I jabbed the down button, I replied with a calm that belied the turmoil inside me, "To get Grace."

"Give me the keys," I ordered Travis when we hit the car park.

"No," he replied, beeping the locks of his mean looking Subaru. It was gleaming black with barely legal tinted windows and a modified turbo, making it one of the quickest cars I'd ever handled. After having rendered control to Mitch and Gabriella these past few hours, I needed to take it back, and that started now, with driving Travis's car.

"Give me the motherfucking keys," I growled.

With what sounded like a deep sigh of regret, he tossed them my way. I caught them easily and we both slid in the car at the same time. I turned the key and the car rumbled to life.

Travis was still shutting the passenger door when I hit the gas hard. I tore out of the police carpark, passing uniformed officers and ignoring their glares. Barely pausing to check if the road was clear, I fishtailed onto the street, heading straight for Morgan's house.

"How did it go with Henry?" Travis asked.

I gunned the engine, shooting through an orange light. "He punched it out of his system," I replied, running a tongue over the split in my lip. It was a throbbing reminder of Henry's aggression.

"And the test for the roofies?"

"Positive."

"Bitch," Travis snarled.

The tyres spun when I took a hard left. "I backed Morgan into a corner but I never expected her to retaliate with something like this."

"Finding out about your parents and what happened with Kelly has been a long time coming," he replied, rubbing at the back of his neck. "Being so close and getting nothing? What choice did you have?"

"Getting nothing is better than losing Grace over this," I replied, for the first time realising just how much falling in love had changed my priorities. It wasn't until the idea of being with Grace and building a future together was snatched away that I realised how desperately I wanted it to happen.

"You're not losing Grace over this," Travis vowed. "We'll find her."

"It's not just about finding her," I said, glancing across at my friend. "Grace has cancer."

Travis muttered a quiet, "Fuck," before tipping his head back against the seat. "How bad is it?" he asked, squeezing his eyes shut, bracing for my response.

"I don't know," I replied, feeling my control start to slip just thinking about it. "I found out last night and fucking lost it. You saw me. What would you do if you found out Quinn had cancer?"

His eyes opened and he paled, looking like the idea made him want to puke. "I'd lose it."

"Exactly," I replied as I spun the wheel, careening into the street that would lead us to Morgan's house. "So I can't talk about it right now. I can't even think about it. I need to focus on the now and getting Grace."

I slowed down, taking in the surroundings as we passed by her house. It would be dusk soon, yet the interior was dark, not lit up like the neighbouring houses. She could've been lying low, but I didn't believe it. The house was empty. An unmarked police car sat further down, keeping watch for her return.

"Call Seth. Get him to put Beck out here on surveillance again," I told Travis. "He'll do a better job than these clowns," I added when we drove by the unmarked car.

Travis began dialling and I hit the gas, roaring away from Morgan's house with satisfying speed. Travis glanced behind us before turning his gaze to me. "Where are we going? We could at least search her house and see if we find anything."

"Gabriella's arranging a search warrant. I don't want to compromise any evidence they might find. Besides," I told him as I planted my foot, barely scraping through another orange light as we left her house behind. "I've got another idea."

Sunday afternoon traffic was full of nine to fivers—all returning home at the same time from their weekend escapes. Dusk had truly arrived by the time we hit our destination. Parking the car a street away, we walked along the back of the reserve until we reached the yard of Graham Bennett's house. Unlike Morgan's, the back half of his house was lit up, highlighting the kitchen and dining area clearly to the backyard.

Travis handed me another Glock. I checked the sight and safety before taking another peek at the house through the car-wide gap in the fence.

"What do you see?" he asked from behind me.

"No one yet."

"Wait here," he told me, palming his own gun. "I'll go around the front, see if Morgan's car is in the drive."

I set my jaw stubbornly. "You wait here. I'll go."

Travis sighed, exasperated. We did a quick rock-paper-scissors. Knowing Travis always chose rock, I went with paper. When he decided to switch it up and came out with scissors, I hissed quietly. "Sonofabitch."

With narrow-eyed satisfaction, he threw a quick, "cover me," my way, and crouched low, running for the back of the house.

He returned five minutes later. "Morgan's car is in the garage. I saw it through a side window. I did a scope of the entire house from the outside. Didn't see Grace," he told me before I could ask.

I huffed with indecision. "What do we do? Storm the place or follow Morgan when she leaves?"

"If we storm the place and Grace isn't there, then we've played our hand. Morgan will know we're on to her and then following her when she leaves will be a crapshoot."

"Hell," I muttered, rubbing a hand over the back of my head.

"My gut's telling me Grace isn't here," he said, shifting his gaze from the house to meet my eyes. "I vote we wait and follow Morgan when she leaves."

"I can work with that." I trusted Travis. His gut had never steered us wrong. "But if she leaves and then just returns home? What the fuck then?"

"Then we're screwed, because the unmarked car the police have out the front of her house will pick her up, beating us to her."

"Fuck it, Travis. I vote we storm the place."

We both turned to stare at the house and as if I'd just said abracadabra, the garage door magically began to rise, the loud clunk alerting us to the activity. My pulse rose right along with it and we turned and began running for the Subaru. I beeped the locks from ten yards away and had the engine growling and the wheels spinning before we'd even shut the doors.

We shot out of the side street at the back of the reserve, just in time to catch the tail lights of Morgan's car turning the corner. I inched off the gas, not wanting to alert her to our presence.

"Speed the fuck up. You'll lose her."

"I'm not going to lose her," I snapped, speeding up a fraction because he was right.

When she hit the intersection up ahead she turned left instead of the right which would've taken her home. I followed carefully, keeping behind other cars, and hanging back when traffic around us eased. Travis rang Mitch for the second time since we left, updating him with our progress. In turn, he kept Gabriella in the loop. Travis had the phone on speaker and she was barking at us to stand down.

When she realised she'd have better luck pushing a snowball up a lava-spewing volcano, she told us they were on their way and to wait.

My response was firm and distinct. "No."

Reaching across Travis, I hit the end button, cutting off her rant.

"Gabriella is a hard-ass," Travis noted as we drove further towards the mountains.

"No shit," was my reply as my gut began to churn, engaging its warning system the further out we drove.

"They've got a helluva history, those two."

"Which two?" I glanced at him, confused. "What?"

"Mitch and Gabriella. You don't remember her? They were tight at uni."

I thought she looked familiar. Mitch had been two years ahead of us at Charles Sturt. They'd been tight for a long time. She'd changed, gotten taller, or grown her hair long. Or something. Whatever. I shrugged his question off because we just started down a familiar street in Blackheath. And screw my gut's early warning system, it was full on screaming by the time Morgan pulled up outside the house where Janie Berg had been abducted.

I pulled to the kerb at the end of the street, both of us seeming to hold our breath as Morgan got out of the car.

Moments later, a Harley thundered down the street, driving straight past us. It pulled up next to Morgan's car and the man swung his leg over and dragged the helmet from his head as he stood, and stood, and fucking stood. He was wearing a Sentinels MC vest and a beard so wild and woolly it was a wonder it didn't smother him in his sleep.

"That is one big motherfucking bastard," Travis breathed.

"Ring Mitch," I ordered, but Travis was already dialling and giving out the address a second later.

"Holy motherfucking shit!" Mitch shouted when it clicked a second later where we were. Gabriella's wild Spanish was ripping someone a new one in the background so he kept yelling over the top of her into the phone. "Don't either of you dare touch this one or I swear to God, I'll—"

"You'll what, tell Dad?" Travis snorted as our eyes fastened on the argument in progress between Morgan and the big-ass biker dude. They started inside, the man roaring at her the entire way. I squinted at the back of his vest, catching the letters BIN on the back of his vest. He turned, eyes scanning the street before I could make out the rest of the letters. "Damn," I hissed, ignoring the bickering between Travis and his older brother over the phone.

Reaching over, I hit the end button for the second time, cutting off Mitch's rant.

I eyeballed Travis. "I'll take the front, you take the back."

Travis narrowed his eyes. "I'll take the front, you take the back."

"Fuck you, Trav," I declared, both of us knowing the front would be more dangerous. "I called it. It's mine." He opened his mouth to argue and I knew exactly how to shut it. "You've got a little boy who needs you."

Knowing I had him, I swallowed around the huge lump in my throat and held up a fist. "Let's do this."

He met my eyes as he bumped it with his. Then he grinned, his smile feral. "Let's do this."

We got out of the car and I popped the boot. Travis reached in, lifting the false flooring to reveal an entire arsenal. As he handed over a bulletproof vest, I strapped it on quickly. While Travis did his, I allowed myself the luxury of thinking about Grace for a brief moment, of her scent and her laugh, of the wild abandon on her face whenever I fucked her hard, of how much I adored every single hair on her head. My chest tightened and my hands shook. She could be just metres away right now, breathing in the same air, hurt, scared, bleeding out.

"Hey," Travis muttered, eyeing me. "You with me?"

"A hundred per cent," I told him, willing it to be true.

"Okay, then."

We both tucked a spare handgun in the back of our jeans, keeping one each in our hands. My breath puffed in and out as we approached the house. The air was cooler near the Blue Mountains, seeping into your bones. I shivered. I hated the cold. It reminded me of hiding in the yard when my father was in one of his rages. Sometimes I would fall asleep, my body pressed up between the fence and the tall eucalypt tree that always smelled good in the summer. When I eventually woke, my fingers and toes would be numb from the frost.

We reached the house and I wiped my mind of the memories. Travis peeled off, heading around the back while I approached the front screen door. It was one of those old kinds. The one that was there simply as a flyscreen, not a security screen. The hinges were flaking with paint and thick with rust, telling me that if I jerked too quickly, they would protest loud and clear.

Surprisingly, it was unlocked, making me pause. They couldn't have seen us coming. Maybe it was missed during the argument the two were having as they headed inside?

With a slowness that made me itchy, I eased the door open, gun cocked and ready, and stepped inside the house.

A quick scan in front of me gave nothing. I took another two steps, opening up the living room to my gaze, and my heart punched to my throat. Grace was bound to a chair. Silver duct tape held her arms and legs in place and a single strip covered her mouth. Her eyes filled the second I appeared.

I ran my eyes over her as I took another cautious step. Her hair was a wild tangle, dirt smudged her cheek, and dried blood covered her arms and dress. I couldn't remember ever seeing anything more beautiful in my entire life. I dragged air into my lungs, suddenly realising I hadn't taken a full breath since last night. "Grace, baby? Are you hurt?"

She shook her head, trying to speak behind the tape. I took another step and that's when Morgan appeared to Grace's left. With a smirk on her lips, she held up a gun in her hand and jammed it against Grace's temple. Raw fear flashed across Grace's face and it took everything I had to hold myself in check and not flinch.

"She's not hurt yet, but that can be arranged," Morgan told me.

My finger caressed the trigger of my own gun. "Put it down and step away from Grace, Morgan."

Grace's eyes went wide over my shoulder and she started screaming from behind the tape. Before I could turn, I felt the cool butt of a gun press against the back of my head.

"You first, Casey," said the voice from behind me.

My arms went slack and for a second I allowed my eyes to close. I knew that voice. It might have roughened over the years, but I knew it. It wasn't just the same voice as mine, it was the voice of my brother.

I swallowed hard and opened my eyes, focusing on Grace in front of me. She was blurred and I realised it was because my eyes were burning with tears.

"Kelly?"

Chapter Thirty-Three
GRACE

Two hours earlier...

"You don't talk much," I announced from my bound position on the dining room chair.

Kelly had taken the liberty of having a nice hot shower for himself while I was trussed up like a Christmas turkey, unable to move and feeling tired and grimy. Now he was moving around in nothing but a pair of low slung sweats, showing off that mile-wide motherfucker of a chest and tanned, rippling muscle. It was obvious he'd chosen commando as this afternoon's dress of choice, highlighting the fact that the man really was big everywhere. I made it a point not to stare.

"Yeah?" Kelly slammed the fridge door shut and cocked his brow at me in true Casey fashion. My breath hitched. I couldn't deny it. The Daniels brothers were absolute sex on a stick—like what sweet, sticky cotton candy was to a poor, deprived child. It was a crying shame that this Daniels brother was completely whacked. "You talk too much, babe."

"Argghhh! I'm not your babe," I told him for the millionth time.

"Not yet." He winked at me. "But you can be if you play your cards right."

The gleam in his eye was downright predatory as he walked over and stood in front of me. Unfortunately, my gaze shifted downwards, suddenly eye level with the giant anaconda in his pants. Not knowing where the hell to look, my eyes began ping-ponging around the room, eventually settling on somewhere in the distance.

"There will be no card playing," I declared in my primmest voice possible.

Kelly took hold of my chin, forcing me to meet his gaze. "Unlucky for you, I'm the one in charge and if I want card playing, there'll be fuckin' card playing."

My eyes clouded over, suddenly apprehensive. "So we're playing cards?"

He let go of my chin and straightened and there went my eyes again, fighting to find somewhere safe to land. "Why? You bored? Because I'm sure I can find something for you to do." Kelly's hand ran suggestively down his chest until it hit the waistband of his sweats. "It would have the added bonus of shutting you up."

My nostrils flared and the subtle reaction made him laugh. "How dare you? If my mouth is going anywhere near a guy's junk, it'll be Casey's and his alone. I'll pass, thanks."

For a second his eyes softened and I got a brief glimpse of the real man that lay beneath the cockiness coating his surface. "Why were you and Casey arguing?"

I blinked, wondering how he knew.

"The party, Grace," he prompted, his tone exasperated because I couldn't somehow read his mind. "You walked in, laughing and teasing him. I saw the light in his eyes and his hand slide under that sparkly dress of yours. You walked out, you're yelling, he's yelling, and that light in his eyes is gone."

My heart squeezed because Kelly was right. I hated seeing that light disappear. I also shivered, because being watched like that was really creepy. "You were watching us."

"You think I just magically stumbled upon you in that airport passageway?"

"No."

Kelly folded his arms, the move making his biceps bulge even more. "So why the argument?"

I made a pointed effort of glancing at the tape binding me to the chair. It didn't hurt, but it itched, and I was pretty sure I'd need to pee soon. "You want me to answer your questions, you can untie me from this chair."

"I can make you answer any question I want without untying you, Grace," he told me, his tone harsh.

"Threaten me all you like. It won't work," I replied, doing my best to suppress the fear. This guy might've been Casey's brother, but I had no idea what he was capable of.

Kelly shrugged and I watched him walk to the kitchen. He opened up the cutlery draw and took out a paring knife. It looked extra pointy and gleamed under the light of the kitchen, forcing my pulse to ramp up a notch. He walked back to me, picking up his phone along the way. "Let's test this little theory of yours."

An unnatural calm took over the fear, impressing me. My mind tried to tell me it was simply adrenaline, but I was too busy being phenomenally calm to pay attention.

Test away, pal, I retorted silently. And coolly.

Kelly pulled out a dining table chair, setting it so it faced me. Sitting down, he carefully placed the knife in arms' reach and then tapped at the screen of his phone. Then he held it up in front of me. I took one look and my calm expired on the spot. It was a photo of Henry in high megapixel glory. He was in the backyard of the duplex, Mitsy in his arms. He was laughing at someone but I wasn't sure who because they were out of camera shot. The focus was solely on my brother.

Kelly took the phone back and cocked his head. "You know that guy?"

I wanted to rip the smirk from his lips. Instead, I shrugged, the movement more feeble than I would have liked thanks to my forearms being attached to the chair. "Never seen him before in my life," I said breezily.

Kelly tapped at his phone and held it up again. It was a photo of Henry and me together at the awards ceremony the very day of my arrival. It was after our performance and celebratory champagne so we were hugging each other close and smiling wide for the camera, busy riding the high. It seemed an entire lifetime ago now. Taking the phone back, Kelly read the beginning of the attached article out loud. "Henry Paterson, lead guitarist of Jamieson and brother of leading international model Grace Paterson, talks to us about rising fame, fortune, and his illustrious sister."

I lifted my chin. "That's not me."

Kelly looked up from the phone. "Of course it's you, Grace." He set the phone down on the dining table to his right and then leaned back in his chair, staring me down. "Your brother's got skills on the guitar. Be a shame to send someone over to break all his fingers, don't you think?"

All the fight went out of me like a deflated balloon. If I wasn't strapped to the chair, I would've sagged from the easy defeat.

"Okay," I said. "You've made your point. You can make me answer any question you want without untying me. Does that make you happy?"

Kelly grinned. "Yep ... So ..." He folded his arms and sat back in the chair. "Why were you and Casey arguing?"

"Why do you even want to know?"

"Humour me."

I sighed, the sound heavy to my own ears. "Because he found out something I was keeping from him." To deflect any further questioning, I asked, "Why did you disappear?"

Kelly stared at me for a moment. "I didn't disappear."

"Casey thought you were dead."

He shrugged, the casual motion making my words appear unimportant. "He thought you were dead," I bit out, repeating myself so he understood the magnitude of those five words.

Kelly's eyes narrowed, flashing anger. "Heard you the first time, Grace."

"Don't you care?" I burst out.

His gazed dropped to his hands, shielding his face from my eyes. "It was better that he did."

My heart dropped to my toes. "Better that he thought you were dead?"

He looked up from his hands. "Better that than knowing how much I hate him."

"Why do you hate him?"

Kelly stood abruptly. "I'm the one asking the questions here." Snatching the knife, he came at me. I shrank back. He took hold of my hand and with a quick flick of his wrist, sliced through the bindings on my left arm. I looked up at him, surprised. "You're letting me go?"

He shook his head, indicating that was a no. "You've been squirming in your seat for five minutes. Lettin' you use the bathroom."

I watched him slice through the tape on my right hand. Then he crouched down and cut through the ones around my legs. A joyful moan slipped out at being able to move. Kelly grinned and gave my ankles a quick massage. "Feel good, babe?"

I jerked from his grip and hissed, "Don't touch me."

Kelly stood from his crouch, crowding over me with his bulk. "I bet I could make you feel even better."

"You don't know when to quit, do you?" I stood up. "Newsflash, pal. You might think you're all that, but you're not."

"You don't think I'm all that?" He gave me a look of mock sadness. "That hurts."

"Arrghhh!" The man was a frustrating brute. Now that I was out of my chair, I was ready to run. I shoved at his chest. He didn't budge. I shoved harder and he snatched my wrists.

"You done?"

My jaw locked from the effort of containing my rage. It was obvious I wasn't getting through. Yelling at him wouldn't help my situation. I would scope out the bathroom, I decided. I was probably slim enough to make a daring window escape. If not, I could just search for a weapon. Hell, I could just undo the shower tap and use it to bean him in the head. "Yes," I replied through gritted teeth. "I'm done. I'd like to use the bathroom, please."

Kelly brushed a thumb across my cheek. "Pretty manners, babe. I bet a man could take you anywhere and be proud to have you on his arm."

I paused. Casey's brother had a soft side. It kept slipping through, surprising me. "Why are you doing this?"

He withdrew his thumb, rolling his eyes. "Already told you, Grace. People want you dead."

"Yes, yes." I waved a hand. I knew that part. "That's why you made it look like I was. What I don't get is why you care, and now that you have me here, what are you planning on doing with me?"

"Let me worry about that."

Kelly took my bicep and dragged me down the hall. Damn, I muttered under my breath when I saw the toilet. It was separate from the bathroom and the window sat high near the ceiling, mocking me with its microscopic size.

Kelly nudged me inside and now that I was there, I realised how busting to go I really was. I spun around, hands ready to slide my dress up, and paused. Kelly was leaning against the doorframe, arms folded, watching me.

"Privacy," I snapped.

"Is totally overrated," he finished for me.

"You're not going to stand there and watch me pee."

He turned around, giving me his back, and leaned against the doorframe again. "Hurry up, Grace. Gettin' hungry."

"I don't give a rat's ass if you haven't eaten for ten whole days. Get out and shut the door."

"Just go, would you?"

"No," I told him.

Bitch, my bladder screamed at me in protest.

"Pretend I'm not here."

My brows winged up. Was he serious? Pretend there wasn't a colossal dude standing right there in nothing but a pair of sweats that were somehow inching lower by the minute? I cocked my head as I stared for a second at the tattoo covering his back. A grim reaper with red eyes stared back. He was standing at the front of Hell's Gates. One skeletal hand was held up, a bony finger pointing at me, beckoning me forward. It was chilling. And familiar.

"You're a Sentinel," I breathed in horror.

Kelly tilted his head, looking at me over his shoulder. "Fuck, babe. You still haven't gone?" Ignoring my comment, he reached for the door handle and shut the door. Suddenly I was alone. I tucked that little piece of information away to think on later and went about my business. When I was finished, he took me to the bathroom so I could wash my hands. I took my time, stalling, because I really didn't want to go back to the chair. In the end, he got fed up and dragged me back.

I eyed the chair balefully. "Don't make me sit down again. My ass is still numb."

"Want me to massage it for you?"

I huffed. "Would you stop?"

"Can't," he said and nudged me into the narrow kitchen instead. He wedged me in the corner, making sure an attempted escape would mean having to tackle him like a linebacker first. "You make it too easy."

Kelly got a loaf of bread out of the pantry and sat it on the counter next to where I stood. Going to the fridge, he came out with butter, cheese and tomatoes. The thought of eating made my stomach growl loudly as I watched him butter the bread.

He looked up, pausing his movements. "Hungry?"

I pursed my lips. "No."

"No?" He raised his brows. "I make a mean grilled cheese and tomato sandwich."

"Of course you do," I retorted. "Because you're a mean person. If you were nice, you'd be making a nice grilled cheese and tomato sandwich."

Kelly barked out a laugh as he started slicing cheese from the block of cheddar. "You worried my sandwich is going to beat you up?"

"I wouldn't put it past anything you made," I muttered snidely.

He chuckled as he layered the cheese over the bread. My stomach growled again. Without even looking at me, he handed over a slice of cheese. His response was a grin when he felt the piece of cheese leave his fingers.

There was no harm in eating, was there? It would give me energy for a proper escape. And maybe appearing amenable might get him to answer the question that had been running through my head on repeat since I first saw him. I nibbled on the edge of the cheese as I watched him slice tomato and add it to the sandwiches.

"Kelly."

"Mmm," he replied, not looking up.

"Your parents. It wasn't a murder-suicide, was it?"

Kelly paused and I almost missed the way his hand shook a little before he drew a deep breath. The tremor stopped when he regained control. He finished making the sandwiches and put them on the pan heating behind him. Then he turned around and gripped the edges of the counter on either side of me, trapping me in. "How 'bout you tell me what you were keepin' from Casey that got him so upset. Then I'll answer your question."

"Really?"

"Yes, babe. Really."

I'd tell him anything to get the answers Casey was so desperate for. "I have cancer," I said simply. "I was going to tell him, but he found out from someone else."

Kelly drew back sharply, looking like I'd punched him in gut. "Fuck."

He muttered the word under his breath, but I still heard it. His reaction didn't make sense. Why would he care?

"How bad is it?"

"That's none of your business," I replied.

Kelly stepped close again, so close I could feel the heat of his body. I tried inching back, but there was no room to move. "How bad is it?" he bit out.

"I'm supposed to be on my way home to Melbourne right now to start chemotherapy. I've already held off treatment as long as possible, so whatever the hell you're doing with me, it's pointless if I don't get home."

Kelly nodded carefully and I could see him absorbing what I was telling him. After a pause, I said, "Your turn."

"No, it wasn't," he told me before he turned around and flipped the sandwiches, his body tense.

"What?"

"Your question. It wasn't a murder-suicide," he told me. Reaching up, he took two plates from the above cupboard and placed them on the counter, the grim reaper on his back glaring at me all the while.

"What was it then?"

"I answered your question," he growled. He put the sandwiches on the plates, sliced mine into quarters, and turned, shoving the plate at me. I grabbed it before it dropped on the ground.

"Quarters? I'm not a child."

"The cheese is hot," he replied. "It'll cool faster for you."

"You're worried I'll burn my tongue?" I questioned, my eyes wide with disbelief. "After you backhanded me across the face?"

"I told you to be quiet and you started screaming. It hurt my fuckin' ears." He carried his plate to the dining table, dragging me along with him.

I noticed his sandwich wasn't cut into quarters. He hadn't cut his at all. "What, your tongue is so badass it can handle hot cheese and mine can't?"

"Babe, you wanna know how badass my tongue is then sit down and spread your legs."

I paused to glare at him, beginning to realise he was a lot more like his older brother than just in looks. "It all comes back to sex with you!"

Kelly snatched the plate from my hand and dumped it on the table. "Sit down, shut the fuck up, and eat."

I sat, and I ate, and I blinked back tears because I wanted Casey and I wanted him now. I wanted him to wrap me up in his arms and hold me close like he loved to do. It made me feel safe when I was burrowed against him, inhaling his warm, male scent.

"Don't cry," Kelly ordered.

"Sure," I muttered sarcastically.

His phone rang where it rested on the table beside him. I saw the name Morgan flash up on the screen before he picked it up. My eyes narrowed. That bitch! Were they in this together? I should've done more than just slap her in the face. I should've throat punched her. And when she went down, because my blow would've felled her, I could've scratched her eyes out and ripped every single hair extension from her head.

"What do you want?" Kelly answered.

I strained but I couldn't hear her reply.

"Shit," Kelly spat. "This ain't the fuckin' mafia, bitch."

I took mild satisfaction at hearing him call her a bitch when all I got from him was babe or Grace. Suck on that, Morgan. The entire world knows you're a mean cow.

"You can't just go around putting hits on people because your brother is the president of the Sentinels."

Oh shit.

And I'd slapped her.

No wonder they wanted me dead.

I was so dead.

So very, very dead.

I tuned back in to find Kelly ending the call.

"I'm dead, aren't I?"

"Fuck." He tossed his phone on the table without answering me and stood quickly. "Morgan is on her way and she's got her fuckin' brother involved."

"What are you doing?" I shrieked, batting his hands away as he began strapping me back down in the chair. "You should be letting me go, not taping me up to await my doom like a Christmas turkey!"

"You don't escape the fuckin' Sentinels, Grace. Shit is about to fly. You're better off here with me while I talk it out." He paused and then picked up the tape. Ripping a piece off, he slapped it over my mouth. "Be better if you shut the fuck up too. If you start flappin' your gums, you'll only make it worse."

On that ominous note, he disappeared down the hall. Moments later he returned, a handgun tucked into the waistband of his sweats and a shirt in his hands. He tugged it on, pulling it quickly over that motherfucker chest.

That's when I heard it. The thunderous roar of a motorcycle coming down the street. My heart began to hammer in my chest in tune with the sound, creating a symphony of doom. As though my fear was audible, Kelly stood in front of me, arms folded, his bulk wiping out my view of the front door.

There was arguing out the front of the house, then suddenly the front door slammed. I flinched. I wasn't sure my heart could hammer any harder until it suddenly hit warp speed.

"Where is she?" I heard Morgan hiss.

"Move," boomed a gravelly voice from the door. There was a shuffle and Morgan came into view, moving sideways as someone came in behind her.

Kelly jabbed a finger at her. "Keep out of this, Morgan."

Yeah, bitch, I added silently from behind the tape.

"This her?" boomed the voice, louder now because it was closer.

Kelly stepped to the side, still keeping guard, but revealing me to the big biker boss dude.

My mouth fell open as I took him in, from the buzzed hair on his head, to the mammoth, woolly beard, to the leather that covered his entire body and down to booted feet that would crunch bones beneath them with ease.

My eyes flew back up, meeting his dark brown ones. That's when I knew that before, when I thought I was dead, I really wasn't. Because that was before I saw this man. Now I was whatever was worse than being dead, because I knew this man.

From the flare in his eyes, I knew he knew me too. The last time I saw this badass biker was at the bonfire after our photoshoot for the Hendrix label. I'd tossed water all over his burning beard before careening away in a hail of gravel, John sideswiping a bunch of Harleys with his car as we made our rapid escape.

"Grace." The single word on his lips was a ball of dread in my belly.

He reached forward and ripped the tape from my lips. I ignored the sting because it was nothing in the grand scheme of things. Not when death was here, knocking on my door.

I breathed his name with horror. "Bingo."

"This is the bitch you ordered a hit on, Morgan?" he thundered, looking at me while he spoke.

"That's her," she replied, her lips pressing in a smirk that I wanted to smack from her face.

He spun around. "What the fuck? Who do you think you are, traipsing around ordering hits on people? What are we? The fuckin' mafia? You want every single fuckin' fed in Sydney tacked to our fuckin' asses? Goddammit!" He jabbed a finger at Kelly. "You shoulda just fuckin' told me what the bitch was up to."

Kelly held up his hands. "You were out of town. I had to do something to keep her safe until I could get a hold of you."

Bingo turned back around to face me. "No one's touchin' this classy piece of ass. Call the hit off," he ordered, staring into my eyes.

"Why?" I blurted out.

"You saved my motherfuckin' life," he boomed.

Morgan's mouth fell open. "She did?"

"I tossed water at you," I told him as if he needed reminding. It was hardly life saving. "Then I broke all your motorcycles," I added. Then I shut my mouth before I could mention the slapping of his sister. Otherwise he might change his mind and put the hit back on.

"You scratched a couple," Bingo admitted, then rubbed at his epic facial hair lovingly. "But you saved me from goin' up in flames when I was being a fuckin' idiot. You didn't stick around to let me thank you. I owe you big, " he boomed.

Bingo turned back to Morgan. "Touch a hair on her pretty head and there'll be trouble." He jabbed his finger at Kelly again, who'd been standing there watching our exchange without a flicker of emotion crossing his face. "I need to take a piss. When I come back, I want her out of that chair and gone."

Bingo disappeared down the hallway.

"Fuck," Kelly growled suddenly as he stalked to the window. "Casey's here. You let him follow you," he accused Morgan.

My heart leaped instantly. Then Kelly snatched the gun from the back of his sweats and engaged the slide. My heart plummeted just as fast.

I opened my mouth to scream when suddenly Morgan was slapping another piece of tape across my face.

Godfuckingdammit!

Chapter Thirty-Four
CASEY

The butt of the gun jammed harder into the back of my head. I blinked and Grace came back into focus. I wanted to turn around, to see my brother, but I wouldn't take my eyes from Grace for anything.

"I should've known the police would let you off quickly," Kelly growled.

"You did this?" I whispered because suddenly it hurt to talk. Every piece of me hurt knowing my brother was alive and hid from me all these years. That he would do something like this. "You took my girl and you made it look like I killed her?"

No answer came from behind me and that was answer enough. Anger coursed through my blood like molten lava. Breathing through it took effort. My eyes flicked from Grace to the gun pressed to her temple. I couldn't look at Morgan because if I did, I knew my finger would press down on the trigger and I'd shoot her and that couldn't happen, because if I fired at Morgan, she might hit the trigger and shoot Grace.

"Call off your bitch before I start shooting," I ordered Kelly, the gun in my hand steady and cocked.

"She's not my bitch," Kelly said from behind me as if the thought made him want to puke.

Movement from the hallway caught my eye and the big biker came into view. I blinked, because he was even bigger up close and that was a lot to take in. He scanned the scene before him with apparent exasperation. "What the fuck is goin' on here?" he boomed. "You!" He pointed at me and my adrenaline spiked. "Get that fuckin' gun off my sister. You!" he pointed at Morgan. "I told you to leave that girl the hell alone."

"Fuck you, Bingo!" Morgan cried out, the words aimed at the biker. "And fuck you," she added, glaring over my shoulder. At Kelly, I realised with surprise. "I wanted you like I never wanted anything in my life. But after everything I did for you, you never gave me the time of day." I felt my brother jolt behind me, the butt of his gun shifting slightly against my head. "So I fucked your brother instead."

"Jesus," Kelly breathed from behind me.

Grace closed her eyes, her chest expanding with a deep breath before she opened them again. I wanted to apologise for making such a huge mistake. I hadn't even met Grace before it happened, yet it continued to taint us anyway.

"But your brother never wanted me either!" Morgan shouted, her eyes red and her body trembling. It made the gun in her hand shake and I held my breath knowing how easily the trigger would fire. "He threatened to destroy everything I ever worked for. Just like that! Everything. That's why this bitch here deserves to die. If he takes everything from me, then I'm going to return the favour. All the better he's here to see it," she sneered.

"Put down the weapon, Morgan!" I ground out. Both my arms were outstretched holding the gun, my eyes squinting as I kept her in my sights. I didn't care how big her biker brother was. As long as Morgan stood there with that gun pointed at Grace, I wasn't putting mine down.

Movement came from the hallway again. I was careful not to shift my eyes and reveal Travis silently making his way towards us.

Ignoring everyone, Morgan ripped the tape from Grace's mouth. Tilting her head at my girl, she asked, "Any last words?" before cocking the gun. The sound was soft, but it rang through my ears like a crack of thunder.

A single tear rolled down Grace's cheek and my heart stopped.

I love you, she mouthed silently, her eyes holding mine.

I locked my jaw, fighting back a sob as time stood still.

"Who do you think you are? Batman?"

She'd been so fierce and bright the day I first met her. From that moment on I knew I'd be whoever she wanted me to be.

"You even think about carrying me, or touching me, or even breathing in the same airspace as me, I'll punch you so hard you'll be spitting teeth for a week."

So damn feisty and beautiful.

My finger tightened on the trigger and I dragged air into my lungs.

"This is my fight! It's mine, and I'm not going to allow what happened to my father and to my family happen to you."

Grace was wrong. It wasn't her fight anymore. It was our fight. I wasn't letting anyone, or anything, take her from me.

A red haze of anger drew down over my eyes.

"You made me love you so hard."

I cocked my head, checked my aim, and I pulled the trigger.

Then everything happened at once.

Kelly knocked my arm from behind and the shot went wild, hitting the ceiling. At the same time, Travis launched himself at Bingo and they both went down. In the middle of all that, Gabriella stormed the front door behind me, rushing past. Her rapid-fire Spanish flooded the room as she went straight for Morgan. Mitch came from the opposite direction, having come through the same back door as Travis. They both closed in from either side.

Morgan's eyes flared wide. She swung the gun from Grace to me and fired three rounds into my chest.

I heard Grace cry out as the force shoved me backwards. I smacked hard into my brother, my legs buckling beneath me.

"No!" Kelly bellowed, catching me. He stumbled, going to his knees as he took my weight. We both went down. I landed hard on the floor, Kelly hitting somewhere behind me.

Then he appeared over me.

"Grace," I gasped at him. My lungs felt crushed and I could hear the ragged breaths escaping my lips.

He looked up quickly and then back down. "She's fine."

I nodded because that was all I could manage to do. Everything else felt impossible. Kelly's face swam in front of me as he ran his hands down my chest, checking the bullet entry points. I stared for a moment, finally getting to see the man my brother had become. He looked just like me and my gut clenched with grief, not because I didn't know him, but because I wasn't sure I wanted to.

"Why?"

Kelly's jaw quivered and he clenched it hard. "Because you left me," he choked out, "and I've hated you ever since."

"I'm sorry," I managed, his words a punch to the gut. I was his big brother. I was supposed to protect him from anything that would hurt him. And I'd failed. But what he'd done today? No apology could fix the man he'd become. I didn't know if I could save him from himself. And the thought broke my heart.

"Casey!"

Hearing Grace cry my name was the best thing I'd ever heard in my life. I tilted my head forward and tried to tell her I was okay, but I couldn't get the words past my lips. Her eyes held mine while Travis cut her free. Travis loved Grace because I loved her, and when I hurt for Grace, he did too. I could see it in his eyes as he untied her with so much care, checking for injuries while she slapped at his hands, impatient to get to me. When the last bit of tape was removed, she was suddenly on me.

Kelly shifted out of the way and stood. Straddling my lap, Grace began patting at my chest where the bullets hit.

"Casey," she sobbed. "Where are you hit?"

"Fine," I breathed, my head falling back with relief. "I'm fine."

Her hands shoved my hoodie up and over my chest where she encountered the bulletproof vest beneath it. "Oh thank God!" she cried. Her arms wrapped around me and she buried her face in my neck. I could feel her tears on my skin, her delicate frame shaking with sobs as she draped her body over mine, unwilling to let go. My arms came up around her, happy to keep her there.

"Casey, you came for me." Grace pulled back, taking my face in her hands. I covered her hands with mine. I looked at her until she blurred in front of me and I knew I'd never find a feeling like this with anyone else. Ever. "You came for me."

"Remember when you told me you loved me that first time?"

Grace nodded, swallowing as she straddled over me, my face still in her hands.

"And when you said that some people leave you in the blink of an eye, and some are with you for years?" She nodded again. "I promise you, Grace, no matter what happens, you'll be with me forever, because you're in my heart, and I won't let you leave."

Her bottom lip trembled. "I don't want to be anywhere else, Casey."

I dragged her face down until my lips met hers. The kiss was fast and hard because it wasn't the time or the place. I just needed to taste her before I had to deal with my brother.

After nipping lightly at Grace's bottom lip, I let her go and Travis loomed over me. "You pussy." He held out his palm to Grace. She took it in his and he helped her to her feet. "Lying down on the job."

"Don't mind me," I said, wincing as I stood without assistance.

Travis raised his brows. "Last time I saw, you didn't have a vagina. You can get yourself to your feet."

I dragged my hoodie over my head and in that split second of inattention, Grace—having decided I was fine—charged towards Morgan. Gabriella had Morgan's front pressed against the wall as she slapped on a pair of handcuffs. Mitch stood by, holding onto a similarly handcuffed Bingo. Grace obviously didn't care. She launched herself without the slightest hesitation and all three girls went down in a pile of body parts. Limbs stuck out everywhere as I tossed my hoodie aside, unstrapped the vest, and waded into the fray with Travis.

"You shot my boyfriend!" came a shriek from the pile.

"Calma el fuck abajo!" was yelled from somewhere and I had no clue what it meant. It sounded harsh though.

Then came the unmistakable sound of a fist cracking someone in the face.

"You bitch!" came another shriek, this one muffled and agonised and sounding a lot like Morgan. "You broke my fucking nose!"

"Come here," was the answering growl. "I'll break your whole fucking face and I'll laugh while I'm doing it."

"Your woman's feisty," Kelly told me as if I didn't already know.

I reached in for a limb like a lucky dip and yanked out a body. I got a glaring Gabriella. "Control your woman, cara de verga!" she snapped, shrugging free of my grip.

"What did you call me?"

Mitch's lips twitched. "She called you a dickface."

"Nice," I muttered.

"I told you to wait," she snapped, brushing hair from her eyes impatiently.

I turned to grab Grace from the pile when Kelly's arms wrapped around her waist from behind. Blood smeared along her arm and across her cheek from the melee as he pulled her back.

"Babe, stop," he growled when Grace struggled.

"Let me go, asshole!"

My eyes narrowed. I left Morgan bleeding on the floor for Travis to deal with. I snatched Grace from Kelly's hold, nudged her behind me, cocked back a fist, and slammed it in my brother's face.

Kelly stumbled backwards, his hands flying to his nose. "Ow, fuck," he hissed.

I clenched and unclenched my fist, trying to relieve the throbbing burn in my knuckles before I went for round two. My brother had a hard fucking face. "That's for taking Grace," I snarled.

He came back at me hard and fast, clipping me in the jaw. I sucked in a breath. The punch packed a hell of a lot of power, surprising me. "That's for leaving me," he snarled back.

From my peripheral vision, I saw Grace step forward and then snap backwards like a rubber band. I turned my head. Travis held her. "Let them punch it out, Grace."

"Are you kidding? Look at them," I heard her say as I turned back, fury taking over the pain of Kelly's punch. "They've got muscles on their muscles. They'll kill each other."

"No they won't," I heard Travis reassure her as I tackled my brother and we crashed to the ground, breaking the side table by the couch when we landed. I reared back for another punch and Kelly grabbed me in a headlock. "See? They're hugging it out already," he added soothingly.

I landed a fist in Kelly's ribs.

"Oomphf," he huffed.

"That's for calling Grace babe. She's not, nor will she ever be, your babe."

Kelly grappled and managed to roll me over, landing a blow to my right eye. It jarred from the impact, blinding me. I shook my head, feeling it swell instantly. "That's for never coming back when I needed you."

I reared up, headbutting him in the face hard. He snapped backwards, toppling off me. Shifting up on my knees, I loomed over him. "That's for setting me up for murder!" I yelled.

"Es suficiente!" Gabriella grabbed my shirt by the neckline and I heard it tear. "That's enough!"

"You!" She pointed at my brother. "You are under arrest for the kidnapping of Grace Paterson."

Kelly's jaw ticked, but he nodded once, stoically. "Fair enough."

"No!" Grace blurted out as I got to my feet, breathing hard and ignoring the ache from where the round of bullets hit my chest. I looked around, noting that Mitch, Morgan, and Bingo were no longer there. Mitch must have taken them out while I was fighting with Kelly.

"You can't," Grace added when the room fell silent.

Gabriella planted her hands on her hips, a frown marring her brow. "Why not?"

Grace looked at me before shifting her eyes to my brother. "Because he saved my life."

Surprise flashed across Kelly's face, but he didn't say a word.

"Slim?" I reached out, taking her hand. Threading our fingers together, I drew her towards me. "You want to explain?"

She looked to Kelly and he nodded imperceptibly.

"Morgan arranged a hit on me. It was supposed to go down last night." My nostrils flared but I kept quiet, letting her speak. "Kelly found out and told her he'd take care of it himself. Only he had no intention of carrying it out. He just made it look like I was dead. He was going to keep me here, safe, until he could talk to Bingo and let him know what Morgan had planned. But somehow she found out what Kelly did and turned up just before you all did."

"If you had just come to me," I growled at Kelly, "I could've taken care of it!"

"Like you did all those years ago?" he sneered.

"Christ, Kelly." I let go of Grace's hand and took a step forward. "You set me up for fucking murder!"

"It was only temporary for fuck's sake!" he yelled, exasperated. "It's not like they could keep you for long without a dead body. It kept you outta my fuckin' hair so I could deal with the situation. You keep stickin' your nose into shit and causing trouble. We had that Janie Berg case handled and you had to go stick your hands in it. Then you kept askin' questions about our parents and you wouldn't leave it alone. Why wouldn't you leave it the fuck alone? This is all your fuckin fault!" he shouted, jabbing a finger at me.

A growl worked its way up from my chest, and I took another step forward, going nose to nose with my brother. "Did you stop to think that maybe if you hadn't gone and disappeared, that none of this would've happened?"

That jabbing finger poked me in the chest, right in the middle of bruised tissue. "None of this would've happened if you hadn't left in the first place!"

I shoved him. "I spent ten years, ten fucking years, thinking you were dead!" I yelled back, my voice cracking. "Godammit!" I spun around, fighting to control the absolute pain of it all.

"Stop it, Kelly," I heard Grace say angrily to my brother. "Just … stop. I've listened to every word you've spoken since the moment I met you and not once, in that entire time, did you stop to consider Casey's feelings or what he went through. He's just as important as you are, but you know what he never had?" she asked him, her voice hoarse and sad and I knew she was crying. "He never had anybody to fight for him the way he fought for you. He never had anybody."

"Babe—" Kelly began.

"Shut it," she hissed and I could sense her temper starting to heat up. "He's got me now, and he's got my family, and he's got a whole pile of friends who love him. We'll fight for him."

I swallowed around the lump in my throat, so fucking proud of Grace I had no idea what to say. "Grace."

"Shut it," she hissed at me, taking my hand. "I'm not finished."

She dragged me back around and lifted my shirt, exposing the tattoo of the ancient sword and dragon covering the left side of my torso. "Can you read what the tattoo says?" she snapped. The words were pretty clear, but she read them out anyway. "Glory is not in never falling, but in rising every time we fall." Grace twitched my shirt back in place while glaring at Kelly. "That tattoo covers a scar so deep it almost killed him. His father almost killed him, and he took that for you." I saw Travis flinch from the corner of my eye. I'd never told him about that scar because I hated the memories. "Then he had it inked over so instead of seeing a scar, he sees the sword of a warrior, and it reminds him that every time he took a hit, it was a hit he was taking for you. You know what I see when I look at that tattoo?"

Kelly shook his head, mute.

"I see a man who doesn't know how to give up and I thank fucking God for that, because while I might be able to fight for him, right now, I need him to fight for me. I need …" Grace choked up, unable to speak.

My eyes burned as I dragged her into my arms wrapping her up tight. I kissed her forehead, and I kissed her temple, and I buried my head in her neck and kissed her there too. "I love you so much, Slim," I whispered against the warmth of her skin. "I'll fight for you. I promise."

I vaguely heard the murmur of Travis and Gabriella talking before they left together, leaving just me, Kelly, and Grace standing in the living room.

"Grace is right," he said. I looked at my stricken brother over Grace's shoulder. "I didn't … I never thought about you or what you did at all. You were just always there and one day you weren't."

My arms tightened on Grace as she sniffled into my shirt. I rubbed her back soothingly as I spoke. "I left to setup a better life for us. It took longer than I'd hoped, but I was coming back for you, Kelly. I was coming back."

He nodded. "I believe you."

"Will you tell me what really happened to our parents?"

Kelly lifted his chin but I could still see the tremor in his chin and the pain in his eyes. "I killed him."

I froze and Grace stilled in my arms.

"It was me that killed dad."

I closed my eyes, reeling, before I opened them again. "Why? What did he do?"

"He hit Mum. She went down hard, crackin' her head against the dresser in their room." Kelly's eyes filled. "She never got back up. She never fuckin' got back up," he bit out, his tone harsh and thick with grief. "So I killed him."

Grace let out a whimper and I realised I was squeezing her too tight. I loosened my arms a little. "Did he come after you?"

He shook his head. "I heard the yellin' and Mum screamin' and suddenly it went real quiet. Then I heard Dad sobbing and I never heard that sound in my life. So I crept towards their room and saw him sittin' on the edge of the bed cryin' and Mum on the floor."

Kelly drew a deep breath, his lungs expanding visibly. "So I went and I got Dad's gun and I walked back to his room, all the while feelin' like I was standing outside of myself lookin' in on it all from above, you know?" He shrugged. "And then I held the gun up to his temple, and I shot him."

"Kelly," I choked out.

Grace untangled me from her arms and nudged me towards my brother. I latched on and pulled him close, hugging him. A sob broke through his chest and his arms came up holding on. "He killed mum. I couldn't … I didn't know what to do. I'd just had enough and couldn't take it anymore."

"Why didn't you call me? Why did you run?"

"I was scared I'd go to jail. It wasn't self-defence, Casey. It was murder." Kelly pushed back from me, wiping tears from his eyes with the heel of his hands. "I didn't want you to know what I did. You were always so fuckin' strong and brave and at the first sign of trouble I lost it. The neighbours called the police after hearing the shot. That's when I met Morgan. She was just a rookie then, on her way back to the station on her own after doing some fuckin' work errand or something. I don't remember." He shrugged. "I begged her to help me. She agreed. Guess she wasn't so much of a bitch then like she is now. She called someone in from the Sentinels, made it so it looked like a murder-suicide. She pulled the records from the system two weeks after they closed the case. Didn't want anyone sniffin' around, knowing the truth, and I didn't want anyone to find me. I didn't want to go to jail. I was fifteen fuckin' years old. I left that day and I've been a Sentinel ever since."

After all this time I finally knew and I had no idea what to say. Grace tucked herself behind me, warming me. I took her arms and wrapped them around my waist. "Show me your tattoo," I asked.

Kelly dragged his shirt over his head, mussing his hair, and turned around. For a long moment I stared at the representation of what he considered his family, and it hurt like a bitch to know he went to them instead of me. I wasn't sure I would ever get over that.

Kelly turned back around. "I didn't think after all these years of turnin' Morgan down that she'd go after you instead. I'm real fuckin' sorry about that."

"I used her," I told him, "and she knew it. So she dangled the case records in my face like a carrot. To be honest, I'm not sure how she got through all the psychological testing to become a detective. She's not right in the head."

"You can say that again," Grace mumbled from behind me.

Gabriella appeared in the doorway, frowning impatiently. "Can you wrap this shit up? You all need to come down to the station. I need statements."

"Tomorrow," I told her. Grace needed a shower, a bed, and me. Everything else could wait.

"No," Gabriella snapped. "Now. This is my first case for the department after my transfer. I want it all wrapped up in a pretty bow because I'm the new team member and a girl. I have to prove myself, comprende?"

Grace dropped her arms from my waist and went to follow Gabriella. "You up for doing your statement, Slim?"

She paused, turning. "You heard her. She's a girl and she has to prove herself. I'll take one for the sisterhood and get it over with."

I lifted my chin at the front door. "Wait for me over there."

"Okay," she said agreeably.

Grace kept within sight so I turned to Kelly taking him in all over again because I was still in shock he was here standing in front of me. I briefly wondered where the two of us would be if he never took off like he did.

"You're not gonna say anything, are you? About Dad?"

"No." Relief flashed through eyes the exact same shade of blue as mine. "That doesn't mean I agree with what you did. Remember that time with the knife? You almost attacked me with it. I've got a hell of a temper, but yours was always worse. You need to work on reining that shit in," I told him.

"Enough with the big brother crap," he muttered, folding his arms.

"Okay," I agreed. "Just one quick thing." I glanced over at Grace waiting by the door, starting to look impatient while trying not to. She was muttering to herself and picking at something on her dress and I was sure I heard Mac's name mentioned. I turned back to Kelly. "I honestly don't know what I would've done in your situation, but when I got the news about losing all of you, his death was the only one I didn't cry over, because if anyone deserved to die, it was him. So if you're carrying around a whole bunch of guilt about what you did, you need to stop that shit now."

Kelly tipped his head to the ceiling. "Easy enough to say."

"Say it for long enough, then maybe you'll start believing it. Now let's go. Grace is waiting for me."

"Pussy whipped," he replied, a slight grin tipping the corners of his lips.

"You're probably right," I conceded, "but if it means having Grace, then I don't really give a shit."

Chapter Thirty-Five
GRACE

Steam built up in the bathroom as the shower ran hot behind me, fogging the mirror and making it a little hard to breathe. After Casey finished checking the temperature, he turned and I used the opportunity to steal a quick kiss.

Casey ran his tongue over his bottom lip and groaned. I loved how his clear blue eyes darkened when he wanted me, as though it was impossible to focus on anything else. He slid his hand around the nape of my neck and pulled me in for another one. I opened my mouth for him. His kiss was deep and consuming, like sinking under water. I got lost in it. In him. His touch, and his taste, uncaring that I couldn't breathe.

He broke off, pressing his forehead against mine. "You okay?"

"I'm good," I replied, as if he hadn't just rocked my world with a single kiss.

He nudged me into the shower. I stepped inside, careful to keep my cast from the spray despite it being wrapped securely. Casey took hold of my hips as he stepped in behind me then shut the shower door. Then he kissed me again while the steam surrounded us. After a moment, he slowed it down and took a step back.

"Turn around," he commanded, his tone husky.

I turned obediently, splaying my hands against the shower tiles. My right arm throbbed and I knew a return visit to the doctor was in my immediate future. I think I did some real damage when I punched Morgan in the nose. It felt surprisingly good at the time. I never truly understood a man's affinity for violence until her bone crunched beneath my fist. It was savage, and disturbing, and overwhelmingly satisfying. I kept replaying how she shot Casey and it brought back the urge to punch her all over again.

"You sure you're okay?" he asked again, running a soapy washcloth over my back.

I hesitated.

"Slim?" He paused.

"I keep seeing her swing that gun at you. I think it will give me nightmares for the rest of my life. She would've killed you without that vest," I said, my eyes burning. I made a mental note to make him wear it every day, even if he was just going into the office or to the corner store for milk. That would be the price he'd have to pay if he decided to keep me. I still wasn't sure if he wanted to. There hadn't been any time to talk about our future. "I'm not a violent person. Not usually," I added, taking past events into consideration. It seems people could be whoever they needed to be when the occasion warranted it. "But I wanted to rip all the limbs from her body."

"I was scared too," Casey admitted, running the washcloth over my hips and down my legs. His words surprised me because he hadn't looked scared. He'd looked hard and cold and more vengeful than a Liam Neeson movie. "When I walked into that house, I …"

"You what?" I asked when he trailed off.

He stood up and his mouth touched the back of my neck at the same time his soapy hands slid around my waist. "I honestly didn't know what to do. In that kind of situation you're trained to talk the person down, but all I could see was you and I wanted to start shooting." Casey's breath was hot in my ear as he pressed up behind me. "Grace, I was scared because I can't lose you. Not when I just found you. You need to talk to me because I'm scared I still might. I need to know what we're fighting."

He ran a slippery hand up my ribs until he cupped my breast in his palm, scraping a calloused thumb gently over the scar. "Does it hurt?"

I shivered at the touch, pressing my forehead against the cool tile. "No."

"Good."

"I got tested regularly because of mum. You're at a higher risk if it runs in the family," I explained. "So they caught it early. Initially, they thought it was benign and then I got the news it wasn't. I threw up afterwards. What happened to my mother was happening to me," I whispered. "My dad, Henry, the twins. How was I supposed to tell them they were about to head down the same path they thought they'd put behind them?"

Casey turned me around and I caught the flash of fear in his eyes before it was carefully banked. He was trying to be strong for me. The very thought had me swallowing around the lump in my throat.

"Is it the same path?"

I shook my head. "They said they got it all, but they want me to do a round of chemotherapy to be sure."

Casey didn't reply. Instead, he reached around and flicked off the taps. The air seemed quiet and still without the hot, gushing water. Reaching for the towel hanging off the shower door, he wrapped it around my shoulders and led me out.

Then he began patting me dry, his touch so gentle and careful I wanted to cry. "I'm not going to break," I snapped, my tone undeservedly harsh from battling emotion and exhaustion.

He exhaled deeply and stopped his ministrations to look at me. "This is all I know how to do, Grace. The doctors can do whatever it is they do, but taking care of you, being there for you through all of it, that's the only way I know how to fight this. So humour me, okay?"

Cancer made people feel helpless. I knew this because my dad went crazy trying to do everything he could to fix something that couldn't be fixed. When something was wrong, men would do whatever was necessary to put their world back in balance, and then they would move on. Maybe I wouldn't break, but I would humour Casey. Not just because it was a man thing, but because I loved him and he, more than anyone I knew, needed his world in balance.

"Okay," I agreed.

He nodded once and went back to drying me off. My eyes fell on his bruised and swollen knuckles. Today I had learned that Casey could hold his own in a fight. But so could his brother.

"Do you think you and Kelly will find your way back to being brothers one day?"

Casey paused as though the question was difficult to answer. "I hope so," he answered eventually.

I opened my mouth to speak and hesitated.

"What?" he prompted.

"I was going to say that maybe a therapist might help the two of you get through everything, but I'm not sure I can see Kelly agreeing to something like that. He seems so … hard."

"He is hard. And you're right. I don't think he'd agree to anything like that. He found his family and I found mine, and I'm not sure how we'll meet in middle. Or if he even wants to."

"But you have to try."

"Of course. He's my little brother." Casey swallowed and shook his head. "He's carrying around so much hurt and anger from everything that's happened. I can't blame him for that and part of it is my fault."

"Casey—"

"No. It is, because he needed me. I should've found another way. It was selfish of me to think I could try and make a life for myself at the same time as getting them both out."

My brows drew together. I didn't like that Casey would carry this weight on his shoulders. "That life you made has saved a lot of people."

"But it didn't save the two people who mattered the most," he pointed out as he wrapped the towel around me, tucking it in at the front.

"It saved you, and after all these years, you have your brother back. I think he's a lot more like you than you realise."

"Really?" Casey looked me with an expression I could almost believe was hope. I knew then he hadn't seen in Kelly what I had. Not yet. He was too busy being angry at his brother, and then heartbroken, and now at an utter loss. I wasn't. They would work it out. Kelly would always be a Sentinel. He would always live in that area somewhere between black and white. That was something Casey would have to accept, but deep down, Kelly had a big heart he hid from the world.

"Kelly saved my life." He might've set Casey up because he was angry and wanted him to hurt, but it seemed he was at war with himself because he also wanted his big brother happy. "He just went about it in a really shitty way. He grew up with bikers," I pointed out.

It was almost the equivalent of being brought up by wolves, wasn't it? I didn't know. All I knew was that Bingo, who'd been released from custody, didn't seem so bad after all. He honestly seemed to think I'd saved his life when all I'd really done was put out his burning beard. Perhaps his mind was hazy on the events of that night because he was drunk. Bingo's sister was another story. She remained in custody after her efforts today, and Gabriella had assured us she was also under investigation for a lot more than what she'd done today.

"He did, in his own misguided way, attempt to save your life," Casey conceded, "but he should've just come to me first."

"You're going to have to let that one go," I advised as Casey took another towel from the rack and dried himself half-heartedly. "You both just need time."

"Yeah?" Casey tucked the towel around his hips. "He could use that time to learn he can't go putting his hands all over you like he seemed so eager to do. Or call you babe. Or be anywhere near you really."

I let the topic go when he opened the bathroom door, steam trailing out behind us in a big wave. They had nothing but time on their side to build a new relationship together.

We passed by a channel-flicking Coby on the couch and walked into Casey's bedroom. He shut the door behind us, peeled off his towel, and tossed it on the floor. I had to bite my tongue because really, Casey was naked, and he was stalking his way towards me with that predatory look in his eye. The one that told me he was done with the talking and it was time to get down to business.

"Enough talking for now," he told me, confirming my suspicions. "On the bed," he ordered. My towel seized, I watched it sail across the room and land on the floor, meeting his in a joint pile of rejection. I looked back at Casey.

"I told you I'd take care of you and there's more than one way to do that," I was informed as he crowded me towards the bed.

The backs of my knees hit the mattress and I went down on my ass. On board with his plan, I began edging backwards. The bed dipped as he climbed on and stalked towards me on his knees. My eyes dropped, my pulse racing as I watched him take his hardening cock in his hand. Then he did something I wasn't expecting. He let go of his erection and crawled further up, hovering over me with both hands planted on either side of my head.

With solemn blue eyes, he looked down at me as though he never wanted to stop, and his next words stole my breath.

"Marry me, Grace."

I stared at him wordlessly, shock and surprise warring inside me. My knee jerk reaction was to say yes, but I held my tongue.

"No?" Disappointment and hurt clouded his eyes and it broke my heart. "You need time or is this something you never want to do with anyone?"

"I want to do all of it," I told him honestly. It wasn't until you had the real possibility of your life being snatched away that you truly believed how important it was to live how you wanted to. From the moment I arrived in Sydney, it was like I'd come alive, and a part of that was due to Casey. He lit me up on the inside, and I didn't want to just give him a lifetime, I wanted to give him forever. "And I want to do all of it with you."

"Is it my job? I know it can be dangerous but—"

"No," I replied vehemently. "It's people like you who change the world." I brushed a hand down the side of his face before letting it fall. "Protecting others is instinctive with you. I would never ask you to change who you are or what you do."

Casey sat back on his heels and I saw the realisation sweep across his face. "It's because you're sick, isn't it?" he said softly. "You don't think you're a sure bet."

"I'm not," I whispered hoarsely. My eyes burned and I bit down on my bottom lip when I felt it start to quiver. How could I promise forever with this man when forever was something I couldn't offer? "There's every reason to believe that after this round of chemotherapy I'll get the all clear. But what about the next time? What if it comes back, bigger and stronger than before? I can't watch you lose yourself like my father did. Mum dying broke him. How can I stand before God and promise to love you when I could break you too?"

"Easy," Casey breathed. He threaded both our hands together and leaned over me again, pinning me to the bed. I was staring directly in his eyes when he pressed his forehead to mine. "You just say the words."

"It's not so easy," I argued.

"It is," he replied stubbornly. "Do one thing for me?" Casey continued before I could answer. "Ask your dad," he told me, his voice fierce. "Ask him if it was hard or if it was easy to stand up before God and promise to love your mother forever. I bet I can tell you the answer."

A tear escaped and ran down the side of my face. It slid off and plopped onto the sheets below. Because of course it sounded easy when he put it like that. Damn Casey for being so logical and so heartbreakingly persistent. My resolve wavered, but it didn't break.

"You're going to marry me, Slim," he vowed when I couldn't find the words to reply. His tone told me he'd brook no argument and I wanted to believe it. "I won't stop asking until you eventually realise that there aren't any sure bets in life. Not for anyone. And it doesn't matter because people don't need sure bets. They just need hope and determination, and I have enough of that for the both of us."

My heart began to pound so hard I could feel the roar of blood in my ears. "Okay," I breathed, feeling his determination as though it was seeping into my own skin just by touch alone.

Casey pulled back, tilting his head slightly as he looked down at me. "Okay?"

"Okay. Don't stop asking me."

It wasn't a yes and it wasn't a no, but it was enough for his lips to curve deliciously. My blood stirred in response, a sweet ache beginning to throb between my legs. He was so masculine in his satisfaction that I found myself returning the smile. "You're beautiful," I told him.

He shook his head, his grin widening. Then he kissed my lips, and my neck, and then down further, until my nipple was in his mouth and he was sucking it deep and hard, forcing a sharp cry from my lips. Moments later, loud music began to pump from the living room. I giggled as the sound of "Sweet child o' mine" by Guns N' Roses pealed through the speakers, informing me Coby was into the classics.

"Oops," I said with a grin at Casey's roommate trying to drown us out.

"You're loud in bed," Casey told me.

A flush climbed my cheeks, making me hot. "I am not."

His next words made me jolt with surprise. "My name's Casey Daniels," he began. We were having another do-over? My heart began to race at this adorable side of Casey he sometimes let out to play. He kissed his way across to my other nipple, tugging it between his teeth. He sucked quickly and then let go with a small pop. "And I'm madly in love with a woman who's loud in bed and snores like a man."

"I do not!" I practically yelled, my face getting hotter.

I felt his answering smile as he kissed his way down my belly, sending goose bumps skittering across my skin. "She's also stubborn, and incredibly sexy, and one day…" he licked the crease of my thigh and my breath hitched "…she's going to marry me, and it won't make me the happiest man on Earth…" his tongue flicked out and stroked my clit skilfully "…because right now I already am."

I cried out again when he took the small button in his mouth and sucked.

The music kicked up another notch and I giggled again.

"You're turn," Casey told me with a laugh, reaching for a condom.

I snatched it from his fingers and forced him onto his back. It was no easy feat forcing Casey to do anything, so the minor exertion had me breathing hard. I took his warm, hard cock in my hand, feeling it twitch under my touch. Before rolling the condom down, I leaned in and licked the head, swirling my tongue and taking him in my mouth.

I drew back slightly, everyone—family and friends—would be descending on the loft soon. "Do we have time for this?"

I gave another quick lick and Casey groaned as I looked up at him. "Slim, if I ever say no to that question, you have my permission to get my gun out and shoot me with it."

My body shook with laughter as I took him deep in my mouth, as far back as I could, then I hummed, letting my throat close tight around his erection. He let out his own shout, jerking his hips, pushing his cock further in my mouth before pulling back quickly.

"Jesus," he panted, gripping the base of his cock.

"He can't help you right now, but I can," I told him as I began to roll the condom down, looking into Casey's eyes as I did so. Their colour was the darkest I'd ever seen them, and I couldn't force my eyes away.

"My name's Grace Paterson," I began, my voice solemn as the laughter died away. "And I'm madly in love with a man who's overprotective and bossy, and spends way too much time on his hair." That last one was a total lie but finding a negative about Casey was hard work.

"I do?" He seemed surprised and I had to laugh. Gripping his cock, I swung my leg over his lap and began to sink down, taking him inside me. A groan rose up from inside his chest as I squeezed him.

"He told me once that he was good with his tongue and the way he looked at me when he said it had me believing it. I think I'd believe anything he tells me when he looks at me that way—as though I'm the only person in the room. So when he promised me he'd fight for me, I knew it was true." I took a deep, shaky breath and swallowed the sob of emotion. "He's also incredibly hot, and a total badass, and one day …" I began to move, rocking slowly. Casey tensed, waiting. "One day I'm going to marry him because he's not only in my heart, he's my goddamn hero."

Casey pulled me off and flipped me underneath him easily, making my earlier efforts of moving him around seem feeble at best. He kissed me hard, his tongue sweeping deep inside my mouth before pulling off.

"Coby better turn that music up louder," he told me, sliding back inside my body. He rolled his hips and I bucked upwards, drawing him in as far as our bodies would allow.

"Why?" I locked my legs around his waist.

As though hearing him, the song kicked over to "Welcome to the jungle" and the walls began to thump.

"Because I'm about to pound the woman I love into this mattress and make her scream louder than a low-flying fighter jet."

I grinned, slightly breathless. "How romantic."

I woke to Coby rapping on the bedroom door, and I rubbed my face sleepily, not sure how long we were both out for. Casey was spooning me and I felt hot and sweaty under the heat of his naked skin.

"Grace," he called out softly. "Your family's here."

My stomach dropped to my toes. The sheets rustled when Casey stirred, as though sensing my tension rather than waking from Coby's intrusion.

"Crap," I muttered. Casey stretched and rolled quickly from the bed.

"I put them off for as long as I could," he reminded me, slapping me on the ass to get me up.

He had. They'd been at the duplex, waiting for news on my disappearance. I knew they knew about the cancer, so Casey rang them to let them know I was okay because I wasn't up for talking. Not right then. He explained to them everything that happened, going into great detail when I heard Dad peppering him with questions. He also told them we would finish with the police, he would take me home to his loft for a shower, and then they could meet us there. Dad had yelled. I heard it. And still Casey stayed calm and forceful, willing to incur the wrath of my father so I could have the time I needed before I spoke to them.

Now my time was up.

I found Casey's old football jersey in his dresser and tugged it on. I added my own pair of sweats to the casual ensemble, and when we walked out of Casey's room, Coby was busy playing host and offering drinks.

I shook my head when he asked what I wanted. How could I think about drinking when I was about to tell my dad I was moving to Sydney? The way he was with Mum and her cancer, he wasn't going to let me out of his sight.

Before I could take a breath, Dad rushed me. My face mashed into his chest as he smothered me. "Dad," I squeezed out.

"Shush," he muttered. "Let an old man fuss over his little girl."

I tried to tell him there was a line between fussing and suffocation, but I couldn't get the words out. I wasn't sure how it happened, but suddenly he was gone and then Henry was there taking his place.

"Gracie Bean." His voice cracked and my arms tightened around him.

"I'm sorry," I told him because I was. I hated seeing him hurting. When it was Mum who was sick, sometimes I would climb in his bed and burrow into his side, like it was us against the world. Now it was me who was sick, and

Henry didn't have anyone to climb into his bed and comfort the pain like we used to do for each other. That made me sad.

He buried his head in my neck, and I felt a tear plop on my shoulder. "Life is so fucking unfair."

"It is," I replied because it was true. I pulled back. Henry looked terrible—his shoulders were slumped and I could feel the heaviness in his heart. It made me realise that I didn't need to be here in Sydney just for me and Casey, but for my brother. I just didn't know where that left my dad.

"I'll be okay," I tried assuring the both of them.

Dad nodded stoically but Henry gave me nothing.

Coby returned from the kitchen with a round of whiskey for each of them. We all sat down in the living room, Casey beside me. He brought the glass to his lips, about to tip his head back when I realised that a little bit of liquid courage was exactly what I needed right now.

Snatching the glass from his hand, I gulped it down in one hit, hissed audibly at the burn, and braced. "I'm moving to Sydney."

Dad reared back as though I'd just told him I was moving to Botswana to become one with the meerkats. Then his lips pressed into a thin line, indicating the famous Paterson stubbornness was making an appearance. "No."

I held my glass out to Coby, indicating a refill with pleading eyes. He must have understood the gravity of my situation because he took it without saying a word and disappeared back to the kitchen.

"Dad," I began.

Casey took over, threading our fingers together. "Sir—"

"Nate," my dad boomed back at him.

"Nate." Casey squeezed my hand. "I can understand the next few months are going to be difficult for Grace but—"

"Difficult?" Dad paled and I knew he was thinking of Mum. Of the months and the years spent prolonging her life and then watching her fade from our lives eventually anyway. "You have no idea what months and years of chemotherapy can do to a family."

"No, I don't," Casey answered honestly and I squeezed his hand in return because the thought made me ache unbearably. I didn't want Casey to know. I didn't want this for him. "But what I was trying to say was that I would move to Melbourne in a heartbeat for Grace if that was what she wanted."

I jolted with surprise, looking at him. All that talk about his brother and him reuniting and the Valentines being his family, and he'd never said a word. He'd walk away from all of that for me? My heart expanded until I thought it would burst right out of my chest.

"You would do that for me?"

He returned my look of surprise with one of his own, as though I should've automatically known of his plans to move mountains for me. "Of course. It's up to you, Grace. Where do you want to be?"

"She wants to be home. In Melbourne," Nate clarified, answering for me.

Henry shook his head, brows drawn. "No, Dad. She wants to be here where I can take care of her."

Dad folded his arms, gearing up for an argument. "You work shit hours, son. How on God's earth do you think you can be there all the time to take care of her?"

I leaned closer to Casey. He let go of our threaded hands and put his arm around me instead, tucking me into his side. Coby returned at that opportune moment with my drink and I accepted it gratefully. Then he went to leave, giving my family privacy, and I grabbed him, making him sit on the other side of me. He sat, tense and a little awkward at being thrust into my family drama, but my hope was that his presence might make them behave.

"I'll figure it out," Henry told him, his voice beginning to rise as he leaned forward in his seat. I knew then that I was wrong. My father and brother were quite willing to embarrass themselves in front of the entire world, or at the least, Coby. "I'll quit the band."

"You'll do no such thing," I declared, leaping feet first into the argument with rising anger. Dad and Henry paused to glare at me. I glared back. "You're living the dream, Henry. Not many people get a chance to do that. I'm not letting you quit!" I told him, finishing with a shout.

"So what, it's okay for Casey to just up and move to Melbourne for you, but when I want to make the grand gesture, you tell me I can't?"

Dad stood up, towering over Henry with the kind of scary intimidation that only a father could produce. "Son, don't talk to your sister in that growly fashion," he growled. "She's fragile right now and—"

"Fragile?" I shrieked, the pitch of my voice high from disbelief and anger as I stood to avoid the intimidation tactic of my dad looming over me. "How dare you assume I'm not strong enough to handle what's coming. You—"

"I don't believe this!" Henry yelled at Dad, cutting me off. He stood up too, thus forming a huddle of three very angry Patersons. "Why is it okay for everyone else to do something and I'm told to just sit back and play my guitar like a good boy?"

The three of us began to argue in earnest when Casey's bellow cut through the angry words. "Enough!"

Casey reached for the drink that was still in my hand. He tossed it down his throat, shook his head once, and dumped the glass on the coffee table.

We all shut up.

"Sit down," he bit out, his voice a smidge calmer now that he had our attention.

We all sat down.

Coby shifted awkwardly beside me. I patted him reassuringly on the knee, a silent thank you for sticking out the drama. Coby grinned at me and I startled, realising how close his face was to mine. I wondered for a brief moment if I should be embarrassed about my earlier noise in the bedroom. I decided to just let it go and hope he didn't mention it.

Casey snatched my hand from Coby's knee and tucked it in his. Then he looked at both Henry and my dad, his expression steely. "Stop making this about you and what you both want. Nate." Dad raised his brows at Casey but held his tongue. Wisely, I thought, because I had come to learn that particular expression on Casey's face. I thought of it as his don't poke the sleeping dragon face. "I can appreciate you wanting Grace home because a father should be there for his little girl." Dad nodded his agreement and then paused because it seemed Casey wasn't finished. "But Grace is going to heal best being where she wants to be, not where you want her to be. And, Henry ..." My brother glanced up from staring at the floor as Casey's voice took on a note of warning. "Have you forgotten everything I said to you at the hospital? Don't make everything Grace did mean nothing."

I looked between the both of them, knowing I was missing something important. I made a mental note to ask Casey what he'd said to Henry.

Dad turned to look at me, his voice quiet. "Is that what you want, Grace? To move to Sydney?"

I hesitated because I didn't want to upset him any further, but I knew I needed to start being more upfront about my life and what I wanted. It wasn't until I eventually replied with a yes that I realised how tense Casey was because I felt him relax beside me.

"It's settled then," Dad boomed at all of us after taking a hefty gulp from his glass.

"What's settled?"

"I'm moving to Sydney too."

"Dad, you can't—"

He held up a hand, halting me. "You're my daughter, Grace, not my mother. Don't start trying to tell me what I can and can't do."

"What about your job?"

Dad shrugged as though the decades of time spent working at the garage was just a blip on his radar of life. "I've got long service leave out the wazoo. I'll give 'em a call. Arrange for six months, and then we can go from there."

The intercom buzzer cut through the loft. We all paused while Casey stood to answer it. He flipped on the video monitor at the wall and Mac's face came to life. "Oh good. You are here."

"Of course we're here," he told her.

I saw her look left to someone off screen before smirking at Casey. "Is it safe to come up or are you busy rubbing one out like you were last time?"

Dad choked on his drink and Coby snorted with laughter from beside me. Henry had to get up and slap dad on the back pretty hard.

I wanted to jump instantly to Casey's defence by saying he wasn't in the habit of "rubbing one out" at all times of the day or night, but talking to your dad about your boyfriend's jacking off habits was a topic best left alone. Besides, it was quite possible Casey did jack off all the time. Then I flushed hot and red because I was sitting in the living room next to Coby, my dad sitting opposite me, and all I could see was Casey naked and stroking his cock.

While I was burning up from embarrassment on the couch, Casey appeared unaffected. His dimples popped when he laughed at Mac. "Have you been talking to Travis?"

"No." Quinn appeared on the screen waving, a grin on her face. "Me."

"Thanks for throwing me under the bus, Quinn," Casey replied.

Quinn disappeared rapidly off screen, giving a little "oomphf" as though she'd been pushed. Mac filled the screen again, booming, "Let us up, asshead."

"Who's 'us'?" Casey asked, suddenly wary.

"Everyone." Evie appeared from behind Mac. "And be quick. I brought Mr Chow's and I'm hungry enough to eat a rhinoceros."

"Who brought Mr Chow's?" I heard Jared grumble.

"You did, baby," came her loving reply.

"And I brought champagne," Mac added.

"You told me to bring the champagne," Travis complained from somewhere within the pile of people out the front of the loft.

"Yeah, but you forgot, didn't you?"

There was a brief pause by the entire group while they waited for Travis to reply. He didn't.

"Let us up, Casey," Mac growled. "I have it on good authority that Grace made Morgan bleed. We need to celebrate. And then we need to discuss why I wasn't called in on the smackdown. I really think—"

Casey hit the buzzer, effectively cutting Mac off and letting everyone in the building at the same time. After flicking open the locks, he took my hand, muttered an, "excuse us for a minute," at my dad, Henry and Coby, and hauled me to his room, shutting the door behind us.

"You can't keep hauling me around, Casey," I complained, even though I secretly liked his bossy side. It was nice letting someone else take the reins for a little while.

Casey pressed me up against the wall near the door. "Or what?" He grinned. "You'll punch me so hard I'll be spitting teeth for a week?"

"Yes," I replied stubbornly. My next question threw him. "How often do you jack off?"

His brows flew up. "Really? You want to talk dirty right now with your father in the next room? Because if you start this conversation, I'll be finishing it, and I don't think you really have any idea of how loud you are when you come." His arms came around me, his hands landing on my ass and shoving me against him. "It's fucking hot."

Loud voices, dog barks, and laughter began filtering in, indicating the loft was filling rapidly with visitors. I knew they were all here to see for themselves that I was okay and to find out about Kelly, the scary-ass biker dude brother of my boyfriend, yet my body was more interested in doing exactly what Casey wanted.

"You can tell me later. Or show me even," I mumbled under my breath.

Casey must have heard me because he groaned and reached down to adjust himself in his pants. "Later," he vowed. "Right now we need to talk about your move to Sydney."

"What about it?" I asked, finding my way underneath his shirt. My happy hands encountered warm, hard abs and began their trek downwards. "I want you here in the loft. With me," he clarified, the back of his head tipping back and hitting the wall when I took his growing erection in my palm.

"Really?" I asked, suddenly breathless and ready to leap on board with the idea. Then I remembered his roommate and I tamped down on the eagerness. "What about Coby? He might not like the idea of me moving in with you. You should ask him first."

Casey paused, panting lightly as my hands stroked over him. "You're right." He opened the bedroom door a fraction and shouted for Coby.

"Oh my God." I whipped my hands out of Casey's pants, flushing when Coby slipped inside, giving us both a knowing look. He shut the door behind him and looked at the both of us expectantly. "What's up?"

"You cool with Grace moving in with us?"

Coby looked at me. "You got lots of hot friends?"

I knew quite a few girls from my modelling years that were based in Sydney. A handful of them were really nice. I shrugged. "Yes."

Coby looked at Casey and nodded once. "Okay."

Then he turned to leave until Casey said to his retreating back, "You're next."

Coby turned, confused for a moment before his eyes suddenly cleared and he paled, making me wonder what Casey meant. "Mate." He shook his head, holding up his hands as though telling Casey to back off. "Don't even."

Casey began to laugh as Coby left, shutting the door behind him.

"That seemed too easy. What did you mean by 'you're next?'"

A smile tugged at the corners of Casey's lips and I sensed a private joke. "Nothing, Slim. I'm just looking forward to waking up every morning with you beside me. I never realised how much I wanted it until I almost lost you."

"It's not going to be easy for us," I warned, knowing that a difficult road still lay ahead.

His lips brushed mine. "Nothing worthwhile ever is."

Epilogue
KELLY DANIELS

I stood at the front door of my brother's building, staring at the intercom. I wasn't sure why the hell I was there. Well I knew, because Casey and Grace had invited me to some party for something. I couldn't remember what. Something about Jamieson returning from tour. I just didn't know why I'd decided to show up. I must have been shitfaced to agree to this. And not only that, I brought a friend with me like I was some kind of whiny chick that needed support.

"Stop staring at it like it's going to bite your fuckin' face off and press the damn thing."

I glared at my best mate of ten years and fellow Sentinel brother. "Shut up, Fox."

"Pussy." Fox shifted the six-pack of beer under his arm with impatience and went to press the buzzer.

"Don't call me a pussy," I snapped. Shoving his arm away, I jabbed hard on the button, almost breaking the damn thing in the process.

My mood could almost be described as joyful when no one answered. I must have got the day wrong or the party was over. Either way, I was outta there. I turned.

"Wait." Fox grabbed my arm and pressed it again.

I shrugged out of his hold and started walking off.

"Hello?"

Goddammit. That was Grace's voice. The sound of a party in progress in the background was unmistakeable. I turned and sighed, feeling the urge to kick something. Fox raised his brows at me, making him the closest target.

It wasn't like I hadn't been here before. I had. Five times. Three of those were to see Grace. Not just because she was sexy and fun to tease, but because she was sick. I hated seeing her that way. It made me feel about as useful as tits on a bull. Two of those times, Casey had been there. And it had been tense. Ten years didn't automatically make him my brother again. Anyone who said blood was thicker than water had never been a biker. The Sentinels were my family, my brothers, and I didn't need Casey anymore.

Too bad Grace kept trying to rectify that. Somehow saying no to her was impossible and I couldn't work out why.

I stalked back and held down the damn button. "Yeah, it's us," I growled.

"Kelly?" Grace sounded surprised.

It was weird hearing her use my real name. Most called me Shade. It was the name my biker brothers gave me because they said only a soulless bastard shot his own father. I didn't have to like it but I couldn't argue that it didn't fit.

"You invited me, didn't you?"

"We did, but if you don't check that asshole attitude at the door, you can just turn around and take a long walk off a short cliff. Preferably somewhere where there are crocodiles. And piranhas," she added.

Fox snorted beside me. "I like her already."

I really didn't like hearing Fox say that for some reason. Annoyance oozed from my pores. "Grace is my brother's old lady. Don't you even fuckin' look at her."

Fox rolled his eyes. "Calm down, Shade."

I jabbed the button again, holding it down as I spoke. "Sorry, babe. Not much in the party mood."

She sighed and I remembered I was supposed to be working on that whole babe thing. Typical chicks, always trying to fuckin' change who you were.

"Showing up is a good start, Kelly," she replied. "Come on in."

The buzzer sounded along with a loud click indicating the doors had unlocked to let us through. I frowned as we stepped inside. There was an underlying exhaustion in Grace's voice. I didn't like hearing it. She told me she was starting a degree at uni in a couple of months. I had no clue how she was gonna manage it with being sick how she was but she said she was starting off part-time. Eventually she'd major in public relations and end up working for Jamieson when she graduated. I had no idea what public relations was, but I told her if she ever wanted to study private relations, I was her man. That statement had the added effect of pissing Casey off which was always fun.

Reaching the loft door, I knocked and some chick I didn't know opened it rather than Grace like I was expecting. Heavy rock music thumped out from behind her, filling the hall and vibrating off the walls.

"I'm Kelly," I told her. "Casey's brother."

She paused, raking me over. I felt the urge to close my eyes for a minute because she was so beautiful it almost blinded me to stare straight at her. If these were Grace's friends, I needed to start coming to more of these parties.

Her blond hair hung in a long sheet, and her tight black jeans had zippers all over the front and from what I could see, they decorated her ass on the back too. I wondered briefly which of the zippers led to the Holy Grail. Who even cared? There would be a helluva lot of fun in finding the fuck out.

"Holy shit," she declared when she was done with her quick inspection. "Grace was right."

"About what?"

Her eyes dropped to my crotch for a split second. It was almost unnoticeable but I was watching her closely. My cock stirred happily at her interest. I grabbed it and smirked. "She tell you I was hung like a horse?"

Her brows rose coolly and damned if that didn't make my dick harden even more. "Does that line work for you a lot?"

I grinned cockily. "With a face like this, babe, I don't need lines."

"Maybe not, but it sounds like your ego needs a kick in the ass." I was suddenly dismissed, her eyes shifting to Fox on my right. They flared wide. "Luke?"

Fox grinned.

I looked at him. "You know this chick?"

"This chick," she snapped, turning her fierce emerald eyes back on me, "has a name."

I sighed heavily. Grace and her friends were high fuckin' maintenance and we hadn't even stepped in the damn door yet. Parties weren't supposed to be this much hard work.

"Mackenzie Valentine," Fox supplied and winked at the hot chick still barring us from coming inside. "We go way back, right, Mac?"

Her nostrils flared, indicating that way back part wasn't sittin' real well with her. "You're a Sentinel now, Luke?"

Fox shrugged at her. "Have been for ten years."

"Figures," I heard her mumble.

After a pause, she swung the door wide, indicating for us to come in.

We stepped inside and I scanned the loft. The living area was full of standing or dancing bodies, the kitchen was littered with people getting drinks, the dining room with food, and even more people spilled onto the big deck out the back. "Where's Grace?"

"She had to go do something," Mac replied, shutting the door behind us. She pointed to the kitchen. "You can put your beer there, or there's a big ice bucket out on the back deck. There's food on the dining table if you're hungry." She also indicated to a big glass bowl shot with cloudy streaks of blue sitting on a cabinet by the wall. "Keys go in there."

"The keys to my Harley are not goin' in some fuckin' bowl," I told her, no matter how fancy it looked.

"We don't tolerate drunk driving here," she snapped. "Keys in the bowl now, biker dude. I decide who gets to drive at the end of the night, not you."

Jesus.

I tossed my keys in, grabbed a beer from Fox's six-pack, and disappeared before she decided my balls had to go in the damned bowl too.

Fox walked with me into the living area, beers in hand. I don't know why I brought him. He'd been the paramedic on Casey's car accident, but he hadn't been real impressed when I told him it was our MC who was behind it.

"You were the fuckhead who rammed their car?" he'd asked, looking at me with a pissed expression.

"No, it wasn't me." He'd relaxed, until I added, "It was Cowboy."

"Cowboy? What the fuck?"

I had to explain then because Cowboy was a peaceful brother and not much into violence, or ramming cars for that matter. "He wasn't supposed to ram the fuckin' car. He was supposed to warn Casey off from buttin' into our business and got some dickwad to do it for him. The dickwad didn't realise Grace was driving and it turned into a giant shit sandwich."

Fox might've been pissed, but he'd had my back swiping the pint of blood I needed to stage Grace's hit. He'd nicked it from the clinic the morning of her check-up. Casey hadn't appreciated it when I explained the details. And he really hadn't liked hearing how I broke into this very loft either and swiped his gun while they were at some party. What could I say? I was fuckin' good with locks and alarm systems.

"Would you just relax, mate?" Fox bitched beside me. "You're makin' me itchy."

"Fuck off then," I replied because I was itchy. I didn't want to be here.

A space cleared on the couch so I sat down and finished my beer while the party went on around me. I was about to stand up and look for Grace when some little dude slid on to the couch beside me. I didn't think he meant to sit so close, so I shifted a little to the right. He shifted with me. I looked at him and realised he was looking at me. The guy had dark girly shit smudged under his eyes and his lips looked suspiciously glossy.

"You a pansy?"

His eyes widened. And this was why I never liked uptight parties. You couldn't say shit without someone getting offended. Then the little guy surprised me by shrugging. "Yeah, I'm a pansy. Of the badass variety," he added.

"You're a badass pansy?"

"That's right." He held out a hand. I shifted my beer from my right hand to my left and shook it. "My name's Tim. I'm Casey's personal assistant. We're tight."

My brows winged up.

"Not that tight," he added hastily. "Unfortunately," I thought I heard him mumble. "And you're his brother Kelly."

I let go of his hand. "I am," I confirmed and downed the rest of my beer.

"I can tell because you look a lot like him." Tim ran fingers through his tousled dark hair while he gave me a speculative look. "You ride a Harley?"

"I do," I told him.

"Damn," he muttered. "Hearing there were two of you gave my dick a stroke. But knowing you ride with some thousand pound vibrating machine between your legs, well that's …" he trailed off, staring unfocused into the distance.

I eyed him warily. "You okay?"

Tim jolted and looked at me. "Never better. Can I get you another drink?"

My eyes fell to his glass of purple liquid with fruit in it and I winced. "Yeah, no." I started edging off the couch. "Thanks. I'm just gonna go get a beer." His face fell and for some reason I felt bad. "I'll be back later, yeah? Just gotta go find Grace."

"Oh." He smiled at me but it was a sad kinda smile. "Maybe try her room? I don't think she's feeling the best tonight."

I grabbed another beer from the kitchen and turned, bumping into a huge blond guy. "Shit." I held up the bottle before it tipped liquid everywhere. The guy turned and I got a look at his face. Double shit, I thought. I gave him a chin lift. "Travis."

He nodded once, his green eyes flat. "Kelly. Thought you'd be a no-show."

"Yeah? I guess you thought wrong."

"Quinn," he said to the sweet looking female he had hauled to his side. She was tiny, the top of her head only reaching his shoulder. She stared up at me with wide, chocolate-coloured eyes. "This is Kelly, Casey's brother."

"It's nice to meet you." Quinn politely held out her hand and I took it, my huge palm swallowing her tiny one as I clasped my fingers around it. "Casey's told me a lot about you."

"He has?" I asked with surprise as I let her hand go. I guess Casey was a lot more open about shit than I was.

She leaned in while Travis stood talking to some other guy that was just as huge as he was. "He doesn't share much with anyone at all, it's just that Casey and I have some things in common."

My eyes whipped to hers, looking a little more closely, and that's when I saw it. That slight lift of defiance in her chin and the wariness in her eyes.

"Oh." She was like a tiny, little fairy. The thought of some big dude beating on her made me want to puke. I swallowed down the urge by downing my next beer and grabbing another. "I'm sorry."

"Don't apologise. I just … can I tell you something?"

I popped the lid off my bottle and tossed it towards the bin in the corner. "Sure thing, babe," I replied with a casualness I didn't feel. Chicks and talking was never a good thing. "What's up?"

"I don't know you, but I know a lot about what you've been through, so I can understand your anger. But don't let it eat you up until there's nothing left. Being angry at the world, and at Casey, is letting your father win. You know why? Because it's hate breeding hate. You're keeping your father's rage alive inside you and you're feeding from it and using it against your own brother. I don't want that for Casey. He doesn't deserve that. Your brother loves you. Don't hate him for that."

"Are you finished?" I bit out, my tone harsh because her words made my eyes sting. Damned if I was going to break down like some bitch in the middle of some classy as fuck party where I didn't belong.

"Hey!" Travis abandoned his conversation to grab my bicep. His fingers dug in hard. "Watch your fucking tone around my wife."

Fuck.

I needed to go find Fox and get the hell outta here.

I shrugged off Travis's hand. The last thing I needed to do after everything Quinn just said was to punch her husband in the face. With the way I was feeling right now, it was a possibility.

"I'm sorry," I said stiffly to Quinn and shoved my way out of the kitchen, knocking some guy in the process and not caring. Needing to take a piss, I made my way towards the bathroom.

I felt everyone's eyes on me as I weaved my way through Casey's friends. Was it the shock of seeing how much I looked like him, or that they sensed I didn't fit in here? I wiped everything from my face—frustration, anger, and the regret Quinn's words induced—and I slipped on a mask of indifference. I even managed to wink at a sexy girl. She flushed, her eyes flaring with interest, and the weight of confidence settled in my chest. This was something I knew. Sex was easy. Women came easy. Getting rid of them maybe not so much, but it was hard to care when you were in the moment. There was nothing like forgetting your troubles in a pair of hot tits and an even hotter pussy.

I opened the bathroom door, slipped inside, and shut it behind me. Then I turned and in that instant, everything flew from my head because Grace was on the floor and she wasn't moving. Her dark fiery hair was spread out in a fan across the tiles and her face so pale that her full lips looked red in comparison.

"Babe. Jesus." Moving quickly, I rushed to her side and dropped to my knees. With shaky fingers I checked her pulse. It was thready and weak. "Grace, babe. Wake up."

She swatted at me like I was a pesky fly and I almost groaned with relief. "Mmmf."

I frowned. "What?"

She let out a long, shaky breath, clearly exhausted. "I'm fine. Just … sick. Needed to lie down 'cause the room was spinning."

"On the bathroom floor?"

"'s near the toilet," she mumbled.

"What can I do?" I asked, thinking that maybe I should go get Casey.

"Hold me up?" she whispered weakly. "Gonna be sick again."

I got on my knees behind her, propping her back against my chest. Her bony arms flopped uselessly and my goddamn heart bled out all over the floor at the sight. How did Casey deal with this? I felt fuckin' useless.

Grace curled over and heaved in the toilet bowl. I held her hair and kept her upright. That's about as useful as it got. She kept apologising over and over until I told her to shut the fuck up. Who apologised for cancer? Fuckin' shit-ass disease. I wanted to smash my fist through a wall.

"'m 'kay," she mumbled again. "I'm over the worst."

It had been worse than this? I wrapped my arms around her waist and held on, thinking that right then I needed the comfort more than she did.

"No more chemo anymore?"

She fell back against me, her head sagging into my neck. "No more for now."

I couldn't resist a quick brush of my lips against her hair. It was still the same deep vivid red, hanging down her back in soft waves. "I thought your hair fell out with chemo?"

"I only needed a low dose," she managed to say as I twisted a lock of it between my fingers. It was so soft. "My hair thinned some but not much."

The door opened and Casey slipped inside.

"Grace! Fuck," he bit out.

"Where the hell were you?" I dropped the lock of hair and glared up at him, feeding that rage Quinn talked about. "Out there having a goddamn party while your woman is layin' in here half dead!"

"You sonofabitch!" he ground out as he dropped beside me. I passed Grace over carefully, smoothing the hair from her face. He wrapped her up in his arms, his anger at me contrasting with the tender way he took hold of her. "You don't know shit. I didn't want this fucking party," he told me, his voice cracking. "Dammit. She was in bed when I left to get some ginger ale for her stomach. When I came back to the bedroom she was gone."

"'s my fault," Grace mumbled, burrowing herself into Casey's chest. "The party. Everyone was home from the tour and I missed them all so much. Felt fine this morning."

"How could you miss Henry?" Casey asked as I stood up and wet a washcloth with cold water. "He flew back every five minutes just to check on you."

I crouched and ran it over Grace's forehead. She looked like she'd passed out. Casey didn't seem to mind that I was wiping down her face so I kept going, pausing briefly to look at him. "Is this how it's been these past three months?"

Casey's jaw ticked. "Yeah. I fucking hate it. We got her a great doctor here in Sydney. Made the appointment and went and saw him a couple of days after all the shit that went down. I sat in that office of his and listened to him talking about injecting her with poison. I had to sit on my hands because I wanted to grab him by the throat, drag him across his desk, and toss him out the window."

"I'm sorry, Casey," I told him, because I was. They were dealing with all that and me being a jackass on top of it.

I'm not sure he heard me, his eyes were on Grace, his fingers tangled in her hair as he brushed it from her face.

"I cried," he choked out as he sat back on the tiles, Grace in his arms. "I fucking cried myself sick the first time they put that needle in her and I watched it drip slowly into her veins."

"But she's gonna be okay, right?" I stood, re-wetting the washcloth. "That's what she told me."

Casey nodded, his nostrils flaring as he drew a deep breath in. "Yeah. She is. She should start getting better from here on out. The original surgeon cut out the cancer before she arrived in Sydney. The chemo was done as a precautionary measure to kill off any cancer cells that might've been left behind."

"Told you I'm fine," Grace mumbled, her eyes fluttering open.

"Hey!" Casey protested when she tried pushing her way up off of the floor. She fell back against him. "Let me carry you."

"No," she replied stubbornly. "I'm fine. There's nothing like a good puke to make you feel better, right, Kelly?" She winked up at me. The effort was puny at best, but it felt nice to be included.

"Right on, babe," I replied smoothly, winking back.

Casey narrowed his eyes on me. I shrugged and grinned.

Grace sighed.

"What?" he asked her.

"You and Kelly. You both have the same pretty dimples."

"Pretty?" we both said at the same time with disgust.

"Yeah." She giggled, starting to sound drunk. The exhaustion must have well and truly set in. Tilting her head back, she looked up at Casey, taking his face in her hands. She smiled sweetly. "I love you so much, Batman."

It felt like I was intruding on a private moment, but really? "Batman?"

"Don't you know?" Grace looked at me, tired and pale, but happiness shone in her eyes. "Casey's my hero."

I knew right then, in that one single fuckin' second, that I wanted what my brother had. It must have felt real damn nice to be someone's hero, for them to look at you the way she looked at my brother. We might've had a shit start to life, Casey and I, but he had Grace now, and that meant he had everything.

At Grace's stubborn insistence, Casey carried her out to the kitchen while I followed behind. He planted her ass on the counter top. Then he stood between her legs with his back to her. She latched her arms around his shoulders while they chatted with their friends. I stood on the fringes next to Fox, beer after beer shoved in my hand until I felt unsteady.

Fox left soon after, catching a cab because Mac refused to give us the keys to our bikes.

"They better still be there in the fuckin' mornin'," I bitched at her.

Her gaze narrowed gloriously and I was drunk enough to start eyeing off her zippers with real interest. "Or else what?"

I paused, my mind too drunk for a good comeback. "Or else I'll be pissed off."

"Good one, Kelly," Mac replied with an eye roll. Then she crooked a finger. "Come with me."

Holy fuck did I want to come with her. I abandoned my beer to the counter and followed her to the living area, barely noticing the party had wound down and the place was emptying fast. She pointed to the couch. It was covered in blankets and pillows. "Lie down."

I dragged my shirt over my head, tossed it on the floor, and stalked towards her.

She backed up a step, but I noticed with satisfaction that her eyes were on my chest and she may as well have licked her lips the way she was staring at it.

Then she shook her head, as though coming to her senses. "Are you crazy?"

I paused. Was I? Or was I just drunk? What was she talking about?

"I have three brothers. Older brothers. They all own guns. They'll shoot you if you touch me."

I shrugged and kept coming for her. "Won't be the first time."

"Wait, what? You've been shot before?"

"Yep."

I grabbed her hips and yanked her towards me. Ducking my head, I pressed my lips on hers, waiting for her to respond. She did for a second and I groaned, one hand reaching up to fist her hair.

"What in the goddamn fuck?"

Mac leaped in the air, letting out a little shriek. "Jake!"

I turned, recognising the drummer from Jamieson that I was introduced to at some stage during the night. My brows rose at the guy, silently telling him to fuck off because I was busy. I had zippers to get to.

Jake shook his head, growled, "Fuck this shit," and left, slamming the loft door behind him. Then Mac burst into tears and this new, vulnerable side to her surprised me. It also left me floundering. I didn't do tears.

Before I could pat her awkwardly on the back, she took off in the other direction.

I sighed, figuring there was no getting any pussy tonight. Flopping on the couch, I closed my eyes and fell asleep.

When I woke later, the loft was quiet and dark. I groaned, rubbing the side of my face and then scratching at the stubble on my jaw. I rolled off the couch, ready to go search for the keys to my baby and take her home when the unmistakable sound of retching came from the bathroom door.

"Hell," I muttered. Had Grace even slept at all?

I opened the bathroom door quietly and did a double take, because it wasn't Grace heaving over the toilet bowl this time. It was Mac.

"Jesus, babe. You okay? How much did you have to drink?"

I sat on the edge of the tub and for the second time that night, I held back a chick's hair and rubbed her back in warm circles while she threw up in the toilet. Classy bitches sure puked a lot.

"Nothing," she moaned.

The door opened and Grace slipped inside, shutting it behind her. Her eyes found Mac first and they flashed with concern. Then they found mine and I saw the banked amusement. "Kelly. Come here often?"

Then her eyes fell on the vanity and they widened like fuckin' dinner plates. I followed her gaze.

"Shit," I muttered. On the vanity sat a pregnancy test. Highlighted in pink neon so bright they stood out like a cock at a lesbian orgy, were two distinct lines.

"You're pregnant," Grace breathed.

Oh shit. And I'd tried fuckin' her. What a douche.

"Who's the father?" I asked because I could be nosy when the occasion warranted it. I wanted to know who'd knock this hot bitch up and then leave her so I could go tell him what a giant cock he was.

Mac swallowed and wiped away the smeared trails of mascara that ran down her cheeks. She looked at me, then she looked at Grace.

"Jake," she rasped, her voice hoarse from puking. "It's Jake."

Books by Kate McCarthy

Fighting Redemption

The *Give Me* Series
Give Me Love (Book 1)
Give Me Strength (Book 2)
Give Me Grace (Book 3)

FIGHTING REDEMPTION

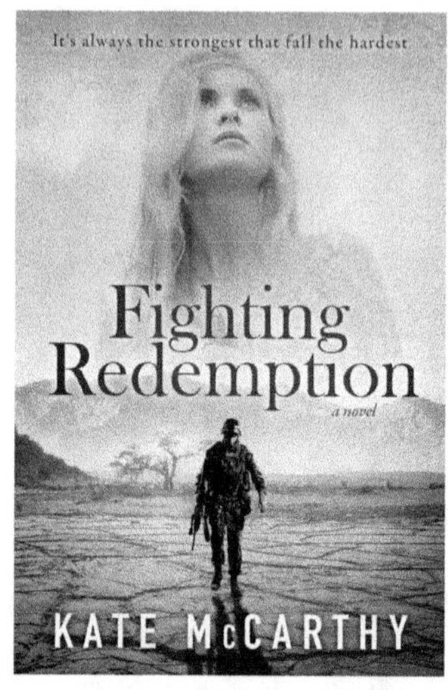

Ryan Kendall is broken. He understands pain. He knows the hand of violence and the ache of loss. He knows what it means to fail those who need you. Being broken doesn't stop him wanting the one thing he can't have; Finlay Tanner. Her smile is sweet and her future bright. She's the girl he grew up with, the girl he loves, the girl he protects from the world, and from himself.

At nineteen, Ryan leaves to join the Australian Army. After years of training he becomes an elite SAS soldier and deploys to the Afghanistan war. His patrol undertakes the most dangerous missions a soldier can face. But no matter how far he runs, or how hard he fights, his need for Finlay won't let go.

Returning home after six years, one look is all it takes to know he can't live without her. But sometimes love isn't enough to heal what hurts. Sometimes people like him can't be fixed, and sometimes people like Finlay deserve more than what's left.

This is a story about war and the cost of sacrifice. Where bonds are formed, and friendships found. Where those who are strong, fall hard. Where love is let go, heartache is born, and heroes are made. Where one man learns that the hardest fight of all, is the fight to save himself.

GIVE ME LOVE

Evie Jamieson, a former wild child, is not only a headstrong, smart-mouthed trouble magnet, she is also a lead singer with a plan. That plan involves relocating her band, including her two best friends guitarist Henry and band manager Mac, to Sydney to kick off their dreams of hitting the big time.

Jared Valentine is the older brother of Evie's best friend Mac and also the man determined to make Evie his. They strike up a long distance friendship which suits Evie because she's determined to avoid the distraction of love, not only because it doesn't fit in with her plan but because twice in the past it has left her for dead. Moving to Sydney however, has put her directly in Jared's path and he has decided it's the perfect opportunity to make his play.

Unfortunately Jared, co-owner in a business that 'consults' in dangerous hostage and kidnapping situations, makes an enemy who's determined to enact revenge. When this enemy puts Evie in his sights, Jared not only has a fight on his hands to make her his own, but also to keep her alive.

Is accepting the love he's so desperate to give worth the risk to both her heart...and her life?

GIVE ME STRENGTH

Quinn Salisbury doesn't think she's cut out for this whole living thing. Even as a young girl she struggled. Just when she thinks she's found a way to leave her violent past behind her, the only thing that's kept her going is ripped away, leaving her damaged and heartbroken.

Four years later, she is slowly rebuilding her life and lands a job as an assistant band manager to Jamieson, the hot new Australian act climbing their way to the top of the charts. There she meets Travis Valentine, the charismatic older brother of her boss, Mac.

From his commanding charm to his confidence and passion, Travis is everything Quinn believes is too good for her, and despite her apprehension, she finds their attraction undeniable and intense.

When her past resurfaces, it complicates their relationship. Instead of reaching out for help, Quinn pushes Travis away, until a staggering secret is revealed that leaves her fighting for her very life.

Torn between running and opening her heart to the man determined to have her, can Quinn find the strength within herself to fight for her future?

Acknoledgements

Tammy I'm not sure how this book would've happened without you. I choked at the start, putting enormous pressure on myself. Casey deserved his story told well and you weren't letting me do anything less than just that. Thank you so much. Your help with the research, and the plot, along with being the best beta anyone could ever ask for, made this book what it is.

To my editor, Max, and my proofreader, Claire, you both, as always, make my words look so much better than they were originally. Thank you.

My beta team was there through every chapter. Thank you for taking the time to read as I wrote. Kim, Kylie, Barb, Shelley, Trisha, Jo, and Natalie.

Thank you to Ellie at Love N Books and Scott Hoover for helping me find the perfect 'Casey' for my cover.

Colby Lefebvre you are an amazing cover model. Thank you.

To Julie and Terrena. My best friends. You've always been there for me and I can't tell you how much I appreciate the both of you.

To my sexy fantastic ladies. As always.

To Author 101 and BJ Harvey for being an amazing resource and support.

To all the bloggers and readers who've supported me through this writing journey. Thank you so very much.

About the Author

Kate McCarthy lives in Queensland, Australia.

Facebook:
https:/www.facebook.com/KateMcCarthyAuthor

Check out Kate's blog:
http://katemccarthy.net/

Follow Kate on Twitter:
https://twitter.com/KMacinOz

Friend Kate on Goodreads:
http://www.goodreads.com/author/show/6876994.Kate_McCarthy

This paperback interior was designed and formatted by

E.M.
TIPPETTS
BOOK DESIGNS

www.emtippettsbookdesigns.com

Artisan interiors for discerning authors and publishers.

www.ingramcontent.com/pod-product-compliance
Lightning Source LLC
Chambersburg PA
CBHW061939130726
47909CB00013B/2044